Warren Tute, the distinguished historian and bestselling author, was born in County Durham in 1914. He was educated at the Dragon School, Oxford, and later at Wrekin College. In 1932 he entered the Royal Navy and retired in 1946 with the rank of Lieutenant Commander. His career included service in Earl Mountbatten's staff and during the war he took part in the North African, Sicilian and Normandy landings. His last Service appointment was as Deputy Secretary at Combined Operations Headquarters in Whitehall.

After the war he was under contract to the late Ted Kavanagh of ITMA fame, writing for radio and television. He then spent seven years making films in England and Greece. Since 1950 over thirty of his works including plays and histories, have been published. World sales of his books are well over the million mark, the most successful of his novels being *The Cruiser* (1955), *The Rock* (1957), *Leviathan* (1959) and *The Golden Greek* (1960). His non-fiction bestsellers include *Hitler: The Last Ten Days* (1973), *D-Day* (1974) and *The North African War* (1976).

Also by Warren Tute

Novels

The Felthams
Lady in Thin Armour
Gentleman in Pink Uniform
The Younger Felthams
Girl in the Limelight
The Cruiser
The Rock
Leviathan
The Golden Greek
The Admiral
A Matter of Diplomacy
The Powder Train
The Tarnham Connection
The Resident
Next Saturday in Milan

History

The Grey Top Hat
Atlantic Conquest
Cochrane
Escape Route Green
The Deadly Stroke
Hitler: The Last Ten Days
D-Day
The North African War

Plays

Jessica
A Time to be Born
A Few Days in Greece
Frost at Midnight (translation)
Quartet for Five (translation)

Warren Tute

Honours of War and Peace

PANTHER
GRANADA PUBLISHING
London Toronto Sydney New York

Published by Granada Publishing Limited
in Panther Books 1977

ISBN 0 586 04632 1

First published by Constable and Company Ltd 1976

Granada Publishing Limited
Frogmore, St Albans, Herts AL2 2NF
and
3 Upper James Street, London W1R 4BP
1221 Avenue of the Americas, New York, NY 10020, USA
117 York Street, Sydney, NSW 2000, Australia
100 Skyway Avenue, Toronto, Ontario, Canada M9W 3A6
Trio City, Coventry Street, Johannesburg 2001, South Africa
CML Centre, Queen & Wyndham, Auckland 1, New Zealand

Made and printed in Great Britain by
Richard Clay (The Chaucer Press) Ltd
Bungay, Suffolk
Set in Linotype Times

For John Ramsay-Fairfax

Contents

1

How it began

There was a fresh wind from the north-east and a sharp autumn tang in the air. The little ketch would not take long to reach the southern side of the Firth of Forth and already Inverkeithing had shrunk into a single lump of houses. He looked back at the familiar outline of the hills backing the coastline, which had been imprinted on his mind since boyhood and which had always brought a surge of warmth to his heart on return from even a short voyage, say, to Norway. Now he had no idea when he would see home again. He felt uncomfortably moved.

'The Cappey will be right sorry to see you away,' the helmsman said, jerking his head in the direction of Burnt Island. The young man nodded but did not encourage a conversation. It was not his father but his mother who most occupied his thoughts. She had always entreated against his partiality for the naval profession. Now she had lost that battle. Ever since he could remember, she had made it her duty to plead anxiously with his father that their only son should finish his education before taking to a maritime career, or, as she put it, 'starting in life'. The Captain, however, had been obstinate.

'All efforts to dissuade the boy serve only to make him the more resolute,' he had retorted to his wife. 'However much you may dread exposing him to the dangers of the sea, I am compelled to yield an unwilling consent to his wishes. He is soon to be a man.'

This decision had been taken when he was but a tender fifteen. Now he had developed into a fully grown man of twenty-three. His disposition in life being thus early determined upon, the father had initiated him into the duties of his profession without delay. Despite Mrs Greig's strong and continued opposition young Samuel had accompanied his father, the Captain, on his very next voyage to Norway in the little ship which he owned. An unfortunate expedition as it turned out, since the vessel had been wrecked in a storm and the Cappey and he had escaped drowning only by the skin of their teeth.

'Shall you be home for the lifting?' the helmsman said, bent on an exchange of opinion or perhaps sympathetic to the melancholy which he knew must be animating the young naval officer-to-be. The 'lifting' took place in the late spring when the sheep and cattle, which had survived an almost fodderless winter, would be half driven, half carried by the farmers out once more to the fields.

'I doubt it, Angus. When one goes for a commission in the King's Service, the likelihood will be a long spell abroad – even if this be merely blockading the French off Brest.'

The helmsman, who had never been further south than Berwick, had but the vaguest idea of what the King's Service entailed. The recent affair of Admiral Byng, however, dwelt in the popular mind as a caution against too romantic a notion of the realities of Royal Naval life. This was the year of Our Lord seventeen hundred and fifty-eight, and the war with France, later to be known as the Seven Years' War, had been in progress a mere two years.

'Have you yet been appointed a ship, Master Samuel?' The helmsman was indefatigable in his friendly curiosity.

'Why no, Angus, nothing as yet has been arranged. I stay with my sister in Edinburgh tonight and then, on the morrow, post to London, there to find my fortune or whatever Providence may intend for my life.'

These noble sentiments helped somewhat to disguise the loneliness he felt privately at the prospect. What, indeed, did Providence intend?

'London!' said the helmsman, spitting out his quid of tobacco. 'They say it's a right wicked city filled with the most shameless Jezebels. A Sodom and Gomorrah of a place.'

'Your smile belies you, Angus,' said Samuel Greig, 'but no matter the morals of London, I go there to get a ship.'

'Then God be with you, Master Samuel, I have no doubt you will be needing His help.'

*

The Edinburgh of 1758 had not yet expanded to any appreciable extent into what later became known as the New Town, but still remained within its ancient limits for safety and defence. The ten to twelve storey houses, each in the possession of a particular clan, whose various members lived on floors appropriate to their grade, reflected an equally ancient French influence and were as alien to the English style, which Samuel Greig was soon to discover, as chalk and cheese.

Samuel's sister had married an Edinburgh bookseller called Charters, and it was to this dwelling that Samuel Greig now repaired with his small portable bundle of possessions for the farewell gathering which, he had been told, had been arranged to celebrate his departure south on the following day. Margaret embraced him warmly. After enquiring about the health of their father and mother, she dispatched him to reserve his place on the coach.

'And cousin Sarah Cook shall be your navigator for this purpose,' she said, 'and shall ensure your return in case you should be tempted to the horse racing on Leith sands.'

'Come now, Meg,' he said, 'is that folly never to be forgotten, not even when I am away to sea?'

But his sister had said it kindly and Samuel sensed that nothing would mar the modest festivity which was to come. Cousin Sarah, whom he had not previously met, turned out to be a slender girl with bright green eyes, freckles and clear golden-red hair which seemed to dance with fire. She had not as yet developed physically as a woman, but it struck Samuel instantly that she had a spirit as lively as a sprite.

'No getting into unexpected scrapes now, Sarah,' his sister said with a frown which she hoped would be taken as ferocious. 'This child is a regular tomboy,' she went on for her brother's benefit, 'just because her father is at sea with Admiral Hawke and she has no brothers or sisters to curb her, her mother finds her more than a handful, I can assure you, and so do we.'

'Come, Sarah,' Samuel said, 'you shall lead me by the hand to the coaching inn.'

And that was how it began. The child took his hard,

calloused seaman's hand and dragged him away like an eager young pony.

'I am coming with you,' she said, as they picked their way through the filthy Edinburgh streets, with the previous night's ordure thrown from the high buildings still left uncleared. 'I am cutting off my hair and coming as a seaman boy to fight the French, even though they say it is an English war and nought to do with the Scots.'

'You will be doing no such thing,' Samuel said, 'and if you are counting on me as an accomplice, you are badly deceived.'

'My father is a Captain in the Royal Navy,' Sarah said proudly, 'and since he has no offspring but me, I must do duty as a son.'

'Do duty for what you are,' Samuel said, returning the squeeze of the hand which she was giving him, 'you will not long be a skinny little urchin. It is bodices and skirts, not breeches and hose, which will best become you.'

'A curse on all women,' Sarah said, with an attempt at bravado, at the same time snatching away her hand. 'I thought you of all people would have had the spunk to help me further my intent – and you about to seek a commission of the King.'

'As to that,' Samuel replied with a smile, 'you are a very forward and outspoken young madam and it is my opinion, on an acquaintanceship of five minutes, that becoming modesty and patience are somewhat lacking in your composition. How many years do you admit to in your life?'

'Why, sir, I am eleven,' Sarah said with a flash of very white teeth and an arrogant toss of her head, 'and my father was a Midshipman at twelve.'

'Well, Sarah, when you yourself attain the great age of twelve, I doubt that your interest will lie in fighting the French attired as a boy.'

'We shall see, shall we not?' Sarah said, and led the way into the courtyard from which the coaches set off on their four hundred-mile stages south to London.

The premises of Mr Charters, the Bookseller, were not

extensive but his inauguration of the new London idea of circulating libraries had forced him to acquire the house next door. Even so, Samuel found himself surprised at the number of relations and friends who came to the farewell party. Of Greigs there were none since Samuel was the last descendant of an old but decayed Scottish family. Of uncles, aunts and cousins, however, no shortage revealed itself and indeed it was to a relative on his mother's side that he owed his forthcoming expedition to London. Or rather it was to Dr Somerville, a kindly but strong-charactered elder of the kirk, that Samuel would be obliged for his essential recommendation to patronage at the Admiralty.

'In this ebullient period through which the country is passing,' he said to Samuel, almost as if addressing him from a pulpit, 'a word from a great officer of state would instantly promote your interests in whatever direction you have set your desires. Since I cannot give you either Lord Bute or Mr Pitt, I an recommending you to a Mr Oswald of Wandsworth whose influence with the Board of Admiralty and with the dockyards of Deptford and Portsmouth I believe to be considerable. You are embarking upon a naval career at a fortunate time. I know of no previous period in the recent history of Scotland and England when the temper and spirit of the British nation was more in unison than today. You will discover that persons of every rank in the southern capital are disposed to mirth and festivity. The general gloom and despondency diffused by the disgraceful events two years ago at the commencement of this war with France have not only been dispelled by the vigorous administration of Mr Pitt but are also daily increased by what is, to my mind, the most brilliant series of naval and military exploits ever to be recorded in the annals of Britain. They afford both pride and exultation.'

'You believe, sir, that Mr Pitt can win us this war?'

'No, Samuel, that is what you are to do. But Mr Pitt is a leader unique to our times in that he possesses that rare ability to give our countries the impersonal service they need. Our Prussian ally King Frederick, no less, has said that, "England has been long in labour but at last she has brought forth a man", and the well-celebrated London writer whose christian name you share has observed that whereas Walpole was a Minister given by the Crown to the people, so Pitt is a Minister given by the people to the Crown. I refer to Dr Johnson, of course.'

He turned to an elderly man with white hair who had joined them, and who seemed to be amused at the 'sermon' the worthy Doctor was preaching.

'And what is the opinion in Muscovy, Mr Cook?' Dr Somerville enquired, following this remark with an explanation to Samuel that Mr Cornelius Cook, uncle to Sarah, had held the post of Consul at Crondstadt and Petersburg almost from the time of Peter the Great, and that he was now about to retire and to induct his son into the same position. Both Cooks intended to sail back to the northern port before the winter ice set in.

'I fear that Grand Chancellor Bestuzhev proved himself to be no William Pitt,' the Consul replied, 'but then nor does he have Mr Pitt's parliamentary troubles with the King. Bestuzhev had the ageing Empress Elizabeth if not in his pouch at least under reasonable control – in so far that a barbarian autocrat can be said to be under anyone's control.'

'And I apprehend that we in our turn had the Grand Chancellor in our pocket,' Dr Somerville observed.

'He was in receipt of an English subsidy,' the Consul corrected him, 'which is not an identical state of affairs. Our newly arrived Ambassador told me that he hopes soon to counter the influence of the Versailles court. But in Russia nothing remains stable for long. Who knows where the whim of the Empress will next direct her attention? Count Vorontsov, who has stepped into the Chancellor's shoes, will no doubt change the scene, as will the Grand Duchess Catherine, so it is said, when her husband becomes the next ruler of Russia.'

He paused and studied young Samuel as if judging his capability to comprehend.

'The Grand Duke Peter,' he went on, 'is of diminished intellectual ability and has only the morality of the barrack room to offer his country. He is reported to play with toy soldiers during the day and retire drunk to his marital bed, clad in his breeches and boots. There is universal sympathy for the Grand Duchess, his wife.'

The young sailor listened with an attention perhaps a little more apparent than real. His mind was on the venture awaiting him in the immediate future down in the south. Moreover there seemed to be a dearth of that leavening to a farewell gathering for which a young man of his age naturally looked – and that was the presence of any personable young ladies. Not even Sarah was there and when he enquired the reason, her mother informed him tartly that the child had been sent to bed for disobedience.

'And I hold you partially to blame,' Mrs Cook informed him,' for encouraging her in this demented idea she has of running away to sea.'

'*I* encourage her?' Samuel said in astonishment. 'But I did nothing of the sort. The truth, indeed, is the opposite.'

'You are not, I hope, accusing my daughter of telling untruths, Mr Greig?'

'Come, come, Martha,' the Consul interrupted his cousin, 'do not tease a sober young man on his way to the war. We are all well aware of the mischief which my niece, Sarah, can contrive even at her tender age. Better to take upon yourself any blame which may attach for her behaviour.'

'She has need of a father,' Mrs Cook replied, 'and the Royal Navy requires her father to be at sea. This is agreeable neither to his wife nor to his daughter.'

'This young man intends the same career,' the old Consul interrupted, determined not to permit 'Mother Cook' her familiar carping. 'Tell me, Mr Greig,' he went on quickly, 'why, when you are already an accomplished Captain of your father's merchant vessel, you should fix your eye upon the Royal Navy as the means of advancement most congenial to your tastes?'

'Why, sir, to serve the King,' Samuel said, caught unawares.

'The English King, Mr Greig? Indeed, to be more pertinent, a German King scarce able to converse in the English language? Your principles do you great credit.'

The old man's twisted smile seemed to reveal a lifetime of assessing and judging the real motives of those with whom he did business or to whom he was beholden. But there was a kindliness in the look which belied any malice, as there was in Dr Somerville who had now joined them again.

'Well, sir,' Samuel said, 'I owe as well to certain ambitious feelings, the gratification of which—'

'In a word, Mr Greig, shall we say prize money?'

Weathered though his young face had already been by the elements, Samuel found an unwelcome blush mounting to his cheeks.

'There is no dishonour in that,' the Consul continued. 'Your parents are now in the decline of life and when misfortune presses, as I understand it does, it is legitimate to endeavour a provision of the comfort their age requires, and thus for this worthy object to engross your thoughts.'

'I thank you, sir,' Samuel said. He had no quarrel with the sentiment, even when thus pompously expressed; it was his ability to put the plan into effect which disturbed him.

'However, Mr Greig, I apprehend that you have not had truck with the English before?' Samuel nodded. 'So you will permit a much older man a word of advice? You will find that matters are ordered in London in a very different manner from north of the border. I have spent the greater part of my life in Crondstadt and St Petersburg, but that does not imply that I have not informed myself of the march of events. Moreover there is a disproportionate number of our countrymen – of varied rank and quality – either in the Russian service or engaged in commerce or in the affairs of the Court whose interest,' he shrugged his shoulders, 'it is not always possible to declare.'

He paused whilst his hostess replenished his glass and gave her brother, Samuel, a knowing wink.

'We Scots have both an advantage and a disadvantage in our union with England, and in what has happened since 1707. As your dominie will have told you, at the time when our Scots Parliament was abolished and the late Queen Anne became the sovereign of Great Britain, a number of changes in our lives took place. Our previous trade with

Holland and Scandinavia expanded into the English colonies. Opportunities for Scottish intelligence and energy opened up to us all and there has been a steady migration to the south ever since. The grinding poverty into which your father and mine were born began to yield sensibly to improvements in agriculture and to an increase in trade imported from the south. When I was your age, tea was known to the Scottish subjects of Queen Anne only as an expensive medicine. Cottage windows were bereft of glass. Even chimneys were rare, since no bedroom but only "the fire room" enjoyed the luxury of heat. Our staple diet remained oats and you will recall the basis on which even this simple food was produced.'

'Ane to gnaw and ane to saw and ane to pay the laird witha', Samuel put in and was rewarded with a nod and a smile.

'Children always and grown-ups often went on their way bare-footed in damp, stinking clothes so that rheumatism has become our national heritage and scourge ... and so on and so forth.'

The old man paused and looked into Samuel's clear blue eyes.

'All now is changed,' he went on; 'why, even the gaberlunzies in their blue gowns with their licence to beg from door to door – even they are in decline. Of such is progress.'

'And what is the matter with that?' Samuel ventured to say.

'Nought that the English can apprehend,' the Consul said, looking into the distance, 'but we Scots maintain, nevertheless, a sour aversion to our purseproud, overbearing, southern neighbours. The English, in turn, to whom every Scot is a Jacobite or a Presbyterian and to both of which they feel incontrovertibly alien, regard us as uncouth, unreliable, bigoted and incomprehensible. That, sir, is the crux of the matter and the climate of consideration in which you will find yourself when you begin to seek patronage in the great capital city of London. But be not discouraged, Mr Greig, this is an age of progress where reason hold sway. You should nevertheless thank a beneficent

Deity for the foreign wars. There lies your fortune and your hope, as the fair heather-clad hills of Scotland dwindle into nothing more than the memory they have been to me these forty-five years through the cruel winters and the burning summers of the Russian realm. Thank you, Meg,' he finished as Samuel's sister replenished his glass, 'this instruction of the young is a thirsty business indeed.'

The next day, shortly after dawn, Samuel Greig set off for England. He had plenty to mull over en route and the journey proved lengthy enough for him to indulge all his hopes and speculations to the full. Before leaving his sister's house, however, a drama had taken place. Cousin Sarah had played truant in the night and could not be found. She had taken a small amount of money from her mother's purse, had cut off her hair, leaving it in a tidy pile with the grey dress she habitually wore, and had disappeared before the household was astir.

'Doubtless she had acquired other clothes,' Margaret opined. 'Probably a shirt and breeches since she was always saying she would run away to sea as a powder-monkey, and she could certainly be taken for a boy.'

Sister Meg was the only member of the family who found amusement in this exploit. Sarah's mother collapsed in a rage and had to return to her bed. The men left the house to try to discover the child's whereabouts.

'She was always threatening a prank of this nature,' Meg went on. 'The girl has her father's dash and spirit. I doubt she will come to much harm. We have guardian angels, do we not? Here, Sam, put away a lock of her hair for luck. Perhaps you will find yourselves at sea in the same man-of-war. She took a great fancy to you yesterday.'

So Samuel set off in the heavy rumbling coach with a curl of Sarah's red burnished hair in his pouch. Like his sister he could not find it in his heart to condemn the child. From what he had seen of the mother, Mrs Cook too easily gave the impression of being a tiresome scold and even their short acquaintanceship was long enough to tell him that Sarah certainly had the temper and the will to set about doing what she had apparently long planned to achieve.

He had imagined she might be lurking somewhere in the coach yard ready, no doubt, to clamber on board at the last moment or possibly, as had happened before, curled up in the baggage. But she was not there and, as the long slow journey began, he put away the lock of her hair and with it the memory of her bright, young smile and her dancing eyes. Providence would decide her fate as it would his own, but he sent a prayer for her safekeeping and success. Providence would take care of them all. The solid old coach with its four horses trundled slowly south to the land of the Sassenachs. Another lean, threadbare Scot had begun the long and dangerous journey towards his individual fame and fortune.

London did not welcome him with open arms. In fact it did not welcome him at all, except to remove from him all his material possessions bar those he carried on his person, by means of one of the oldest 'tricks of the trade'. He had been deposited tired and hungry at a coaching inn near Holborn and was immediately set on by three porters in vociferous competition for the privilege of taking his effects on the final leg of his journey to Deptford. There he was to seek out the Collins family who were ship chandlers of long standing and, as his uncle had advised him, 'Mrs Collins keeps a decent house, from which no doubt you will get your bearings.'

However the problem was to reach Deptford from Holborn together with his grip. The three porters bid angrily and noisily against each other for Samuel's custom – at times threatening one another with violence – but when finally Samuel had settled on one particular man, it was discovered that his effects had been neatly removed whilst his back was turned. Everything he possessed was gone and he was alone in a strange and hostile city. It took him a moment or so to realize the full enormity of what had happened, and by then the three bawling contenders for his custom had melted away. When he applied for help to the innkeeper, he received a look of scathing contempt and was told there was no beadle or authority to whom he could refer. 'Those who cannot mind their own property, deserve to be parted from it,' he was advised and so, angry and despondent, he set about walking to Deptford as night fell, nurturing strong feelings of hostility to all Londoners and their filthy city, which had afforded him so scurvy a welcome.

Mrs Collins did much to put this right. She was a stout motherly woman who had prepared him a room at the top of the house and who tried to restore his flagging spirits with an excellent cut of roast beef washed down with Kentish ale.

'And tomorrow,' she said, 'Mr Collins will accompany you back to Holborn. I hold out but little hope of recovering your portmanteau. However you may be able to identify the rogues who distracted your attention and this in turn may lead to discovering the thief.'

'It is unco' guid of you,' Samuel said, at the foot of the dark winding stairs. 'I'm just a wee bit exhausted by the journey and distressed to arrive in such a plight.'

Mrs Collins patted him on the shoulder.

'You'll just have to get over it,' she said, but in a kindly tone of voice, 'it's not the end of the world.'

'But I am recommended, you understand, to a Mr Oswald of Wandsworth who may be able to advance my naval ambitions, and now I have nae decent clothing in which to wait upon him.'

'I have no doubt we can remedy that. Tomorrow is another day. Now away with you upstairs for a good night's sleep.'

In spite of Mrs Collins' care and attention, Samuel dropped off to sleep that night in a state of lonely despondency. Before turning in he looked out of the dormer window at the small forest of ships' masts and rigging which lay below him bathed in the moonlight. He felt not only a long, long way from home, which was undeniable, but also gripped by a fear of the unknown. To be friendless and deprived of his worldly goods in a great city like London, did not augur well, and his prayers to that Providence in which he had been taught to put his trust were that night of a somewhat plaintive and melancholy nature.

However, he consoled himself, he still had a small amount of money in his pouch, together with the lock of Sarah's hair, and in a vivid dream which visited him that night, the bright child who had made him her confidant came dancing back along what seemed to be Leith sands and again took him shyly by the hand to lead him towards the great shining sea. Together they advanced into the waves as they broke upon the beach, and it was with a feeling of tremendous joy that they stepped into the sea, hand in hand – at which point Samuel woke up to discover the rain beating in on his bed from the open window of his room.

The visit to Holborn the next day proved to be lively and all but disastrous. However it did result in the Collinses having to reassess their initial impressions of the young man from the north. That very first night as they had reclined into slumber, as Jenny Collins usually phrased it, or slid into the arms of Lethe, as the more poetic Mr Collins had it whilst accommodating his own ample proportions to those of his wife, they had exchanged opinions about Samuel.

'As young men go, he is agreeable enough,' Mrs Collins had remarked. 'He is of a polite disposition, mild in temperament and no doubt when we have come to an understanding of the Scottish brogue in his speech, we shall the better appreciate his qualities.'

'How would you rate him as a fighting man, Jenny? After all, he seeks a Commission of the King with that end in view.'

'You can never be assured of the shy ones,' Mrs Collins replied. 'On the face of it, he seems to be gifted with little of the swashbuckling seafaring arrogance you and I know only too well in Deptford.'

'Dull,' Mr Collins murmured as he dropped off to sleep. 'Worthy enough, but something of an honest jog-trot man, I'd say . . .'

The next day was to alter all that. Samuel and Mr Collins made their way to Holborn and, advised by the landlord who was disposed to be helpful once he saw in Mr Collins a man of substance like himself, the three rascals who had purloined Samuel's effects were identified as to name although no trace of them could be found in the vicinity of the coaching inn.

'Nor will they show their faces here until another coach comes in from the north. They are adept at the trickery they put over on this innocent young man, but they rarely apply their ruses to anyone coming from south of York. However were you to go to the *Nag's Head* in Covent Garden and ask for Jack Ratcliffe, you might discover their whereabouts.'

Jack Ratcliffe, it seemed, specialized in the arranging of 'Fleet marriages' which were illicitly-legalized unions conducted in tavern courtyards, usually by clergymen confined in the nearby prison for debt and who split the fees with those who organized the trade, such as Jack Ratcliffe. Samuel, privately shocked but determined to put a good face on it, found a hot-blooded anger taking possession of him with each flagon of ale which he and Mr Collins drank. This seemed to amuse the ship chandler but Jack Ratcliffe made it clear they were wasting his time and as soon as the bloated go-between finally decided that Samuel was not likely to be a prospective client, it took a sizeable gratuity from Mr Collins to secure the information they sought.

At that moment one of the three thieving porters slipped into the *Nag's Head*. 'Ha!' said Samuel, springing to his feet. Without a moment's further hesitation, he seized the blackguard by the arm, twisting it behind his back and threatening to break it if the whereabouts of his portmanteau and its contents were not revealed. But the porter denied all that had happened and continuously called for help. Since he seemed to have plenty of friends in the tavern, in no time at all Samuel found himself in the middle of a maelstrom of fighting men, of thrashing arms and of doubled-up fists. This affray moved first into the yard and then out into the street. Samuel suffered a black eye and a cut lip but, in the considered opinion of Mr Collins, he was giving his adversaries as good as he received before 'Mr Fielding's people' – that set of brave fellows who pursued malefactors from nearby Bow Street – arrived on the scene and attempted to make arrests.

At that point the crowd melted away like a puff of wind, and Samuel was taken along to the lower front room of the magistrate's house where he then had to explain himself to the blind Mr Fielding, a daunting experience in itself. Luckily there were those present who spoke for him, and ably assisted by the jovial Mr Collins who had skilfully avoided the mêlée but who had nonetheless stuck closely by his young charge, Samuel was released with a caution and on the payment of a small fine by Mr Collins.

Somewhat the worse for wear, Samuel returned to Deptford with his mentor, who saw fit to congratulate Samuel on his fighting courage. 'I also advise you to pass it all off in your mind as merely a part of the experience necessary to acclimatize yourself to London life,' Mr Collins went on. 'Were you already a man-of-war's man, I would say you was begotten in the galley and born under a gun – every hair a rope yarn, every tooth a marline spike, every finger a fish-hook and your blood right good Stockholm tar.' To this Samuel found little to say, not being entirely sure that to be born under a gun was a complimentary reference.

That night in bed, Mr Collins remarked to his wife, as Lethe set about the work of claiming him again:

'He is neither dull nor worthy, as we both of us thought, but a game little fighting-cock. Ho! yes, he has spirit enough for ten. I would not care to face that one were I a Frenchy Frog and the King's enemy.'

'Yes, yes,' said Mrs Collins, patting her husband's stomach in a comforting way, 'he is a brighter young man than either of us thought.'

So the next day, Mrs Collins whose motherly instincts had now been sensibly increased by a ready admiration for 'a true fighting man' made every effort to assuage the physical damage Samuel had suffered, and at the same time to restore his flagging spirits. Not in fact that he had much need of this. Indeed he seemed almost to be preening himself.

'There is a remedy for every disaster,' she said, applying

a poultice of raw meat to his blackened eye, and with a nod at her husband, went on: 'Mr Collins will advance you the necessary funds to secure replacements of the clothing you had stolen. Moreover once you have been appointed to a ship, you will need to equip yourself with a suitable naval uniform. Our good friend Smolley, the tailor, can take care of that on a credit basis. Both Mr Collins and I feel it shameful that a fine, upright young man about to go to the wars in a King's ship should receive such a shabby welcome in London town.'

'Och! away,' Samuel said with a grin, 'now that it is behind me, I must admit to enjoyment of the scrape. I think I gave as good as I received.'

'You broke his nose,' Mr Collins said, 'and maybe also his pock-marked jaw. He will think twice before taking on another young innocent from north of the border. I do not fancy you will be lingering long in Deptford, my boy. Go and see your Mr Oswald who is, if I mistake it not, a high Government official on the look-out for just such a fighting man as yourself.'

'I had better delay the visit a day or so,' Samuel said, looking at himself a little ruefully in the glass. 'I doubt a black eye is the best visiting card to present.'

'Nevertheless – with the backing of a man such as Mr Oswald, you will soon be set on a great naval career. Now let us go and drink some ale until Jenny has our dinner prepared.'

Mr Oswald of Wandsworth, the placeman to whom he had been principally recommended by Dr Somerville, turned out to be a sharp-eyed, round-headed person of substance, judging by the house to which Samuel was admitted at Wandsworth. Mr Oswald, in fact, was a Junior Lord of the Treasury and lived in some style.

'You are fortunate in finding me here,' he told Samuel when he had bidden him into his study. 'A slight indisposition has kept me from Whitehall this day so that I am in a position to attend to other affairs.'

Judging by the number of interruptions which there were to this first encounter, it became clear to Samuel that Mr

Oswald's other affairs were extensive and of a personal concern, such as his share of an importation of brandy from France, rather than those strictly concerned with the state. However it was soon evident to Samuel that in spite of – or perhaps because of – the subtle questions he was asked, Mr Oswald had taken a fancy to him.

'Sturdy new arrivals from Scotland are never in short supply,' Mr Oswald remarked taking a little snuff and obliging Samuel with a piercing look, 'but you are highly spoken of by Dr Somerville who declares you possessed of a strength of mind, a decisiveness of character and a strict integrity. Excellent, excellent. To this he adds that strong religious feelings have been inculcated in you from an early age by Dr MacFait of Inverkeithing – a dominie of some renown north of the border.'

'And by my mother and father,' Samuel put in nervously. He did not wish the role his parents had played in this matter to be overlooked.

'Yes, yes,' Mr Oswald said, impatient at the interruption. 'However it is your naval talent which must now be examined.'

'I have had several years' experience in my father's ship,' Samuel said eagerly.

'Service in a merchant vessel carries but little weight with the Lords Commissioners of Admiralty,' Mr Oswald remarked in a lofty tone of voice. 'However I shall be mentioning your name to some of my acquaintance in the naval service, so if you were to pay me another visit in, let us say, ten days' time I may have some news for you.'

'Ten days?' Samuel said, an acute disappointment showing on his face. 'I had hoped for a more rapid . . .' he faltered into silence as Mr Oswald rose to his feet and indicated that the interview was at an end.

'You have a great deal to learn, Mr Greig, as to the way in which such matters are arranged here in London. However,' he went on, with a smile at Samuel's crestfallen appearance, 'there is a requirement in this war for persons of your calibre however uncouth their manners may be. Do not despair. You are young and all is ahead for you. I will make it my business to see that you get a ship but you must learn patience. Now, sir, do you come back as I have suggested you should in ten days' time, and perhaps you will do me the honour of staying to dinner.'

'I am greatly obliged to you, sir,' Samuel managed to blurt out, suppressing with difficulty the disappointment he felt, and was shown politely to the door.

When later he recounted to Mr Collins what had happened, the ship's chandler gave a guffaw.

'So you have had your first encounter with a high personage of government,' he said, 'and you are only offering your services. Imagine what it is like when you are tendering a supply of stores or of victuals to the fleet! Patronage is all, Master Greig, in this world we live in today and the acquiring of patronage can be a lifetime's study. But do not be downcast. It appears to me that Mr Oswald is prepared to help you, no doubt with a future reward in mind.'

The intervening ten days between his first and second meetings with Mr Oswald were as difficult a time as Samuel had ever experienced. Samuel regarded himself as a man of action, a practical seaman accustomed to giving a ready and practical answer to any problem he was faced with on board ship. To have to kick his heels and wait upon the efforts and the good nature of others was something else. However guided by – and at times gently mocked by – the benevolent Collins family, he survived this period of trial.

Smolley the tailor fitted him out with a coat appropriate to the rank of Master's Mate which, he was told, was the most he could initially hope for in the King's service and, to the amusement of the Collinses, he withstood the blandishments of the dockside ladies who frequented the nearby tavern, walking many, many miles through the London streets and contriving to wait with as good a grace as he could muster until the evening arrived when he was to present himself once more at the Wandsworth residence of the Junior Lord of the Treasury.

This time he was greeted by Mrs Oswald, a lady of some

affability who condescended to put him at his ease and provided him and some ten other guests with a dinner which in Inverkeithing would have been considered a feast. He was plied with an excellent claret and when the ladies had withdrawn, Mr Oswald drew him to one side and said:

'I have, as I promised, mentioned your name in the right quarters and there is a prospect of employment.'

'I am greatly obliged to you, sir,' Samuel said, 'but when shall I receive the appointment?'

'I have no doubt you will be at sea before the summer is out,' Mr Oswald said blandly.

'Before the summer is out ...' Samuel echoed, feeling as if he had fallen through a hole in the ground.

'Come now, Mr Greig, I warned you that patience is necessary in these matters. Perhaps you would care to take a turn with me in the new conservatory which I have just had constructed. I should like to give you a little advice before we rejoin the others.'

Without waiting for Samuel's reply, Mr Oswald led the way through into a glass edifice the like of which Samuel had never before observed, and then taking him by the arm, walked him slowly up and down, interrupting his discourse from time to time to point out some exotic plant for which he had great hopes.

'You are an eager, impatient young man,' Mr Oswald began, 'and there is no harm in that. However you will be entering a service where merit, alas, has to struggle hard and often unsuccessfully with the patronage of the great. It bears heavily upon every aspect of our lives and you will be no exception to this long-standing rule. You have seven years' experience of the sea and indeed have captained your father's ship. You will find this of little avail when you seek advancement under the naval regulations. There the purchase of a Midshipman's place at birth by some nobleman for his son will block your progress on the seniority list.'

'How, then, am I to succeed?' Samuel asked.

'By the courage, audacity and obvious skills you possess,' Mr Oswald answered. 'These in the end will secure you the preferment which others, less talented, will have had dropped into their laps. It will take you longer, that is all. England is at war with the ancient enemy and the King has need of every trained fibre you possess, whether of mind, spirit or body. The rewards are there and shall be yours when they have been duly earned. Moreover as you do progress in the Service, you will yourself acquire the friendship and patronage of the Captains and Admirals under whom you serve. They are not monsters of selfishness and greed – at least not all of them are. Moreover, as Mr Pitt has discovered in the prosecution of this war, and despite a frequent and powerful opposition from the King, which you may find surprising, nothing succeeds more expeditiously than success itself. Your fate is perhaps more in your hands than you imagine. But you must propitiate – or at least not offend – the custodians of Mammon. It is a wise chandler who knows where best he should hamper in the Royal Dockyards.'

Since Samuel had no clear idea of what Mr Oswald meant by 'hampering', he had to have some of the intricacies of tendering for a warship's stores explained to him. It seemed that the apt arrival of a suitable hamper at the home of the purchasing official ensured the success of the tender, however outrageous the price. Leading the way back into the main room where the other guests had reassembled, Mr Oswald indicated an older man to whom Samuel had been briefly introduced before sitting down to dinner.

'Enquire of Mr Patterson,' he murmured, 'as to how the perquisites of office can provide many an interesting competence. Mr Patterson trades into Muscovy, where hampering might be said to be on a national scale.'

It seemed to Samuel, as he was being given these sidelong views into the common corruption of government, that he had already come a million miles from the simple commercial practices of Inverkeithing and Burnt Island.

'However,' said his host who appeared to be watching him closely and even reading his thoughts, 'such matters do not concern you at this stage of your career. But as I would hazard a guess that you will go far in your chosen profession, it behoves you to learn the ways of the world in that same chosen profession with all despatch. The conduct of affairs in London is markedly different from that in our own country, Mr Greig.'

'You are a Scotsman, sir?' Samuel asked, his surprise evidently displeasing Mr Oswald. It would have displeased his host even more had Samuel gone on to say, which was on the tip of his tongue, that Mr Oswald sounded as if he had been born and bred a Sassenach.

'That you should have discovered before presenting your letter of recommendation,' he said severely. 'Yes, Mr Greig, I am a Scot hailing from Dunikeer, a kinsman of Lord Bute to whom I naturally owe my place and favour. And Mr Patterson, here, is related by marriage to Consul Cook whom I believe you saw recently in Edinburgh.'

'And related by commerce as well,' Mr Patterson put in. He was a jovial, round-faced man, with almost a replica of himself for a wife. 'My son, over there, has just returned from Crondstadt and Petersburg where we ship in a variety of goods to the Russian Court, and from which we receive furs and timber, there being little else of value which the Russians can offer by way of trade.'

Young Clarence Patterson, to whom Samuel now found himself presented, seemed to be as open and likeable as his father. Another young man of military bearing who was with him turned out to be a Captain Keith, the son of the new English Ambassador to the Court of Imperial Russia. He, too, had just returned from a visit to his father and he, too, was Scottish.

'So you see, Mr Greig, our countrymen are disposed in strategic places all over the world,' Mr Oswald remarked, studying him through somewhat crafty-looking eyes as if he were all the time assaying his quality, which in fact was exactly what he was doing.

'How does this come about?' Samuel asked with an assumed innocence and remembering the dissertation to which he had been treated by Consul Cook.

'We Scots have a special position in the continent of Europe.' Mr Oswald clearly enjoyed hearing himself speak on what was evidently a favourite topic. 'I take it you are not a Jacobite, Mr Greig?'

Samuel nodded. 'I would not take up arms for Prince Charles Edward,' he said, 'but fortunately the decision was not a difficult one to reach. At the time of the rising, I was but ten years old.'

'You will find many Scotsmen about the world who are of a different persuasion. They become of use to England's enemies, since often a Scotsman is accepted where an Englishman is not.'

'That is correct,' Captain Keith broke in. 'My father has recently been forced to protest to the old Empress against the presentation at the Imperial Court of a certain Monsieur or as he prefers to call himself Chevalier, Douglas whom the French King had sent, accompanied by a strange lady called Lia de Beaumont, both of whom my father knew to have been enrolled by the Prince de Conti in le secret du Roi.'

'And what is that?' Samuel enquired.

'In a word, sir, they were spies reporting directly to King Louis.' Captain Keith pronounced it 'Lewis'. 'The French King may be known disparagingly as "La Pompadourette", but he is well informed through his private spies working to the Prince de Conti and le secret du Roi. By this means he is enabled to check on, and if need be to rein in, his accredited Ambassador.'

'And why was your father so concerned to keep Mr Douglas at bay?'

'Because the English Ambassador had at last persuaded the Empress Elizabeth – who has never been a real friend to England – to send some fifty thousand troops on our behalf to Hanover to prosecute the war.'

'Why should she do that?'

'Why, sir, for a hundred thousand pounds from King George's treasury,' Captain Keith replied; 'which scheme the Chevalier Douglas and his strange companion were ordered to disrupt.'

'What was so strange about the companion?' Samuel asked, his interest thoroughly aroused.

'Some say she was a man in disguise and that she was

in reality a Chevalier herself. The Chevalier d'Eon by name and notoriety.'

He looked at the naval officer-to-be wondering how this would strike him. Samuel pondered it all for a moment or two and then said:

'I confess I am glad to remain no more than a simple sailor and to be going to sea in a man-o'war. Diplomacy is not for me.'

'Defer a judgment on that matter for a while,' Mr Oswald said. 'You may wish to reverse such an opinion once you have made your way in the King of England's Navy. Indeed, Mr Greig, you will soon discover that every naval officer at some stage or other must act as his country's Ambassador in unforeseen but compelling circumstances.'

Then with a further smile, he proceeded to attend to other of his guests.

2

'This is Russia ...'

The Grand Duchess Catherine moved slowly across from the window of the Winter Palace, from which she had been contemplating the Petersburg scene, nodded at her lady-in-waiting with what struck the English Ambassador as a conspiratorial look and then, when Maria Ivanova had closed the door firmly behind her, remarked in a low, somewhat husky voice:

'You have undertaken a grave risk in calling on me here – and I, also, in permitting you the visit.'

'I was told that there is an excellent prospect of the new formal garden from the window of your apartment,' Robert Keith replied. Both he and the Grand Duchess spoke in French and had drawn very close to each other. 'I was also informed that Her Imperial Majesty is making one of her rare visits to her naval establishment at Crondstadt.'

Without wasting further time he took the Grand Duchess in his arms and sought her lips in a willing and passionate embrace. Then leaning slightly back he went on: 'And your husband, the Grand Duke, I gather is with his Holstein troops.'

'Whose company he so evidently prefers to that of his wife,' the Grand Duchess murmured, a sadness overcoming her countenance. She was wearing a loosely fitting blue gown which served more to reveal than to conceal the gently heaving bosom. The Ambassador was pleasantly aware of the heady perfume she had daubed on her shoulders and neck, and once again their mouths met eagerly and hungrily. Then, as his fingers began to explore the full, swelling breasts beneath the gown she bent her head backwards, pressing her body against his, and asked in a mocking voice: 'You wished to have a prospect of the garden, Your Excellency?'

'It strikes me that the prospect there,' Keith replied, nodding at the great bed with its flowing drapes, 'is better worth our attention.'

The blue dress was conveniently buttoned down the front and in a matter of moments Keith had these buttons undone so that her splendid nakedness was revealed. It was an ample, though well-proportioned body and, as she slipped her arms out of the sleeves, letting the dress fall to the ground, it seemed to Keith one which was made for love. She had put up but a token resistance to his cavalier approach and now as she lay on the bed, still with that faintly mocking smile on her lips, the prime centre of attraction lay open to the fierce, thrusting invasion for which it was designed.

'Your Excellency belies the reputation the English appear to have acquired for a coolness of passion,' Catherine observed as later they lay in each other's arms, for the moment contented with a mutual ecstasy of feeling.

'I may be the English Ambassador,' Keith answered, 'but I am still a Scotsman. We order these matters differently north of the border.'

'And I, too, am still a German,' Catherine said, a strange sadness in her voice, 'although the whimsicality of Fate has transposed me into this Russian role I am required to play. Outwardly I am the Grand Duchess Catherine, wife to the next Tsar of all the Russias: but the woman you hold in your arms still sometimes thinks of herself as the Princess Sophie-Frédérique of a more civilized Anhalt-Zerbst.'

She fell into silence and a little later Keith became aware that she was quietly crying.

'Come, come, madame,' he whispered, 'tears are not an appropriate reward for a lover – unless of course, they reveal a disappointment in the attentions paid to your feminine magnificence.'

For answer she clutched him to her with a renewed passion.

'You are not the cause of my tears, except they be those of fulfilment,' she said, kissing him tenderly in the intervals of speech. 'I cry not for you but for myself and this prison life I am compelled to live.'

The Ambassador set about comforting with words the passionate creature he had until now found it dangerous even to address in public, unless it were with the express consent and under the eye of the ageing Empress Elizabeth.

'You are not the first Princess to be procured for the purpose of assuring succession to a throne,' he said, 'and that mission you have twice fulfilled. I do not suppose – from the present state of Her Majesty's health – that your slavery will long continue. Soon, perhaps sooner than you think, you will no longer be wife to the Heir Apparent but Tsarina in living fact.'

This did not appear to please Catherine at all. She disengaged herself from his arms and sat up with a snort.

'My husband is a dolt – a brutal dolt. He would dispose of me like that if he could.'

She snapped her fingers, and suddenly she was all anger and fire.

'He wishes to replace me with my lady-in-waiting,' she went on, tossing her head, 'and with that end in view he never ceases to give the Empress the worst possible impression of my behaviour on every possible occasion.'

'Not Maria Ivanova surely?'

'Not that sweet girl – the only close companion on whom I can rely – no, it is another of my ladies-in-waiting.' She glanced at him sideways to see if he already knew this fact, but Keith's smile gave nothing away. 'The Countess Elizabeth Vorontsov it is that he has taken to his bed and into what confidence he still has the wit to possess.'

Keith nodded in agreement, thinking back to his own arrival at the Russian court.

'This has all been contrived by the French party,' he said, 'as well I know. When I first came here from Vienna I found those two Ambassadors – the French Marquis de l'Hôpital and the Austrian Count Esterhazi, in complete possession of the whole credit at court.'

The Grand Duchess again snorted like an angry horse.

'They have the Grand Duke absolutely in their power. Their instrument in this is a fellow countryman of mine, the Count von Brockdorff. That sodden lout ingratiates himself with my husband day after day. There is not a debauch in which they do not indulge. I complain to the Empress but to no avail.'

'Do your troubles not partially stem from the disgrace of the late Chancellor Bestuzhev?' Keith suggested. He had little wish to talk politics whilst he still had this naked Juno at his side, but the responsibilities of his Embassy were never far from his mind. Catherine nodded, a hard look in her eyes.

'He was alleged to have entered into various intrigues with me – the whole plot was an entire fabrication of his enemies.'

'But the Elizabeth Vorontsov you have just mentioned – is she not one of the daughters of the present Chancellor?'

'She is indeed, and I suspect feels herself to be as much entrapped as I do myself.'

'She is not a willing accomplice?'

'This is Russia, monsieur,' the Grand Duchess said, getting out of bed and indicating that the Ambassador should soon depart, 'a barren land ruled by an old woman known as a tyrant unparalleled in the modern world.'

Of this fact Ambassador Keith was only too well aware. He had been warned in his early days, he reflected ruefully as he dressed, he could not remember whether it was by Baron de Golz, the envoy of Frederick of Prussia or by Baron Merci from the Austrian court, that it was a custom in Russia to regard the Empress's bed as a place of pleasure which could easily be reached. One is allowed to aspire to it freely, he had been told, and it is even a mark of good taste to show that it is desirable.

He shuddered slightly at the disagreeable memory which the exercise of this 'privilege' – undertaken in the course of duty – had entailed. As if his thoughts were being read, he became aware of the Grand Duchess Catherine, who had just summoned the faithful Maria Ivanova to show him out, looking at him with her piercing blue eyes and with a wry smile round those full lips he had so recently devoured.

'I trust your enjoyment this afternoon,' she indicated the

window giving on to the garden, 'at least matches your experience of – other imperial prospects?'

He was astonished at her insight and perspicacity, and for a second or so he felt himself nonplussed. Then quickly pulling himself together he replied in a low voice:

'The prospect here, madame, is a thousand times more agreeable than the retrospect to which I think you refer, and about which I was not aware that you knew.'

'In this country, Your Excellency, there is very little that is not known by someone who would be better off without the knowledge. You must not visit me again,' she added, dropping her voice so that her lady-in-waiting could not hear, 'unless and until I specifically send you word.'

The Ambassador nodded formally and then took his leave. He would have a most interesting, though difficult, despatch to write to the Foreign Secretary in London who would undoubtedly discuss it with another German – King George II of Hanover and England.

A problem common to all envoys at St Petersburg was the acquisition of confidential information from a reliable source. The following day the English Ambassador was putting the finishing touches to his report whilst awaiting the arrival of Bernardi, the Court Jeweller, who had become one of his more valuable informants. Bernardi could move about between embassies and all levels of the court without attracting any undue attention.

'The Grand Duchess Catherine intends to rule Russia,' Keith had written, 'about that there is no doubt whatever, though whether as consort to the brutish Peter or in her own right, only Fate will declare. She has summed up her role to me as being "an aristocrat by duty and profession" and she is unique in that, alone of her contemporaries, she has opened herself to ideas from abroad which can only be described as highly advanced. She has passed on to me in confidence a part of the correspondence she maintains with Monsieur de Voltaire at Ferney. She has a grasp, both instinctive and informed, not only of Russian affairs but also of the entire continental balance of power. She is romantic, ardent, prepossessing and affable. She has also already developed an arresting presence – a precursor, no doubt, of the power she intends to wield. I have acquired a copy of a confidential despatch recently compiled by the current spy sent by King Louis of France to the Russian court. In it the Chevalier describes his impression of the Grand Duchess with which I find myself in at least partial agreement.

'"... her eyes are brilliant, their look fascinating and glassy – the expression of a wild beast. Her forehead is lofty and, if I am not mistaken, a long and terrifying future is written on it. When she comes close to me, I instinctively recoil for she frightens me...."' Keith allowed himself a smile when he copied this out, '"... she will be the first Intellectual to occupy the Russian throne and she thus combines the brain of a Philosophe with the will, not yet in full flower, of an autocrat to which must be added the many frailties of a full-blooded woman."'

Keith laid down his pen and reflected for a moment or so on the public and private images of this extraordinary woman, so obviously waiting in the wings of this far northern theatre. How best could he sum her up for the polished, evolved and percipient reader of his dispatch in distant London, who would want to know above all if the delicate balance of power in Europe was in danger of being disturbed?

'Unquestionably,' he finished by saying, 'this woman is unique. She intends to be – and doubtless will succeed in becoming – a formidable ruler of this primitive land unless, like the luckless Ivan VI, the prisoner of Schlusselburg, she has been put away by the present incumbent of the throne before she grasps the power in her hands.'

'Signor Bernardi is here,' his factotum informed him in the conspiratorial voice which caused the Ambassador to suppress a smile. He had trained his staff with discipline and care, making it clear that on many occasions their lives would depend on it. The arrival of the sly Florentine jeweller, however, could scarcely bring with it many uncharted dangers the limits of which could not be observed.

'Show him in here,' said the Ambassador, carefully closing and locking the inlaid escritoire which he had had made to his own design whilst in Vienna. He entertained little doubt about Bernardi's reliability. However, it was also prudent to ensure complete security.

'Well, now, *signor maestro gioielliere*, what news do you bring today?'

The little jeweller settled himself in a chair and accepted a glass of brandy with a servile bow of the head.

'The Grand Duke's infatuation for the lady-in-waiting continues to rival his love for all things German, and also to scandalize the court,' Bernardi began. 'As you know, sire, the Countess Elizabeth is Grand Chancellor Vorontsov's eldest daughter, so no doubt there is method behind this particular madness. She has a more prepossessing sister who has not yet been seen at court and who is reputed to be as fascinated by literature as the Grand Duchess Catherine herself. The Countess Elizabeth, however, has all the rough peasant attributes of her maternal grandfather whose sister, as Your Excellency is aware, was the servant Martha Skavronski and became wife to Peter the Great. The Grand Duchess Catherine has ceased to be so openly incensed as she let it appear when the liaison first began. She is reputed to have said that if it keeps her husband from attempting to play the violin and from thrashing his spaniel dogs, then it is a small price to pay. May I recall to Your Excellency a remark the Grand Duchess made concerning a predecessor in that same role, the Princess of Kurland – "the fact of her being hunchbacked could not repel a Prince of the house of Holstein – no deformity has ever been repulsive to them. In fact, the King of Sweden, my maternal uncle, never had a mistress who was not hunchbacked, lame or one-eyed." '

'I am not interested in ladies-in-waiting,' the Ambassador said, 'but in any embarrassment which can be caused to the Marquis de l'Hôpital and the French party.'

'As to that, sir, the Grand Duke's heart and soul, if he has such articles, are fixed on Holstein and Prussia – as always – and not on France. When he marshals his toy soldiers into military formations, it is always the French who must lose the battles of the day. But as to the French party, sir, I am told that Mademoiselle Lia de Beaumont, whom some claim to be the Chevalier d'Eon, has been appointed "a private reader" to the Empress Elizabeth and has taken up residence with the other ladies-in-waiting. It is rumoured that this influence – and no doubt a private understanding privately conveyed from the French King – may make the Empress reverse her present alliance with England and Prussia, and join with France and Austria.'

'That would be delicate indeed,' said the Ambassador, 'seeing that France and Austria support the Turks in their present squabble with Her Imperial Majesty.'

'At all events I have a commission from the French party for a circlet of diamonds, sapphires and rubies which it is intended to present to the Empress in token, doubtless, of some forthcoming scheme they will wish to advance.'

'I have a letter for the Grand Duchess Catherine,' the Ambassador said, his tone and smile indicating that the audience was coming to an end, 'and I would be obliged if you would deliver it into her hand without knowledge of the private chancery.' The Russian inquisition was universally feared even by foreigners protected by their letters of credence.

'Your Excellency can rely on me,' the jeweller said, 'as did your gracious predecessor. Is Your Excellency still requiring a local factotum who speaks Russian and who knows his way around the more menial court circles? Such as I understand in Austria is called a *Haus Jude*?'

The Ambassador inclined his head.

'I think I can procure you the ideal man. He has recently been employed by the Marquis de l'Hôpital but there was, I believe, an unfortunate misapprehension over remuneration. The French King, as I know to my cost, is notorious for signing bills on the future but not, alas, for producing a few hundred louis from the Treasury in cash.'

When the English Ambassador's letter arrived, the Grand Duchess Catherine had been about to make her weekly visit to Peterhof to see her four-year-old son, the Grand

Duke Paul. She could not recall a time when she had been more unhappy, in a lifetime of scarce interrupted spiritual and emotional misery. She locked away the diary she had kept since a girl in Zerbst-Stettin, placing in it Keith's little expression of sympathy and understanding, which could hardly be regarded as a love letter from a man of his age, nationality and position to a person such as herself. Nevertheless it warmed her heart.

As with her letters from Ferney, words of affection and encouragement were one of the few lifelines to civilization to which she held on in the all-pervading tatterdemalion manners which framed her existence. The tone of her life seemed to her then to be like the dark, dank Petersburg marshes which surrounded the royal palaces. She walked across to the window and gazed at the melancholy Russian landscape. Soon the snows would come, and this at least would secure a temporary release from the wretched autumn she had endured.

Although she had no doubt that the Empress would comment cruelly on her subsequent appearance, she made no effort to stop the tears from coursing down her face, as she stood there at the window, praying in a blind, wordless way for divine help in her distress. In the adjoining apartments, the Grand Duke Peter, who no longer shared her bed nor her daily life but who was equally a prisoner of the Empress, had been devoting the afternoon to court-martialling a rat which he had secured by its tail to a gallows, whilst the Holstein court-martial procedure was enacted prior to the animal's slow execution.

But at least nowadays Peter left her increasingly alone, and for this she rendered thanks to the ugly Countess Elizabeth, 'her' lady-in-waiting whom her husband would paw and pleasure and in whose company he would by night become hopelessly drunk. That at least was an alleviation. Moreover she still acknowledged a few sentiments of compassion for the clumsy, simple-minded man whose freedom, like her own, had been so circumscribed.

Never once, since their marriage, had he or she ventured to town – indeed neither had dared even to leave the house openly without first getting permission from the Empress. In this they were in no better condition than the mindless serfs who comprised the rest of the native population of Russia. The Imperial court and the society of St Petersburg remained, in her opinion, little more than the pigsty it had been on her arrival in Russia fifteen long years ago. How far, far, far was this stale, slow, unending decay from the philosophy of enlightenment propounded by her invisible friend, Monsieur de Voltaire.

She dried her eyes, called for her carriage and proceeded upon the weekly routine of visiting the plain little boy, her son, who would one day – perhaps sooner than anyone could conjecture – inherit the imperial crown. She sent up a pious hope that the Empress would have had a satisfactory lover the previous night or perhaps that very afternoon. She might not then be so critical of her unhappy self.

Across the bay from the Winter Palace lay the fortified harbour of Crondstadt and beyond that the distant coast of Finland. Admiral Ivan Talytsin walked one of the upper 'decks' of this wooden fortress built by Peter the Great, awaiting with a somewhat crusty impatience the arrival of the British Ambassador whom he had invited to dine. He had private reasons for this visit apart from the normal exchange of courtesies attendant upon their respective ranks and positions.

The Commander-in-Chief of the Imperial Russian Navy was far from content with the state of his fleet. The vagaries of the old Empress, the foreign – mostly German – influence bearing on the Russian armies and the general state of affairs at court, affected the fleet more in the form of a stultifying neglect than in active measures or events which the Admiral could approve or contest. Stagnation had become the order of the day.

The creative impulse of the Great Peter, his vision and energy as applied to naval affairs had long since exhausted itself. Indolence, corruption and greed on the part of purveyors of stores and victuals, added to corresponding defects in the seagoing fleet – such as it was – all combined to cause a continuing and insidious decline in discipline and efficiency similar to that which was taking place in Holy Russia itself.

Principle, never a strong factor in the rude, brutish life of the Russian medieval state, had come to be consistently overlooked in the selfish debaucheries of those at the head of affairs. All could be laid at the feet of the tyrannical, failing, officially unmarried Empress, with her eight illegitimate children; and with the prospect of the defective Grand Duke Peter, incapable of controlling either himself or the realm, being brought to power on her death. Chaos reigned under a thin blanket of despair and by the time this swamp had degenerated into a morass, which it had done on previous occasions, it would be necessary as a matter of urgency to invite in foreign aid or the state would collapse.

'The Prussians, sir, conduct and control our military affairs,' the Admiral said to the British Ambassador, once they were over the formalities; 'for the Navy we must look to you.'

'That is flattering to the Royal Navy,' the Ambassador replied, 'but the war with France has yet to be determined. Our resources are stretched to the utmost. I am told by Admiral Keppel and other of my naval friends that it takes seven years to make a naval officer of any competence.'

'The war with France will not continue for ever.'

'We had one lasting a hundred years. However, Admiral, I agree. The war must sooner or later come to an end. What, then, did you have in mind?'

'The Anglo-Saxons and the Scots have assisted us before. I would like them to do so again. Especially the Scots. We have a long tradition of being officered at crucial times by Scotsmen on a mercenary basis. So far as I am concerned, I would welcome a freshening of the blood. I dare not, however, promote this cause in the present dubious state of Her Majesty's health.'

'I agree that human beings, like wars, do not continue for ever. I will, if you wish, consult their Lordships of Admiralty – not, as you say, for immediate response but with an eye to the ending of the war with France.'

'In turn, I shall write privately to the Russian Ambassador in London. I will also mention the matter to Dmitri Volkov who heads the special Government committee dealing with military and other matters. Beyond that no one must know. As Your Excellency will be aware, there is strong feeling in certain court circles against any further foreign encroachment on the Russian state, whatever the expediency. Moreover the officers concerned must needs be chosen with the greatest care. Nowhere are people quicker to notice weakness, absurdity or error in a foreigner than in Russia.'

The Ambassador smiled.

'It is said in London, Admiral, that anyone who is successful in Russia, can be certain of succeeding in Europe.'

'Then, sir, let us set our sights on achieving both objects with a single aim.'

The jaundiced view of the Russian Court held by the Admiral and the Grand Duchess was not universal even in St Petersburg. The foreign community, headed by educated, aristocratic men from every country of import in Europe, had grown perhaps ten times in size since Peter the Great had first opened up Russia to civilization at the beginning of the century.

The material fabric and etiquette of the Court certainly could not compare with that of Versailles, which it attempted lamely to ape and, as the British Ambassador noted in one of his despatches, the attitude to the fair sex was still vulgar and primitive in spite of – or possibly because of – the old woman on the throne.

But there was a hunger, except amongst the military faction, for the rich fruits of education and art. Fine imported wine was replacing the coarse native spirit as the accepted beverage. An Italian architect, Rinaldi, had been invited to design houses and to advise on palaces. Imperial and private art collections were developing apace. Fine silks from France, woollens from England and from the Flemish weavers, and jewels from Amsterdam were, with difficulty, to be procured. Even an elephant from a Chinese Ambassador had been marvelled at in St Petersburg. The hot, steamy summers and the bitterly cold winters made the maintenance of a healthy constitution more of a daily problem than it would have been in temperate England. Even so Ambassador Keith found he could adapt without too great a hardship to the byzantine intricacies of the Russian character and the life it led.

Naturally he had not spend a lifetime *en poste* abroad, in the service of his country, without acquiring a sharp nose for intrigue. He found no shortage of rascals in Petersburg at that dangerous time. Insincerity, hypocrisy and treachery stalked the shadows, but then so they did in Potsdam, Vienna, Versailles and even at the Court of St James. Loyal though he was to the English King, his Scottish background proved always to be a sane adjustor of any tendency he might once have had to believe and trust in the bright innocence which disguised a trap waiting to be sprung. He was watchful and alert.

In all these endeavours, Ambassador Keith built on the strong foundations which his predecessor, Sir Charles Hanbury-Williams, had laid. The English influence and its culture already occupied a special place in Russian life. No educated people from any other country travelled Europe as did the English milords of that time. Like the butterflies and the bees, they fertilized the various societies, courts, mansions and estates which they visited. Not many of them, alas, came to St Petersburg, but those Russian noblemen and diplomatists who themselves travelled abroad in the service of the Empress invariably brought back with them acquaintances or friendships with the island race.

There were also qualities, at times unique, in the English and the Scot who, whether courtiers, soldiers or merchants, inhabited St Petersburg. In general they were honest, just and disdainful of the greed and corruption into which they had been pitched. If the English aloofness might seem to some a rich seedbed for malicious pleasantries, nevertheless it would be to an Englishman or a Scotsman that many turned in the daily crises which occurred in that unhappy town. Of this reliability, and of the power it brought, the Ambassador was well aware.

The agony of Catherine's weekly visits to see her children, under the aegis of the Empress, could sometimes be lessened by those persons present at the time. Today the Grand Duchess was in luck. The Empress Elizabeth had a spiteful tongue and this she exercised on any suitable victim, provided that there was an audience at hand to enjoy the humiliation. Present that afternoon were two members of the Orlov family, only one of whom was known to the Grand Duchess Catherine through the fact that he was a member of her husband's bodyguard. This was Count Alexis Orlov, a good-looking officer of twenty-one, who had already indicated to the Grand Duchess in a number of subtle ways that his sympathies both as a man and as a courtier favoured herself rather than her boorish husband. To this Catherine had been careful enough to make but a guarded response.

The Orlov family was rich and powerful, Alexis alone owning some thirty thousand serfs. Today he had brought for presentation to the Empress and, of course, at her command, his younger brother Gregory, a handsome boy of fifteen well advanced for his age. He was resplendent in his uniform of an Ensign in the Imperial Guards and the cruel eyes of the Empress watched the effect of this dashing youngster on the Grand Duchess Catherine.

Also present was Ivan Shuvalov, the crafty and dangerous courtier whom Catherine knew to be a lover of the old Empress, but whose interest in education and the arts had nevertheless drawn from her a reluctant understanding and a sympathy. Shuvalov had created the first Russian university in distant Moscow and had plans as well to found an Academy of the Arts here in Petersburg. He greeted the Grand Duchess with what she took to be a friendly smile. No doubt he had pleasured the Empress the previous night, so there might now be hope for a reasonably peaceful encounter. No sooner had Catherine entered the Presence, however, than the Empress went into the attack.

'We shall have to forbid these weekly visits,' she remarked with a smile totally lacking in warmth, 'if a mother cannot see her offspring without emerging red-eyed with tears – or is there some other reason for the Grand Duchess's sorry demeanour?'

'I beg Your Majesty's pardon,' Catherine said, 'I must excuse my tired appearance on the grounds that last night I had but a few hours' sleep.'

'We would suppose that that depends upon the company you were keeping.'

'As to that, Your Majesty is no doubt better informed than I am myself,' Catherine said insolently, but also warning herself for the thousandth time of the obvious dangers of standing up to a bully. 'I was referring, however, to the Grand Duke my husband's increasing habit of carousing all night in the company of his Holstein friends. I can only suppose that the hilarity occasioned by Count Brockdorff's wig, constructed as it is rumoured out of brass wire, was such that it was considered necessary for the noise and festivities to continue until dawn.'

'Count Alexis,' the Empress said, turning to the elder Orlov, 'you were doubtless in attendance on His Imperial Highness last night . . . ?'

'No, Your Majesty, as Count Shuvalov here will confirm, I was present at a concert and afterwards at a reception given by His Excellency the Austrian Ambassador.'

Whilst this exchange was in progress, Catherine became conscious of what appeared to be a burning-eyed devotion from Gregory, the younger Orlov. She noted this fact but made no answering sign. In any event the Empress had not yet had her fill of blood.

'Does His Imperial Highness then have no right to intercourse with his friends?' the Empress asked, twiddling a locket around her raddled throat. 'Are we to issue instructions concerning behaviour as between man and wife?'

'As to that, Your Majesty must be the better judge,' Catherine answered. 'I would only remind Your Majesty that when the Grand Duke and I were first espoused you gave him directions on how to treat a wife. Among the qualities you urged upon him was that of discretion and, at the time, I do recall your comment that by nature the Grand Duke was about as discreet as a cannon-ball.'

This remark drew a spontaneous laugh from Shuvalov and the elder Orlov. From Gregory there was nothing but a frown.

'That is enough!' the Empress said curtly. 'If you cannot control your husband with the feminine wiles God has given you, then we may see fit to accede to your earlier request to return you to Zerbst-Stettin.'

'As Your Majesty decrees,' Catherine said. She had, in fact, reached very nearly to this point herself.

'Now, madame,' the old Empress continued, 'what do you say to this young man who has been requested by our cousin Frederick of Prussia as an Aide-de-Camp? Come now, madame, you were born a German yourself. How would you advise him on his behaviour at the Prussian court?'

Catherine gave the young man a dazzling smile which was returned as a mirror reflects the sun.

'Your Majesty is gracious enough to invite comment on a matter which is not by any stretch of the imagination within my powers to give.'

'What would your friend Monsieur de Voltaire advise?' the Empress needled her, an unpleasantly scornful tone in her voice. 'Did he not visit the Prussian court himself for three years? A visit which ended in a violent and scandalous quarrel?'

'I cannot speak for Monsieur de Voltaire. I do believe, though, that His Prussian Majesty declares himself to be "the first servant of the State", a notion fostered by the philosophy of enlightenment which, Count Shuvalov will doubtless agree, is the one continually preached by Monsieur de Voltaire.'

'Liberalism,' said the Empress, breaking wind in a loud and objectionable manner, 'is a dangerous food for our northern taste. It smacks of these alien ideas of freedom which Sir Charles Hanbury-Williams and now Mr Keith have been urging me to introduce. Your Monsieur de Voltaire went to England, too.'

'So did your distinguished ancestor, the Emperor Peter. And that, I believe, was also the wish of King Frederick – to whom you are to be attached,' Catherine said, turning to Gregory Orlov with a glance not observed by the Empress.

'Well, madame,' said the Empress in a triumphant manner which disposed of any further argument, 'your scribbler Voltaire had his book on England burnt by the public executioner in Paris as a danger to the state. King Frederick had an even more appropriate reward – his father caused him to witness the execution of the dear friend who had plotted his escape to England. I do not fancy we shall import many liberal English ideas into our Russian realm. The climate is not suitable for their growth.'

'But English soldiers and sailors, Your Majesty – would they not go some way to counterbalance the Holstein influence, which I understand Your Majesty to have said disturbs the equilibrium of the State?'

'Soldiers and sailors are another matter,' said the Empress, 'they are only men. Ideas are to be guarded against with every weapon in the armoury. Remember, madame, that the English are the first and only nation in our modern world to depose and to execute their King.'

Abruptly the Empress brought the audience to an end. She rose, taking the younger Orlov by the hand and saying, 'Come, boy, your brother tells me you are well practised in the military drills. Now show your Empress how well you can stand to attention.'

When the Grand Duchess returned to her apartment she summoned her lady-in-waiting, but Maria Ivanova did not appear. Instead another tearful lady-in-waiting reported to Her Imperial Highness that an officer from the secret chancery had called and had started to question them about the visitors, especially foreigners such as the English Ambassador, whom the Grand Duchess had received. He had also demanded the key to the little French writing-desk in the boudoir and had refused to believe that it was always, as they had assured him, on the person of the Grand Duchess herself.

He had ordered Maria Ivanova to borrow the key on some pretext so that a duplicate could be made, and when she refused, he had ordered her to go with him to the secret chancery building. At first she had also declined to do this, hoping to delay matters until the Grand Duchess should have returned, but the officer had struck her several times on the face so that she had broken down crying. One of the other ladies-in-waiting had run to His Imperial Highness to implore his protection. But the Grand Duke Peter was drilling his toy soldiers in the company of Count Brockdorff, who appeared to be drunk, and was not to be disturbed.

So they had dragged Maria Ivanova away screaming in terror until a hand had been clapped over her mouth, and ever since she had gone the retinue had been in tears.

'This is monstrous,' Catherine said and sent for Alexander Naryshkin, the Grand Marshal of the Court, whose brother Leo was a member of her inner circle of friends. The Grand Marshal was some time in coming, but when he did so, he agreed that it was a clumsy, insolent and disgraceful interference in the personal affairs of the Grand Duchess.

'However,' he observed, 'it would certainly not have been done without the direct authorization of the Empress Elizabeth Petrovna herself. I will do what I can to secure the girl's release, but it is to the Empress you must complain. And you are the best judge of the wisdom of such a course.'

'Why don't they imprison me?' Catherine demanded. 'Why spare *me* this last indignity? My present life is no better than that of a prison without bars.'

'It is still better than a prison with bars,' the Grand Marshal said. 'Remember that wretch whose name we must not mention – in Schlusselburg – the rightful Tsar,' but even the Grand Marshal had dropped his voice to a whisper in case he should be overheard.

'I shall ask to be returned to Germany,' Catherine said. 'I have fulfilled my duty here. I have provided an heir to this kingdom of serfs and tyrants. Now I shall go.'

To her surprise the Grand Marshal clasped her hand and went down on one knee.

'I pray Your Imperial Highness not to do that. If you leave us now, there will be no light in the darkness at all. All will be lost and we shall return to the barbarity from which the Emperor began to rescue us. Pray do not go . . .'

She looked down and raised him to his feet.

'Come now, Alexander Petrovich,' she said, 'it is unbecoming for the Grand Marshal to have tears in his eyes.'

'Promise you will not abandon us now.'

'I promise,' Catherine said with a sigh, 'but you must return me my Maria Ivanova.'

However even that proved to be impossible. A few days later the mutilated, naked body of the lady-in-waiting was discovered in the murky waters of the Neva. No one could then know that the Empress Elizabeth Petrovna had but two more years left of her turbulent reign.

3

'A little hauling upon the ropes'

The patronage of a Junior Lord of the Treasury eventually proved invaluable to Samuel Greig and he was appointed almost at once as Master of the *Princess of Wales,* an armed ship belonging to the Greenland Company, which had been commissioned by the British Government for the purpose of protecting the trade in the northern seas against the attacks of the French and their allies. This was not exactly the glamorous war service for which he had hoped before leaving Scotland, and he determined to offer his services to the Honourable Augustus Keppel who, as Commodore, was fitting out an expedition against Goree, at that time the only settlement which the French possessed upon the coast of Africa.

By good fortune the *Princess of Wales* was shortly paid off, and Samuel again found himself established at Deptford and in pursuit of his new endeavour. During this period he received a letter from his youthful admirer, Sarah Cook, which was delivered to his lodgings by a young naval lieutenant. The writing, he thought, was surprisingly mature for one so young.

> 'Dear Lieutenant Greig,' the letter began, 'I take the liberty of addressing you thus since I am sure you will already have prospered and by now have attained to this rank in the King's service. I, alas, got no further than the port of Leith where I was ignomminously (? spelling) trapped by an agent of the Sheriff and returned to Edinburgh where I received the most fearsome thrashing it has been my misfortune ever to suffer. However what matters physical distress when set against the high purposes of the spirit? I have been made to promise no further acts of bravado of this kind, but I had my fingers

crossed when I was thus under duress and I do not consider, therefore, that it counts.

Anyway, for the present no opportunity is forthcoming since I am watched day and night by my mother and my uncle. I am thus driven into the mind and to imagine the life at sea which my much longed for father and now you, sir, have the good fortune to enjoy. What it is to be born a girl with the spirit and inclinations of a man! However I will not weary you by continuing in this vein – but do, I pray you, write me a word of your adventures. I think of you many times during the day – and for that matter at night – and my aunt tells me she gave you a lock of my hair. I am pleased you should have it, though I would not have been so forward as to proffer it to you myself.

This letter will come to you by the hand of Lieutenant Fortescue Fynne. He was at one time in my father's ship, but was put in charge of a prize frigate captured from the French, and in consequence of its successful conduct to Deptford, where I understand you are lodging, was given leave of absence. This he has employed by coming to Edinburgh in amorous pursuit of my cousin Matilda – who fancies her looks and is well known in the family as a "tease".

'I hope you will like Lieutenant Fynne whose gaiety makes all in his company laugh though he has not your own high seriousness of purpose. Dear Lieutenant Greig, I hold you close in my thoughts and long to receive from you a word in return. Your faithful comrade in feminine form.

Sarah.'

When he had finished reading the letter, he looked up to find himself being studied by the goodlooking, fair-haired naval lieutenant who had brought him the epistle.

'She loves you,' said Fortescue Fynne.

'You have read the letter?'

'Of course not. However before pressing it into my hand, she discussed you at length. A somewhat one-sided discussion, since I had not previously had the pleasure of making your acquaintance.'

Samuel tucked away her letter, but he was amused at, and touched by, her earnest entreaties for correspondence with him.

'She is only eleven years of age.'

'And of what import is that? I have a grandmother who fell in love with her coachman at the age of eighty. He himself was seventy-eight.'

'Do you mean to say they married?'

'Marriage, as I understand it, is for the bearing of children and their subsequent upbringing. My grandmother had fulfilled those functions some years previously. The coachman – I do not know – may perhaps still have been able to force his horses into a gallop. What does that matter? They adored each other and since Fate had mercifully cast them both into roles where a daily contact was possible, they spent the rest of their lives in a condition of bliss.'

'You propound a strange philosophy,' Samuel said, not quite knowing how to react.

'Strange only to you, with your Presbyterian ideas,' said Fortescue Fynne, with a touch of arrogance in his voice. 'Why do we not drink a few stoups of claret together? I know of an inn where the wine has not been adulterated.'

So this was what they did. It transpired that Fortescue Fynne was the younger son of a younger son of an Earl. The law of primogeniture being what it was, he had little money with which to satisfy the expensive tastes which were the heritage of his blood. After having a place bought for him in the Navy, he was now in the receipt of an allowance – 'an exiguous pittance' was how he described it – which his father paid into his bank account quarterly.

'I am much afeared that within the week it is gone. Indeed were it not for this blessed war with the French – and the requirement it brings of going to sea – I would by now be in a debtor's prison, since my father has long since refused to honour my commitments. Do you, in fact, have sufficient funds for our dinner tonight?'

'I do,' said Samuel, somewhat formally, 'and I shall be honoured for you to be my guest.'

'Honour be damned!' said Fortescue Fynne, 'it is the ladies who cost the money and, indeed, why should they not? Their work may be of a pleasurable kind conducted in a comfortable position but it requires its reward.'

'Do you mean to say . . .' Samuel began and then laughed. 'I am afraid you find me somewhat innocent of the delights of the town.'

'Well, sir,' said Fortescue Fynne, 'I know of a number of establishments where that can be put to rights and whilst we are dining, which shall be your sole expense since I naturally do not expect you to cover my other disbursements, we can discuss the child Sarah and also the prospects of the naval career you have embraced. I understand you have volunteered for Commodore Keppel's expedition to Goree. I have done the same, so with a little hauling upon the ropes we may yet contrive to be shipmates together.'

The 'little hauling upon the ropes' referred to by his new friend proved to be more tedious and dispiriting than any shoreside activity Samuel had yet embarked on since coming south to London, even including the delays and disappointments he had suffered through Mr Oswald.

'I confess I do not understand the way in which matters are ordered in Admiralty,' he complained one evening to Mr Collins, when they were drinking ale together in a Deptford tavern. Around them in the small ill-lit room were the usual collection of dockside and longshore men, sailors on leave and the local Revenue man in his corner seat. Only Samuel, it seemed to himself, had no employment or purpose.

'Hope is a good breakfast, it is a bad supper,' Mr Collins remarked, shooting the young Scotsman an appraising look. 'Console yourself now until tomorrow's breakfast.'

'See here, Mr Collins,' Samuel said angrily, 'the principal matter on which all my thoughts and endeavours are bent is to get myself to sea in a ship on the King's service. I was reliably informed that Commodore Keppel is in need of officers with exactly my seagoing experience. I am well equipped with the qualifications and yet I cannot make my mark.'

'Did you not meet the Commodore today?'

'I did not. I kicked my heels in that damned Admiralty Waiting Room whilst those better recommended than I came and went – but when I put myself forward, I was told to be patient. "Do not press too hard, Mr Greig, or the verdict will not be in your favour" – so what am I to do? I was advised that Commodore Keppel is to command a fleet of four line of battle ships, two frigates, two bomb ketches, a fireship and a number of transports for the troops who are to possess the island of Goree off Cape Verde. I would give my right hand to be on that expedition. It is rumoured he will sail from Cork in November. Surely there must be some post in that fleet for me? Does one have to despair before securing a place? Should not some roster be honestly kept? Or is the whole Navy run by bribes and privilege?'

Mr Collins raised his eyebrows and smiled at the Revenue man who had overheard the complaint. Both had had a lifetime's experience of the way naval affairs were arranged and Mr Collins had no wish further to discourage this eager young man.

'Did you not learn the names of the Captains of those ships?' he asked shrewdly.

'I have the list here.'

Samuel passed over a piece of paper to the old ship chandler who glanced down it quickly.

'Why, here is one you may try,' Mr Collins said. 'I see Captain Orrock is to command the *Firedrake* – a bomb vessel. Captain Orrock is an old friend of ours and, if I mistake not, can be found of an evening at the *Hind's Head* at Rotherhithe. I will write a word to him now and you shall take it after your supper.'

Reluctant though Samuel was to set off again after his long, fruitless day, he nevertheless grasped at the chance which the ship chandler gave him, walked to Rotherhithe, discovered Captain Orrock as directed in the *Hind's Head* and then made himself known. Captain Orrock turned out to be a sharp-featured, red-cheeked man of fifty years or so, much addicted to the brandy of which he had clearly consumed a large quantity by that time of night, and yet by no means so bemused that he could not give Samuel the most intense scrutiny he had yet received since his first meeting with the devious Mr Oswald. This was followed by a brief but penetrating examination of his navigational knowledge and Samuel then found himself clapped on the shoulder and told he would be taken on as Master's Mate of the *Firedrake* and was to report at a certain Admiralty room the following day.

So, at last, Samuel got to sea on the expedition he had been so eager to join, and the fleet sailed on 11 November 1758, more or less as planned, for the Barbary coast. Lieutenant Fortescue Fynne was serving on board the *Litchfield*, a fifty-gun ship. So the new friends were together, yet in different vessels.

Exceedingly foul weather was encountered off the coast of North West Africa and this resulted in the stranding of the *Litchfield* and of two of the transports. However by 28 December the squadron had anchored in the harbour of Goree. The island was about two miles in circumference and was within cannon-shot of the African shore.

The following day Keppel attacked. The English squadron pressed home the assault on the forts and batteries of the island with such vigour that the French Governor was soon desired to capitulate. However since he demanded that his troops should be allowed to march out of the garrison with the honours of war, Keppel rejected the offer, promising to oblige him with a further attack on the morrow.

'And *Firedrake* is to lead the van,' Captain Orrock informed his officers after returning from a conference on board the flagship. This was to be Samuel's first experience of action and it proved to be an especially hot and hazardous one. Although the two men to one side of him were both felled by a single shot, Samuel came through the ordeal of battle unscathed and when the French Governor had surrendered at discretion, yielding the British force three hundred prisoners, Captain Orrock sent for Samuel on his diminutive quarterdeck, clapped him on the shoulder (an action which seemed to be his favourite way of showing approbation) and said:

'I intend to report to the Commodore on your remarkable coolness and intrepidity in battle, Mr Greig. You have set your brother officers an excellent example.'

'I am grateful to you, sir,' Samuel replied, flushing with unexpected embarrassment, 'but it was done without conscious thought. I simply acted at the time as the situation seemed to demand.'

'Do not denigrate yourself, Mr Greig. If there is a will to conquer it will animate and reveal itself in the circumstances through which we have all so recently passed. Our lives are in the hands of Providence which alone decrees our survival or collapse. However, Mr Greig, as I think you have already discovered for yourself, a man's training and instinct can lend Providence a helping hand. Chance does little that has not been prepared beforehand.'

Later Samuel set down his feelings in a letter to Sarah. He began by thanking her for writing as she had done and for the lock of her hair which he had carried through the battle next to his heart 'for luck – the which it must evidently have brought me', and he then went on to recount his impressions.

> 'To say that one of my education was entirely unconcerned upon such a prospect would rather argue me to be stupid then brave. Most of the concern I felt was *two days* before the attack when I was pondering the sum of things in my mind.
>
> 'I assure you that my friends had not the least share in my thoughts but amidst all my thoughts I felt an eagerness of mind prompting me on. I recommended my spirit to its Maker and left my fate entirely in His hands to whom the issues of life belong and resolved to discharge my duties whatever the event might be.
>
> 'When the danger drew nearer, my concern abated and I felt a secret pleasure when I learnt that we were to lead the van and were to sustain the fire of all the forts as we

went along, and I think I was never more master of myself than that morning when we were bearing down upon the place and bringing the ship to before it.

'After we brought her broadside to bear upon the island and had her cable secured, I then gave my whole attention to working the mortars and, being engaged in the noise and hurry of the battle, every thought vanished but that of annoying the enemy. When the two men fell by my side, both by one shot, one killed on the spot and the other with his arm shattered to pieces and his entrails torn out, surviving a few minutes – a sight which at other times would have been shocking and ready to raise pity and sympathy – I found my heart too obdurate to feel any such tender emotion and I only considered it as any other indifferent accident that I was prepared for. I have since considered it in a quite different light and have sympathized for them as I ought to have done then.'

Samuel went on to explain that her fond hope that he might already have obtained the rank of Lieutenant was, alas, far from being fulfilled. 'The established rules of the Service which my senior officers tell me are strictly adhered to are that an officer should have been two years in command of a merchant vessel and for four years on board a King's ship to entitle him to pass as Lieutenant.' As to the first requirement, he had in fact served three years in command of his father's ship and he entertained some hope that this might be taken into account in dispensing with the usual period of service on board a King's ship. 'This I shall know when I am again in London and can have the decision direct of Admiralty. I am already twenty-three.'

It was not to be. Well into the following year after Samuel had returned from Goree, he applied for his pass as Lieutenant, but did not obtain it. The obstacle of four years' service on board a King's ship was found to be insurmountable and his application rejected. This was but one of many setbacks which he was to endure in the early part of his extraordinary career. Patronage might have done it but Mr

Oswald's power did not – or he did not wish it to – extend to this.

However with his firm belief in Providence, Samuel accepted this state of affairs with a good grace and, determining not to remain inactive, he resolved to embark with the first foreign expedition which should sail from England. There were two reasons for this. In the first place it was easier to obtain employment in ships going abroad and secondly, as he had long suspected and as was confirmed by his friend Fortescue Fynne, 'a better opening is afforded for the exhibition of your nautical skill and consequently your chances of promotion will be increased.'

Now, when in London, he no longer put up at Mrs Collins' establishment at Deptford but accepted the offer of accommodation in the town house of the Earl of Braddenham, who was Fortescue Fynne's uncle. This was not the secure nor even the palatial residence which he had imagined when Fortie had first mooted the idea – 'so that our combined resources will benefit by not having to pay for an address and there will then be more funds to be put into that joyful bank, topped by delicious thatch, which is concealed between a pair of luscious thighs.'

The reason for this insecurity lay in a fatal predilection on the part of Fortie's uncle to gamble at the establishments in St James Street so well run by Mr Brooks, Mr Boodle and Mr White. It proved quite possible for His Lordship to lose not only his town house but also his estate in Wiltshire in a single evening. It was true that he usually got these properties back a few nights later, whereupon the arrangements to sell up the furniture and quit were rescinded, but the interim periods when a search for more credit had to be undertaken at great urgency were black with uncertainty.

It was also a long time before Samuel had a reply from Sarah, but this was explained in a letter he received shortly after he had had the good fortune of obtaining an appointment as Master's Mate on board the *Royal George*, a hundred-gun ship wearing the flag of Admiral Sir Edward Hawke, who then commanded the Channel Fleet.

*

'At last I know where you are in London,' thirteen-year-old Sarah wrote in a hand which seemed fuller and firmer than before, 'and I have only lately secured the letter you wrote me after the Goree Expedition. The reason for this is that my mother in her wisdom had decided it to be unsuitable for a young lady in my position to correspond with, or even to receive letters from, a man of your age and station. So your letter was intercepted and I never had it direct. Only the good services of your sister who interceded on my behalf have now allowed me at last to have in my hand the treasure which it is to me. Pray write to me in future, dear Samuel' (it was no longer Lieutenant Greig) 'in care of your sister who has promised I shall not be deprived as I have been for reasons – misapprehended reasons – of etiquette. I do not wish to be ungrateful or disloyal to my mother who has only my best interests at heart but I am now becoming a woman, as you said I would, and wish to determine my life as I myself see fit.

'If only my father were back from sea! I miss him as I miss you, but I do not think I am long intended to remain a child locked away in gentility as I am now. I fear that by this time there must be dozens of other ladies in your life, all far better endowed than I am, also that it is presumptuous of me to lay any sort of claim to your attention, yet this I do. Wait for me, Samuel. I shall not be long in catching up. In the meantime I send you my fondest affection and hope you will spare an occasional thought on a calm night at sea for your adorative and lonely

Sarah'

This letter touched Samuel with a surprisingly tender emotion, and he forthwith placed it with the lock of her hair next to his heart. Fortescue Fynne, who had been present when the letter was received and who had been covertly watching his friend's reaction to it, asked if there were mention of cousin Matilda.

'Not in this letter from Sarah,' Samuel replied, 'but there

was a brief reference in another letter which I had of my sister.'

'She does not write to me now and I fear my chances, which were never strong, must be diminishing.'

Samuel looked at him with a smile.

'I believe you are even more romantically inclined than I am myself, Fortie. Did you really go overboard for Matilda MacFee? I cannot believe it.'

'Neither could I,' said Fortescue Fynne, 'but those pert pretty features haunted my dreams. I was determined to possess her. That was why I went to Edinburgh.'

'Well, Fortie, I'm afraid she has fallen from grace as far as Edinburgh society is concerned. She has taken up with a visiting actor, and you know what the generality of the inhabitants think of theatrical amusements.'

'Och! away mon,' Fortescue Fynne said in a poor imitation of a Scottish accent, 'that famous stool your distant ancestor, Knox, threw in the cathedral is still having a repercussion. It is time theatrical entertainments became respectable in Edinburgh, instead of having to advertise themselves as concerts of music.' He paused and thought about Matilda. 'So I am rejected for a man who puts greasepaint on his face!'

'Well,' Samuel said, 'I do not suppose that will last very long. And then you can return to the attack. But do you want Matilda as a wife?'

'Passionately – and also those rich lowland acres that go with her hand.'

'Ah! now I see the cut of your jib. I am told she has a wart on her groin and is something of a tease.'

'Wart or no wart, I desire her with an undying passion. And as to being a tease – two can play at that game. Shall we in the meantime repair to the *Bell Tavern* for our evening refreshment? I am still in funds.'

'I think it is just as well we are to go to sea again,' Samuel said with a smile, 'we have been in enough scrapes as it is for a while.'

Late in 1759 it became apparent that the invasion of

England, which had long been projected by the French, was not likely to be abandoned because of the losses the French had sustained in the engagement off Cape Lagos. Shortly after Samuel had joined the *Royal George*, the Admiral saw fit to call together the officers of his flagship and brief them on the current situation.

'The preparations for a naval armament in the harbour of Brest continue without interruption,' he said. 'It is a dull business for the Channel Fleet to be kept thus on constant observation of this French port, and if there were any signs that our ancient enemy might be about to give up his aggressive ideas, I would be the first to recommend to the Lords Commissioners of Admiralty that we, in turn, abandon the watch. But this is not so. I have no doubt that Monsieur de Conflans is hoping that the winter storms will compel us to take refuge in our own harbours and thus afford him an opportunity of coming out unopposed. In the meantime we remain in position off Brest.'

The weather did, however, intervene in the French interest. Early in November 1759 a violent gale caused Sir Edward Hawke to quit his watch on Brest and bring his whole fleet to anchor in Torbay. This was the moment for which the French were waiting. On 14 November, Monsieur de Conflans put to sea with twenty-three ships of the line and two frigates. An advice of this move was brought express to Sir Edward Hawke who, in spite of the weather, sailed from Torbay with a fleet somewhat superior in numbers. This was to be Samuel's first experience of a fleet action from the deck of a battleship of the line.

On the morning of the twentieth the French fleet was discovered betwixt Belle Isle and the coast of France. Previously Samuel's navigating experience – and he was the Master's Mate and thus responsible for this duty – had been limited to the small merchant vessels owned by his father and the bomb ketch *Firedrake* in the action off Goree. Now the circumstances and the weather were very different. Now Samuel had to control a hundred-gun ship of the line in a strong wind blowing on to a lee shore. Indeed they were navigating in an exceedingly dangerous area, peppered with rocks and shoals, and in addition to the natural hazards with which they had to contend, Samuel was now to have his first experience at sea of the fighting spirit of a very determined British Admiral.

'Lay me alongside the *Soleil Royale*,' Admiral Hawke commanded. The *Soleil Royale* was wearing the flag of Monsieur de Conflans, the French Commander-in-Chief.

'Sir, we have a gusting squall taking us hard down upon a lee shore,' the Master remonstrated, exhibiting some trepidation in thus standing up to the ferocious Hawke. 'To reach the French flagship puts us in danger of stranding the ship. I must – with respect – give warning . . .'

'You have done your duty in this remonstrance,' Admiral Hawke snapped back. 'Now obey my orders and lay me instantly alongside the French Admiral.'

The action commenced at half-past two in the afternoon with the French ships turning for refuge into Quiberon Bay. As at Goree, Samuel forgot his every fear and anxiety in the heat of the battle, and Admiral Hawke's aggressive spirit inspired him in a way he was never to forget. The Admiral found time not only for the strategy and tactics required of a Commander-in-Chief in battle but also for the personal, intimate and immediate encouragement of the officers and men with whom he came closely into contact. Samuel watched him out of the corner of his eye and was astounded at the strength of leadership he evinced. Admiral Hawke appeared to have no thought for his own safety, leaving this matter entirely in the hands of the Almighty. So had the somewhat 'brandified' Captain Orrock at Goree, Samuel reflected, but a small bomb craft was one thing, a hundred-gun ship of the line – and the flagship at that – quite another.

Indeed such was Admiral Hawke's fighting spirit that he was only with difficulty prevented from himself leaping on board the French flagship once she had been grappled by the *Royal George*. Instead Samuel led this attack, watched closely by Hawke, and he so distinguished himself throughout that at the close of the engagement, which only ceased with the daylight, by which time four French ships of the line had been destroyed and one taken as prize, the Admiral embraced him, thanking him most energetically for his valour and conduct.

Sir Edward's compliment at the time was rough, though expressive. To Samuel this would have been reward enough, especially as he knew he would henceforth carry in his mind's eye, as the epitome of leadership, the picture of the Admiral exhorting, lambasting and otherwise encouraging his officers and men. Had he not been on board the British flagship and close to the Admiral, he would never have acquired this prime example of how best to behave in action – an example he determined he would himself try to set his own subordinates for the rest of his life. But the initial compliment paid him on deck by Admiral Hawke in the heat of battle was to be followed by an even more moving one later that night, when he was sent for to the Admiral's cabin. He knew that the senior officers of the ship had been previously summoned to the after-cabin, with its swaying lanterns and polished oak bulkheads, but when Samuel entered this 'holy of holies' to his great pleasure and somewhat bashful confusion the Admiral threw his arms round him and exclaimed:

'Greig, fight eternally!'

The next day, and as a further testimony of his approbation, Sir Edward appointed him an Acting Lieutenant and gave him command of the cutter *Portland*.

'I desire you to remain here for the present, Mr Greig,' said the Admiral, 'and maintain a watch on the motions of those French ships which have escaped into the river Villaine. In addition you should scour the coast between Quiberon Bay and the Isle of Aix.'

Thus for the remainder of that long, hard winter Samuel cruised up and down the French coast.

'It is not the danger, considerable though that is, which preoccupies us here in our little ship,' he wrote to Sarah, just before he was recalled in the spring of 1760, 'it is the tedium and the parsimonious attitude of our victuallers, who keep us on hard tack and an absence of fresh vegetables and porter. Indeed I cannot but sympathize with our brave seamen. A few days ago they allowed me to discover the following satirical squib, addressed to the people of England, which it was hoped might be forwarded to Sir Edward Hawke:

Ere Hawke did bang Monsieur Conflang,
You sent us Beef and Beer,
Now Monsieur's beat, we've naught to eat
Since you have naught to fear.

'I am afraid it is true,' he added, 'and gratitude to those courageous men who risk their lives at sea would seem to be in inverse ratio to the threat of invasion. Once that is removed, we are of little consequence.'

On his return to England, Samuel felt confident that now at long last his appointment to the rank of Lieutenant would be officially confirmed. Admiral Hawke had recommended his advancement in the highest possible terms and had privately let Samuel know, through his Secretary, that of the three gentlemen 'in the running', Samuel had been the most strongly recommended. The other two had returned to England with the principal fleet whilst Samuel remained at sea watching his 'villainous' French ships. He now learnt that these other two had been immediately confirmed. There could be no reason why he should not be similarly treated. So, on his first day home, Samuel visited the Admiralty office already planning in his mind the celebration he would have with Fortescue Fynne, to be followed by a triumphal journey to Scotland to see his parents and, of course, Sarah.

However the clerk in the Admiralty office, a snivelling little rat of a man and insufferably pompous in Samuel's opinion, not only kept him waiting two long hours but, when Samuel was eventually admitted to his presence, addressed him as if he were some recent and minor recruit who had, perhaps, been 'pressed' into the service and who was emitting an unpleasant smell.

'Your expectations of advancement', this clerk remarked, elegantly taking snuff and avoiding Samuel's stare, 'are I regret to inform you destined to further delay. The Board of Admiralty are not empowered to alter the regulations for the naval service which have been laid down by Parliament for the benefit of all. You have indeed received a commendation from – let me see, ah! yes – Sir Edward Hawke. However ...' he coughed in a deprecating way and again solaced himself with snuff, 'your record reveals that you have not yet completed the period of service required for advancement to the rank of Lieutenant. The regulations, I would observe, are exact and cannot be relaxed.'

Unable to contain his rage a moment longer, Samuel turned abruptly on his heel and swept out of the office without saying a word.

'I could not stand the mortification,' he later confided to Fortescue Fynne, 'nor the unctuous and gloating tones of that mean little scrivener who had clearly never been nearer to danger than the edge of the Thames.'

'And I see you have been restoring your equilibrium with brandy ever since.'

'I have indeed,' Samuel said, 'and I trust you will join me in this negative celebration.'

His friend laughed and sat down at his side.

'The mortification will soon be forgot and you will be an Admiral yet.'

'That is easy to say – somewhat harder to accept.'

'I think it was Dean Swift, was it not, who complained that the cards were always ill-shuffled till he had a good hand. You constantly claim a belief in Providence – so why not hold fast to it now? You are simply being put to the test.'

'If you have no more comfort for me than that, I think we had better go our separate ways. Unfortunately I do not have an uncle who is an Earl.'

'Do not despair, Sam. Volunteer your services to Admiral Saunders in the Mediterranean Fleet. He is a distant cousin of my father's and would, I am sure, accept you on board the *Neptune*. He is also empowered to commission officers on that distant station under his own authority.'

'Very well,' Samuel said with a sigh, 'I will do as you suggest.'

So for the greater part of 1760, a year which saw the death of King George II and the ascent to the throne of the first Hanoverian King to speak English, Samuel found himself Master's Mate on board the Mediterranean flagship. He took with him a strong recommendation to Admiral Saunders and almost at once distinguished himself in action, as he had done with Commodore Keppel and Admiral Hawke.

However it was not only in action against the enemy that his qualities and aptitudes became noticeable to his superior officers. He had been sent ashore to a village on the Barbary coast called El Arache to secure corn and other supplies for his ship, from the friendly natives who, during this transaction, were suddenly threatened by an attack in some numbers from across the river by another Berber tribe with hostile intentions.

'There are several pieces of rusty cannon,' said the Chief of the friendly tribe, 'which could no doubt be brought into use if the old cannon-balls lodged inside them could be freed. But they have been rusted into their present condition over many years.'

'Aye, but their carriages, too, are in a state of utter decay,' Samuel said after he had inspected this ancient armament. 'If we introduce fresh powder into the touch-holes, the balls will either be blown out or the guns will split or the carriages collapse. However it is worth taking the risk. Quartermaster, fetch me a long match on the end of a pole and the rest of you stand well to the rear.'

His orders were obeyed and, somewhat to his private surprise, the guns were brought back into use and the hostile Berbers driven away. Samuel then returned to his ship with the supplies he had acquired. When they were about to sail, an English merchantman approached the port and requested a pilot to enter harbour. By now a heavy swell was running over the bar and the village Berbers declined to put to sea. The English ship then decided to enter the harbour unaided, but promptly grounded on the bar.

Seeing that unless assistance was at once provided the ship would break up, Samuel had a boat manned, threw her a line and succeeded in pulling her clear. In this process, however, his own boat capsized in the surf and it was only by clinging to an oar that Samuel was able to avoid a watery grave. All this bravery and skill had been observed by his Captain who wrote an appreciative report to Admiral Saunders, which in turn was entered on Samuel's record of service. Before returning to England, therefore, at the end of 1760, Admiral Saunders saw fit to award Samuel his Passing Certificate for Lieutenant, back-dating it to 6 November.

'Now surely my advancement can no longer be delayed for any conceivable reason,' Samuel observed to Mr Oswald when he called on him after his return. 'I have obtained the mark and public approbation of every commander under whom I have served, and my experience and professional acquirements have been noted by all who have the means to judge them.'

This observation was met with an ominous silence. Then after taking a turn up and down the room, the Junior Lord of the Treasury said:

'I have bad news for you, Mr Greig. I made enquiry before your arrival, hoping in this way to have matters settled once and for all but—'

A thundercloud seemed to pass across the younger man's face.

'I cannot believe there is yet another valid excuse for shutting me out.'

'Unfortunately there is. Your period at sea in the *Princess of Wales* cannot be reckoned as service in the Royal Navy. She was classified merely as an armed ship not as a man of war. You will therefore need to serve another year to make up the time required to gain your promotion.'

'By then,' Samuel said, with difficulty suppressing an oath, 'the war may well be over – with myself still in this continuing second-class position. To hell with you all!'

'It is a bitter disappointment to greet your return,' Mr Oswald retorted as blandly as ever, 'but you cannot change the world, Mr Greig. You came to London as a poor Scottish youth, as indeed I was once upon a time. You must wait patiently on the favour of the great. Greed is one thing:

misplaced philanthropy another. Your concern for your ill-nourished sailors did you great credit but your reward is likely to be in heaven ...' he shot a sly look, 'and that is also likely to be the only credit you will gain.'

'If my promotion depends on the half-men I see sitting in Admiralty offices – men who have never been in a greater danger than that of falling over their own feet – how am I ever to progress?'

'You *will* progress, sir, because the world of patronage is not entirely one-sided, as you evidently consider it in your present unfortunate circumstances. Patrons also need good men on whom to bestow their favours. An Admiral does not work his own ship. Your qualities will in the end draw to themselves the recompense they deserve.'

'Subject, of course, to the Naval Regulations,' Samuel said bitterly.

'Indeed, Mr Greig, subject to the regulations which protect you to the same extent that they seen to favour others less gifted than yourself. They can assist a stripling Earl to a position his talents do not admit: they cannot get him to the top of the tree. And I am informed by Sir Edward Hawke and others I have consulted that the top of the tree is assuredly for you. But do not dissipate your energies in pointless impatience. Trust in your Fate and in the meantime give thanks that I have secured for you the recommendation of Lord Anson to an appointment on board the *Albemarle*, to be commanded again by Commodore Keppel in the fresh expedition now being mounted against Belle Isle.'

'And what is so important about Belle Isle', Samuel asked sourly, 'that we need to go back and do again what was so excellently done last winter?'

Mr Oswald gave him another shrewd, courtier's look.

'Why, sir, this is the largest of the European islands now in the possession of the French. It is embarrassingly near one of their major ports. Do you not think that if it be captured – and a peace with France subsequently concluded – it would make an admirable exchange for – shall we say – Menorca?'

Since such an idea, and the political thinking behind it, had never occurred to Samuel and since this fact had long ago been grasped by the egregious Mr Oswald, the discussion was brought to an end. It was clear to a rueful, depressed Samuel that he still had a great deal to learn.

If Samuel could legitimately feel aggrieved, disgruntled, hard done by and generally the victim of an unfair system – which is what sea-going sailors have so often felt when the fruits of their labours appear to be devalued by the administrators of Admiralty – things were no better in Edinburgh where the 'bright-spirited girl', who was to his surprise, becoming the object of those of Samuel's waking thoughts and dreams which were not devoted to maritime matters, found herself hedged and thwarted by an 'Admiralty' of a different kind, to wit her dragon of a mother. Indeed it seemed to Sarah these days that she had but one friend in the world and that was Samuel's sister. Already Meg Charters had become the willing Post Office through whom Sarah and Samuel conducted their clandestine correspondence.

'But I cannot continue like this,' Sarah said, when Meg had come to her little room at the top of the house to deliver the latest epistle from the south. 'I have again been sent up here supperless for a disobedience I did not know I had committed, but now that I have, I would do again – and again – and again.'

'As to the supper,' Meg answered, 'that can soon be put right. How have you offended now?'

'I refuse to "co-operate" as mother says. She wishes to enter me in the Edinburgh Marriage Stakes and I have no intention of taking part in any such race.'

Meg studied the girl who was sitting on her bed with the traces of recent tears on her face. Meg could well understand her brother's feelings for 'the little sprite'.

'But your mother only has your best interests at heart. Every mother wants a good marriage for her daughter, the more so when you are all she has.'

'If my father were here . . .' Sarah began and then shrugged her shoulders, 'but what is the use? My father is at sea and so is the man on whom I have set my heart.'

'You are very young for such talk.'

'Do we not come of age at different times?' Sarah said. 'What does age matter, if two people love each other and know what they want?'

'Well ...' said Samuel's sister with a smile, 'the circumstances of life do not always arrange themselves to suit a couple of star-crossed lovers, however determined either or both of them may be. My brother is in no condition to make a proposal of marriage – even if he wanted to. He has difficulty enough in keeping his own head above water – in matters of finance, I mean. He cannot take on a further responsibility at present and in any event, Sarah, you would need your parents' consent. You are not yet of an age, a legal age, which would enable you to kick over the traces as you so clearly intend. You will have to acquire the benison of patience, however painful that process may turn out to be.'

'I shall run away to London,' Sarah said, getting off the bed and impetuously walking up and down the room.

'You will do no such thing,' Meg said firmly. 'You may be too old for the thrashing you previously received; you are still young enough for the application of plain commonsense.'

'What can I do?' Sarah said, bursting into tears again. 'How long have I got to wait?'

'You must do, of course, what my brother has taught himself to do. You must trust in Providence. It is all we can rely on in this very uncertain life.'

'Oh! go away!' Sarah said, burying her head in the pillow. 'Leave me alone! I am only fit to be by myself when I am overcome in this way.'

'Very well then, I will smuggle you up some food and we will try to reason with your mother anew. After all you are both guests in our house and she will have to do us the courtesy of listening to what we have to say.'

'My mother is a determined witch!'

'She is no such thing, Sarah, and you will not make such

remarks in my presence again – even when we are by ourselves and no one else can overhear such a wicked remark.'

'Oh! I am sorry, I am sorry,' Sarah said, throwing herself in the older woman's arms, 'I do not mean what I say. I am only desperate for the man I love.'

'Well ...' Meg said gently, stroking her hair, 'there is a time on everything, you know. Nothing can last for ever. Now get you into bed as your mother has ordered and we will see what can be done.'

At the end of March 1761 Samuel duly accepted the appointment to the *Albemarle* which Mr Oswald had got him, and sailed from Spithead in the flagship of a fleet of seventeen ships of the line, eleven frigates, three bomb and two fireships, arriving off Loch Maria Point on the south east corner of Belle Isle on 7 April. It was decided to effect a landing on the following day, and a gallant attempt was duly made.

Commodore Keppel, an impetuous aristocratic man with dark humorous eyes, surveyed the hostile coast they were approaching, stuck his telescope under his arm and said to Samuel:

'If I recall matters aright, Mr Greig, it was Captain Orrock of the *Firedrake* whom you last advised when sailing under my command? To Goree was it not?'

'Aye aye, sir,' Samuel replied, wondering what was to follow.

'And Sir Edward Hawke had the benefit of your navigational knowledge off this very same coast?'

Again Samuel assented.

'I do not consider my intentions towards the enemy any less aggressive than Sir Edward's,' Keppel continued, 'but I like neither the coast nor the wind in the quarter it lies. What say you to that, Mr Greig?'

'Sir, I am not yet a Commissioned Officer,' Samuel replied, taking advantage of the twinkle in his Commodore's eye, 'so my advice can be of but little account.'

'You can safely leave a judgment on that to your Commodore,' Keppel replied. 'Do we attack or do we not?'

'You should stand out to sea at once, sir,' Samuel replied, 'or your transports will all capsize in this swell.'

'You are right, Mr Greig. Signalman, hoist the general recall.'

But they had left it too late. Although the fleet turned away from the coast, several of the flat-bottomed transports continued inshore either because they could not read the flagship's signal hoist or because, being within striking distance of their target, they felt it better to proceed. All who did so were wrecked. That night, whilst the British fleet was hove to in the gale which then blew for the following three days, Samuel was sent for by the Commodore.

'You are the only one of my officers who proffered me the correct advice,' Keppel said. 'How does it come about that you know more than the Master of my fleet?'

'Sir,' said Samuel, looking him squarely in the eye, 'if I may speak freely ...'

'You may speak in no other way.'

'I have been longer at sea than the Master of your fleet and, to hazard a guess, have been through more vicissitudes and in worse conditions than any of your staff. A man who has worked his way up since boyhood in the sort of ships in which it can never have been your misfortune to serve, is likely – in my humble opinion – to tender you more practical advice than any you will receive from a man who has merely walked the King's decks since his father bought him a place on the Seniority List.'

The two men looked at each other as the ship heaved and rolled, the lantern in the after-cabin swaying as if manipulated by some invisible conductor of an orchestra.

'There are not many men who would risk speaking to their Admiral in the way you have just done, Mr Greig, the more so since it is my own judgment which is really in question. You shall have your commission, Mr Greig, if I have to prise it out of the King himself.'

'Then may I ask you a further favour, sir?'

The Commodore nodded.

'Allow me to land with the Royal Marines when the assault takes place.'

'You shall have that honour, Mr Greig, provided you do not get yourself killed. I have need of your services afloat.'

The intrepidity of the Royal Marines, a newly raised corps of soldiers who had in addition been given some practical training at sea, had already been established and Samuel took full advantage of the privilege he was now accorded. As soon as the storm abated, a landing was made under Samuel's direction at a point where the French had relied on the natural impediments of the coast for their defence rather than on man-made fortifications. The skill of the actual disembarkation was such that there were no casualties to men, boats or material and, quickly pressing this advantage, the town of Le Palais, the capital of the island, was invested despite a gallant defence by the Chevalier de Sainte Croix. Now only the citadel held out.

This was Samuel's first experience of the chivalrous conduct of war which was soon to disappear for ever from the world. In the early days no shots were fired at single persons in the embrasures or on the walls. The task was to reduce the fortification with cannon brought ashore from the ships and thus to provoke a surrender of the whole. On several occasions, at the start of the siege, Samuel approached to within twenty yards of the ditch surrounding the citadel. He thus gained a very distinct view of the battlements and on one such visit received a genteel bow from a monsieur among the officers, which he returned.

However as the siege continued and the French began to lose more and more men, the courtesies disappeared. By now the British batteries had been brought to bear within pistol shot of the walls. Thus a continual fire of musketry took place whenever anyone appeared to be unprotected. The carelessness of Samuel's early approach to the point of action abruptly ceased when another British officer, Sir William Piers Williams, was foolish enough to strut up to within hailing distance of a French sentinel, who promptly shot him dead.

So went the summer of 1761. 'The energy, presence of mind and versatility of talent displayed by Mr Greig,' Commodore Keppel reported, 'have raised him in the estimation of his superiors and brother officers. Whether superintending the disembarkation of the troops, and, when driven back, carrying them off in the face of the enemy though a gale was blowing on a lee shore, whether bearing a part in the siege, directing the bombardment or cheering his men on to the attack, Mr Greig has discharged his duties to my unqualified satisfaction.'

On his return to England, therefore, after the brave surrender of the citadel by the French, the required period of service having now been accomplished beyond any possible doubt, Samuel Greig received his commission as a Lieutenant in the Royal Navy.

A few days later war was declared against Spain.

4

The end of an era

The Empress Elizabeth Petrovna, Her Imperial Majesty Elizabeth II of all the Russias, died on Christmas Day 1761. Outwardly little had changed during the preceding three years. The European war, later to be known as the Seven Years' War, still continued. Frederick the Great in Prussia and 'the Royal Boa Constrictor', Louis XV, dominated the western world on land. Elsewhere the British Royal Navy had gained, and was holding fast to, a command of the seas.

In Russia an almost putrid deterioration seemed to grip the country so that nothing moved, nothing grew and life remained virtually at a standstill. In Petersburg, as the English Ambassador, the Scottish mercenaries and the various merchants of the town all individually reported, it was as if society were holding its breath against the inevitable changes which the passing of the Empress would bring.

'Corrupt stagnation is the order of the day,' the English Ambassador had written in one of his later dispatches, 'illiterate superstition among the serfs and unbridled tyranny and greed among the so-called educated classes will make the task of any reforming monarch, such as I expect the Grand Duchess Catherine intends to be, very nearly impossible of fulfilment. When the Empress Elizabeth took a bath in Holy Week, she scandalized all Russia. The Grand Duchess, on the other hand, is very careful to avoid doing the slightest thing that might shock. She told me herself that she was "all the more anxious to conform, since I know very well that in matters of this kind, it very often does more harm to neglect trifles than essentials. There are many more minds susceptible to trifles than there are sensible people to despise them." It will be both interesting and dangerous to see the impact of such liberal ideas as she will continue to cultivate in this society where the inclination to tyrannize is greater than in any other inhabited part of the world. If, that is, she is ever permitted to ascend the throne.'

Now that Ambassador Keith had been *en poste* for over three years, his knowledge of and acceptance by the St Petersburg court had become firm, and the intelligence he secured was wide ranging and of considerable reliability. This intelligence was procured from a number of sources. Krevitsky, the *Haus Jude* recommended by Signor Bernardi, seemed to be *persona grata* with the minor officials of the court and with the merchants both Russian and foreign upon whom the court depended for its supplies. The Consul at Crondstadt, the young Mr Cook who had taken over the appointment from his father, establishing himself with a Russian wife, had also become another fruitful source of information and, in the reverse direction, a growing influence on the variegated personalities who visited or traded in the port.

By this time, also, Admiral Talytsin and the Ambassador had become trustworthy friends. The Admiral had still not succeeded in obtaining further mercenaries from Great Britain for the Russian Fleet, but at least the necessity had had been accepted in principle, the proposition had been put to the Russian Ambassador to the Court of St James and discussions initiated with the British Admiralty. Only the naval requirements of the war against France, now extended to Spain and the Spanish possessions in the West Indies, made the execution of such ideas impossible to achieve.

'Consul Cook's wife is a distant cousin of Grand Chancellor Vorontsov,' the Ambassador wrote in a despatch in the latter part of 1761, 'and thus provides a valuable connection with the Russian court. They have done me the honour of asking me to stand godfather to their second son and this has given me the opportunity of making the acquaintance of another Vorontsov cousin, the Princess Dashkov, younger sister to Countess Elizabeth, the somewhat dull-witted lady-in-waiting to the Grand Duchess Catherine who has replaced her in the Grand Duke's bed. There is so much scandal concerning the Grand Duke Peter, now that the demise of the Empress cannot be distant, that his relationship with this Countess Elizabeth Polyansky, *née* Vorontsov, passes almost unnoticed.

'But whereas this lady is not only sluggish of intellect but also enjoys a considerable ugliness of physique – an essential recommendation to the taste of the Grand Duke – her sister the Princess Dashkov seems more than ever to be a rare flower in these harsh northern climes. She is a cultivated, personable young woman of seventeen, agreeably attached to her husband who is a Captain in the Preobaginsky Guards and an Aide-de-Camp to the Grand Duke. The Princess Dashkov speaks French and Italian fluently, in addition, of course, to the obligatory German which the Holstein faction requires. She can also converse in Russian when she condescends so to do. She is very well read and when her brother Alexander was attached to the Russian Embassy in Paris, they corresponded, so she informs me, at least twice a month, conveying to each other the main news of the court in both countries.

'She has also become an intimate, in so far as the Secret Chancery allows, of the Grand Duchess Catherine since their common interests of the mind and spirit draw them together. "I may venture to assert," she told me when we were conversing at a reception recently given by the Grand Chancellor, "that there are not two women in the empire except the Grand Duchess Catherine and myself who occupy themselves at all in serious reading." Both she and the Grand Duchess exhibit an unusual understanding of the Russian mind. Her husband, Prince Dashkov, is by birth a Muscovite and when she married him in February of last year, she journeyed to Moscow to meet his family. "Here," she told me, "a new world opened upon me: new engagements and new circumstances. The members of my husband's family were for the most part elderly people and I could not help perceiving that had I been a Muscovite, I should have pleased them better. I spoke Russian – then – very imperfectly and to add to my other embarrassments my mother-in-law spoke no other language. I resolved, therefore, to apply myself with diligence to my native language."

'She is also becoming practised in the diplomatic procedures of the court. Given the fact that her sister is a lady-in-waiting to the Grand Duchess and her husband an Aide-de-Camp to the Grand Duke, she must tread delicately in the company she keeps. When her husband was ordered to Oranienbaum by the Grand Duke, she contrived not to stay in the palace, preferring to put up at the house of her husband's father which is between St Petersburg and Oranienbaum. This did not please the Grand Duke. "Though you are determined, I find, not to live in this palace, I hope to see you every day and I expect you to spend more of your time with me than in the Grand Duchess's company."

' "I was in a dilemma," she said, "since I greatly preferred the company of the Grand Duchess Catherine to the drunken capers of her husband, and marshalling all the tact of which I was possessed, I indicated this preference to the Grand Duke. He was greatly displeased. "You would do well to recollect," he told me with a scowl, "that it is *much safer* to deal with honest blockheads like your sister and myself than with great wits, who squeeze the juice out of the orange and then throw away the rind."

'This observation,' the Ambassador's despatch continued, 'coming as it did from "the honest blockhead" himself shows a somewhat surprising pertinacity and the incident reveals the Princess Dashkov to be an impetuous, headstrong young woman. She is certainly a fresh element in this midden of a court. Yet she endangers not only herself and her husband but others with whom she is connected by the unbridled character of her outspokenness. I was present at another reception given by the Grand Duke, whose habitual arrogant and drunken behaviour passes comprehension. There she had the courage, as some would say, or the gall, as others did in fact declare, to stand up and remind His Imperial Highness that his aunt still sat on the throne of Russia, ill and debilitated though she might be. The effect was dramatic, the party being brought abruptly to a close. I later drew the Princess to one side and warned her of the danger of speaking the truth to sovereigns, a transgression which they, perhaps, themselves may pardon but which, I am very sure of, their courtiers never can.'

The British Ambassador's shrewd assessment of the little Princess Dashkov and of her impact on the court scene, was uncomfortably, perhaps even dangerously, close to the mark. Her independence of mind, her courage and her generosity of heart would all require the discipline of experience if they were not to be jeopardized by foolhardiness.

Since the Grand Duchess Catherine shared a number of these qualities and the perils they brought in their train, and since it had become apparent to both of them – though independently – that a risky period of change, incalculable in its effects, would follow upon the death of the Empress, the two women, one nearly double the age of the other, were drawn together. Their meetings were hazardous and communication clandestine. Even during the last few months of her life, when the Empress scarcely ever left the Palace, the system of spying, gossip and intrigue had taken on such proportions that no one could feel safe from the Secret Chancery.

However the virtual confinement to her room of the ailing Empress, because her legs were now so swollen that she needed assistance even to hobble a few steps, diminished to a great degree the outward, official life of the court. Functions, of course, continued but these days usually without the attendance of the Empress. From time to time the old lady would dress laboriously for a ball and then, catching sight of the finished result in a looking glass, would refuse to go. The study of her gorged body and decayed looks had an inevitable and deeply depressing effect on her spirits which her vanity and the thousands of gowns bolstering this up could not allay. Towards the end of 1761 it became less and less likely that the Empress would ever attend another ball.

On the last of these occasions, the whole court having assembled, the Grand Duchess Catherine, surrounded by members of the Orlov family, espied the Princess Dashkov in conversation with the Grand Chancellor and beckoned her across.

'Your Imperial Highness did not honour our house with your usual visit after seeing your son last week,' Princess Dashkov said after she had bowed.

'But you received my word of explanation, did you not?' the Grand Duchess said, with a meaningful glance at Alexei Orlov.

'Alas, no,' the Princess replied, also looking at the Orlovs.

'Well, Alexei, and what have you to say to that?'

'Your Highness's commission was faithfully executed,' Orlov said. 'I delivered the note to Count Vorontsov's house but I was not permitted to give it into Princess Dashkov's hand. You were, I was informed, indisposed.'

'Rubbish!' said Princess Dashkov. 'I was eagerly awaiting the arrival of Her Highness. I had recently received a copy of Monsieur Rousseau's *La Nouvelle Héloïse* and I was looking forward to discussing the rupture between him and "our" Monsieur Voltaire.'

Count Orlov politely suppressed a yawn.

'Then you should question your servants,' he said, 'since I delivered the letter myself.'

'The Princess will do as she sees fit,' the Grand Duchess remarked stiffly, and with a nod dismissed her entourage. Then when they were out of earshot, she went on in a low voice to the Princess:

'He is speaking the truth. I am afraid the Secret Chancery still interests itself in the innocent communications between two lonely women. We must behave with even more circumspection than before.'

'Does Your Highness trust the Orlov family? I am told that might be unwise.'

'I trust everyone and I trust no one,' the Grand Duchess replied. 'I consider that the vilest of all situations is that of being made a dupe. As a child I used to cry bitterly when I was deceived but I obeyed implicitly, even if resentfully, when the true reasons were given to me. I apply this experience to my present circumstances.'

'You shall never be deceived by me, madame,' the Princess

said, looking straight into the Grand Duchess's cold blue eyes. 'Destiny intends you for the throne and me to be at your side.'

'Princess, this is neither the time nor the place for that kind of opinion. The immediate future is dark indeed. There is no question but that the Grand Duke would like me away from here. He wishes to replace me with your sister.'

'Never! My uncle will take care of that.'

'If the Grand Chancellor finds himself in a position to take care of anything,' Catherine said. 'We are none of us safe with Ivan Shuvalov and Alexei Razumovsky in the apartment next door to the Empress.'

'As to that,' said the Princess, 'if an old woman wishes to have her lover and her morganatic husband together in adjoining apartments at the end of her life . . .'

She faltered into silence, alarmed at the look on the Grand Duchess's face. Catherine studied her young companion for a moment or so, and then said with authority:

'I trust, for your sake as well as mine, that you speak in this fashion to no one other than to me. The truth is sometimes better left unsaid. Outspokenness must be kept within bounds or it ceases to be a quality. We are all of us entering a period of very great danger.'

Princess Dashkov bowed her head.

'I simply wished Your Highness to know that in me you have both a trusty servant and a faithful, and I hope understanding, friend.'

The Grand Duchess touched her hand.

'Whose warm heart and eager spirit are fully appreciated,' she said. 'I am only concerned that your impetuosity should not result in an unfortunate miscalculation. Ah! here is Prince Trubetskoy, no doubt with news of Her Majesty's health . . .'

With a glance of dismissal the Grand Duchess disposed of the young Princess and turned her attention to the fifty-seven-year-old Boyar who had always had a special position in her thoughts. He had indeed come to discuss with her the Empress's health but as she watched the Princess return to her husband's side across the room, she wondered how much the girl knew about her present companion Prince Trubetskoy. Did she, in fact, know that thirty-three years ago this same Prince had presented to the French court at Versailles the Grand Duchess's mother, the Duchess of Anhalt-Zerbst? Did the girl further know the gossip and the rumours that this same Prince had been her mother's lover a year or nine months before she, the Grand Duchess Catherine, had been born? The Dashkov girl had offered her friendship and loyalty. For this she was grateful. It could not, however, approach in warmth and understanding the relationship she enjoyed with the Prince Trubetskoy.

'Now Sophie,' he said, using as always the name with which she had been christened, 'we have a number of urgent matters to discuss.'

These urgent matters came to a head on the evening of 22 December. A few days previously the Empress had suffered a high fever and had vomited blood. Doctor Karl Friedrich Kruse and the other Court Physicians had held an emergency conference and had expressed a mounting alarm but, as had happened so many times before, death's approach rallied the corpulent old lady into a final resistance. Bernardi, the court jeweller, had also contracted a fever and the Empress sent her doctors to advise on his recovery. She was incorrigible.

Indeed she would not even release her grip on minor matters of state. She signed an order reducing the salt tax and also, perhaps as a last hostage to Fate, an amnesty for tax evaders. Her own unpaid bills plagued her thoughts and she enquired of the Grand Chancellor as to how, in his opinion, she and her reign would be remembered.

'For the beautiful palaces you have constructed,' he replied; 'for your victorious armies and for the position of respect and fear in which mighty Russia now finds herself held *vis-à-vis* the rest of the world.'

'And not for the corruption and laxity of our public administration? Not for the arrogance of our nobles and the neglect of their serfs?' she countered.

'Those are factors common to the whole civilized world,'

the Grand Chancellor remarked. He was careful to make no mention of the prisoner without a name – the Emperor Ivan, whom she had locked away in Schlusselburg these last twenty years and who had now gone off his head.

At ten o'clock on the night of 22 December, the Empress suffered a relapse. Delirium attacked her, and on the following day the priests were sent for to administer the last rites. This resulted in a lucidity and calmness of spirit, whereupon she summoned the Grand Duke Peter and his wife to her bedside.

'I have not long now to go,' she said, 'and you shall inherit the throne. Take good care of the Grand Duke Paul and secure the succession in the manner I have decreed.'

By now all Russia knew that the end was near. The palace, upon which she had lavished so much love and attention, had filled with nobles and commoners, many of whom were on their knees wailing and crying in the traditional way of showing grief. Others began making such arrangements as they could to ingratiate themselves with the man who would soon be Peter III.

The agony and the vigil lasted until the middle of Christmas Day. Then, shortly after three in the afternoon, Prince Trubetskoy left the royal bedchamber and announced in a loud clear voice: 'Her Imperial Majesty has fallen asleep in God. God save our most gracious Sovereign, the Emperor Peter III.'

So a new era began. The Grand Duchess Catherine, in concert with the more responsible members of the Imperial court, retired to her room and proceeded to fulfil the ceremonial of mourning appropriate to her rank. In contrast, the new Emperor Peter caused a lavish supper party to be organized in the hall of the palace next to the chamber where the dead Empress Elizabeth lay. The carousal continued into the early hours of the following day.

There are certain years when the fires of history seem to be mysteriously stoked up and the contents of any cauldron sitting on the top, instead of gently bubbling, come almost explosively to the boil. 1762 was such a year. If it be true that the future dictates the present, then in that year the ferment of ideas and the resulting actions achieved a peak not only in Russia but in France, Germany and Great Britain as well.

Samuel Greig, as yet completely unaware of the main course of his future destiny, had volunteered for service in the West Indies under his old Commodore, Keppel, and found himself commander of a sloop on the expedition mounted by the Earl of Albemarle to reduce the Spanish power in Havana. In France a rearguard action against the assorted liberal ideas of Voltaire, Diderot and Jean-Jacques Rousseau resulted in the burning by the public executioner of the latter's *Emile* and an order by the Parlement of Paris for the wayward philosopher's arrest.

In Russia, Peter III continued the drunken and irresponsible behaviour which had characterized his life as the Heir Apparent. In this he scandalized all Russia. 'Tradition', as Voltaire observed, 'must be subjected to the criticism of reason,' and both criticism and reason were patently missing in the doltish and insecure occupant of the Russian throne. To maintain, as was fashionable at the time, that nobody did anything very foolish except from some strong principle did not explain the brief, unhappy reign of Peter the Third, most of whose foolish actions derived from no principles at all.

'Indeed,' as Ambassador Keith observed in one of his private dispatches written at the end of February, 'there is but one decision of merit the new Emperor has so far taken, and that is to abolish the Secret Chancery. Last night the Emperor did me the honour of inviting himself to dinner at my house in the course of which he remarked that "that abominable tribunal (the Secret Chancery) was in all respects as bad as, and in some respects worse than, the Spanish Inquisition." Whilst I cannot but agree with this sentiment, the Emperor may well have jeopardized his own position by thus summarily disposing of one of its major supports.

'Over all the watchful intelligence of the Grand Duchess Catherine anxiously broods. She is beloved by the common soldiery and also by certain of the more daring and younger of the officers. The court intrigues, the corruption and the open venality of all who surround the throne, however, continue unabated. The country is not so much governed as manipulated by greedy and selfish men for their own interest.

'Indeed one of the few glimmerings of light in an otherwise darkening scene is that the Emperor Peter cordially and openly detests everything French. He has discharged the French company of comedians at court and declares himself a dozen times a day to be more Prussian than Frederick II himself. Whilst this in no way harms the interests of the English throne, it makes him more enemies than any such gesture is worth. And the time may not be too far distant when this German corporal of an Emperor will have need of every friend upon whom he can rely. The only thing certain is that matters cannot continue in their present hapless way for very much longer.'

'Well, Sam,' Fortescue Fynne remarked when they met at the *Bell Tavern* for an evening meal, 'it is rumoured around that you have at last been given a command of your own.'

Samuel flushed with pleasure and responded with an evasive smile.

'Where did you gain that intelligence, Fortie? I have only this very afternoon had confirmation myself.'

'Why – in that graveyard of hope, the anteroom in the Admiralty we both know so well. Captaincy of the Armed Vessel *Laurel*, I believe, sailing from Spithead for the Caribees.'

'Indeed that is so. I heard that my old Commodore Keppel was requiring a powerful armament to assist him in striking an early and effective blow against Spain in the West Indies.'

'So you are no longer averse to a little pulling of the strings? Mr Oswald would be proud of his shy apprentice. And what powerful armament does the *Laurel* bear?'

'She does have one four-pounder gun, I am told. The rest is properly a matter of prayer.'

The two friends studied each other as they settled down to their wine. There was no jealousy in Fortescue Fynne and no offence was taken by Samuel at the ribald denigration of his first command which followed. A command was a command, even if the vessel in question were no greater in size than a soap dish.

'I had occasion to glance at the Recommendation whilst the clerk's attention was elsewhere,' Fortie went on. 'It said you were Bold, Upright and Responsible – a young man with a brilliant potential. Well, well, well, I said to myself, so that is what that threadbare, lovesick Scot has got himself described as. And myself off to the Mediterranean again! How do you manage it, Sam? Is it all for King George?'

'And Sarah,' Sam said, looking into the distance. 'I must get the prize money before I can indulge in thoughts of marriage.'

'Marriage! Oh, my God!' said Fortie, 'there is no end to the idiocy of man.'

It was the spring of 1762 and the decision had been taken to attack Spain at her most vulnerable point. So the Royal Navy assembled a greater force than had ever yet been dispatched to the West Indies, with the object of capturing the island of Cuba. This was the keystone to Spanish commerce and navigation in the New World.

'And Commodore Keppel's brother, the General, is to command a large part of the ten thousand troops which the Earl of Albemarle is going to throw against Havana,' Samuel said. 'It is something of a family affair as you can readily see.'

But Samuel's prognosis of destiny proved in this instance to be faulty. As he had indicated to Fortescue Fynne, the *Laurel* was not exactly a battleship of the line. Indeed when he first stepped on board, he had doubts as to whether his little command would stand up to a Channel breeze, let alone an Atlantic storm. From this point of view, therefore, it was perhaps fortunate that this dubiety was never to be put to the test. No sooner had the *Laurel* heaved anchor with the rest of the fleet at Spithead, than several large Indiamen seized the opportunity of taking advantage of the convoy and started at the same time. One of these, the

Haughton, a few cables away from the *Laurel*, was got under way in such a clumsy, unseamanlike manner in the bustle of starting that:

'She's running foul of us, sir!' Samuel's boatswain called out with an oath, as the great merchantman bore down on them and rammed the *Laurel* just aft of the forepeak, splitting her in two. It was at once apparent that the little craft would founder in a matter of minutes, so it was ironic that almost the first order Samuel gave as a Captain was 'Abandon ship! Every man for himself!'

'Thus ended my first proper command,' Samuel wrote to Sarah, 'without our ever quitting Spithead and this was the fourth occasion on which I have narrowly escaped drowning. The annoyance at the loss of my vessel is very great' (it was perhaps lucky that Fortescue Fynne was not present to read this description, or he might have ribbed him on its pomposity) 'although I derive some consolation from the united testimony of the whole fleet that the fault was none of mine but resulted from the careless and disgraceful manner in which the huge Indiaman had been worked.'

So, from being Captain of his own ship, Samuel dropped down to taking passage as a supernumerary under Captain Elphinston, an officer later to distinguish himself in the Russian service. A conjunction of the fleets duly took place off Cape Nicola at the end of May – one from England and the other from its successful operation against the French island of Martinique, a victory which had resulted in the English becoming possessed of the immense chain of the French Caribees extending from the eastern point of Hispaniola almost to the continent of South America. It was 1762.

The British Armada now consisted of nineteen great sail of the line, eighteen smaller ships of war and nearly one hundred and fifty transports with, in addition, bomb vessels, fire ships and victuallers. The problem which Admiral Sir George Pokoke, the Commander-in-Chief, had urgently to face lay in bringing his force to the point of attack before the advent of the hurricane season.

'I am sending you over to the flagship, Mr Greig,' Commodore Keppel informed him. 'The Admiral has need of every skilled navigator in the fleet, as he intends the short but dangerous passage through the old straits of Baja Mar. I have recommended you highly to Sir George, so pray endeavour not to run us all aground.'

It was no small achievement on the part of the Masters and their Mates – the Navigators of the fleet – that this vast convoy of ships of all sizes proceeded to make the Bahama passage without a single mishap, the whole being brought to about five leagues east of Havana in preparation for the landings intended. The voyage duly completed, Samuel was returned to Commodore Keppel with a commendation from the Commander-in-Chief and the suggestion that 'this officer having been instrumental in keeping the fleet off the rocks, may now be employed in putting the soldiery on to the rocks.'

This was to be easier said than done. Together with General Keppel, the Commodore's brother whose responsibility it was to invest El Moro, the fort commanding the entrance to the harbour and the town of Havana, Samuel surveyed the landing places from a cutter and concluded that he had never yet been given a harder task. There could now be no element of surprise and although they were protected by the Commodore's guns, the terrain on which Samuel landed his eight hundred Marines – 'his' in the sense that he had been made responsible for getting this detachment safely ashore with their guns – was so inhospitable that at first sight the difficulties appeared all but insurmountable.

'We can land the material and the men,' Samuel informed his superior officers, 'there are no insuperable problems in that. However the labour of forming a communication through the woods leading up to the fort and of drawing along the artillery will be excessive in this heat.'

'Nevertheless it shall be achieved.' The Commodore and his brother studied the young man with appreciative smiles. 'Self-confidence, it has been said, is the first requisite to great undertakings and you do not lack self-confidence, Mr Greig, nor for that matter do any of us in this squadron. We look to your stubborn audacity to carry this operation through to a successful conclusion.'

It was bad in prospect, it was worse in the execution. The soil proved to be so lacking in cover that Samuel and his men were compelled to protect their approach with bags of cotton, pieces of old canvas and any other similar articles which could be spared from the ships. No fresh water was to be found in the vicinity and the troops, many of whom dropped dead from the heat and exhaustion, soon had to depend on depleted supplies from the naval vessels.

By now it was June. The rigorous perseverance demanded of Samuel and his fellow officers had resulted in a sufficient number of batteries being placed in position ashore to effect a breach in the walls of El Moro fort when the order should be given. The operation had so far cost the disablement of some three thousand of the sailors and the troops employed, mostly from the vile climate they had had to endure, but by the last day of the month all was ready for the opening assault.

'And now that your work is done,' Samuel was informed, 'you should return to the ship.'

'Never!' said Samuel, with difficulty suppressing a rage which threatened to overcome him. 'I have stood by my men up to now, as they have stood by me. At the risk of insubordination, I insist on taking part in the assault.'

'Your value as a naval officer –' the Commodore began, when Samuel abruptly interrupted.

'Sir, there is a spirit of generous rivalry between soldiers, seamen and marines which has got us to the present point. I cannot leave them now.'

'Cannot, Mr Greig? And should I give you a direct order?'

'Pray give it to someone else,' Samuel said. 'I will see this matter through to a successful conclusion if it is the last thing I do – sir.'

The Commodore smiled. He was a tall, distinguished-looking man and although he affected a somewhat languid speech had nevertheless a commanding presence. After a slight pause he turned away, saying:

'I find I am become somewhat hard of hearing these days, Mr Greig. I have no doubt you have just made a report of some consequence but, alas, I did not take in its import. You had best return to your post ashore and report to me again when Don Luis de Velasco has surrendered the fort. And God be with you,' he added as he walked away.

So the mines were sprung, a lodgement was effected and the fort was then stormed with what the General described as 'irresistible intrepidity'. A shell splinter carried away some of the flesh of Samuel's right arm but he bound this up quickly and mounted the ramparts with his loyal men in one common impulse, clearing them of the enemy.

The Spanish now fled on all sides leaving four hundred killed and as many prisoners. Only the citadel – the innermost strong point of the whole fortification – yet remained in Spanish hands. Don Luis, the Governor of the fort, had died fighting gallantly in defence of his colours and the Marques de Gonzales, his second-in-command, had also fallen in a brave attempt to rally his troops.

By mid-August in an almost unbearable heat the Spanish who remained in the citadel had been reduced to some seven hundred men and, their water and food being almost entirely depleted, a flag of truce was displayed. The garrison was then accorded the honours of war and the British were put in possession of Havana. When the count was made, the money, goods and stores found at the time of surrender amounted to nearly three million pounds sterling, an altogether extraordinary prize.

'A sad disappointment, however, attends the distribution of this prize money,' Samuel wrote to Sarah, 'which is not to be made according to the rules hitherto observed. The Admiral receives the enormous share of £122,697. The Lieutenants of the fleet £234 each. This is scarcely proportionate to the bravery they have shown and the hardships they have endured.'

This meagre sum was not going to afford his aged parents the relief he intended to give them, nor would it allow him to consider marrying. It was a sorry material reward for the exceptional efforts he had made. However once more he received the unstinted approbation of his senior officers. 'The skilful and judicious manner in which Greig effected the disembarkation of the troops deserves the highest praise,' wrote Commodore Keppel, himself promoted Rear-Admiral of the Blue for this operation; and Admiral Pokoke showed his sense of Greig's services by appointing him third Lieutenant of the *Hampton Court*, a sixty-four-gun ship of the line. He was then allowed to go ashore for a short time to recover his health.

'I took up quarters at the house of a priest of the neighbouring village,' Samuel wrote to Sarah, 'and found this priest to be one of the most kind, obliging men I have ever met with. Religion is a topic we never enter upon but few men talk of morality better or practise it more than he does. I have the benefit of riding out morning and evening on a horse which I have had as a present from an officer on this service and have also the priest's chariot at my command. I do not know when I shall return to the United Kingdom but Sir George Pokoke will soon sail from here and I shall endeavour to send this letter to you at the same time.'

This in fact took place. The Commander-in-Chief left Rear-Admiral Keppel in charge of the long drawn-out process of clearing up and restoring the captured port. During this period Greig was employed in making a survey of the harbour and adjacent coast. This exhibition of his powers as a draughtsman resulted in a chart 'which gave entire satisfaction' and when Keppel himself sailed for home, he appointed Lieutenant Greig as Commander of the captured sixty-gun ship *Conquistador* with orders to fit out the ship so that it could proceed to Europe. Here again the short time he took to put the prize into perfect order was an indication of the great skill he possessed in naval economy, which was to stand him in such good stead in his later service under another flag.

Sometime after the *Conquistador* had been made ready for sea, Greig was directed by the Admiral to receive on board the Admiral's brother, Major-General the Hon George Keppel, his retinue, officers and troops. With these exalted passengers, Lieutenant Greig sailed for England on what was to be his final service under the British crown. If hitherto he had seemed to lack an adequate patronage of the powerful and the great, his distinguished actions in the West Indies had now put this essential asset within his grasp.

5

Autocrat and Empress

Russia in 1762 endured a convulsive year. It began uneasily enough. The death of the old Empress caused all at court first to reassess themselves and their positions individually and then, as events in the spring and summer galloped towards disaster, to coalesce together as a whole. No one could feel secure. Each kept careful observation on his neighbour, unsure of friendship, dubious even of blood relationship, watchful, suspicious, insincerely smiling, inwardly distrustful, always on the alert. Only Catherine succeeded in keeping herself above the morass, her mind and spirit clear, her instinct sharper than ever before and turned, it might fairly be said, to the demands of her extraordinary fate.

'You nourish your soul with books,' she observed to the Princess Dashkov early in that ominous spring. 'This is also what I have endeavoured to do since I was an ugly girl of less than your age.'

'That I cannot believe,' the Princess politely replied, 'I mean that you were ever an ugly child . . .' But before she could proceed with the flattery, which in any case the new Emperor's consort did not desire, she was interrupted by an imperious gesture and a hardening of the blue eyes which seemed to stare right through her and yet retain the trace of a twinkle.

'I do not know if I was actually ugly as a child, but I recollect that I was so often told that I was, and that because of that I should try to acquire wit and other merits, that until the age of fourteen or fifteen, I was convinced I was a regular ugly duckling and tried much more to develop these other virtues than rely upon my face. It is true that I have seen a portrait of myself, painted when I was ten. It was excessively ugly so that if it were a good likeness, then I was not being deceived.

'However I recall my father's Adviser discussing with my Governess the marriage of the Princess Augusta of Saxe-Gotha, who was my second cousin, with the Prince of Wales, son of George II of England. Monsieur Bolhagen said to my Governess, "Really this Princess has been much less carefully brought up than ours: she is not beautiful either but there she is – destined to become Queen of England! Who knows what future faces ours?" He then proceeded to teach me wisdom and all the moral and Christian virtues which would make me worthy of a Crown, if it were to be my fate to wear one. This idea of a crown', the Empress went on with a smile, 'began running in my head then like a tune and has been running in it ever since.'

'In the achieving of which it will be my privilege to assist.'

The Empress seemed slightly to withdraw, as if she found this expression of determined loyalty a little too strong for her.

'What idea compels you to speak in this way?'

'An image of perfection,' Princess Dashkov said, her eyes afire, 'a striving towards the light. We shall not have it from the present Emperor.'

Instinctively both women looked round to make sure that they were not overheard, but Catherine was no longer bothering to admonish her proselyte or caution her to control her tongue. Both knew the eleventh hour would soon be at hand.

'It has always been my endeavour to please the people among whom I have been destined to live,' the Empress said, looking into the distance as if going back into her memories. 'I therefore adopted their way of living and their manners – or shall we say some of their manners. I wanted to be Russian in order that the Russians should love me.'

'They already do.'

'They are a dangerous people upon whom to practise improvement,' the Empress declared. 'The inclination to tyrannize is cultivated here more than in any inhabited part of the world.'

'When my brother was at the French court,' the Princess Dashkov said, 'he told me that it was an understood thing amongst the Ministers and Ambassadors that second journeys to Russia were extremely hazardous to undertake.'

'For that the French King himself must bear the main responsibility. He is the very progenitor of intrigue,' the Empress said scornfully.

'Would you not agree that King Frederick of Prussia runs a close second in that particular race? My brother Michael tells me the Emperor drinks a toast to him every night and did so even whilst the war with Prussia was in progress.'

'You are well informed.'

'Michael is a Captain of the Guard and my uncle the Grand Chancellor,' the Princess Dashkov said simply. 'But I fear my husband is to be sent away.'

This took the Empress by surprise.

'So soon after your second child has been born? I did not know.'

'He made a mistake in the ceremonial parade on Tuesday which occasioned the Emperor's rage and displeasure. He is to be banished to Constantinople as our Ambassador.'

'I am not informed of such matters,' the Empress said, and then, touching her hand, 'That will be a hardship for you. How old are you? Still seventeen?'

'No, I am turned eighteen,' the Princess replied, 'but I shall not be accompanying my husband, dearly though I love him. Matters must soon reach a point of decision here.'

The abrupt banishment of a Captain of the Guard was but a minor event in the almost headlong lurch to disaster on which the new Emperor had embarked from the very earliest days. This had begun whilst his aunt, the late Empress, had still been lying in state. He had long been an autocrat of the nursery and now that he was Tsar, Peter indulged each and every passing whim which pressed into his mind. Exhibiting an almost total lack of discretion, his drunken capers first offended, then disgusted and finally revolted the courtiers, the soldiers, the sailors and the foreign community of St Petersburg. On all of these he nevertheless had to depend in different ways for the operation of the power which the accident of his birth had dropped into his lap.

'Never has a man had more acquaintances and fewer friends,' Keith said to Catherine on one of the increasingly rare occasions when she had allowed him the pleasure of her bed. Now that she was Tsarina, she had perforce to be more circumspect than ever. 'Never did a newly installed monarch receive more lip service to his face,' the English Ambassador went on as he caressed what he now referred to privately as the Imperial Breast, 'and be subjected to a more cruel denigration behind his back. Although,' he continued with a smile, 'denigration is not the only thing going on behind his back.'

Catherine tossed her head impatiently. She had little taste for a discussion of her cloddish husband whilst being pleasured by a lover of whom she had become inordinately fond.

'For that state of affairs,' she murmured, looking up at the canopy of the bed with a sigh, 'the Tsar must bear the entire responsibility himself. The things which amuse him result only in raised eyebrows and *sotto voce* sneers from those they are meant to impress. I have told him so to his face, but advice from his wife is something the Tsar of all the Russias will no longer accept.'

'His conduct at the funeral must have shocked all Europe,' Keith said as reluctantly he obeyed Catherine's indication that it was time to leave. 'By deliberately varying the pace of the cortège, by alternately running ahead and then dawdling so that the mourners knotted themselves into lumps of confusion, he delighted no one but himself. Admiral Talytzin informed in confidence . . .'

'You and the Admiral have become as thick as thieves,' Catherine interrupted as she watched him climb into his breeches and regain the outward appearance of a foreign ambassador.

'For the benefit of Russia,' Keith retorted. 'If the Royal Navy is to supply officers and material to Russia whilst our war against France and Spain continues in full spate, it will need a very hard argument from its Ambassador at St Petersburg.'

'Who will not, alas, be *en poste* for very much longer,'

Catherine said softly, watching him with a sad look in her eyes. Keith stopped abruptly, remaining completely still for a moment or so.

'You are sending me away?'

'Not I, of course, but the Tsar. Do you not think it wise? Your attentions delight me,' she went on, quickly leaving the bed and taking him in her arms, 'as your true friendship has warmed my spirit, but this is still Russia. We cannot behave as two castaways on a desert isle. Your visits – the memory of which I shall always hold dear – excite increasingly hostile criticism from those who would destroy me. Have you not yourself reported to your King that I have a thoughtful and crafty mind and that I maintain – that I must perforce maintain – a dignified aloofness from my husband's antics whilst awaiting the right moment to present itself for a seizure of power?'

'You are indeed well informed, madame,' Keith said somewhat formally, realizing that she must have had a sight of at least one of his more secret dispatches to London. Catherine acknowledged this remark with a nod and a twist of her ample mouth.

'You said, if I recall correctly, that I involved myself in these matters of state with the caution of a man-of-war approaching a foreign, possibly hostile and certainly well fortified coast. Some suitable opening to a welcoming port must be sought out and discovered, you went on, I trust with an unintended irony – ' she glanced down at her voluptuous naked hips and at the welcoming port they sheltered, and then smiled at him in reassurance, 'whilst all this time the ship remains under threat. At any moment the enemy may decide to open fire and sink us both. It will do as a passable analogy. In the autocratic conditions of this "midden of a court" – as I think you described it – the Tsarina can disappear like that.' She snapped her fingers and picked up her robe. 'No one would find her. No one would rescue her from banishment or imprisonment any more than the prisoner without a name will ever leave Schlusselburg alive. A despot has but to say the word and life is forfeit. The Emperor comprehends this sombre fact and so do I.'

Keith examined his well-manicured nails, playing for a little more time.

'Then is this the last time I am to see you?' he said eventually. He found himself strangely, surprisingly moved, almost like a stripling boy near to tears. He looked at this very remarkable, passionate woman with the great blue eyes who had done him the honour not only of taking him as a lover but also of admitting him to a very real and intimate friendship, respected by both of them.

'My dear Sir Robert,' Catherine said, continuing to restore her toilette, 'a new and dangerous ferment has begun to work in this court which pretends to be a civilized society but the standards of which would scarce do honour to a Tartar tribe. We have Field-Marshal Munnich, exiled to Siberia these last twenty years by the late Empress, suddenly reappearing in our midst. We have the intrigues between the old Count Razumovsky – to say nothing of his elegant son – the Panins, State Secretary Teplov, the Naryshkins and the Orlovs all in full spate. We have the Preobaginsky Guards throwing off their Prussian uniforms, so beloved of my husband, and reverting overnight to the traditional uniforms of Peter the Great. What is the answer to it all? Assuredly there is foreign money and influence at work. The Princess Dashkov tells me she has received many overtures of unbounded credit from the French Ambassador.'

'To which she assures you she has replied strongly in the negative.'

The Tsarina obliged him with a quizzical look.

'I cannot but think you are involved in similar proposals on behalf of His Britannic Majesty ... So, my dear Sir Robert, I suggest that now perhaps it would be expedient for you to request your own recall to London before – shall we say – others demand it.'

This aerating process, similar in some ways to that of ploughing up and turning over the hardened winter soil of the previous reign, did not stop at the British Ambassador. Other of the Imperial lovers were banished by promotion in rank followed by appointment abroad. The world might see Catherine as little more than an appendage to her husband at this stage of her life; she had, however, already learnt to distinguish between the gratification of her private desires and the management of the affairs of Empire, which had their own rules. It was a distinction the Russian court would soon acquire for itself.

Principles, indeed, had been forgotten or overlooked. They had been allowed to lapse by the Empress Elizabeth, a continuing neglect which was accelerated by the abysmal ignorance of her successor, Peter III. All this was soon to change. Catherine was well aware that crafty men condemn studies, simple men admire them and wise men use them.

In this endeavour Catherine, and her young protégée, the Princess Dashkov, had the assistance of a strong, innate and masculine will. This was to be put to the service of high motive, disciplined by what she understood to be the requirements of an elementary but burgeoning social justice, as recently and somewhat headily defined by the French Philosophes.

Impelled by such powerful ideas, Catherine set herself to face and to fight the appalling barbarity of Russia. This vaguely Christian morality, however, did not extend entirely to the amorous side of her nature. This was a horse which throughout her life was to be curbed only with the lightest rein.

'I do not know where my wife gets her pregnancies,' the Grand Duke Peter, as he then was, had remarked a few years previously in one of his rare flashes of perception, 'and I am by no means sure I shall accept paternity of her latest child.'

But the child in question had turned out to be a daughter, and since an heir to the throne had already been procured in the Grand Duke Paul, and since this birth had pleased his aunt, the Empress Elizabeth, Peter had promptly lost interest and had returned to his deformed mistress and the military games which, in the main, occupied his life. He and Catherine led separate lives, and although he attempted to control her outward behaviour with the full 'corporalism' which characterized his reign, a lazy disinclination to have any physical relationship with his wife left Catherine free, provided she remained discreet, to seek such a fulfilment elsewhere.

Thus immediately before the death of the Empress Elizabeth, Catherine's current lover had been, and continued to be, Count Gregory Orlov, a hussar of undoubted courage but perhaps over-endowed with that male arrogance which it was Catherine's pleasure to tame. Gregory Orlov, several years younger than the woman he loved, shared his mistress's ambition for power and at least some of her high principles. But to whatever degree he dominated her in bed, he and his equally dashing brother Alexis could in no way escape the fact that Catherine had now become the Emperor's wife, and as such must be above reproach.

Nature, however, can provide her own inescapable hazards. On becoming Tsarina, Catherine found herself in the last months of a pregnancy by Gregory Orlov. This she had so far been able to conceal from the new Emperor. The voluminous black garments decreed by court mourning had suited her well though for another purpose.

'However I have still to give birth,' Catherine confided to her lover, 'and that could well be the end of us both.'

It was not a sentiment to which much argument could be opposed. The new Emperor had already been freely exercising his boundless power. He was unstable and his many whims, especially if obeyed in anger, were highly dangerous. A stratagem would be urgently required to provide a solution, the more so since by mid-April, which was the expected time of birth, revolutionary plans for deposing the Emperor might well be mature. The Orlov brothers had principally contrived these plans: it would, therefore, become increasingly important for none of the main protagonists to be temporarily or permanently removed from the arena, least of all Catherine herself.

'I have a suggestion I would humbly urge upon Your Majesty,' one of the Emperor's valets murmured in Catherine's ear, after delivering a written edict from the Emperor concerning the court-martialling of one of her dogs which had accidentally strayed across a parade ground whilst Peter was inspecting some troops.

'Speak freely, Ivan Ivanovich,' Catherine encouraged the young man, whom she well knew to be more devoted to herself than he was to his royal master.

'I understand that the middle of April is likely to be a critical time for certain eventualities – a time when it might be appropriate to arrange some distraction for the Tsar.'

'Pray continue,' Catherine said, nodding her head.

'My royal master is, as you know, much addicted to a spectacle, especially one involving the element of fire. Any blaze, if it should threaten our great wooden city, will secure his presence as fast as a horse will take him.'

'That is so.'

'Your Majesty, I have a wooden *isba* on the outskirts of Petersburg. It is a building I cherish but I have no doubt that it will one day go up in a spectacular blaze since the fabric is dry and in parts rotten. Now, Your Majesty, were I to receive word from you of a certain urgency, I have a sad presentiment that my *isba* will suddenly be found to be dangerously alight, calling for the attentions of our gallant fire fighters, an event I am sure His Majesty would wish to witness, indeed one I am quite sure he would never miss.'

'You are a good and generous man, Ivan Ivanovich,' Catherine said with an understanding smile, 'and we shall see to it that should such an eventuality take place, your generosity shall not be in vain and shall be suitably rewarded.'

Thus it came about that on 11 April 1762 when Catherine's labour pains began, a fire of great proportions was reported on the road to Gatchina. An immediate commotion began and a large crowd gathered at the scene of the outbreak to which, as had been planned, the Emperor felt himself inevitably drawn, the more so since a misfortune attending one of his own servants was a treat to be especially relished. During his absence from the palace the birth took place and a son, to be named Alexis Gregorievich Bobrinsky was born.

No sooner was the umbilical cord severed and the afterbirth disposed of, than the babe was removed and the mother, assisted by her ladies, dressed and got upon her feet. When the Emperor returned after the conflagration had been duly subdued, he visited the Empress but finding her disinterested in his joyous description of the destruction he had just witnessed, he at once retired in a sulk and embarked on yet another of his drunken carousals. Thus was this particular point of danger passed.

The moment of decision in Russian affairs came on 28 June 1762. In the preceding six months Peter III had strained to breaking point the loyalty of all who came in contact with him. The new English Ambassador, watching from his privileged position, remarked to the Governor General of St Petersburg, 'Do you know the Emperor is quite mad?' Even the Empress herself had commented to him privately, 'Peter III has no greater enemy than himself: all his actions border on insanity. Besides this whatever arouses the sympathy of other people moves him to anger. He takes pleasure in beating animals and men. He is not only insensible to their tears and cries but they enrage him, and when he is in this state he quarrels with everyone that comes near him. His favourites are very unfortunate on this account. They do not dare to speak with each other without arousing his distrust. When this is awakened, he beats them soundly before everyone.'

An instance of this took place at Oranienbaum in the presence of the diplomatic corps and about a hundred spectators, both men and women, at a festival ordered by the Emperor. The Grand Master of the Horse Naryshkin, Lieutenant General Melgunov and Privy Counsellor Volkov were all soundly cudgelled by the Emperor himself in public and for no reason that anyone present could perceive. All were left speechless with amazement.

Thus a groundswell arose that the Empress should seize the reins of power and save the Empire. The reasons had long been patent for all to see. The motives were of the highest and the means were secured by the ill-expressed but genuine feeling of the troops who called Catherine 'their little mother' and who looked to her to rescue them all from the downfall of the Fatherland.

Many propositions, all of them dangerous, all filled with risk, had been made to her since the old Empress had died. In the early days Catherine held these differing factions apart and bade each of them wait. As the general situation grew worse, however, she let the separate groups know that the time had now come for them to combine and to consider ways and means.

This process was touched off on 9 June 1762 at a banquet given to celebrate the peace with Prussia. Peter drank to the Imperial family of that nation but, whilst all others present stood on their feet to honour the toast, Catherine remained seated. At this Peter sent over his favourite, Gudovich, with an insulting message, and to rub salt in the wound he shouted loudly across the table a word euphemistically translated as 'silly bitch'. This brought proceedings to a tense and awkward halt, whereupon Catherine rose to her feet and departed from the banquet.

A few days later Peter removed himself to Oranienbaum and Catherine to Peterhof. Now the matter was *au point.* During this period, the revolutionaries decided that on his return from the country, the Emperor should be arrested in his apartment and declared incompetent to reign. This deed had been planned for 30 June but three days previously, because of imprudent talk by a soldier, one of the principals of the plot, Lieutenant Passek of the Guards, had been abruptly arrested. The three brothers Orlov went into action. All were now in dire peril. The Hetman, Count Cyril Razumovsky, and Privy Counsellor Panin thought it all too early. Nevertheless they sent a coach to Peterhof with one of the Counts Orlov to summon the Empress without further delay.

Accordingly Catherine was awoken from her sleep at six o'clock on the morning of 28 June by the arrival of Alexis Orlov.

'Passek has been arrested and there is now no time to lose. For the sake of your own safety and the success of our plans, Your Majesty should drive to the city now.'

The Empress at once decided to risk her life and commit herself to the plan. Aided by the Princess Dashkov, she drove straight away to the barracks of the Izmailovsky Regiment, where she was received by the elder Orlov brother and Prince Bariatinsky. Only twelve men were present at this initial meeting. The rest of the regiment knew all about it but remained in their rooms until summoned. When the call went out, however, they gathered in the barrack square and hailed her as 'Autocrat and Empress' with a joy and a fervour which were all but indescribable.

Catherine was next conducted by them to the Semyonovsky Regiment where a similar reception awaited her, and the soldiers, joined now by large numbers of the common populace, escorted her to the Kazan Cathedral, to which the Horse Guards and the Grenadiers of the Preobaginsky Regiment also came. After being blessed in her endeavour the by now enormous but not unruly crowd of soldiers and civilians conducted her to the Winter Palace, where the Synod, the Senate and all the high dignitaries of state were assembled. A manifesto was drawn up and the oath administered, those present recognizing her as 'Sovereign Empress of all the Russias'.

Catherine now gathered together a kind of council which decided itself to go with four regiments of the Guard to Peterhof in order to secure the person of Peter III.

'And should he then be abandoned by the army,' Admiral Talytzin remarked, 'he will doubtless throw himself on the mercy of the fleet at Crondstadt.'

'Go there, then, yourself,' the Empress commanded, 'and forestall any such move.'

Whilst the council was in session, the Grand Chancellor Vorontsov arrived. He had been sent by the shaken Emperor to reproach the Empress for her actions and to demand her reasons. Catherine listened in silence, ordered the old man to withdraw and told him she would let him know her answer. Vorontsov duly left her presence, and when in an anteroom was generally advised to take the new oath of allegiance. This was unquestionably a hard matter for an honourable man to settle.

'May I make a report on the outcome of my mission to the Emperor,' he enquired, 'to relieve my conscience?'

This permission was given him and he then took the new oath of allegiance to the Empress. Prince Trubetskoy and Field-Marshal Shuvalov now came and prostrated themselves at Catherine's feet, informing her that they had been sent by Peter to kill her. She bade them rise and they, too, then took the oath of allegiance.

By now it was night. Putting her small son, the Grand Duke Paul, in the care of the Senate, Catherine donned the uniform of the Guards to which she had had herself appointed as Colonel-in-Chief and marched through the night towards Peterhof. On this trek her closest companion remained the Princess Dashkov, who had been with her since the beginning of the day.

Meanwhile the wrath of the soldiers and of the people against the unfortunate Peter continued to mount. Of this fact the deposed Emperor gradually became aware, but when he had first arrived at Peterhof from Oranienbaum and had learnt of Catherine's early morning departure, he reacted in a typical manner. He looked for her everywhere, even under the bed. He then questioned all who had remained but could come to no decision. Those surrounding him suggested a variety of different plans of action, of which he chose the weakest. He then walked up and down in the garden and demanded that dinner be served.

In the meantime Admiral Talytzin, privately thinking himself lost, had reached Crondstadt. This citadel lay not more than a mile by water or four miles by land from Oranienbaum. When he arrived he found Crondstadt in the possession of General Devier, with two thousand men. This officer was loyal to Peter.

'Why have you come and what do you want?' the General enquired of the Naval Commander-in-Chief.

'I have come to hasten the departure of the fleet,' the latter answered.

'And what are they saying and doing in the city?'

'Why – nothing,' the Admiral lied.

'Then where are you going now?'

'I am going to take a rest. I am dying of the heat.'

The Admiral was then allowed into the fortress. There he at once summoned to him Commandant Nummers who was on General Devier's staff. They met in private and the Admiral said to him:

'Hark you! In the city the news is quite different from here. Everyone has taken the oath of allegiance to the Empress. I advise you to do the same. I have four thousand sailors here and you have only two thousand men. Here are my orders. Now make your decision.'

'Very well,' said the Commandant, 'I, too, will take the oath of allegiance.'

'Then go and disarm General Devier.'

This Commandant Nummers proceeded to do. He called the General aside, explained the reality of the situation, asked for and received his sword. Then all of them took the oath of allegiance. Of all this procedure Peter naturally remained unaware.

The deposed Emperor lingered in his indecision until the evening of that day. By now only the aged Field-Marshal Munnich, General Izmailov and about thirty women in his retinue continued at his side. Taking the women's advice Peter boarded a galley and set off for Crondstadt. When he reached the fortress at about one a.m., he demanded to be admitted. The officer of the Guard, Lieutenant Michael Gabrilovich Koshukov, refused him admittance.

'Turn back, sire,' he commanded, 'or I shall open fire.'

For this the Lieutenant possessed no authority whatever and had the Emperor not obeyed, he would doubtless have forfeited his life. By this time, however, Peter realized that all was lost. He returned forthwith to Oranienbaum and retired to bed.

The following day Peter dispatched General Izmailov to the Empress, offering to renounce the throne and pleading for his life. He added that he wished to be allowed to withdraw to Holstein with his mistress Elizabeth, and that he still had with him some fifteen hundred armed Holstein troops, together with more than a hundred cannon. When

General Izmailov entered the presence, he threw himself at Catherine's feet and said:

'Do you regard me as an honourable man?'

'I do.'

'Very well,' he replied, 'depend upon it, I am yours. If you will trust me, I will save my Fatherland much bloodshed. I give you my word that, if you will release me, I will bring Peter here. I am quite alone.'

To this the Empress agreed. General Izmailov was ordered to procure the deposed Emperor's abdication in writing and to bring him, his mistress and his favourite Gudovich to Peterhof. These orders were scrupulously obeyed. The document of abdication proved to be surprisingly lucid and clear.

> 'In the short period of my reign as autocrat of the Russian Empire, I have realized its hardships and burdens, to which my powers are not equal, so that neither as autocrat nor in any other way can I rule the Russian Empire. Thus I perceived that inward changes were leading to the destruction of its safety and would necessarily bring lasting disgrace to me. I have therefore, taken counsel with myself and herewith solemnly declare without hatred and without compulsion, not merely to the Russian Empire but to all the world, that I renounce the sovereignty of the Russian Empire for my whole life. As long as I live I will never reign over the Russian Empire as autocrat nor in in any other way, and I will never myself nor with anyone's help strive for it. I swear this sincerely and without hypocrisy before God and the whole world. This entire abdication I have written and signed with my own hand. The 29th day of June in the year 1762.
>
> Peter.'

Aware of the loathing of Peter and of his German troops which the Russian soldiers and the common people bore him, Catherine provided him with a guard of Prince Bariatinsky and three other officers, the whole under the command of Alexei Orlov. Later she sent a hundred picked men from regiments of the Guard, to Ropsha a remote place some twenty-five versts from St Petersburg – a *verst* being two-thirds of an English mile. She gave orders that they were to make life as pleasant as possible for the monarch and that they were to provide everything he wished for his entertainment. It was her intention to send him from there to the fortress of Schlusselburg and then, as circumstances developed, to allow him in time to depart for Holstein with his favourites.

It was just as well that she made these moves. The seizure of power and its consolidation depended in these critical moments on such slender threads that the snapping of any one link could have endangered the chain.

'After his departure from Peterhof,' Catherine wrote, 'I was advised to go straight away to the city. I foresaw that the troops would be disturbed at this. I sent forth a rumour to this effect under the pretext of wishing to know at what hour they would be ready to start after these three fatiguing days. They said: 'Towards ten o'clock in the evening but you must come with us." So I started with them and half-way there I withdrew into the country house of Kurakin, where wholly dressed I threw myself upon a bed . . . Amid a never-ending jubilation I entered the city and went to the Summer Palace where the Court, the Synod, my son and all those who were entitled to appear at court were awaiting me. I then went to mass. This was followed by a *Te Deum*. Afterwards I received congratulations. Then having scarcely eaten or drunk or slept from Friday morning at six o'clock until Sunday evening, I went to bed and fell asleep.

'At midnight, when I had scarcely fallen asleep, Captain Passek entered my room and waked me with the words, "Our people are terribly drunk: a hussar in that condition has just been running about crying out: 'To arms! Thirty thousand Prussians are coming and wish to take our Mother.' Thereupon they seized their weapons and are now coming here to enquire about your welfare. They say they have not seen you for the last three hours and they will go home peacefully if they see that you are well. They will not listen to their leaders or to the Orlovs."

'I went to them and told them I was well but that I wished in future they would hearken to their officers. They replied that the alarm had gone out among them on account of those accursed Prussians and they were all ready to die for me. I said: "Fine. Thank you but now you must go to sleep." Thereupon they wished me good-night and a good health and went away like lambs, frequently turning back as they went to look after my carriage.'

Things did not go so well with Peter. He wrote with a sad dignity in July:

> 'I beg Your Majesty to rest assured on my account, and have the goodness to give orders that the guards be removed from the second room: because the room in which I am is so small that I can scarcely move about in it, and because you know that I always run about in the room and shall get swollen legs from it. Then I beg you further to order that the officers shall not remain in the same room when I have necessities; that is impossible for me. Finally I beg Your Majesty not to treat me like a great criminal; I am not aware that I have ever offended you. I commend myself to your generous consideration and beg you at least to let me go to Germany with the persons I have named. God will certainly reward you and I am . . .
>
> Your very devoted servant
>
> Peter.'

But the good God was to arrange it otherwise. Anxiety had caused Peter to have a diarrhoea which lasted for three days, even continuing to the fourth. On that day he drank immoderately for he had everything he wanted except his freedom. He had asked for his mistress, his dog, his negro and his violin. In order to avoid a scandal and to prevent exciting the guards, the Empress only sent him the last three of his requests.

Peter then suffered an attack of haemorrhoidal colic, worsened by fever fantasies. For two days he remained in this condition, which was followed by a great weakness. Then at what was clearly the worst possible moment, he had an altercation with his guards. This was accompanied by physical violence, all concerned being partly or wholly drunk, when suddenly it was realized that he had breathed his last.

Fearing that the officers might have poisoned him, Catherine ordered the body to be dissected and to her relief it was possible to prove that not the least trace of poison was there in the body. His stomach was quite healthy, the doctors reported, but an inflammation of the intestines and a fit of apoplexy had carried him off. His heart, they added, was unusually small and quite shrunken.

So Peter died, whether the apoplexy had been caused by his years of excess or by the drunken brawl or possibly by a combination of the two. His departure from this world, though it relieved Catherine of a continuing anxiety on his account, posed questions which remained publicly unanswered until she died. Then following the death of Catherine herself, a letter was discovered among her papers. It was dated 6 July 1762, was on a dirty grey sheet and was in the handwriting of Count Alexei Orlov.

> 'Little Mother, Merciful Empress! How shall I tell you, how describe what has happened? You will not believe your faithful servant but before God I will speak the truth. Little Mother, I am ready to die, but I do not know myself how the mischief came about. We are lost if you do not have mercy on us. Little Mother, he tarries no longer on this earth. But no one would have believed it and how could we have thought of laying hands upon the Emperor! But, Empress, the misfortune has happened! He fell into a quarrel at table with Prince Feodor (Bariatinsky). We could not separate them and already he was no more. We ourselves could not remember what we had done, but we are all guilty to the very last one and deserving of death. Have mercy upon me, if only for my brother's sake! I have made my confession and there is nothing to investigate. Pardon or else command quickly that an end be made! I do not wish to see the light; we have angered you and hurled our souls to eternal destruction.'

'My horror at this death is inexpressible,' the Empress said to the Princess Dashkov. 'It is a blow which strikes me to the earth.'

To this the Princess, who disliked and distrusted the Orlov clan, replied:

'It is a death too sudden, madame, for your glory or for mine.'

The long extraordinary reign of Catherine II of Russia had begun.

6

'If you will only wait'

It was now high summer in Petersburg. The swamps and quagmires from which the city had risen yielded in that season a plague of flies and mosquitoes, which seemed to the inhabitants to be increasing each year. The Neva, it was true, carried away into the bay much of the ordure thrown into it by a native population in total ignorance of the first principles of hygiene – or even of the necessity for it – but as the town had spread, so did the breeding grounds of the pests which made the hot steamy summers as difficult to endure in their different way as the hard frozen winters.

Such then formed the humid background to the first startling days of the new regime. Once the excitement of revolution had died away, the whole of Petersburg watched with a tense anticipation to see how the young Empress would establish herself on the throne. They did not have long to wait.

'We shall have an audit,' Catherine told her Grand Chancellor. 'We shall attend the Senate daily to hear our Treasurer tell us the condition of the Exchequer and of the country's finances.'

'That will not consume much of Your Majesty's time,' Vorontsov answered with a wry smile. 'The Exchequer is bare. The late Empress left debts of seventeen million roubles and the entire taxes of Empire have for many years been variously licensed to private persons for some two million roubles. Even these latterly have not been paid since coming. Two-thirds of the Army have not been paid since the death of the late Empress, and many others for some considerable time before that.'

'Summon the Senate for tomorrow,' the Empress commanded, 'the Secretaries to bring with them all documents required to support the explanations we shall require.'

'Tomorrow is a Saint's Day, Your Majesty. It is not seemly to do business on such a day.'

'I shall decide what is seemly and what is not,' Catherine said tersely. 'We shall first attend the Cathedral and then continue to the Senate. Pray arrange matters as I command.'

The Grand Chancellor bowed and quickly put word of this exchange about the court. It was as if lightning had begun to flicker in one of the frequent Petersburg thunderstorms, only now the lightning and the storm itself were centred on the Palace. The Empress had already caused her three Secretaries to attend her more than two hours earlier in the day than had been their wont. She was prepared to work and she would make others work for her. Moreover she had begun to give decisions on matters so long deferred as to have passed from scandal into oblivion.

The meeting the next day at the Senate astonished those present and, after they had survived the shock of being roundly berated for their past behaviour, augured well for the future. The Senators, who were in no sense representative of Russia but only of themselves, stood expectantly while Catherine seated herself upon the throne. As the Grand Chancellor had forecast, the 'audit' or hearing of the country's finances did not take long. Russia had for many years been in a state of disguised bankruptcy. Indeed the late Empress had endeavoured to float a loan in Holland which, though insufficient, might perhaps have helped to restore the country's finances. But this had totally failed, since no one would take up the risk or any part of it on the security which had been offered. No taxes were being collected which could have serviced such a foreign loan.

'Very well,' Catherine said when she had considered this matter, 'read out the roster of the cities with such taxes you estimate each can pay.'

An uneasy silence fell. The State Treasurer glanced from his principal secretary to that of the Grand Chancellor and then to other courtiers and officials. A blank look of distress lay on every face.

'Answer!' the Empress said.

'Your Majesty,' the Treasurer eventually faltered, 'no such list exists.'

'Am I to understand that this Senate does not possess knowledge even of what towns and cities the Empire is comprised?'

Since no one answered, the Grand Chancellor reluctantly stepped forward.

'Never, since our inauguration, has the Senate been given even a map of all the Russias, Your Majesty. Such a map does not exist. The various Nobles can, no doubt, supply details of their own estates: as to the rest ...'

'And the rest is Russia,' Catherine said and then rose to her feet. After a short pause in which the threat emanating from the throne permeated all in the Senate, Her Imperial Majesty went on in a firm voice:

'Take note, whoever you be and wherever you are, that I intend to continue my reign in the way it has already begun. I shall govern with gratitude to those who helped me, mercy to those who opposed me and with justice to every man. From today all private monopolies are abolished. Let trade now flourish as it will. I conceive that this may not be to the taste of many of my nobles whose private wealth has hitherto been distinct. However it is our will that business should henceforth enjoy a free development, and anyone who stands in the way of this command shall stand before me as an enemy of the state. Taxes will henceforth be collected by the Exchequer. Debts will be paid and we shall contrive a code of law applicable to all.'

There was a murmur amongst the assembled Senate, though whether of approval or dismay it was impossible to judge. Since until then the Empire of all the Russias had in fact been no more than a collection of large private estates each individually governed in its own particular way, Catherine's statement might be taken as pretending to a greater importance than in reality it had, a notion unquestionably held by the majority of her court and senate. However what the Empress now proceeded to say marked the beginning of a new era, and for ever changed the Russian life.

'Know you, also,' she said in a loud, clear voice, 'that all I possess, down to the last rouble and the last serf, is no longer mine but Russia's. I declare this irrevocable decision before God and in front of you all.'

There was an outburst of spontaneous applause and as Catherine surveyed the scene she observed several of the more elderly Senators brushing tears from their eyes. The atmosphere was highly charged with emotion. Hope fired them all and then, like an actor who knows when to quit the stage, she stepped swiftly down from the dais and left the hall.

Thus the Empress settled herself with style and confidence into the commanding position which she was to occupy for the next thirty-four years. She began to gather about herself advisers upon whom she could rely, and military and naval officers who would execute her orders.

Admiral Talytzin, for example, who had played so essential a role in her accession to power, now took his place among those high officers of state whom the Empress felt she could trust. When, therefore, he came to her after a year of her reign to request a strengthening of the fleet by the seconding of naval officers from Great Britain, the prime naval power in the world, she listened to his reasoning and dispatched an Envoy Extraordinary to the Court of St James, charged with this commission. The timing of this could not have been more apt.

The preliminaries of a general European peace which had been signed at Fontainebleau the preceding November, were ratified on 10 February 1763 and peace had been proclaimed in London on 22 of that same month. In consequence of this a great reduction of the Royal Navy took place. The fleets on foreign stations were ordered home to pay off and everything began to be placed upon a footing of peace.

Once again Samuel and Fortescue Fynne found themselves at loose in the capital with somewhat negative prospects. As they had done previously, they soon adopted the habit of meeting for an evening meal at the *Bell*, where a good mutton stew might be had for sixpence, including the wine, and where if they felt so inclined feminine company could be procured without too much bother. On the first of these occasions, they examined the pros and cons of the peace which had just broken out. Both had been several years at sea and felt they deserved a break from hard tack and rotten meat. As always it was Fortescue Fynne who vented the more optimistic opinion.

'You will thus have the opportunity, my dear Samuel, of enjoying a private life and of indulging yourself in the gratification of those warm feelings of affection both inside and outside the family which danger and absence have only served to strengthen.'

He paused for a moment or so and then added:

'You will also be in receipt of half-pay, at the rate of two shillings a day.'

'And when the prize money is gone,' Samuel replied, 'where shall I look for further employment? I have been five years at sea in the King's service. I am not fitted for very much else.'

'As to that,' Fortie declared, 'you should do what you are always urging others to do, namely regard the brighter side of the problem. You are no longer the gawky, threadbare young Scot who came south five years ago.'

'That is true,' Samuel said. 'I am now a gawky, threadbare, middle-aged Scot whom no one wishes to employ.'

'Nonsense! You have been present at almost every action of importance which has taken place. You have commendations from Admirals Hawke, Keppel and a bagful of other nautical nobs. You have Mr Oswald still patronizing himself and others at the Treasury, for what that is worth. You will not be long unemployed, I would hazard a guess, and in any event there will no doubt soon be another war to occupy the national attention.'

They were encouraging words but, as Samuel shortly began to realize, they buttered no parsnips. The prize money he had gained amounted to but a few hundred pounds. It might enable him to supply his parents with some little comforts which their age and infirmities rendered necessary, but not much else.

As he sat in the stage-coach rumbling north from London

to Edinburgh, he could not but help wonder what he had really achieved in the years since he had first made that decisive journey south. Perhaps the world was passing him by. Certainly, judging by the increasing number of turnpikes and the general improvements to houses and roads which he observed as the week's journey continued (he could have reached Edinburgh more quickly, but only at greater cost), it would have paid him better to have stayed at home. The unfair distribution of the prize money so hardly earned in the Spanish West Indies amounted in Samuel's eyes to a swindle, and it rankled in him as the English countryside went slowly past. 'Those Royal Naval Captains,' he had overheard his Boatswain remark to a Gunner with an expletive, 'licensed pirates that's all they are! Happen they should wield a cutlass for their own proper share.' It was a mutinous remark and a few years ago he would have admonished them to guard their tongues or answer for it with the lash. Now he felt the injustice as acutely and depressingly as they did themselves. They had all been shabbily treated. And what was his own future to be – in reality – now that the war had ended?

On arrival in Edinburgh, his sister Meg Charters gave him a warm welcome. In the northern capital as in the south, business had been expanding and successful merchants, professional people and others were beginning to move out of the ancient walled city into the terraces of the New Town. Sam Charters, whose circulating library had become more popular than ever, had bought a suitable plot of land on which he intended to build a house and into which 'we shall invite mother and the Cappey if ever they wish to leave Inverkeithing, but they are as insular as ever on matters such as that. They say they will never wish to move. Shall you go there on the morrow?'

Samuel nodded and then asked why his sister had begun to laugh.

'Because your thoughts were so clearly elsewhere,' she said, 'and from the way you keep looking past me – over my shoulder – up to the ceiling – into the corner – there must, I presume, be a certain person whose presence you were expecting to find awaiting you here. Well, Sam, your expectations are justified. She is here and awaiting you. Sarah!' she called out and almost before the sound had left her lips, Sarah Cook burst into the room, her long red hair flowing behind her like a mane, and then after a second's pause whilst they studied each other, dashed into Samuel's arms, embarrassing him with the warmth of her welcome. Sarah had turned into a mature young woman, still somewhat lean and stringy in body but with a firm and determined jaw and those sparkling green eyes, the memory of which he had carried with him across half the world. Samuel found himself responding with an unexpected awkwardness to the passion of her welcome, but when his sister left them alone in the room, they looked at each other, hardly daring to touch. Samuel was amazed at the upsurge of his feeling for this creature he had previously seen only as a child.

'Nothing matters,' Samuel declared, 'so long as we can be together.'

'We have suffered a tragic loss,' Sarah murmured after a moment or so. 'My father was killed in an action against the French off the Barbary coast. So now there is only my mother and me.'

'And how is your mother?'

'She threatens at any moment to go into a decline.'

Samuel gave up the struggle to keep out of her arms, and comforted her as best he could, then asked what was to happen to them both. He pointed out a fact already apparent to Sarah and her mother, namely that the gratitude of the country to those who give their lives to it but rarely expresses itself in anything approaching munificence. Sarah nodded glumly, the fragrance of her hair nevertheless intoxicating his nostrils. He had no wish ever to leave go of this eager young creature he now held in his arms.

'There is to be a wee widow's pension,' she told him, 'but that is all.'

Still clinging to him, she pressed her body against his and leaning back looked up at him with a smile. 'And my mother is no wee widow,' she went on; 'she has great difficulty in accepting our changed circumstances.'

'Well, Sarah, to be fair they were never exceptional.'

'I know it and now they are sadly reduced.'

Later that evening, Sarah and her mother being invited to dinner, it became only too apparent to Samuel that the widow Cook intended giving back to the world as good as she received. She had been treated hardly, at least in her own opinion, and she was determined to return the compliment. She made it clear as soon as she set eyes on Samuel that he was her instinctive enemy and that she resented, as if she had been personally insulted, the strong feelings which her daughter and Samuel entertained for each other. She contrived never to leave them alone, and it was only with the active connivance of Meg and Samuel Charters that the lovers were able to steal a few minutes together during the remainder of his visit.

'She intends me to make a "good" marriage,' Sarah said. 'She says it is our only hope.'

'And what is your answer to that?'

'Never!' Sarah said. 'I would rather go south, as you did, Samuel, and seek my fortune in the great city of London.'

'There can be only one result of doing that,' Samuel replied, 'and such a course I would never countenance in any daughter of mine. Such an action is certainly not for you, Sarah.'

'Do I not have the looks, sir, for such a procedure?'

'It is because you have been so well endowed in that respect, and because you are to me so rare a person that I speak in this way.'

A silence fell between them, since they found themselves at a loss to know what to say next.

'I would ask for your hand in marriage,' he eventually blurted out, 'but I have nought to offer except what these rough seaman hands of mine can garner, and at the present time they are garnering scarce enough to keep my own body and soul together.'

Sarah again clutched him to her bosom and burst into a flood of tears.

'You have said the most wonderful thing I have heard in the whole of my life,' she declared through her tears.

'Well,' said Samuel, 'I am afraid it is not of much practical help.'

'Who cares about that? If only you will wait . . .'

'For ever,' he replied, astonished to discover the tears starting to his own blue eyes.

Thus perforce it was left. Sarah and her mother had taken lodgings a few doors away from the Charterses and remained under their benevolent protection. In Meg Charters the lovers had an ally on whom both could rely, but the problems of security and sustenance remained for the time insoluble. The slender prize money which Samuel had given to his elderly parents could not also provide him with a competency in the south. Reluctantly he would have to return to London and renew his search for patronage.

'Your mother and I are doubly grateful,' the Cappey remarked with a quaver in his voice, as they bade each other farewell – perhaps for the final time, who could tell? – 'since your gift comes from one who is the pride of our hearts and in whom all our hopes and wishes have been centred.'

'You would do well to centre more of those hopes on Meg,' Samuel said drily but not unkindly. 'She has been better rewarded by Fate, to be born a girl and marry a bookseller, than I to go to sea for King George.'

A few days later he set off once more for London to undertake all over again the dispiriting task of securing a suitable employment for himself. It was late in the year 1763.

He was grateful to find his friend Fortescue Fynne still in the capital, engaged – though somewhat more casually – on the same mission as himself, namely the procurement of a *modus vivendi*. However the Earl of Braddenham appeared to have had a lucky streak at the gaming tables, so that his town house still remained in his possession and Samuel was again afforded accommodation.

'But there have been unexpected changes in Government and especially at the Admiralty,' Fortescue Fynne observed, 'which will make our task the harder. There is, of course, a sensible advantage in being here on the spot and you are more likely to succeed than I since you have energy and experience.'

He accompanied this remark with a somewhat deprecatory gesture and a knowing smile which Samuel took to be a goodnatured jeer.

'I am obliged to you for that opinion,' Samuel said. 'Doubtless with your patronage and my energy—'

'We can cruise the streets of the capital till the beer runs out.'

This was an ironic reference to the stinking beverage usually supplied to the seagoing fleet, described by one exasperated seaman as capable of 'putting the souls of three butchers into one weaver', and which had decided both Admirals Hawke and Frobisher that their endurance at sea could only be as long as the beer lasted. It was not of much comfort as a precept. They were having to accustom themselves – as did all such half-pay Lieutenants – to a long delay.

'Have you observed the lines put up in one corner of the Admiralty waiting room?' Fortescue Fynne enquired, and when Samuel shook his head, went on:

'In sore affliction, tried by God's command,
Of Patience, Job, the great example stands;
But in these days a trial more severe
Had been Job's lot, if God had sent him here.'

Samuel smiled ruefully. 'I cannot stand in for Job for very long,' he said.

The absence of any well-defined plan to gain employment militated against both Lieutenants. It mattered little, in the conditions obtaining in 1763 and in the following year, that Samuel's reputation as an officer stood higher than most others of the same rank in the service; his prospects still presented an undeniably gloomy aspect. Although Mr Oswald still remained in office and was applied to for his assistance, this gentleman did not appear to possess as much influence as his friends and dependants imagined, or it may well have been that his high sense of etiquette precluded a Junior Lord of the Treasury from interfering in the patronage of another department.

'Be that as it may,' Samuel wrote to his sister in Edinburgh early in 1764, 'I dine with him occasionally at his house at Wandsworth and receive other civilities from him, together with many warm promises of support, but, alas, I find him to be very backward in submitting my claims for employment to Lord Egmont, the First Lord of Admiralty. As an example of this, I dined with him on New Year's Eve and as it happened to be a foul evening stayed all night. He told me he has been a little out of order this week past. He has not yet shown Lord Egmont the plans nor mentioned me to him a second time. I told him that General Keppel was to wait upon Lord Egmont this week on purpose to recommend me to him and tell him of the marks of distinction which his brother, the Admiral, had showed me and if he, Mr Oswald, would immediately back it, it might perhaps have the desired effect, which, he said, he would willingly do and would come into Town some day next week on purpose. But this he omitted to do. There must certainly be some reason why Mr Oswald does not make application to Lord Egmont for me the which he does not choose to explain.'

However other of Lieutenant Greig's friends, from whom he had the least right to expect such kindness, willingly exerted their influence to procure him employment. Such a one was General Keppel, referred to above, who had returned from Havana in the *Conquistador*, then temporarily under Samuel's command. 'I am so pleased with the society of this young Commander,' he had written, 'with the true neatness of his vessel and the attention he paid to the comfort of myself, my guests and my suite that I count him from now on as a friend.' It was all to no avail.

At this time there were several fine large cutters being built in the Royal Dockyards, the construction of which had been begun on the assumption of a continuing war. One of these which had just been launched at Woolwich, Samuel declared himself to be very anxious to have in command.

With this end in view, he again applied to Mr Oswald and also to another friend, a Captain John Lindsay, whose scientific acquirements he shared and who had himself just been appointed to the *Tartar* frigate. This officer employed the utmost exertion on Samuel's behalf but also, and again perhaps because of Mr Oswald's negligence to fulfil his promises, without effect.

Whilst thus endeavouring to avail himself of the influence of his private and political acquaintance, Samuel's active mind devised other modes of procuring occupation. In this he differed from his friend Fortescue Fynne, whose reaction to such setbacks and disappointments took the form of recourse to a suitable tavern and to the ladies who frequented it. Samuel, having neither the money nor the inclination for such matters, devoted himself to the preparation of a plan for submission to the Lords of Admiralty, which he was pleased to call 'A Nursery for Seamen'.

'I propose', he wrote, 'that 250 sail of such of the frigates, armed craft etc as are best calculated for the Greenland fishery, making altogether 125,000 tons of shipping, should be fitted out for this purpose at the expense of Government. These should be commanded by Lieutenants having under them 1,500 Petty Officers and 1,700 seamen, all to be paid by Government and to be subjected to the same regulations as for the King's service. As a further encouragement, they should be entitled to the same bounties and privileges as seamen employed in the Greenland and Davies Straits fisheries. I estimate that this undertaking would produce a clear profit of £100,000 yearly and I base this on the experience and information I acquired not only in command of my father's trading vessel but also whilst fulfilling a cruise of thirteen months in the North Sea in the King's service.'

There again the plan failed to attract the attention of Their Lordships, if indeed it was ever properly submitted for their consideration.

Nothing daunted, Greig now proceeded to employ his mathematical talents in devising two machines, both of which he considered would be useful to men-of-war. One was a device to keep a ship's bottom constantly clear at sea. The other was an ingenious pump designed to deliver three times more water than any chain pump and which could be worked by half the number of men, when calm, or entirely by the wind if it blew, so that the stronger the wind the more effective its operation.

'Captain Lindsay was to have come to see the plans,' he wrote despairingly to his sister, 'and would, I am sure, have introduced both them and me to Lord Egmont, but he has been making ready for his departure this some time past. So all my endeavours have proved to be of no avail and the means of earning a livelihood seem to be as distant as ever.'

His naturally sanguine disposition now sank under the influence of adversity and of prolonged inactivity and suspense. Feeling the irksomeness of a situation without influence and without resources, he knew not what course he should pursue. Determined not to become a burden upon those friends who had the power of affording him assistance, his bright hopes gradually disappeared. Want stared him in the face, and now, for the first time, despondency laid its heavy hand upon him. Then unexpectedly an incident occurred which opened to his mind a gleam of that shining destiny which he was afterwards so fully to realize.

At a dinner party given by General Keppel, and attended by his brother the Admiral, he met Count Alexander Vorontsov, the elder brother of the Princess Dashkov, who had been dispatched to the Court of St James with the title of Russian Commissioner. His especial task was the recruitment of skilled professional officers to the service of Her Imperial Majesty the Empress Catherine II of all the Russias.

By that peculiar chemistry which draws human beings to, or repels them from, each other, Count Vorontsov and Lieutenant Greig took an instant liking to one another. The purpose of his mission having been explained, Count Vorontsov drew the young naval officer to one side.

'You have been recommended to me, and through me to the Russian Commander-in-Chief, in the highest possible terms,' he said with a smile, 'so that if we can secure the assent of the Lords Commissioners of the Admiralty and, of course, of the English King, I am authorized by Her Imperial Majesty to invite you to enter her service with the rank of Captain.'

The offer seemed to Samuel so dazzling in its implications as almost to be a direct intervention in his somewhat bedraggled affairs by that munificent Deity before whom he had so often laid his prayers. For a moment or so he could find no words with which to express his gratitude. The young Count then continued:

'You will not be the first Scotsman to accept service under the Tsar. Indeed the present Governor-General of St Petersburg is none other than Count James Bruce of whose name and lineage you will no doubt be aware. You will find Her Majesty both generous and rewarding of your loyalty and skill. Moreover I am sent here because Admiral Talytzin is endeavouring to re-establish the high naval principles introduced by Peter the Great, the which have sadly lapsed through ensuing reigns. It is no easy life we offer, but you have the reputation of rising excellently well to a suitable challenge. I have a certainty, now that I have met you, that you will distinguish both yourself and the Russian Crown in your acceptance of this offer. Naturally your duties will be fulfilled initially at Crondstadt, but I am also of the opinion that it will not be overlong before you see action against the Turkish Sultan – or the "Sublime Porte", as he is often addressed. Does that appeal to you, Mr Greig?'

'It does indeed,' Samuel said, 'if, as you say, I am considered suitable for the duties you have in mind.'

Then, on the spur of the moment, he went on:

'Permit me a question, though. I have no knowledge of the Russian language and you put me to shame with your fine command of the English tongue. How is it you speak it so well?'

'We are not all barbarians in Muscovy,' Count Vorontsov replied with a smile. 'My father employed both English and French tutors in the upbringing of his family. Moreover I have had a high respect for the English race and its civilization since my nursery days. Do you not speak French, perhaps, in addition to your native tongue?'

'Alas, no,' Samuel said, 'my only contact with the French has been at the other end of sword and shot.'

'Then you will need to remedy that defect,' Count Vorontsov said. 'French, as you know, is the language in common use amongst civilized people over the whole continent of Europe. But I am sure you will not find such an acquisition to be an insurmountable obstacle.'

'I shall apply myself to the task without further delay.'

'But not in too solemn a fashion,' the young envoy counselled. 'If we succeed – as I am determined we shall – in securing your services, then it will not be difficult to find one of the many personable young French governesses in St Petersburg to undertake your instruction. Now that we have an Empress capable of reading a book, I have no doubt that she will enhance the process, begun by the great Peter, of hauling Russia into the eighteenth century however reluctant some of our nobility may be to see this happen. It is said, for instance, that she is already herself devising a code of law based on Monsieur Montesquieu's ideas.'

'Is there, then, no justice in Russia?' Samuel asked in astonishment.

'Not as it is understood here. I am afraid that your Habeas Corpus would be simply a cause for derision in Russia.'

'Then how are matters put to rights?' Samuel enquired. 'Other than by force?'

The Count smiled.

'You can petition the throne – should you have the good fortune to secure access to the Empress. As my uncle, the Grand Chancellor, would confirm, it is a costly process and not one to be undertaken in a hurry. At the time of her coronation, the Empress had three secretaries and each of them had three hundred petitions long outstanding.'

'How then is anything procured for the fleet?'

Count Vorontsov paused before answering and finally replied with raised eyebrows:

'That will doubtless be one of the tasks you will be helping Admiral Talytzin to achieve. I think the Admiral would add – and he is a sharp-witted man – that if you can supply the energy and the honesty, we can provide the guile.'

Samuel thought about this for a while, watched carefully by the Russian.

'I have one further question to ask in view of what you have just remarked. How secure would be my own emoluments?'

'As secure as the Empress herself since she will make them her personal charge.'

'In that event,' Samuel said, 'I am ready to sail tomorrow.'

It was not to be as simple as that. In the rigmarole of uncertainties which have assailed the Royal Navy throughout its long, chequered history, the seagoing Fleet has always been able to rely on one constant factor – the obdurate meanness of Admiralty.

Now, in 1764, in the matter of supplying trained naval officers to a foreign power, although it was to the clear benefit both of the officers concerned and of the country itself that Lieutenant Greig and others who had been selected should be allowed – indeed encouraged – to accept the offer which had been made them, their Lordships, no doubt with a shrewd and private eye to their stewards' individual pockets, decreed it not to be in the national interest for a small handful of unemployed Lieutenants on half-pay to be spared from the King's service.

This decision was naturally disguised by a lofty recourse to patriotism. It would never do, the Admiralty maintained, to furnish a foreign monarch with skills which might one day be turned against the British crown. Only the fact that the Russian fleet was negligible, that the majority of those selected were Scotsmen and furthermore that an adequate hampering in the right quarters had been discreetly arranged, enabled a reluctant agreement to be secured at long last for the handpicked mercenaries to sever their allegiance to the English King and sail for St Petersburg. *Sic transit gloria belli.*

Before Samuel had quit the United Kingdom, possibly as he then thought never to return, he proceeded north once more to take leave of his parents, of his boyhood friends and of Sarah. His heart became filled with a mixture of hope and foreboding. Adventure awaited him in the Baltic sea. His material prospects looked to be more promising than ever before and he comforted himself by reflecting that he would still remain a British subject and could, if the Russian venture did not prosper, return to England and the near-starvation status of a Royal Naval Lieutenant on half-pay.

Even then, and despite Mr Oswald's fulsome assurance that the matter could be considered as good as signed, sealed and delivered (and for which he naturally claimed the kudos), Samuel no longer put any trust in the verbal promises of placemen. In his frequent attendance in the ante-rooms of Admiralty he had chummed up with an aged clerk called Pike with a long pointed nose – 'my name deriving, I fancy, more from the fish than from the weapon' – who had a soft heart and often took pity on the many frustrated fighting men mulling around the Secretary's Office in search of employment. Mr Pike, if lubricated with porter, could always be relied on to discover the truth behind any of the statements and promises loftily handed down by authority so frequently and so distressingly, it seemed, merely in order to be rid of the petitioners.

'Precisely as possession is nine points of the law,' Mr Pike remarked, removing the perennial drip on the end of his nose with one of the quill pens on his desk, 'so the receipt of a "By Command of Their Lordships" letter is nine points of a certain fact. The reason, Mr Greig? Because on nine occasions out of ten, a "By Command" letter means the expenditure of cash from the Admiralty coffers – or, put the other way round, those mean-minded skinflints as inhabit the Pay Office pay out nothing except it be by command of Their Crafty, Wily and Parsimonious Lordships. Now sir, the procurement of such a letter can be a complicated and – er – thirsty matter.'

'In my case,' Samuel said, ignoring the obvious hint, 'such a letter can only mean the *non*-payment of further cash from the Admiralty coffers since from now on it will be Russian roubles and not sterling pounds I shall be paid.'

'Yes, yes,' said Mr Pike with a deprecatory cough, 'quite so, quite so. However the – er – thirst factor remains.'

'That can be covered by sterling from my private purse,' Samuel said, 'and the sooner the receipt, the greater will be the assuagement of thirst.'

'*Aha!*' said Mr Pike, 'now that I have that understanding, we shall see what can be achieved.'

He was as good as his word and on 7 May 1764 handed Samuel the letter by which the rest of his life was changed. It was headed 'Admiralty Office' and read:

> Sir,
>
> I am commanded by My Lords Commissioners of the Admiralty to acquaint you that, agreeable to your desire, they are pleased to give you leave to go into the Dominions of the Empress of Russia.
>
> And, in pursuance of His Majesty's Pleasure, Their Lordships are also pleased to give you leave to enter into the service of that Empress, if you think proper, taking care to transmit hither a certificate from the British Minister of the time you do so, as your Half Pay will be discontinued from that time.
>
> I am, Sir, Your Very Humble Servant
>
> (sd) Stephens.

With this letter in his hand and having satisfied Mr Pike who had contrived a somewhat wistful smile and had also volunteered the opinion, which Samuel did not believe, that he wished he were going with him, Samuel made arrangements to proceed to St Petersburg in a merchant vessel departing the Port of London in ten days' time and calling in at Leith, at which port Samuel would join the ship, after taking leave of his family, of friends in Edinburgh and, most important, of his beloved Sarah.

He did not preannounce this visit to the north. Clearing up his affairs, which were not extensive, in London; taking a somewhat boisterous farewell of Fortescue Fynne who declared he was minded to follow him – to which statement Samuel attached but little credence – he put his effects on board ship in Millwall and then took the stage coach to Edinburgh, intending to surprise them all.

What a change he felt in himself between this journey and the previous one! Now with his career settled, at any rate for the present, his heart seemed to overflow with a mixture of hope and foreboding. Adventure undoubtedly awaited him in the Baltic sea and the Gulf of Finland. Material prospects were promising and he even dallied, as once more he rumbled his way north through the English countryside, with the idea of marrying Sarah there and then and of proceeding to Russia a married man.

Caution, however, intervened at this point and made him consider the possibility of the Russian venture coming to grief. Should this occur – well, then, he would still be a British subject and could return to the United Kingdom. Perhaps he would delay a decision on Sarah until he had amassed sufficient roubles to make the wedded state a practical proposition. This particular delay proved in the event to be inevitable since on arrival in Edinburgh his sister told him:

'Your Sarah and her mother are gone.'

'Gone?' said Samuel, as if struck by lightning, 'How? And where?'

'There is the younger son of an Earl on whom the Widow Cook has fixed her intentions for Sarah,' Meg answered, 'so an invitation to stay at Balcarrigh Castle was with some difficulty procured and they are gone to Perthshire, mother and daughter, the one in high hopes and the other as if being dragged off to the hulks.'

'My God!' said Samuel, 'this is the worst piece of news since the signing of peace.'

His sister touched his hand affectionately.

'All is not lost,' she said. 'Sarah has too much character to allow herself to be married off against her will and as you well know, Sam, the younger sons of our Scottish nobility are not possessed of overmuch of this world's wealth. Since Sarah's own dowry will be little more than a drawerful of linen, I do not imagine her mother's plans will prosper. Moreover the old Earl is renowned through Perthshire for his unco predilection towards economy, so I do not fancy Sarah and her mother will be enjoying too gay a time.'

'Shall I not see her, then, before I depart?'

His sister shrugged her shoulders.

'So it would appear – but go you to Inverkeithing to say your farewells to mother and the Cappey, and I will send word to Balcarrigh on the chance that they might return to Edinburgh before you set sail for Russia.'

So with a heavy heart Samuel crossed the Firth of Forth to say his adieus to his aged parents and spend a little time in the simple stone house in which he had been born. He found the Captain and his mother to be undoubtedly nearing the end of their lives and this provoked two days of tearful reminiscence coupled with what was to Samuel an embarrassing pride in his career so far.

'Whilst I cannot but agree that it is the great ideas which animate our lives,' he was compelled at one stage to comment, 'I have not single-handed won the late war against France and Spain.'

'So far as Inverkeithing and Burnt Island are concerned, you did so,' his father said, removing his clay pipe and smiling, 'but your mother and I do admit to the fact that there must be a time for everything, a time to be born and a time to die. She and I are a pace or two nearer this latter time and therefore all the more reluctant to see our only son depart to the land of the *moujiks*, be it never to return.' Whereupon his mother burst into tears and Samuel, thinking of Sarah, felt almost on the point of doing so himself.

On the evening before he should have returned to Edinburgh – his ship being due at Leith the following day, wind and tide permitting – the old folk and Samuel had just seated themselves for a farewell meal in the late afternoon, together with some close friends and neighbours, the little room being filled to overflowing, when there was a rat-tat-tat on the door and there was Sarah, holding by the rein a horse that had clearly been hard ridden.

'I had news of your arrival from Meg,' she said in a breathless and yet strangely composed manner, 'so as we were out riding this morning I contrived to hang back for a private necessity and then did a bolt.'

'Shall they have followed you?' Samuel asked after they had embraced and he had then introduced her to his parents and the company.

'Aye, for the horse,' Sarah said. 'They'll be wanting her back. I doubt the rider would be considered of any great import to the Castle of Balcarrigh. Or they to me. Meg tells me the Admiralty have given you your release and that you are bound for Muscovy, Sam.'

He nodded, devouring her with his eyes.

'Well, I have a mind to come with you, if you will have me.'

This startling suggestion, and the runaway action which had preceded it, so overwhelmed Samuel that initially he could see no objection to the idea.

'But you are still not of an age,' his mother observed to Sarah as she sat her down to the evening meal. 'You will still be needing your parent's or guardian's consent. How would that be received by your mother?'

Sarah looked dolefully at her Samuel.

'We both know the answer to that,' she said. 'I tried once before to run away to sea, when I was shaped more as a boy than I am today. Will you not abduct me out of the realm?'

'I will abduct you back to Edinburgh,' Samuel said, 'and we will discuss it with Meg and her Sam.'

'Discussion will not get me to Petersburg,' Sarah said, tossing her head. 'Discussion will merely get me sent to my room without supper.'

Samuel put his arm round her shoulders and smiled over her head at his parents.

'You see what a creature this is,' he said, 'the memory of which has preserved me through all sorts of perils at sea. They like you, Sarah,' he whispered in her ear, 'there will be no opposition here. However I am going to a strange, uncouth country in the service of an unpredictable Empress. Do you not think it wise if I do duty first for both of us as a pioneer?'

'Would I be such an encumbrance then?' Sarah asked, seeing her brave plan disappearing into thin air like a puff of smoke.

'That is not a fair question. I will not accept such a responsibility in foreign parts without I first find out for myself the conditions we are likely to have to endure. That is but elementary wisdom.'

'Well,' said Sarah with a puckish smile, 'then I will go with you to Edinburgh tomorrow and face the consequences of today's exploit. I doubt my mother and I will be invited to Balcarrigh Castle again.'

The next day, after Samuel had made arrangements for the return of the horse, he and Sarah sailed across the Firth of Forth and presented themselves at the Charterses' house in Edinburgh, arriving shortly before Sarah's determined mother who was in a highly disturbed condition. The Widow Cook had scarcely penetrated the living quarters behind the bookshop before she was stridently upbraiding her daughter whom she discovered standing under the large and comforting protection of Samuel.

'Remove yourself from my daughter,' she snapped; 'you shall both of you pay for this folly.'

'And what folly is that, ma'am?' Samuel answered calmly. 'I know of no folly. However I would like your formal consent to our marriage.'

The Widow Cook gave a convulsive jerk as if, in naval terms, she had been 'brought up all standing'. This was immediately followed by a shivering rage.

'Certainly not, Mr Greig,' she spat out at him with all the crisp authority of a Captain's widow. 'Not only will I never consent to your scandalous proposals, I further forbid you to communicate with my daughter whose tender feelings you have already sufficiently outraged.'

'I see nothing indecent, madam, in a proposal of marriage.'

'Sarah is still a child, sir. Do you see nothing improper in that?'

'I am not attempting to ravish the girl, madam, I am proposing to secure her as a wife.'

'*Secure*, Mr Greig? And what security can a penniless sailor of fortune presume to offer a young lady of quality?'

'To that I can answer that I certainly have no designs upon her *fortune*,' Samuel remarked, matching the Widow Cook's asperity. 'Sarah could scarcely be described as a "catch" in that respect.'

'How dare you address a mother in so insulting a fashion?'

'As to that, madam, the boot might well be on the other foot.'

'Oh! ...' cried Sarah's mother, 'oh! ... oh! ... oh!'

The Widow Cook was well known in her immediate circle for her ability to put on a 'theatrical performance' whenever she felt herself or her interests to be especially at risk.

'Come, come, madam,' Samuel said with authority, 'I am no monster. I understand the predicament. I am not, as you appear to believe, merely trying to deprive you of a daughter: I can at the very least furnish you with a son-in-law and add responsibility for your welfare to my slop chitty.'

'Thank you, Mr Greig,' said the Widow Cook with a haughty toss of the head, 'I am obliged to you for the use of your naval jargon.'

'Was your husband not himself a naval officer?' Samuel said with a smile. 'Do not use anger on me, madam, it is the wrong armament for the matter in hand. Sarah and I intend to be married. You have the power to delay but that is all. Would it not be more propitious for all of us, were you not to admit to this fact? Then peace can be declared and a suitable plan devised which will satisfy the requirements and wishes of all of us.'

He had spoken gently, indeed almost humbly, but Sarah's mother was not to be wooed in this way.

'Certainly not, sir,' she said, indicating that the interview was at an end. 'My daughter is not for you and as long as there is breath in my body, I shall forbid the marriage.'

'As you will,' Samuel replied, a somewhat wistful look in the eyes. 'It is sad that I am to be thus sent away with a flea in my ear. However I shall contrive to bear it.'

Sarah, who had been a silent witness of this exchange, turned away to hide her tears, whereupon the Widow Cook either because she had gained her way or because of a belated compassion, relented now to the extent of a softening of her expression.

'I am no monster, either, Mr Greig and I cannot see you depart for Russia in this unsatisfactory manner. At least allow me to wish you well and once you have made your fortune in the service of the Empress, perhaps you will return when I myself have departed this world. Then, of course, it will be for Sarah herself to decide – if she is prepared to wait so long.'

'I shall wait,' Sarah said, giving him an intense look which was to imprint itself on his dreams over the long difficult years ahead.

'And so shall I,' he replied, his heart full to overflowing with the longing for her which he felt.

After checking that the ship which was to take him to Russia had safely arrived in the port of Leith, Samuel now took his final farewell of his sister, of her husband and of their friends. The night before the ship sailed Meg arranged a gathering at the bookshop to wish him Godspeed. This proved to be fortuitous in that one of the guests happened to be the Cooks' relative, the Consul from Crondstadt who had returned to Scotland on a temporary visit to acquaint his mercantile friends of the new climate in Russia consequent upon the ascent to the throne of Catherine II.

'We are well met,' Consul Cook told Samuel, 'and it is excellent news that you will soon be bringing some Scottish commonsense into the higgledy-piggledy bog of Russian naval affairs. I trust we shall see much of each other once you have established yourself. My house shall be your home for as long as it suits your convenience.'

Samuel thanked him warmly and recounted his meetings with Count Vorontsov, and all that he had contrived so far to ascertain about the Russian scene. Some of his conclusions brought a smile to the Consul's face.

'Do not assume that you will find in St Petersburg the

probity of purpose you would expect here or in London town,' the young Consul said. 'There is certainly a new wind blowing in our affairs and the Empress makes herself felt in a great variety of matters hitherto thought unworthy of attention except by underlings whose integrity left much to be desired.'

'And is this a good or a bad procedure?' Samuel asked, thinking of Mr Oswald and of his recent experiences at the Admiralty. The Consul considered the question for a moment or so.

'One has always to bear in mind the Russian temperament. The Empress works with a zest which not all the world admires. She is pleased to inspect things for herself. She insists on a total obedience to her every whim but fortunately does not indulge herself in the excesses of her predecessors – except, perhaps, in a private capacity and you will understand what I have in mind by that.'

'I think I can hazard a guess,' Samuel said. 'I believe there are great risks attendant on that department but that is not likely to be of much concern to me. As to the Navy—'

'You will find the Empress to be better informed than you may imagine,' the Consul cut in. 'Should she find her orders not carried out, or only partially so, she is ruthless in the extreme and punishment is hard and immediate. She is a full-blooded absolute ruler and fear, nay terror, is the weapon closest to her hand. You, Samuel, will have nothing to cause you anxiety except, perhaps, the jealousy of those who must be driven rather than led. You and your fellow mercenaries have been commissioned for a purpose and if the Empress can be described as a *chef d'orchestre*, I would advise you to study the orchestra itself with the sharpest eye. Mercy is a quality all but unknown to the Russians, and a mistake can very often cost a life.'

'You paint a somewhat alarming picture.'

'I speak from experience,' the Consul said with what struck Samuel as a cynical smile. 'However all is not black. There is a warmth of heart which compensates to a great degree for the follies and the apathy. The Empress treats her people as children and they in turn call her their little mother. It is an apt description, as you will soon discover for yourself.'

'I am indebted to you for your advice,' Samuel said formally and then, with a twinkle in his eye, 'but I shall further risk your indulgence if I may?'

The Consul nodded, watching him carefully.

'You will have heard about your cousin Sarah and myself?'

'I fancy all Edinburgh is *au fait* with that little matter.'

'Suppose that I am successful in getting the mother to relent—'

'It is the wish of all of us. However between the wish and the fact there seems to be an almost unbridgeable gap.'

'Would you consider accommodating in your household, on a temporary basis, your young cousin, were I to secure permission for her to visit St Petersburg?'

'I should be delighted to welcome her for as long as she cares to stay,' Consul Cook declared, 'but how do you propose to prise the young lady away from the dragon who guards her day and night?'

'Why – by marriage,' Samuel said simply.

'I doubt you will succeed. No widow in the severely reduced circumstances in which Mother Cook now finds herself would willingly stand to one side while her only prop and mainstay is knocked away from beneath her.'

'Then I shall have to wait.'

'You will indeed. Are you prepared for that?'

'I am. And so, I am assured, is Sarah.'

'She will certainly add lustre to our northern scene,' the Consul said, narrowing his eyes, 'and that, in itself, will create one or two problems you would do well to consider once you have settled yourself into St Petersburg society. The morals are not those of Edinburgh.'

'Is there, then, no respect for the normal conventions?'

'Once you have safely married the girl. Until then both you and she should proceed with the greatest care. Foreigners are neither liked nor welcomed in Muscovy. The Russians tolerate us – no more and no less – and this is simply because without us they would lapse, in the time it takes a samovar to bubble, back into the primeval slime from which the Empress and a handful of enlightened souls are trying to rescue them. We live in dangerous and changing times.'

'Well,' said Samuel, 'danger has long been a familiar companion in my own life. As to change, is that not preferable to a fixed rigidity so far as business and social affairs are concerned?'

'You may doubtless be right. In theory, at least, and always provided that there is enlightenment at the top.'

'Which you claim exists in the person of the Empress?'

'That is so. But never forget that the Empress Catherine the Second is what she is herself pleased to call an "autocratrix". She has seized the reins of power by force and she has had her husband murdered – or so the world thinks. Be guided by caution in any dealings you may have with the throne. Above all beware of the brothers Orlov. They are as wolfish a gang of predators as you and I are ever likely to encounter.'

7

‘They contrive matters differently here’

So, in the late summer of 1764, Samuel Greig arrived at St Petersburg, after calling in briefly at Copenhagen and at Dantzig. The great adventure, as he described it to Sarah, had begun. His *acceuil* from the Empress of All the Russias took the form of an Ordinance to the Admiralteisty Collegia which stated:

> ‘For the purpose of acquainting himself with the order existing in the Russian Navy, Greig is appointed a Volunteer for the prospective summer campaign, to the squadron under the command of Admiral Poliansky, and should there take oath to loyally serve Her Majesty Catherine II, Empress of Russia.’

‘However,’ he wrote to Sarah, ‘there is very little order existing in the Russian Navy – at least little apparent to us new arrivals. We are not to have the honour of presentation at Court until our Russian superiors certify that we have acclimatized ourselves to the local life, a process which will clearly take one or two of my brother Volunteers somewhat longer than they had calculated before leaving home. They do, indeed, contrive matters very differently here – when things can be said to be subject to any arrangement whatever. My first task, therefore, is to acquire some working knowledge of the Russ for the purpose of exercising command of my ship. This is officially described as a frigate but on first inspection I had serious doubts about taking her to sea in any sort of adverse weather conditions at all, let alone facing an enemy with her. I am also learning French and German so that I can communicate with my superior officers. I speak English only with the British contingent here at Crondstadt and with those members of the British community at St Petersburg to whom I am introduced by the Ambassador and by your Consul cousin, who returned here a few days after my own arrival and who has an elegant Russian wife – the which causes me to yearn inordinately for your presence even though we have been parted but for a matter of weeks.'

He was twenty-eight and as the young Captain began to make his way in local society, he soon became aware that there was a demand for the flesh, blood and bones of civilization from the west exceeding anything he had experienced abroad before, the which was kept in check only by the malevolent suspicion with which all foreigners were regarded. It was a strangely hybrid existence. He also acknowledged himself to be as lonely as he had ever been at sea. However he wasted no time in moping but instead set about visiting and acquainting himself with the city, the port and the environs of that region which would henceforth provide the background to his life.

'With the exception of the Royal establishments such as the Winter Palace and Tsarskoye Selo,' he went on, 'some fifteen miles from Petersburg, with its grand staircase, chapel, gardens, grottos, the Empress's private zoo and her Hermitage with its new picture gallery, the buildings of the city of Petersburg are not remarkable. They might generally be said to be of an Italianate style amongst which one or two impressive edifices stand out. I suppose the city to be some two miles from end to end, the whole interspersed with tributaries and canals. Cobblestoned wharves and prospects paved with timber abound. Oats are still being grown in the fields abutting the Winter Palace and there are still a mass of flimsy buildings of wood in which the poorer classes swarm like vermin so that one is forced to remember that it is not many years since this artificially created city – for all its present-day expansion – was once no more than a primitive fortress village built insecurely on a marsh.'

As time went on Samuel and his fellow volunteers began to be entertained, initially by the foreign community of doctors, architects, musicians and painters and then, as they gradually became accepted, by the nobles attendant on the court.

Sarah herself back in Edinburgh overcame as best she could the emptiness she felt in her life after his departure. She recovered her wit and her spirits. She stood up to her mother in the daily tussles which seemed currently to be her fate and she set about building her relationship with Samuel by means of a frequent correspondence. Clearly she had no relish for hearing about her cousin the Consul's 'elegant wife' nor about the other feminine influences to which Samuel was now exposed, but from a somewhat faltering start her letters soon developed the firm spiritual link which she had decided there should be between them.

In these letters she gave evidence of her lively intelligence and of her virile determination to order her own affairs. It could all be summed up as a grudging acceptance of the conditions in which the Good Lord had seen fit to place the far-separated lovers, but which neither would accept for ever.

'It is all very well,' she remarked in one of these epistles, 'for the notorious Dr Johnson to declare from the comfort of a London tavern, as Sam Charters claims he does, that no man would go to sea who could better find himself in prison, for what is service afloat but that of a prison with the added risks of being drowned? There are those, such as my late father and yourself, whose lives require them to go to sea, just as there are those of my own wretched sex who must patiently await the sailor's return. I trust in the Lord', she went on, in the strong handwriting which it gave Samuel so much pleasure to receive, 'and that He will in his great goodness see fit to draw our two lives together in the passage of time. Meanwhile, dear Samuel, take every precaution to maintain your health both of body and of soul. Remember also that in your native land there is ever one who constantly prays for your welfare in the belief that however impossible it may appear at times, a benevolent Fate will in due course bring us together, never again to part, and that that person is your lonesome, patient but ever loving Sarah.'

She made no mention of the fact that her mother, now

that Samuel was gone, had again set about procuring, or attempting to procure a suitable husband for her only daughter. This time the choice had fallen on Donald MacFee, Matilda's brother, who was reading for the Bar. He was as sober as his sister was flighty and since those rich lowland acres, which had so attracted Fortescue Fynne, would be divided between Donald and his sister, Mrs Cook already saw herself in the Dower House enjoying a rather more comfortable old age than seemed to be at present in prospect.

This idea did not commend itself to Sarah. In her opinion, although Donald MacFee was agreeable enough as a young man who would no doubt make an adequate husband for some conventional young lady, she herself did not find him prepossessing. She liked him neither for his physique nor on account of his strong Jacobite views and the life which she suspected she would be forced to lead as his wife. Luckily, in her opinion, Donald MacFee also directed a firm eye to material advantage and whilst she was aware that he found her engaging enough as a young female person, the lack of any suitable dowry kept her mother's plans severely in check.

Meanwhile in distant Petersburg, Samuel and his brother mercenaries were having to establish themselves, with a mixture of firmness and tact, into the Russian naval way of life. To Samuel this seemed an extraordinary process. Each day brought a new and unexpected challenge. Each day he and his brother officers faced problems which in the Royal Navy had long ago been settled and for which there were generally agreed customs and precedents. Here, in spite of the fact that foreign naval and military men had effectively officered the armed forces of Russia for over a century, the organization for building ships, for supplies and for victualling proved to be rudimentary where in existence at all. Discipline was tyrannical, brutal and untinged with any colouring of British fair play.

'It is a long haul from Inverkeithing,' Samuel commented to Consul Cook, when one day they were discussing affairs after dinner. The Consul had provided Samuel with a room in his house for use whenever duties at Crondstadt or at sea allowed him to visit St Petersburg. This, he had told him, was to be his home until such time as he could acquire a mansion of his own.

'Even allowing for my imperfect knowledge of the Russ tongue,' Samuel continued, 'it is daily apparent that the Admiralteisty Collegia is no Board of Admiralty in the sense that I have experienced it until now.'

The Consul smiled in the somewhat crafty way which prevented his companion ever being perfectly sure what he was really thinking.

'The Russian character', he began, '– if such a thing could be defined – does not generate from itself any illumination, any desire to progress. As the great Peter discovered, civilization is an alien matter imposed from above or imported from without. A few *versts* from this city with its Italian architects, its Prussian soldiery, its Flemish merchants and its general apeing of the French court in all its least desirable detail, a passive and animal barbarity obtains. A short journey into the interior will reveal an appalling condition to our more tutored eyes. I doubt but that the serfs on any nobleman's estate between here and Moscow have more than a hundred words to which any meaning could be ascribed. Life – no, that is too strong a word – existence is conducted by the emission of certain sounds conveying basic requirements based mainly on fear. These achieve a limited and temporary result. But that is all that has been required from birth to grave since time immemorial.'

'It could be said that the British sailor, pressed into service by trickery and force, is in much the same condition,' Samuel remarked, 'and yet he adapts. He has, you may say, no alternative to an acceptance of his fate once he has been got to sea. And yet the Naval Discipline Act, for all its harsh provisions, does in its turn give him certain rights – a recourse to justice of a kind – and a protection.'

'Rights!' the Consul said with a slight sneer. 'The very word has no meaning here. Rights in Muscovy are a cutlass and an arm strong enough to wield it.'

'And yet the Empress, I have heard it said, has great

humanity and would be a fine agreeable woman, were she a private person.'

'That may well be so, but she is not a private person. She is an autocrat of autocrats and, as I told you before ever you arrived, you would do well never to lose sight of that fact.'

'It is scarcely likely to have much bearing on my life,' Samuel said. 'I am but an indentured servant in a cadet service.'

'You are ill-advised, sir, to underrate yourself in such a manner. You have friends at court, even though you may not know who they are. Your reputation preceded you here and you should remember that the Russian envoy to London who procured your services, Count Vorontsov, is a member of one of the most powerful families in Russia. I also have it on authority that your conduct, honesty and bearing so far have provoked a favourable report to the Empress, not only from Admiral Poliansky but also from the Commander-in-Chief himself. Your qualities have attracted attention in the place where it matters the most – the immediate entourage of the Empress herself. Indeed,' and again the Consul paused with another smile which an unkind person would have described as a smirk, 'whether by intent or by chance, you have become *persona grata* with the Orlov brothers and that is an advantage not lightly to be thrown away. You are to be commanded to be present, I understand, at the next levée at the Winter Palace at the express suggestion of Count Gregory Orlov. I do not need to remind you, I trust, of the particular asset this dashing officer enjoys.'

'You mean his instrumentality in bringing the Empress to the throne?'

'That is so, and with his brother Alexei, in the disposal, if that is the word, of an unnecessary encumbrance to Her Majesty's absolute power. Count Gregory, however, is instrumental now where it matters most – in the Imperial bed.'

'Honest Sam', as one of his brother Scotsmen called him behind his back, approached this meeting with the Empress, to whom he had sworn allegiance, with more trepidation than he had experienced before going into battle. By now he had acquired enough aptitude in the French language not to feel any longer the blunt Scottish boor which he had appeared to be to his friend Fortescue Fynne. He was no longer threadbare. Had he so wished he could have indulged himself in the accepted fashion of those whose company he now kept. He could have gambled and wenched. His emoluments were adequate – indeed lavish by the standards of Inverkeithing – and since it was known that 'the foreigners' roubles' were guaranteed by Her Imperial Majesty, there were plenty of bankers and merchants only too anxious to advance him credit. He chose to avoid this trap and, when accused of complacency, retorted that he would rather be complacent than bankrupt.

'Be pleased to inform the Lords Commissioners of Admiralty', the British Ambassador had written in one of his dispatches, 'that of all the naval officers seconded to the Russian service, the most likely to succeed in reaching a significant position of authority in the maritime forces of this nascent realm is Samuel Greig. He has already distinguished himself in small local actions of a protective nature against the depredations of the Swedish King and he has shown himself proof against the machinations of the local victuallers and purveyors to the Russian fleet. This "swimming against the tide" is not calculated to make him popular in commercial circles but, it must be remarked, has promoted his reputation with the Empress herself whose attitude to such matters I have previously reported.'

Meanwhile the Empress herself, who knew more about Samuel and the other foreign officers whom she had caused to enter her service than ever they were to learn about her, had established her style and authority in a manner not so vividly apparent in Holy Russia since the days of the great Peter.

It was now abundantly evident that the Empress would stand alone. No one, be it Gregory Orlov who enlivened her leisure or the Princess Dashkov who, alone of her sex, shared her intellectual interests, was to be allowed in any way to presume upon the friendship of the monarch. She took care to establish and to maintain a clear distinction between her public and her private life.

Her public life followed the pattern of her predecessors' but at a greater pace and intensity, whether it were hunting or hawking at Tsarskoye Selo, inspecting the green-coated Guards with their glittering swords or the cuirassiers with their gleaming golden breastplates, whether she happened to be exercising at the St Petersburg Riding School, attending the Opera or the various Court Entertainments – amongst them the "Metamorphosis Balls" instituted by the aged Elizabeth, where the gentlemen had to wear whaleboned petticoats and unmanageable crinolines, with the ladies dressing as men – or whether it was simply a matter of passing a critical eye over the fifteen hundred rooms of the vast Winter Palace with its Corinthian columns, its caryatids and its silver ornaments displayed to such effect against the turquoise and white painted walls – wherever the Empress moved, whatever she did or caused to be done, her presence had an electrifying effect. She radiated her own brand of divinity like the summer sun – or so the common people imagined. The activities in the Imperial bedchamber were something else. That was her private life. During the early years of her reign she took pains to keep the two lives apart.

This was not easy with a man as violent and ambitious as Gregory Orlov. It was known that he wished to marry her and that he would not be content merely to remain her lover. But whatever took place in the private apartments – and it was rumoured that he frequently beat her in his fits of passion – Catherine had become fully apprised of the jealousy and unpopularity which her favourite aroused in other powerful members of the Imperial court. She had once confided in the Princess Dashkov that she had not cared about her husband Peter, but that she did about the Crown. So now in the first ten years of her reign, she exhibited an equal tenacity in never swerving from this principle in the conduct of her public affairs.

'She is determined to please the nation,' the British Ambassador had observed in another confidential report, 'and she is the more skilled in this endeavour by her ferocious application to matters of state, by her willingness to listen to and to consider reports from every quarter, indeed by her determination to acquire knowledge whenever possible at first hand on every subject which engages her attention. Monster she well may be but not a monster which will permit itself to be caged.'

In fact she worked from ten to fourteen hours a day. She even drew apart from 'the little Dashkov'. In this there was a certain personal jealousy. The Empress felt that the role played by the young Princess in the events of June 1762 had been overvalued. It may have been true that in those early turbulent days she had presented the girl to the old Chancellor Bestuzhev with some such expression as 'This is young Princess Dashkov – would you have imagined that it was to the daughter of Count Robert Vorontsov that I am indebted for the throne?' but if those words were indeed used, then their expression was ironic and when this statement was later repeated back as a fact by none other than her correspondent in Switzerland, Monsieur Voltaire, a coolness between the two women began.

This was increased by the strong opposition, expressed by the Grand Chancellor Vorontsov, to any suggestion that the Empress should take Gregory Orlov as her official consort. 'The nation would be outraged,' he said, and whilst Catherine agreed, she had no wish to have it noised abroad by anyone other than herself.

Samuel Greig had early on presented himself to Princess Dashkov, since it had been her brother who had been responsible for his appointment to the Russian service. There had been an instant rapport between them. He had called on her by appointment, being privately surprised at the modesty of the establishment she kept.

'I have had an excellent report of you from my brother,' the Princess told him, 'and I am pleased you are here. I am sorry to receive you thus in my reduced circumstances but on the death of my husband, the Prince, I found myself alone at the age of twenty with little to call my own but my children and my husband's debts. Sir, I value my independence as much as you British are reputed to do. I therefore became my own steward, my children's nurse and governess, as well as their guardian, and have contrived to reduce my annual expenditure to 500 roubles, and at the same time to pay off my husband's debts. I doubt that you will find another Russian woman of my station who would behave in this way, but I am telling you this because I know you are shortly to be presented to her Majesty and because a scrupulous behaviour over finance is a quality the Empress and I have in common, and one she values to an exceptional extent in her servants, especially her servants from abroad.'

'Why are you telling me this?' Samuel asked. He was forced to admit to a lively feeling which she was engendering in him. The Princess gave him a sharpish look, similar to those he received from Consul Cook. Despite her physical youthfulness here was no innocent young girl, but a watchful and wary woman.

'Have you not been approached by the notorious Stryalokov concerning supplies and victualling for your ship and the squadron? I know you have. In Petersburg there are few secrets of that kind which remain secrets for long.'

'I sent him away with a flea in his ear.'

'I know that as well – and so, you can be sure, will the Empress. That is greatly to your credit.'

'I am here to sail and fight ships, madam, not to become a commercial entrepreneur.'

She looked him in the eyes.

'Your Scottish honesty will make you enemies,' she said, 'and in Russia you may not always be aware of whom you can trust. English freedom of speech is unknown in these northern climes. Not only unknown, but unwise were you to import the custom. And I would not want you to make mistakes without knowing that you do.'

'Pray do not think me impertinent,' Samuel said, 'if I enquire as to what you know of the English freedom of speech?'

'I have a brother in London, sir. Of that you are aware. No doubt you in turn have informed yourself about the Voronstov family. If not, then I would make so bold as to suggest that you do.'

She looked at him coolly but in such a way that his blood seemed suddenly to be on fire.

'Finally,' she went on, 'I have acquired the habit of study. Indeed I sometimes fancy that the Empress and I are the only women in all Russia who occupy themselves in serious reading. We each own to a taste for discovering what may be afoot in other parts of the civilized world. We absorb the best from abroad. We subscribe to the works of Voltaire, Diderot and Jean-Jacques Rousseau. We have even heard tell of the man you call "Dictionary Johnson". Our Court may have the manners of a pigsty but the Empress, with my full and loyal support, is having that changed. We follow the proceedings of the Académie Française, of the Académie Royale de Prusse and the Académie Royale des Belles-Lettres de Suède. It is Her Imperial Majesty's intention to propagate a Royal Academy here in Petersburg. In short, sir, we have been uncivilized in Muscovy for too long a time.'

The enthusiasm which lit up her features struck Samuel as one of the most refreshing sights he had witnessed since coming to Russia. She was not in his opinion a beauty, certainly not when judged against his incomparable Sarah, but the vigour of her speech, the light in her eyes and the self-evident courage with which she conducted herself all combined to delight and to stimulate his spirit. He had looked away, thinking about what she had just been saying, and when his gaze returned, he found her smiling at him as if she had been reading his thoughts.

'You are not married, are you, Captain Greig?'

'No, madam, I have been too much occupied with making my way at sea.'

'Then we must find you a wife.'

'I . . . with respect, madam, I need no assistance in that direction.'

The Princess turned slightly away. He felt a strong impulse to embrace her but contrived to resist the magnetism she seemed to exude.

'May Fortune smile on you,' she said, 'and grant you a longer married life than has befallen my lot.'

He felt it indelicate to pursue this with any questioning. He knew that Prince Dashkov had been appointed Commander-in-Chief in Poland but had died unexpectedly before taking up the post. He felt a wave of compassion towards the young widow who had already made him privy to so many of her thoughts.

'You have left her in England?' the Princess enquired.

'In Scotland, ma'am,' Samuel said and then, unable to help himself, proceeded to blurt out the whole story of his relationship with Sarah, her age, her mother, his own lack of financial resources – in short of the hazards and vast loneliness of a life at sea.

'Then we must send for her here,' the Princess said and immediately, and to Samuel's immense surprise, took him in her arms with a completely unintellectual fervour. 'And in the meantime,' she continued as she led him gently towards her bed, 'we must improvise with such as we can find to hand. Come, come, Captain, you have stumbled upon an unmanned fort. Strike whilst the door to the citadel is still ajar. And do not look so rueful. You have found a friend upon whom you can rely, provided, of course, that your discretion matches your virility.'

His experience with the little Princess astonished and somewhat unnerved him. This uncertainty, fired by a raging guilt, was in no degree lessened by the way in which the Princess mocked him as they lay in each other's arms.

'You are thinking of your Sarah,' she said, brushing his lips slightly with hers, 'but that will only make you more doleful than you already are. You must take life as it comes, Samuel Karlovich, a gift is a gift whether from a serving maid or a Princess, and had you been a lady-in-waiting in the last reign, as I was, you would soon have adjusted your scruples to the situation into which the Almighty has seen fit to pitch you.'

'I am a fighting man, madam, not a courtier.'

She smiled, indicating gently that he should leave her bed.

'Well now you are both,' she said, 'and you are under oath to an Empress who will demand from you – if it so happens that she finds you agreeable – a service other than at sea. I am sure,' she went on, as she watched him pulling on his breeches and buttoning up his coat, 'that with a little instruction you will navigate the dangerous shoals of Peterhof and Oranienbaum, even of the Winter Palace itself. But see if you can manage it with a smile. A pleasure taken on the wing is a pleasure enhanced. It is also an effective means of banishing remorse – and we have enough to endure in Petersburg without adding remorse to the tally.'

8

Her Majesty proposes

It was just as well that extended naval manoeuvres – and it was soon apparent to Samuel that there were no manoeuvres in Russia which were not extended – necessarily intervened between Samuel's encounter with the Princess Dashkov and his formal presentation to the Empress. He thus had time in which to recover his equanimity. Hindsight, he discovered, colours experience with a pleasant afterglow.

It was true that a feeling of his not having been entirely faithful to Sarah nagged at him from time to time, but another voice in him pointed out that Sarah was a long way away and inaccessible. What the eye does not see, the soul does not suffer, he told himself, and from this derived a necessary comfort. Nevertheless he found himself a trifle disconcerted when Consul Cook casually enquired just before the fleet sailed on manoeuvres:

'And does the little Dashkov lie as nimbly as she is known to speak the truth?'

For a moment or so, Samuel made no reply and the Consul studied his naval compatriot with a smile as they walked along the quayside to Samuel's ship. The young Captain certainly looked resplendent in his uniform, except for a somewhat crestfallen expression in the eyes.

'Come, come Samuel,' the Consul continued, 'there is no cause for embarrassment in this quarter. Have I not warned you that in Russia everything is known, though perhaps only partially revealed?'

'That may be so,' Samuel retorted; 'however I would prefer certain matters not to be known.'

'It is a little late for a proviso of that kind,' the Consul remarked. 'All Petersburg pays close attention to, and can lay wages on, the Bedchamber Stakes. How could you be any exception to that? Think yourself lucky, my dear Samuel, that you have not yet been entered as a runner in the Imperial Handicap. Your little Princess—'

'She is not my little Princess,' Samuel interrupted indignantly. 'One swallow does not make a summer.'

The Consul brushed aside this remark and continued with his train of thought:

' – the little Dashkov made a common and pointless error in speaking to you about the Empress as she did.'

'And how is what she said or did not say to me known?'

'Such a puerile question deserves no answer,' the Consul snapped. 'There is not a wall in Russia but has its ear, as well you know. The Dashkov is jealous – and that could be dangerous. The Empress is an exceptional woman, coming into the fullness of her powers. She has no intention of allowing anyone to snatch the reins from her now that she has them finally in her hands.'

'Not even Gregory Orlov?'

'Least of all a member of that clan. King of the couch he may be, he will never be Tsar of Russia.'

'I hope you are correct.'

'You will discover that for yourself, once you have been presented to Her Majesty and have established yourself in the manner on which the Ambassador sets his hopes. The Empress has grappled herself to the throne, however much she dallies in the few leisure hours she allows herself to enjoy, and unlike the two previous reigns, dissipation is not the order of the day. The Empress – this Empress – has more important matters to decide than the gown she will wear for the evening ball. As you will soon come to realize, she decides matters of state entirely herself. She listens and then she makes up her mind. After that the door clangs shut.'

He smiled and shook hands at the bottom of the gangway.

'In the meantime, Captain, bon voyage and good hunting.'

A further two months were to elapse before the fleet returned to Crondstadt from its cruise and prepared for the approach of winter with its annual freezing-up of the port. An invitation to dine with the British Ambassador awaited

Samuel and his brother mercenaries, and at this dinner their forthcoming presentation to the Empress was touched on and an unofficial 'briefing' given to each of them. So after another few days had passed, the levée duly took place.

By now it was late autumn and soon the first snowflakes would turn the outside of the great Winter Palace into the white fairyland scene which Samuel was to know so well for the rest of his life. Inside there was a blaze of light from the crystal chandeliers illuminating the long rows of portraits and the rich decorations which Jean Baptiste le Prince and Louis Joseph de Lorraine had so lavishly and so expensively executed for the late Empress. It had been intended as 'the perfect setting' for the aged Empress who had not lived to see it completed, and it had materially assisted the bankrupting of the Exchequer which faced Catherine when she had herself mounted the throne.

The grandeur of Versailles had set the tone for this northern copy, and on his long approach to the Throne Room Samuel's eyes were dazzled by the luxury and the ostentatious evidence of a wealth which was in such sharp and painful contrast with the life outside. His recent experience in trying to 'work up' a crew of illiterate serfs in his frigate under the harsh conditions of the Russian naval service underlined the waste and indulgence of this oriental splendour, which impressed itself on him in every salon and corridor through which he passed en route to his first meeting with the Empress. He could not but call to mind the reports he had recently been given in private discussions, of the peasant rebellions on certain noblemen's estates which had been serious enough to require whole companies of troops with artillery support to quell them. Here in the Winter Palace all was of a florid magnificence he could scarcely have projected in a dream.

When Samuel was eventually brought forward for presentation, together with his brother officers, he was struck by two things – the comparative plainness of the Empress's appearance (she wore a dark blue gown with a single diamond brooch as adornment), and the almost hypnotic quality of her gaze. Whether by accident or intent, Samuel found himself the last of 'the foreigners' to be presented and after the formalities were over, Count Alexander Naryshkin, the Grand Marshal of the Court, drew him to one side. With him was Count Nikita Panin whose advice, Samuel knew, was mainly relied on by the Empress in matters of foreign policy and the relationship with other kingdoms.

'The Empress wishes to question you on the condition of the fleet,' he said, 'but feels you would be reluctant to speak freely in the presence of Admiral Talytzin. She therefore wishes you to wait on her in one of the antechambers to which Count Nikita will now conduct you.'

Was 'a service other than at sea' about to be demanded of him? Samuel felt both wariness and a dread, but decided it would be wiser to keep as close a counsel with himself as possible. The less said the better for all concerned. The older Russian courtier, who for some twelve years had been Ambassador to Sweden and who was now acting as Tutor to the Grand Duke Paul, Catherine's legitimate heir, watched the young naval Captain with a smile as they made their way to the antechamber.

'If you will accept advice from a non-maritime man,' said Panin, 'you will answer the Empress directly and truthfully in every matter on which she seeks your opinion. She knows that you are not activated by malice and you may therefore speak your mind for the betterment of all.'

'And if I should seem disloyal? Surely it is to her Admirals she should look for advice concerning the naval service?'

'This is not England,' Panin observed drily. 'I have no doubt but that you order things differently in the United Kingdom.'

He paused as if expecting this remark to be capped, but as Samuel remained silent, the Count went on with a sideways glance:

'Senator Elagin has suggested to me that, provided you yourself concur, he would agree to your admission as a freemason to one of our lodges, and he has asked me to enquire of you in this respect.'

This did not take Samuel completely by surprise. But he considered his words carefully before he replied.

'Since Senator Elagin is Her Majesty's Personal Secretary and since you yourself do me the honour of asking me the question,' Samuel said, 'I must tell you that I was approached in this connection before leaving the service of His Britannic Majesty. I came to no decision at that time, however, as I considered that my becoming a freemason might conflict in some way with my oath of loyalty to the Russian Empress.'

'Well spoken, sir, said Panin with, it seemed to Samuel, a somewhat mocking tone of voice, 'you confirm an opinion already held by Senator Elagin and myself. Perhaps you will now accept reassurance that so far from conflicting in any way with service to Her Majesty, it is a proper and expedient way of, shall we say, further shoring up the ramparts of your already established loyalty. Therefore I urge it upon you, sir, and I can assure you without, I trust, being required to specify the matter in further detail, that your decision to accept this invitation would find favour with Her Imperial Highness.'

'In that event, sir, I am indeed honoured to accept.'

At that moment the Empress entered the room, followed by Count Razumovsky. This distinguished soldier Samuel knew to be a person of considerable weight in the inner councils of the Empress. He had risen from abject poverty, as the youngest son of a small farmer, to be for fourteen years the last Hetman of the Ukraine. This unusual preferment had come about collaterally, so to speak, with the rise of his brother from choir boy to lover and morganatic husband of the late Empress Elizabeth. Razumovsky and Panin both shared, in Samuel's opinion, that hard watchful look in the eyes which characterized those who flourished from positions of power in close proximity to the throne. The Empress, however, naturally dominated the scene and wasted no time in coming to the point.

'Now that we have surprised the King of Sweden with an ability to make him keep his distance,' the Empress began, walking slowly up and down, brushing aside the proffered seat, 'and in addition now that the affairs of Poland appear to be settled, for the moment, to our satisfaction and to that of the Prussian Emperor, we intend to look east. This entails a fresh challenge to the Turkish Sultan, the Sublime Porte.'

She paused and fixed Samuel with the most calculating, steely glance he could remember receiving since facing Admiral Hawke in the hour of battle. Here was no feminine tenderness, no wavering doubt but a ruthless and regal self-confidence, which Samuel found to be compulsive and inspiring.

'In your opinion, Captain Greig, is the strength and preparedness of our Navy such to warrant the sending of an expedition through the Mediterranean to achieve this end? You may speak freely. We shall not employ anything you tell us against your superior officers in such a way that you yourself will suffer any evil consequence. But you are, we are told, the officer in our service the most experienced in battle and generally in the art of naval warfare. So how say you, Captain Greig?'

'Your Majesty,' Samuel began, 'in my country the British sailor considers himself the equal of ten of his hereditary enemy the French – not only in courage but in skill. On that basis and from what I have already observed of the Russian fighting man, one Russian sailor could equal ten Turks, provided, ma'am, and this is elemental – provided that he is actively and efficiently led. There is no such thing as a bad sailor, only a bad officer – in my opinion, that is,' he added with a touch of defence.

'Captain Greig must meet Count Suvorov,' the Empress remarked aside to Razumovsky; 'their points of view have much in common.'

On a slight nod from the Empress, Razumovsky explained for Samuel's benefit that General Suvorov was a soldier of the Spartan school who believed that training was 'light', lack of training 'darkness'. A trained man was worth ten not so enlightened. If a peasant did not know how to plough he could not grow bread.

'Alexander Diogenes may not make a pleasing courtier,'

the Empress commented, 'but he achieves greater results in the field than any of my other Generals. And he is harder on his officers than he is on his men, we are told.'

She looked at Samuel and raised her eyebrows.

'That is a principle which should also be applied at sea,' Samuel agreed, 'but it is not one which finds universal favour at Crondstadt ...' He hesitated and then plunged on, 'Since Your Majesty has indicated that I should speak as I think, I would opine that it is mostly the "foreign" officers who are possessed of the qualities needed for victory at sea – and not all of them are paragons of virtue.'

'You are a severe critic of our native Russian talent,' the Empress observed, pursing her lips.

'It is generally considered that it takes seven years to make an efficient naval officer,' Samuel went on, 'and not seven years spent hugging a harbour quay.'

'Perhaps we should execute a few senior officers to encourage the others?' the Empress enquired. 'You British shot one of your Admirals a few years ago.'

'No ma'am. It is not their courage which is in question. It is their indolence.'

A silence fell on the four people in the room, of whom Samuel was the youngest. It crossed his mind that even though invited to talk in this way, he might well be putting his own future in jeopardy. The Empress herself he knew to be of German birth, but both Panin and Razumovsky exhibited that Asiatic stealth he had been forced to acknowledge, even to respect, since entering the Russian service. Eventually the Empress herself broke this pause in their deliberations.

'We have invited another of your fellow countrymen, a Captain John Elphinston, to take command of a squadron for this proposed Turkish adventure. Are you acquainted with this officer?'

'Indeed I am, Your Majesty. We served together under Commodore Keppel at Havana. This is an excellent piece of news.'

'He has been highly recommended, as you were yourself,' the Empress said with a smile, 'but of course he is your senior by many years. How would you say to being put under his command?'

'I could ask for no better officer to serve, Your Majesty. Captain Elphinston entered the Royal Navy, as I did myself, after several years of merchant service. He is – you might say – a thoroughly practical man. It is his opinion – and mine – that walking the decks of the King's ships can never make so expert a sailor as working up from a common seaman.'

'And how will he conduct himself, would you consider, with a Russian Admiral such as Spiritdoff?'

'As to that ma'am, I am not in a position to conjecture,' Samuel said. 'Captain Elphinston, however, is a commander of pronounced, perhaps even rigid, views. He is diligent in the preparations he undertakes. In my experience he is not a man to suffer fools gladly.'

'I trust you do not classify the entire Russian High Command in that category,' the Empress said, moving to the door and indicating that the audience was at an end. 'I am obliged to you, Captain Greig, for your advice which remains confidential to the four of us in this room. I have given instructions,' she added before quitting the antechamber, 'that you are to have direct access to us whenever, in your discretion, circumstances so demand. We therefore rely on your discretion, Captain Greig, to an unorthodox degree. Are we fully understood in this?'

'I am Your Majesty's devoted and completely confidential servant,' Samuel said, bowing low and privately wondering how safe his own future might be in what lay so soon ahead.

The failure of the Widow Cook's plans to secure her daughter's betrothal to Donald MacFee, which failure had to be admitted when the young gentleman married another, threw the lady into a decline but greatly relieved Sarah. When this became known to Samuel, he discussed the problem one evening with Consul Cook.

'As I promised you in Edinburgh,' the Consul said, 'Sarah shall be invited here to Petersburg whenever you choose to say the word, but we were agreed, were we not, that the chances of the mother allowing such an invitation to be accepted are negligible to the point of non-existence? However I am now seized of a better idea on your behalf. There is a Muscovy merchant who resides both in London and in Chislehurst in Kent. My father and I have long maintained a friendly relationship with the Bonars, who are also known to your Mr Oswald of Dunnikeer and therefore also to the Bute faction. Mr Bonar and his wife are now in the evening of their lives. He is a rich and benevolent man and I would hazard a guess that, if approached in the right manner, he would invite Mother Cook and her daughter to stay in his house.'

'With what object?' Samuel asked suspiciously.

'Why, to find a suitable husband for Sarah,' said the Consul, a foxy look in his eye.

'And suppose they should succeed?'

'I will acquaint Mr Bonar with the real purpose of our plan,' the Consul said. 'The Bonars will know how best to stretch the matter in time whilst keeping the Dragon well fed and quiescent. Then perhaps at a suitable moment Mr Bonar may find it necessary to make a Baltic voyage in pursuit of his commercial interests, and since we are currently at war with no one but the distant Turk, there is but little risk of local hostilities endangering such a voyage – in which it might intrigue Mrs Cook and her daughter to join. This could doubtless be manoeuvred in such a way that it could coincide with the arrival here of those ladies attendant on one of the coming influxions of British naval officers. Captains Boyd, Roxburgh and others will, I have reason to believe, be establishing their families here in Petersburg. Admiral Elphinston may even bring his lady with him. Let your mind consider these possibilities, and if you are agreeable, I will write forthwith to Mr Bonar. It is an uncomplicated strategy in which it would please him to engage, since he has always been of a romantic disposition in addition to being a skilful man of affairs.'

It took Samuel but a moment's thought to concur in this plan, which was then got under way. Samuel writing in confidence to his sister in Edinburgh to secure her co-operation behind the scenes. It was thus that Sarah found herself translated to London in what, at first sight, appeared to be a miraculous fashion.

This move south became for Sarah as exciting an adventure as his appointment to Russia had proved to be for Samuel. The Bonars were wealthy, and the comfort of the Chislehurst house was in marked contrast to that of the modest Edinburgh dwelling to which Sarah and her mother had been reduced since the death of Captain Cook. The Bonars also gave the Widow Cook and her daughter a genuine welcome. Initially even Mrs Cook felt a diffidence in accepting this hospitality. However the round and jolly Mrs Bonar soon put this matter to rights. The good lady of the house had entered into the plot proposed by Consul Cook with a private gusto. This stemmed not only from a natural benevolence but also because Mrs Bonar had been made fully aware of the humiliations of patronage in her own early life.

Sarah later discovered – but never told her mother – that Mrs Bonar had once been in service in the household of Mr Bonar's father. On their first evening at Chislehurst, their hostess drew mother and daughter to one side and, after bidding them to behave as if they were in their own home, folded her hands across her ample stomach, smiled at them and said:

'I should perhaps explain that good fortune has for long shone upon Mr Bonar and myself except in one important department. A family has not been forthcoming. This absence of progeny has, alas, been the only cloud in the clear sky of our lengthy married life. Moreover Mr Bonar, who has derived his prosperity from mercantile activity upon the high seas, considers himself more than usually beholden to the brave sailors of King George who protect us all from the depredations of our enemies ...'

Mrs Bonar evidently enjoyed the sound of her own voice and once started had difficulty in stopping even to draw breath, as the Cooks were soon to discover.

'Therefore – dingledy-dum, dingledy-dee' (a phrase the

meaning of which Sarah never ascertained, but which Mrs Bonar would drop into her speech like an extra egg into an omelette) ' – it is a pleasure and a privilege to Mr Bonar and to meself to welcome into our humble home the family of a distinguished officer who has given his life to his country ...'

'What a common woman!' Mrs Cook remarked afterwards to Sarah. 'No wonder they're pleased to entertain us. I don't suppose many of the County call at this establishment.'

As in so many matters, the Widow Cook again stood in error. The Bonars turned out to enjoy a high popularity in the district both among the quality and also lower down on the social scale. Of course there were those who sneered behind their backs, in the manner of Mrs Cook, but the real warmth which both Bonars exuded, their lavish hospitality and the ready concern they exhibited for anyone in trouble gave them a unique reputation, and they were received, somewhat to the Widow Cook's surprise, as easily in the Lord Lieutenant's castle as they were in the local village shop. The Bonars were always having people down from London, and anyone connected with the sea whether in the King's service or in commerce could be sure of an evening's entertainment and a bed for the night should the weather happen to be inclement.

Some two weeks after Sarah and her mother had arrived at Chislehurst, Mrs Bonar announced that a Captain and Mrs Elphinston were coming to dinner that evening.

'Together with an acquaintance of yours, Lieutenant Fortescue Fynne.'

'Fortie!' cried Sarah, 'what a lovely surprise!'

'That dissipated rake!' her mother interjected, but was stopped by a gesture and a frown from Sarah.

'All three are being driven down from Town in the carriage of Count Vorontsov, the Russian Commissioner for Naval Affairs at the Court of St James with whom Mr Bonar – dingledy-dum dingledy-dee – does business on behalf of Her Imperial Majesty, the Empress of All the Russias, and of course of the Muscovy Company.'

As they prepared to go down to dinner that night, the Widow Cook said to her daughter:

'Now, Sarah, do not take me for a complete fool. I begin to see what is behind all this, but I warn you not to try any of your tricks.'

'What tricks, mother?' Sarah asked, the epitome of innocence. 'Sam is a couple of thousand miles away in Russia. If Elphinston and Fortie are going to join him, where is the trick in that?'

'I do not know,' said her mother, 'but equally I do not trust that look in your face. You are too old, now, to run away to sea.'

'Oh! dingledy-dum,' said Sarah, 'what a mountain of rubbish you talk.'

'That is no way to address your mother,' the Widow Cook began in a tearful voice.

Fiddlesticks!' said Sarah. 'Dingledy-dum, dingledy-dee!'

From the warmth with which Sarah greeted Fortescue Fynne, a stranger might have been excused in imagining that they were in love themselves. This effusiveness was watched by Count Vorontsov, himself but little older than Fortescue Fynne, with a somewhat reserved smile. Many years later he confessed to Sarah that he had found her at this first meeting to be so very engaging that had it not been for the mission with which he had been charged, he would himself have entered into competition for her favours. Captain and Mrs Elphinston were nearer to the generation of Mr and Mrs Bonar, and had not been made privy to the real reason for the gathering at Chislehurst that night.

Outside it was blustery November weather which made the blazing fires maintained by the Bonars, the gleaming silver on the highly polished mahogany dining table and the excellent roast duck provided for their dinner, the more enjoyable.

'So you are joining Sam in Russia,' Sarah said to Fortescue Fynne, a wistful look in her eye. 'I would that I could be bundled into the baggage train and accompany you.'

She dropped her voice so that her mother, who was at the other end of the table with Mr Bonar and the Elphinstons could not overhear their conversation. Fortescue Fynne and Count Vorontsov exchanged a quick glance, the significance of which was not apparent to Sarah.

'It is indeed what our French cousins would call *une bonne nouvelle* that Captain Fynne, as he will soon be, has decided to accord the Empress the benefit of his vast nautical experience,' Count Vorontsov said, in a somewhat supercilious tone of voice. 'Once the formalities of Admiralty have been duly completed.'

'I understand it is Her Majesty's intention to annoy the Turk,' Fortie said, 'and doubtless the arrival of the "Elphinston Eccentrics", as I gather we have been dubbed, will astonish the Sublime Porte into an instant surrender without our being put to the necessity of opening fire. The mere threat will be more than sufficient.'

'Perhaps a few fireworks will also light up our northern skies,' the Count continued, studying the craggy physiognomy of Captain Elphinston who was propounding some theory about marine encrustation on the hulls of ships and the reduction of speed which this entailed. 'The gallant Captain's determination and his aggressive fighting spirit may perhaps be put to better use *before* we take on the Turk. The chandlers and ship repairers of Crondstadt are not given to bestirring themselves except under threat.'

As the evening wore on, the prospects facing the Elphinston Eccentrics were thoroughly talked out in a serious vein by Elphinston and in a much more lighthearted manner by Fortescue Fynne. The latter, whose sense of mischief increased with the wine he drank, could not resist countering Sarah's incessant concern with Samuel by dropping into the conversation outrageous snippets of tavern gossip. He also suggested that his old friend had adopted the Orthodox religion, changed his name to Gregovsky and was making off with a Russian Princess – a sally accidentally nearer the mark than anyone except Count Vorontsov believed.

The overall effect on Sarah was to depress her young spirits so that a melancholy settled upon her. What did it matter to her that Fortescue Fynne was amusingly describing the final collapse of his uncle under the weight of his gambling debts? That the Earl of Braddenham should be forced to sell his town house and retire to Wiltshire in an attempt to recoup himself and his fortune was of little import to Sarah. Her mind was entirely on Samuel in distant Russia and it was of no consolation to her, since she did not hear it said, that as soon as the ladies had left the men to their port, Count Vorontsov remarked to Fortescue Fynne:

'You were entirely correct, my friend, in describing the girl as a raging beauty. She will undoubtedly enhance the Petersburg scene. I am only surprised that you haven't mounted a "cutting out" operation and made off with the prize yourself.'

'There are two reasons for that. In the first place she would not have me even were I Bonnie Prince Charlie himself. She is entirely obsessed with her Samuel. Secondly I am minded to acquire for myself some suitable Petersburg maiden, preferably of noble provenance and with a few million serfs, whose hand I would seek in marriage. You see how altruistic I am?'

'Such cynicism is the better part of wisdom,' Vorontsov said. 'However I must not delay the execution of my mission tonight,' and, excusing himself to his genial host, he left the table and by a previous arrangement with the Bonars summoned Sarah and her mother to a private conference in another room. This they attended with some trepidation and surprise. Once the three of them were alone and the ladies had duly been seated, Count Vorontsov looked at them for a moment or so in silence and then said:

'I am here upon a mission of some delicacy, and pursuant to the direct and confidential instructions of Her Imperial Majesty the Empress Catherine.'

This portentous statement caused the Widow Cook to stand up and blench to such an extent that Sarah rushed to her side, fearful that she might be taking leave of her senses. She supported her back into her chair, receiving a glance from the Count which was both friendly and mocking. When her mother had again been settled and the sal volatile applied, the Count resumed:

'I am not accustomed to my remarks producing such an apparently devastating effect, but then neither did I expect to find two such amiable and enchanting ladies the object of my visit.'

On this he found himself in a position to smile at Sarah behind her mother's back and for good measure added an engaging wink. Feeling, perhaps falsely, that some disloyalty to her mother was intended, Sarah drew herself up haughtily and looked askance. She was fully aware that whatever the Count's mission, he found her attractive and instinct warned her that she was not likely to be safe in his hands were they alone.

The Count then went on to explain that he had been some years an envoy to the Court of St James, that he had executed various commissions on behalf of the Imperial Russian Navy of which Captain Samuel Greig, with whom he knew them both to be acquainted, was now one of their most distinguished officers. Captain Greig, he continued, enjoyed the personal trust and consideration of the Empress to a wholly remarkable degree. At the mention of Greig's name the Widow Cook showed signs of a returning attack, and the smelling salts were again somewhat hastily rammed under her nose by Sarah.

'I must inform you, madam,' the Count continued in a more severe tone, 'that Captain Greig has no knowledge whatever of this visit nor of its intent. I come, as I said before, on the personal authority of Her Majesty, and, since there is no longer any point in disguising matters further, to ask you an exceedingly personal question. I therefore crave your indulgence for the abrupt manner in which it is put. Her Majesty makes it her business to discover a very considerable amount of detail concerning anyone from abroad who enters her service, the reasons for which I have no doubt you will comprehend, and she has been informed – not, I hasten to say again, by Captain Greig – that the gallant Captain is enamoured of Miss Sarah Cook and has long desired her hand in marriage.'

'Oh! Oh . . .' the mother began, at which Sarah abruptly took charge and said with surprising force.

'Now, mother, that is enough of that. I am, as you know, past the age of consent.'

The Count saw that it was a politic moment in which to press the advantage.

'Then may I enquire if you would marry the Captain should a proposal be forthcoming?'

'I have waited to do nothing else these last ten years,' Sarah said, an almost steely tone in her voice.

'Therefore,' the Count proceeded, 'I would be correct in assuming, would I not, that if proper arrangements were to be made for you to visit St Petersburg, accompanied by your mother, you would raise no objection to such a manoeuvre?'

An ecstatic joy crossed Sarah's face, followed by a cloud of doubt the cause of which had perhaps been guessed at by the Count, who added with a smile:

'The expense of this proposed visit, I am authorized to inform you, would be borne by Her Imperial Majesty's Privy Purse. My only present concern is to be able to assure the Empress that you are not being procured against your will – and should you take a natural objection to the use of such a word, permit me to remind you that this is precisely what happened to the Empress herself when she was no more than the Princess Sophie-Frédérique of Anhalt-Zerbst. You are, in fact, the recipient of a very considerable honour since, as I do not need to remind you, the Empress has other and more important matters on her mind than the conveyance to Russia of young ladies such as yourself.'

Then, with a polite obeisance to them both, the Count indicated the meeting to be at an end, and without giving Sarah and her mother a chance to discuss the matter further, suggested that they rejoined the others. As they did so, the Count said:

'There is one condition, however, on which Her Majesty insists and that is a complete and utter secrecy. Not a word is to be said to anyone – least of all to Captain Greig. If this requirement is not met, then the event in question will not transpire.'

*

Meanwhile in Petersburg, the now imminent arrival of the Elphinston Eccentrics seemed, to Samuel, to be but one of the many indications that the foreign ambitions of the Empress had moved into a new order of magnitude. Russia was coming of age. Trained observers such as the various ambassadors to the Petersburg court reported to their governments, with differing degrees of approval or misgiving, on this expansion and in particular on the drive eastwards to establish Russian power in the Black Sea. Once started, they said, such Empire building might well be difficult or even impossible to halt, and this had to be aligned with the fact that the other great European powers such as Prussia, Austria, France, Spain and Great Britain were all themselves involved in a similar dynamic process. Would Russia get out of hand?

Luckily for Samuel these great matters of state did not concern him except in the naval sphere. Initially unsure of himself, he had gradually come to accept what the Petersburg world was saying, namely that he did appear to have been chosen as some sort of special person upon whom Her Imperial Majesty was relying to an unusual degree for expert naval opinion, the which no Russian could be trusted to provide. This might well be the hand of Providence. It seemed to Samuel to be none the less daunting for that. Above all it demanded tact, wariness and a strong self-discipline.

'You are under watch with a jealous attention given to no other foreigner at Court,' the British Ambassador informed him, 'and this power is a two-edged sword. I would hazard a guess that there is nothing you can demand of the Empress for the naval service, which she will not make it her business to give you. This is highly satisfactory from one point of view but do not imagine that you have only friends lurking in the shadows. You are constantly rumoured to be venal – to be turning yourself into some Russian nabob – and when there can be found no evidence of this, you are still not excused except, of course, by the monarch herself. Proceed with the utmost care, my dear Captain Greig. There are many personages, especially purveyors to the Court and not all of them of the merchant class, who would be only too willing to contrive your fall.'

He kept well away from the Princess Dashkov and, although sorely tempted at times, did not establish himself with a mistress. This absence of one of the more usual areas of scandal seemed only to infuriate his enemies the more. They began taunting him, always behind his back, with accusations of secret vices, of complacency, and when all else failed, of not even being a proper man. Luckily he was known to be no stranger to wine, to brandy and to the native brewed spirits, such as vodka and schnapps, and he showed himself convivial enough with his brother officers, even accompanying them from time to time into the brothels of Petersburg. However he took good care to steer well clear of any permanent or semi-permanent liaisons.

All this time he pined for his Sarah. He wanted a wife and a home, but he was already beginning to suspect that he was not to be granted this solace by the Providence in which he had placed his trust. He had accustomed himself to long periods of personal solitude at sea, but he had little wish to continue for ever in this way, nor to endure a lonely old age. He had plenty of work with which to occupy his mind, he was active and his health remained good. Yet without Sarah he knew in his bones that he would never achieve the fulfilment he sought.

Then with what seemed to his inward eye an iridescent, miraculous, unexpected stroke of Providence, his whole life changed. As preparations for an important naval assault upon the Turkish fleet continued at an increasing pace, the Empress had desired him to attend on her weekly for the purpose of rendering a confidential report of the progress – or, as was often the case, the lack of progress – which had been achieved.

At these meetings no Admiral or naval officer superior in rank to Samuel would be invited to be present. Count Gregory Orlov, it is true, considered himself immune from these strictures and in the early days strode in and out of Her Imperial Majesty's private council chamber as if of right. He wished to acquaint himself with the topics under discussion, but as the Empress invariably began questioning her naval adviser in detail and as Orlov saw in the person of Samuel Greig no threat to his status as the morganatic consort of the Empress, he soon lost interest in the world of anchors and cables and such like naval 'baubles', as he put it. The Empress took quick advantage of this, and with the aid of other of her closest advisers such as Prince Trubetskoy, the influential Gregory Teplov who had risen from being the son of a stoker to become one of the best educated men in Russa, the wily but honest Nikita Panin, and the all powerful Field-Marshal Razumovsky, she ensured that the Orlov influence became gradually and progressively diminished. It was not long before she received Samuel alone, or in the company of such as her entourage as she herself elected to invite.

It was now late in 1768, and although Samuel had at first approached these audiences with a mixture of anticipation and dread, the Empress had never given him the slightest indication that she was interested in him in any respect other than that of a naval adviser. And yet, from the way she would look at him from time to time, Samuel could not but feel that his innermost thoughts were known. If this were 'the divinity which hedges a king', Samuel found it at best disconcerting and, when he dared to think in such a manner, an assault on his manhood, yet not one which he could either rebuff or understand. The Empress in his consideration remained unquestionably the most powerful and enigmatic woman he had ever encountered. They were talking these days of the strange 'hypnotic' powers of an Austrian physician called Mesmer, but from what little Samuel understood of such matters, the powers Mesmer possessed were nothing compared with the forces directed upon himself at these weekly encounters with his Empress.

At the conclusion of the meeting on the day which Samuel afterwards described as *mirabilis*, the Empress transfixed him with an even more magnetic and dynamic gaze than he could recall ever having received before.

'Was it your intention now to ride back to Crondstadt?' the Empress enquired.

'If Your Majesty so concurs. The arrival of Admiral Elphinston and his party is hourly expected and I must be present at Crondstadt to welcome them in an appropriate fashion.'

'You are too late,' the Empress said with what Samuel mistakenly took to be an angry flash of the eyes. 'They are already arrived and we do not concur in your departure to Crondstadt.'

She paused, staring at him as if he were on trial, and also as if she expected him to volunteer some petulant comment on this. But he had long ago learnt, whenever he found her in a mood such as this, to await the next statement from the Imperial Majesty in patience and in silence.

'Is it not a defect in your system of intelligence, Captain Greig, that these foreign naval officers can arrive in our fortified naval base without your being so informed?'

'Doubtless the winds have proved more favourable since I departed from Crondstadt to attend upon Your Majesty,' Samuel said, privately determining to institute his own inquisition into this embarrassing lapse, and compiling in his mind a short list of those whom he would first have on his quarterdeck.

'Or it might be that we ordered you not to be furnished with this intelligence?' the Empress went on and then, with a sudden smile which seemed to transform her into a girl, she rang for her secretary and when he appeared said curtly, 'Command the Chamberlain to bring in the British Ambassador.'

'Your Majesty,' Samuel put in quickly, 'may I not be given the opportunity of first discovering the reason for—'

'No, Captain Greig,' the Empress interrupted sternly, 'you are about to be given an opportunity of a different kind.'

He fell silent briefly until the door was opened to admit the Chamberlain and His Britannic Majesty's Ambassador – followed by none other than Sarah Cook and her mother, both wide-eyed with wonder, anticipation and a very natural apprehension. For the first time since he had been wounded in battle, Samuel felt that he might be about to swoon and it certainly appeared from her unsteady gait that Sarah was in a similar condition. However the awesome experience of a first presentation to the Empress of All the Russias, seated upon her gilded chair, took possession of them all and this was evidently a moment which gave great pleasure to Her Majesty.

Mistress Cook and her daughter curtsied deeply and somewhat awkwardly, as the Ambassador bowed. The presentations made, the Empress bade them rise and then, turning to the Ambassador, remarked with a smile:

'We are obliged to Your Excellency for the services rendered, in this mark of esteem we are pleased to bestow upon Captain Greig,' and then with a smile which Samuel was never to forget till his dying day, indicated that the audience was at an end.

'We shall be pleased to have Captain Greig confer with Admiral Elphinston tomorrow,' the Empress said as they were leaving her presence, 'and subsequently for the presentation of these newly arrived volunteers to be effected under the normal propositions of protocol, as soon as the gentlemen shall have been acclimatized after their voyage from England.'

9

Pursuit of the Turks

A month later Sarah and Samuel were married. Lord Buckingham, the British Ambassador, gave the bride away which greatly pleased the Widow Cook, and for the ceremony they were offered either the French Reformed Church in Petersburg, which was the Protestant church used by the English community, or the Presbyterian Chapel at Crondstadt which Count Bruce, the 'senior Scotsman' in Russia, had had constructed for the use of the Scottish maritime community.

They chose the latter. This disappointed Mrs Cook, who now saw herself via this marriage as an *ipso facto* leader of Petersburg society – an idea which unfortunately for her was not received with much warmth by those who already comprised that society – but the wedding did mark the final acceptance of Samuel by his mother-in-law, and was followed by a changed and better relationship, although the good lady was to go to her grave under the firm notion that her daughter had married beneath her.

Sarah looked radiant in her white silk dress, which one of the Court ladies had given her and against which her burnished red hair seemed to shine like the sun.

'She is become arrestingly lovely, that wee lass of yours,' Fortie, who was Samuel's best man, had commented at the reception, in what he fondly imagined to be a Scottish accent. 'So you had best get her quickly with child, my friend, or take her to sea with you. She will not be safe in this jungle when her guid mon is awa'.'

The Empress gave Sarah a small emerald brooch and sent the Court Chamberlain to represent her at the wedding, which was also attended by the Orlov brothers and many of the court. The Commander-in-Chief organized a reception at his official residence, and the officers and men from Samuel's ship formed a guard of honour at the church.

Altogether it was an occasion Crondstadt would long remember.

After the honeymoon, spent at a hunting lodge on the Naryshkin estate, Samuel and Sarah settled down in a small house near the dockyard in Crondstadt, a cottage being added to one side for the Widow Cook.

'I am anxious to treat her with the deference and respect which is her due,' Samuel observed to his new wife when they had come to this decision, 'but I do not want her to be always fussing and fretting about the house when I am back from the ship. You are the mistress now. This new routine may be a wee bit painful for the old lady – nevertheless I shall want to see her in this house only by invitation.'

Sarah quickly set his mind at rest on that score, and from then on there was no doubt about who was in command of the Greig shore establishment. Sarah had come into her own.

By now the Elphinston Eccentrics had more or less settled themselves into their adopted service. This proved to be a contentious and bellicose process which made the new foreign contingent even less popular in the event than they had been in prospect. A definite decision had been taken in the summer of 1769 to mount and dispatch a naval expedition against the Sultan of Turkey without further delay. This, as always, was upon the personal order of the Empress. However between the edict and its execution lay a turmoil of administrative troubles which were far worse than the most disreputable embranglements of any of the Royal Dockyards of England.

'We are respected but much disliked by the Russians,' Samuel remarked when Elphinston, exasperated by the forms of office which he was required to observe, called a conference of the foreign officers to demand that pressure be brought to bear on the ship chandlers and other dockyard officials at Crondstadt. 'They are jealous of our knowledge and contemptuous of our experience,' Samuel went on, 'although naturally they are careful not to be too forward in showing it. Instead we are regarded as the naval equivalent of the Holstein troops so much admired by the late Tsar and so hated by the Russians themselves. Russian naval officers are unwilling to take instruction unless expressly directed to do so by the Empress.'

'They are as obstinate as mules,' Elphinston commented morosely, 'and invariably they make pretence of a lack of communication, imputing it to my faulty knowledge of the Russian tongue. This may be so, I admit it, but there is also a sorry reluctance to learn.'

'Given the fact that at the end of the last century, in the early part of the Great Peter's reign, they could not even get one ship to sea,' Samuel replied, 'the progress now visible is, I submit, remarkable. But once we have put to sea, I confess to a grave misgiving as to how they will fight. Ready obedience to command is not their strongest characteristic.'

'Why then,' said Fortescue Fynne, 'let us "Byng" one or two of them for good measure.'

For this remark he received an impatient scowl from Admiral Elphinston, whose already shortened temper had so far not been improved by his experience in Muscovy.

'Yet they bear the Tsarina a fanatic adoration,' Samuel concluded. 'For her they will gladly go through fire.'

'Then the Empress must come to Crondstadt and inspect the Division,' Elphinston said. 'She must observe for herself and in turn be observed. And she must be requested to this purpose here and now.'

In the event this was what happened. Her Imperial Majesty, foreseeing the necessity of dispatch, exerted her authority in removing every obstacle and delegated to Admiral Elphinston such power as no commander before him had ever been honoured with.

By now it was the autumn of 1769. The confidence reposed in him by the Empress gave new vigour to the active and spirited Admiral and not even the fact that once in the Mediterranean the expedition would be under the overall command of Count Alexei Orlov, whose knowledge of naval matters amounted to that of a child with a toy boat, could dampen the ardour of the Elphinston squadron.

Yet whether it took place by guile or as part of a deliberated plan to which they were not made privy, Samuel and the other British officers, who had already established themselves in the Russian Navy, were in no way encouraged in their endeavours by seeing Admiral Spiritdoff sail away with the three most efficient sixty-six-gun ships of the line before Admiral Elphinston and his party had properly got to grips with the immense task of fitting out the rest of the fleet.

'You had best tell Her Majesty,' Fortescue Fynne remarked to Samuel, 'of the bad effect on the rest of us caused by Admiral Spiritdoff spiriting off in this way.'

Samuel was unable to translate this English pun into passable French or Russian, but he did speak plainly to the Empress, observing to her that it was comparatively simple for her to impose her will in general terms, but not so easy to discover – until it was too late – the many omissions in the execution of her orders. Increasingly she had come to rely on her faithful and meticulous Scotsmen, and once Admiral Elphinston, to whom she did not warm but whom she respected, informed her that ready or not he must sail with the remainder of the fleet or risk being iced in for another winter, she authorized him to depart with a fair wind and God's blessing. Samuel, however, was held back and to him she gave a special assignment.

'You, Captain Greig, shall be Commodore to Count Orlov. You are to proceed independently to Leghorn in your ship *The Three Bishops*' (a sixty-six-gun line of battle ship). 'You are to sail now with all dispatch, overtaking the other two divisions of the fleet and making as direct a voyage as possible. At Leghorn you will await the arrival overland of your Commander-in-Chief. This will enable us to co-ordinate the advances east made by our armies with such naval action as may be necessary to assist the Greeks in the Archipelago to throw off their Ottoman yoke, and if fortune smiles on your endeavours, to penetrate the Dardanelles and to capture Constantinople where our Ambassador has been imprisoned.'

The auguries at the start of the expedition were scarcely of the best. The premature departure of Admiral Spiritdoff, taking with him, as he thought, most of the stores and the best sea officers, revealed also that he had omitted to load on board certain armament stores without which his guns could not be effectively used. By stealing a march he had secured himself no real advantage. He had left behind the code books which had been agreed. He had taken a year's supply of vodka but his surgeon's stores were discovered unpacked in a dockyard shed.

'I shall have something to say to that feckless impostor,' Elphinston remarked gruffly to Samuel as he took his own farewell. 'That is to say, if either of us reaches the Mediterranean in one piece. Of one thing at least we can be sure; we shall need the expert attentions of a dockyard before we set out to harass the Turk. Ensure, therefore, that you are at Leghorn before we arrive and that the Grand Duke of Tuscany will oblige Her Majesty by cobbling this so-called fleet together.'

Sarah had an augury of a different kind. The joyful, though not unexpected, news she conveyed to her husband on the eve of his departure meant, in effect, that he would not be able to attend the birth of their first child. It was a lonely prospect for both of them. At her special request Sarah spent the night before they sailed on board *The Three Bishops*. There was not room enough for the two of them in Samuel's bunk so they slept in each other's arms on the deck of his cabin, although neither got more sleep than a fitful doze. In the morning Sarah clasped herself to him with a fierce desperation, unable any longer to hold back her tears.

'I'm frightened,' she whispered in his ear, 'as scared as I never have been before. If I could find some reason to delay your going . . .'

Samuel comforted her as best he could, reminding her as he always did that they had both of them survived already many adventures and vicissitudes, that they were in the hands of Providence, and that, as he put it:

'We cannot have been brought thus far together in our lives for it all to end at this point – and if it does then it is God's will – but I sense that much lies ahead for both of us, we both have many tasks yet to achieve.' He wiped the tears from her face and kissed her tenderly. 'You must play your part, Sarah, and I mine.'

'Shall I come with you?' she murmured, burying her head in the crook of his arm. The pathetic, childlike tone of her voice made him laugh.

'Will you never give up this idea of running away to sea?' he said, remembering the little red-headed girl who had once cut off her hair and made a dash for it all the way from Edinburgh to Leith. 'You are shortly to be a mother. What woman would choose to have her babe on the heaving deck of a man of war?'

'I would,' Sarah cried and burst out into uncontrollable tears all over again, clinging to him as though she were drowning in sorrow.

'No,' said Samuel, gently disengaging himself and kissing her already ripening breasts for the last time for many, many months. 'My son may follow me to sea, but the ship has first to be built on land. There are enough hazards in life without adding to them in that way.'

Silently they dressed, as the ship stirred around them in the cold and windy dawn. Then Samuel poured out two good measures of brandy, and together they drank to the coming child and to the success of the expedition. A few moments later he was watching her being pulled away to the shore in a long-boat, a tiny miserable figure set against the craggy background of the fortress of Crondstadt, waving in a desolate fashion as the great ship of the line began setting her sails and preparing for the unknown adventures ahead.

Meanwhile Admiral Spiritdoff had been rewarded for his hasty, ill-found departure with hard weather in the Baltic and worse in the North Sea. This caused his squadron so much damage that he was obliged to seek shelter in Hull where temporary repairs were effected.

'I am beholden once more to these damned British,' Spiritdoff remarked to the Master of his ship, as they set sail again for the south. 'It was an evil day for all of us when the great Peter acquired the shipwright's art. A curse on all foreigners!' he added, as he remembered the steep repair bills he had been forced to pay in the Yorkshire port, 'this foray will deplete our exchequer before ever we sight the Turk.'

Admiral Elphinston fared even worse. No sooner had his division left Crondstadt, than one sixty-six-gun ship disobeyed every signal hoisted in the flagship and returned to port. A frigate sank. Straggling in a thoroughly lax and unseamanlike way, the squadron encountered bad weather on leaving the Baltic and put into Copenhagen, where the shoreside attractions of that amiable port so captivated the Russian officers as to make them forget the service they owed to their country and the most generous of sovereigns. As had further to be reported – and to the immense displeasure of Admiral Elphinston – 'they even grew remiss in their duty, and expressed a dislike to the expedition, having, as they said, been forced into it against their inclinations.'

Elphinston was therefore compelled to seek the active influence and authority of His Excellency Monsieur Philosophe, the Russian Minister at Copenhagen, so that the unhappy squadron could be got to sea a mere two days before the harbour iced up for the winter – which probability his dissident officers no doubt had in mind in their attempts to delay the sailing. They were immediately paid off in kind. A severe tempest struck them in crossing the North Sea, the ships were all separated and forced to seek shelter in different English ports. Indeed, Admiral Elphinston found himself unable to collect together his gaggle of goslings until Christmas. This was at Portsmouth where an examination of the ships proved them to be in a sorry condition, equalled only by the grave dispiritism of their crews. To this Admiral Elphinston applied two remedies. One was to get the Russian Ambassador at the Court of St James to secure full Admiralty assistance for repairs so that 'an order was despatched to the officers of the Yard to be on the most friendly terms and to render every service in their power'. The second was to maintain, or rather re-establish, morale with drills and disciplines under the somewhat critical and occasionally disparaging eyes of the British jack-tars.

A part of this latter process subsisted upon firing morning

and evening guns in the harbour and at Spithead. This soon proved to be a nuisance to Vice Admiral Geary, the Portsmouth Commander-in-Chief, and he requested the 'temporary Russian Admiral' to desist from the practice. To this Admiral Elphinston replied that it was the Muscovite custom to set watch in this fashion. 'Be that as it may,' he was tartly informed, 'you are now in a British home port and if you persist in this annoyance, orders will be immediately given for you to quit the said port.' Since Elphinston's substantive rank remained that of a Captain in the Royal Navy, whatever flag a foreign power might permit him to wear, he decided discretion to the best remedy to hand and the saluting procedure was brought to an end, the squadron remaining impatiently under the Dockyard care until April of 1770.

Samuel enjoyed better fortune in that *The Three Bishops* and her sister ship, the *Rasa Slav*, made an uneventful passage in company with a bomb ketch to Leghorn, where the Grand Duke of Tuscany had agreed they should remain until Count Orlov's arrival. Here a pause ensued. The expedition depended upon its two main divisions, that commanded by Admiral Spiritdoff and the other by Admiral Elphinston, and since both had in varying degrees become casualties of winter storm and inadequate rehearsal, Samuel and his two ships had little to do but wait in anticipation of a successful outcome to the repairs being effected in England.

Very nearly a decade had passed since Samuel had served in the Mediterranean. In comparison with the winter rigours of Crondstadt, where the port and its installations remained frozen up for several months, the mildness of the Mediterranean, even making allowance for the sudden and violent storms which blow up in the Leghorn area, presented to Samuel a pleasant contrast with the northern life he had adopted. He considered sending for Sarah, but in view of the long journey and the imminent birth, decided against it.

A lowering of tension and the enjoyment of climate are poor preparatives for a coming battle, and Samuel as Commodore employed his small squadron in daily drills and exercises. These were not popular with his Russian ships' companies and a constant guard had to be maintained against the insidious and creeping laziness which he had long recognized as a prime Russian defect. But he was also wise enough to grant shore leave from time to time, the abuse of which he punished with even more severity than he would have visited upon a British ship's company.

The thriving port of Livorno, which the British called Leghorn, did, however, provide the Russian officers with many of the civilized facilities to which the British Royal Navy is accustomed and which existed – alas – in little more than embryo state at Crondstadt. The Grand Duke of Tuscany chose to maintain a friendly relationship with the Russian Empress, and although Leghorn stood at a considerable distance from the target area which was the Morean peninsula, Natolia and the Dardanelles, the only practicable substitute, Menorca, lay even further away. The Russian Empress had endeavoured to obtain use of the Grand Harbour at Valletta in Malta and for this purpose had despatched thither an envoy to the Grand Master of the Knights of St John, furnished with a portrait of herself as a gift. This, however, had come to nought. Perhaps through a fear of allowing into the port any warships not under the Grand Master's control, perhaps to avoid the over-use of the island's limited resources – whatever the cause, the mission politely but definitely failed. The Grand Master kept the portrait but required the envoy to depart. The Russian fleet, therefore, could not look for succour there.

Count Orlov arrived in Leghorn in April 1770 with a considerable retinue and the news that Sarah had lost the child she had been carrying, in a premature birth. This intelligence distracted Samuel from his duties and threw him into a melancholia from which he extracted himself only with a great effort of will.

'It was my wish,' Orlov told him, 'to bring your lady with me from Petersburg but Madame informed me, with a firmness of intent the equal of the Empress herself, that she was not minded to undertake such a long journey in such a joyless circumstance. She also drew my attention,' he went on with an understanding smile, 'to the fact that you have work to do. Indeed we both of us have tasks to perform for our great Empress but your lady was too polite, I suspect, to include me in that general ordinance. She merely observed that it was you who would have the work to do.'

He paused and the smile broadened.

'I feel that your wife shares with Her Imperial Majesty one quality at least which bears upon us both. She knows her own mind. We are mere men, Samuel Karlovich, and it is our function to do as we are told.'

This seemed to afford the Lord High Admiral considerable amusement, and from his behaviour during the first few days after his arrival, the Commander-in-Chief appeared to be more concerned with social activities ashore than with naval duties afloat. Personally courageous though he undoubtedly was, the Count struck Samuel as something of a dilettante in the art of war.

'This is not going to suit Elphinston,' he commented in a letter to Sarah, 'nor does it your husband. We shall not defeat the Turk by a ceaseless round of receptions in Leghorn, when we should be better employed in seamanship and gunnery drills afloat. However as a mere Commodore in charge of his flag squadron, I must proceed with tact. I have long been of the opinion that once we can persuade these Russians into a great action, we may well find them to be exceptional fighting men. But they do not exert themselves either for me or for Orlov, but only for the Little Mother herself. If ever this fact is lost sight of, then we as a fleet are lost. The British officers are well aware of such realities. I feel, however, that the jealousies, arrogance and apathy of the Russian officers with whom we are in harness must, in some way, be kept in check, or disaster will stalk our wake.'

He did not expatiate on the grief he was suffering at their mutual loss but simply reiterated the belief to which both he and Sarah held. 'If it is the intention of Providence to enrich our union with a family, then Providence will arrange our lives to that effect. In the meantime, beloved Sarah, pray for your Samuel in the burdensome task which now lies immediately ahead.'

He was soon to be too occupied for any continued dwelling upon melancholy. Both Elphinston and Spiritdoff arrived with their component parts of the expedition, and early in May the Russian battle fleet sailed east. Of this the Turks had been duly warned but their Levantine habit of thought did not induce them to believe that such a squadron would ever materialize. No Russian warships, organized into a fighting fleet, had ever penetrated into the Mediterranean before – the Crimea and Black Sea ports being still in Turkish hands – and although the Turks entertained a healthy respect for the British Royal Navy, this did not extend to a foreign line of battle merely officered by the British. They were in for a nasty shock.

The Turkish fleet was known to consist of some fourteen battleships with attendant frigates and traders, amounting in all to nearly a hundred ships. Naturally it was Orlov's first purpose to seek out the whereabouts of this conglomerate mass. In this he was aided by Greek intelligence furnished to him by neutral ships plying between the Bosphoros, the Morean peninsula and western Mediterranean ports.

Accordingly on a Sunday morning, 20 May 1770, the Russian fleet passed between Cape Matapan, the most southerly promontory of the Morea or Peloponnesus, and the island of Cerigo or Kythera, once thought by the ancients to be the place where Venus and Helen of Troy had been born. That same afternoon they anchored at the entrance to the bay from which they discerned, on the top of a hill, the flag and the fire which were the signals agreed on to be made by the Greeks.

Shortly before dawn the next day, Admiral Elphinston dispatched his barge into the bay for a fuller intelligence, and about one o'clock in the afternoon, the boat returned with an old man and a Greek priest who instructed them on the proper anchoring places and on the disposition of the inhabitants. The Admiral then hoisted his flag in the frigate *Nadisda* and sailed boldly in, followed by the rest of the squadron. Their reception was tumultuous, the local Greeks flocking round the ships in their boats 'giving the most pleasing proofs of their sincere joy at our arrival, by bringing to us all sorts of fresh provisions in the greatest plenty.'

The troops on board the Russian ships were in high spirits and desirous of engaging the enemy at once. Admiral Elphinston expressed his opinion, therefore, that all the land forces borne by the Russian squadron should march at once to Missistra, the capital of the Morea, which was in Greek possession, and there attack Tripolitza, 'a very populous town and easy to be carried', continuing over the mountains to Napoli di Romani – or Nauplia – where they would assist the naval squadron which, in the meantime, would have sailed round the Cape to take possession of that fortress.

These plans, in the opinion of Admiral Elphinston, would produce a general revolt in the Morea in favour of the Russians. 'But they require a vigorous execution,' his dispatch to the Commander-in-Chief stated, 'and it must be done now.'

'There is nothing equivocal about the gallant Admiral,' Orlov remarked to Spiritdoff in the hearing of Samuel, who was only too unhappily aware of the mounting jealousy between the Russians and their British mercenaries. Orlov had decided to keep Spiritdoff's squadron under his own and Samuel's eyes – Samuel being his Commodore and right-hand man – and to allow Elphinston to forge ahead. In a sense this was only meeting circumstances half-way, since the natural fighting spirit of Elphinston took him whenever possible into the van.

'Perhaps it is fortunate that the troops on board his ships are not under Admiral Elphinston's command,' Spiritdoff remarked. Samuel noted that whenever Spiritdoff essayed a backhanded criticism of his British colleague in this way he conveyed the sentiment in Russian. Samuel's Russian was by no means fluent but he understood more than he could say in the language.

'Why do you speak like that?' Samuel asked. 'Were you not so eager for the fray yourself that you left Crondstadt with your squadron ahead of your orders? What is the objection to Admiral Elphinston's aggressive proposal?'

'Because by risking our troops in such a hazardous and relatively unimportant operation thus early in the campaign, we may jeopardize the whole.'

'The troops are there to fight,' Samuel retorted. 'What is in jeopardy should they succeed?'

The Russian Admiral glowered in silence for a moment or so and then shrugged his shoulders.

'Admiral Elphinston, you and I can do no more than advise the Commander-in-Chief,' Spiritdoff said in a somewhat surly tone of voice; 'it is for the Commander-in-Chief alone to decide.'

'The Turks have but a minimum force in the region,' Samuel addressed himself to Orlov. 'They are thus incapable of any great resistance.'

'I see you are siding with your British colleague,' Orlov replied, a slight sneer in his voice. Samuel raised his eyebrows and stared back at his Russian superior. A voice in him said that he knew ten times more about fighting on land or sea than this court playfellow, but he chased away this thought by reminding himself that his function was currently to draw these high commanders together into one fighting whole, not to increase their divisions.

'Admiral Elphinston is not here to defend his plan in person,' Samuel said, 'and whether he is British, Russian or Chinese is not to the point. We are all here to serve Her Imperial Majesty to the best of our ability under your overall command. As Admiral Spiritdoff has observed, we can only advise. But in my opinion it would be an excellent forward move. If it succeeds – and I see no reason why it should not – then it will put a new invigorating spirit into the troops which will stand them in good stead for the greater campaign ahead.'

'I appreciate the excellence of your thinking,' Orlov replied with a slightly disdainful glance at Samuel and then at Spiritdoff, who was affecting what Elphinston had once called his 'Russian smirk', 'however to go marching about the Morea for a dubious reward when our proper task is to search out and destroy the Turkish fleet, is not in my view what the Empress would wish us to do. So I regret we must hoist the negative to Admiral Elphinston's splendiferous plan.'

This disappointing decision was duly conveyed to Elphinston, who vented his rage on his Russian subordinate officers. They in return pointed out that they could scarcely be blamed for their Commander-in-Chief's opinions, and the upshot was a sorry worsening of relations between the Russian and British elements. However a new move was now to be made.

On Tuesday 22 May, a Greek vessel came into the bay which had been in company but two days previously with the Turkish fleet. 'It consists of eight ships of the line,' the Master informed the Admiral, 'besides zebecs and gallies, and it is gone into Napoli di Romani, there to await the arrival of six more of the line on passage from Constantinople with reinforcement of troops for the Morea and especially for Navirina.' This latter seaport was then being besieged by Count Orlov with Admiral Spiritdoff's squadron. In consequence of this intelligence, Admiral Elphinston summoned all his captains on board his flagship for a conference of battle and the next morning the fleet put to sea in order to round Cape Malea and engage the enemy before he could be reinforced. This movement was delayed for two days by an adverse wind blowing full into the bay, and it was not until Friday that the squadron was got out to sea.

On the following Sunday, pursuant to the Admiral's calculations, the Turks were discovered at the entrance of the gulf of Napoli di Romani and the signal for a general chase hoisted by the Admiral. At about five in the afternoon, the *Netromena* and the *Saratoff*, both sixty-six-gun line of battle ships, and the *Nadisda* frigate, bore down upon the enemy all colours flying and with the drums and trumpets animating the Russian sailors to battle. The Turkish flagship of eighty-four guns was closely engaged, as were the Turkish vice and rear admirals, After the fourth broadside had caused a havoc of destruction, confusion set in among the Turks who, imagining the Russian squadron to be much stronger than it was, ran for safety into the harbour of Napoli di Romani.

At this point the aggressive intentions of the British Admiral received a setback, in that the Russian ships did not pursue the Turkish fleet into the harbour, where they might well have destroyed them, but decided not to continue the fight. The Russian captains were severely reprimanded by Admiral Elphinston but since, under an extraordinary article in the Russian regulations, a captain is not obliged to follow his commander to attack a superior force, or even stay with him should he choose to wait for an enemy, the reprimand had but little effect other than enraging Admiral Elphinston himself.

Accordingly the British admiral dispatched an officer express overland to Navarina to acquaint Count Orlov and Admiral Spiritdoff with the situation, and to request a speedy reinforcement of two more ships of the line and the bomb ketch, with which he did not in the least doubt of destroying the whole Turkish fleet. Urged on strongly by Samuel, the hesitancy of Admiral Spiritdoff was overcome and the ships were sailed to the assistance of Admiral Elphinston.

In the meantime the Turks, no doubt concluding correctly that the Russian force was not as powerful as had at first been apparent, regained their equipoise and themselves put out to sea. Admiral Elphinston observed these motions and was resolved to await them at the mouth of the harbour, which was very narrow, and then to annoy them with a further destructive fire. The Russian captains, however, remained of a different opinion. They sent word that if Admiral Elphinston was resolved to lay to and would not make sail to retire and join Admiral Spiritdoff's squadron, they were determined to leave him.

Thus Admiral Elphinston discovered himself to be the hare instead of the hounds and was chased by the Turks, only being saved from destruction by a sudden and severe gale during which contact with the enemy was lost. Accordingly a somewhat crestfallen and angry Admiral Elphinston rejoined his Commander-in-Chief in the area of Navarina, and as soon as he had dropped anchor stormed on board the flagship.

'It is apparent, sir, that I no longer enjoy your confidence.'

'Why, sir,' Orlov replied genuinely surprised, 'what is the cause of this?'

'The Captains of the ships detached to my command found every excuse to avoid action, and when I questioned their insubordination, they declared themselves to be only subject to Admiral Spiritdoff's command – he being a Russian and not a damned foreigner. Since we were facing a superior force, they chose to invoke that extraordinary regulation by which they are not obliged to follow their Admiral should there be the slightest danger involved ...'

'I am obliged to you for the sarcasm,' the Commander-in-Chief interrupted, 'but pray come to the point.'

'Aye aye, the point,' Elphinston spluttered, his normally weather beaten cheeks now a vermilion red, 'the point is, sir, that no fighting force can be conducted on such a lily-livered basis – and certainly not by me. I therefore request you to subordinate me and my squadron to Admiral Spiritdoff's command, should he think it proper and not too indelicate to pursue and attack the enemy. Only thus will you secure obedience at that critical stage of affairs when obedience is essential.'

Orlov turned to Samuel and asked him to summon Admiral Spiritdoff on board the flagship, and in the meantime to remove his British colleague to his own quarters for refreshment. By the time Admiral Spiritdoff was brought face to face with Elphinston, it was evident that Orlov had used persuasion on him since he was 'all sugar and smiles'.

'There has been a misunderstanding,' Spiritdoff began before Elphinston could even open his mouth, 'and for any part of that for which I may be held to blame, I apologize. Since we are all loyally sworn to Her Imperial Majesty whom we must endeavour to please to the best of our ability, I submit for the Commander-in-Chief's approval that not only would it be undesirable for Admiral Elphinston to be put under my command, it would better serve the interests of the Empress if I were myself to be subjected to Admiral Elphinston's direction. He should lead the whole, sir, and I promise that whatever signals Admiral Elphinston shall make, I will repeat them.'

'Very well,' said Orlov, turning to Samuel who was trying to disguise his astonishment at this move, 'I agree to this proposal. See to it that Admiral Spiritdoff be provided with Admiral Elphinston's signal code so that we may all enjoy the fruits of this British diligence and activity.'

Although Samuel had quickly realized that Orlov was speaking with his tongue in his cheek, this was mercifully not apparent to the bluff Elphinston, who forthwith returned to his own ship and lost no time in hoisting his signal for a general chase to be made.

However it was one thing for the order to be given, another for it to be obeyed. Despite a sharp acrimonious prompting by Samuel acting in the name of the Commander in-Chief, Admiral Spiritdoff took no notice of this order for a general chase, his squadron remaining under close-reefed topsails in a very light breeze whilst Admiral Elphinston's division carried all the sail he could crowd on.

The pursuit of the Turkish fleet thus became, in Samuel's view, somewhat similar to that of a lame man running. Admiral Elphinston was for ever drawing ahead and then having to wait for Admiral Spiritdoff to catch up. During this time a French polacre and a Venetian frigate were both brought to and intelligence of the enemy gained from them. The Frenchman said that he was bound to Malta from Salonica with a cargo of tobacco, and had been boarded the day before by the Turks who told him that they every day expected to be joined by eight more stout ships and then they would fight the Russians; and that an army of eight thousand men, commanded by four Pashas, was ready in Salonica to march to the defence of the Morea. On learning of this, Admiral Spiritdoff became alarmed for the success of the expedition but his fears were not well received by the British officers nor indeed by Count Orlov himself.

At last, the enemy having been pursued into the bay of

Chesme on the Natolian coast, the stage was set on 7 July 1770 for the battle which was for ever after to illuminate the reputation of Samuel Greig. On the previous Sunday Samuel had received intelligence that the whole united force of the enemy was awaiting the Russian fleet between the Natolian shore and the south-east end of the island of Scio, having received positive orders from the Sublime Porte not to shelter themselves any longer in their harbours but to fight at all events without delay and upon pain of death.

Accordingly all the Russian sick were put on board Count Czernichoff's armed ship, which was ordered to proceed with them directly to Menorca. Various command changes were made by which proven officers were put in control of the prime ships of the line. Admiral Spiritdoff hoisted his white flag with a blue cross at the main topgallant mast head, Admiral Elphinston hoisted the same at the mizzen, Count Orlov, on board Commodore Greig carried the Union, and on Saturday 7 July at eight o'clock in the morning, the entire Russian fleet brought to within two leagues of the fort commanding the harbour of Scio. Here they had a full view across the bay of the Turkish fleet as it lay at anchor in a line of battle, some four leagues distant. In all, and including neutral ships at anchor off the port, some two hundred sail were counted.

10

'A fresh and honest eye'

As soon as the Russian fleet had anchored, the Commander-in-Chief summoned his Admirals and Captains to the flagship to give them his orders for the coming attack. There was a fair wind blowing from the south-west, bringing with it across the eastern Mediterranean the heat and indeed some of the sand of the Cyrenaican desert. Even at this early hour Samuel realized it was going to be a hot day, in every sense of the word. Certainly heat of a human kind was generated as soon as Admiral Elphinston came on board.

'The enemy being embayed on a lee shore,' he began briskly to Count Orlov, who was flanked on one side by Samuel and on the other by the shifty-looking Spiritdoff, 'I propose leading in my own ship to bring her abreast of the Grand Bashaw. I shall then let go my anchor with a spring on the cable, in company with two other of my ships on the bow and quarter of the Turkish Admiral, who appears to have positioned himself in the harbour more for his own convenience of a shore communication than for any resistance to a possible attack.'

Samuel watched Orlov out of the corner of his eye. The Commander-in-Chief was not enjoying this brusque address by his subordinate Admiral.

'I am obliged to you, sir,' Orlov began coldly, with a glance at Spiritdoff, 'however—'

'By this arrangement, sir,' Elphinston cut in, having taken another breath and in no way to be stopped, 'our nine battleships shall be engaged against but five or six of the enemy, the rest of their numerous fleet, which I have studied through the glass, being rendered useless as they could neither come to the assistance of those ships engaged, nor attempt to get out of the situation they are in, without the greatest peril of running on shore.'

The Count made an imperious and angry gesture of the hand which momentarily stopped the British Admiral.

'I would remind you, sir,' he said in a peremptory tone of voice which struck a chill into Samuel but appeared only to increase the scarcely-controlled rage welling up in Elphinston, 'that you are addressing your Commander-in-Chief with what appears to be the deportment and manners of a rigger. I have summoned you here to give you orders and not to receive them.'

He paused to allow the force of his personality to take its effect. Anger flashed from Elphinston's eyes but he contrived to remain silent.

'We have already observed the Grand Pasha's ship ourselves. Our conclusion is not that he has positioned himself for the convenience of a shore access but to be under the cover of batteries which I have no doubt he has raised on that small flat island to the west of the harbour mouth.'

'Precisely,' Elphinston interrupted, 'but his line of battle is so formed—'

'Sir, I must request you to keep silent and pay attention to your Commander-in-Chief.'

This reprimand had the desired effect and Spiritdoff rubbed salt into the wound by creasing his face into the sly smirk which so infuriated his British comrades.

'Now draw near, the rest of you, and I will outline the order of battle and my plan of attack.'

Samuel kept a wary eye on Elphinston as Orlov detailed his orders for the coming action. He could see that in no way did they commend themselves to Elphinston since Spiritdoff was to have the honour of leading the van, Orlov in Samuel's own division would follow in the centre and Elphinston was to bring up the rear. When the Commander-in-Chief had finished, he looked calmly at Spiritdoff and said:

'Will you then, sir, lead on both tacks?'

'Aye aye sir,' Spiritdoff replied, in a firm and pleased tone of voice.

'And you, sir,' Orlov went on turning to Elphinston, 'will you bring up the rear as I have ordered?'

'Had my plan been thought eligible,' Elphinston replied with a look at contempt at Spiritdoff, 'I should consider myself bound in point of honour to carry it into execution. But if the considered views of an officer of my experience are not to find favour, then I must inform Your Excellency that, in my opinion, the method of attack you intend to adopt is too uncertain of success for such a risk of reputation. I cannot do it by choice and desire you to stand me excused.'

'What say you, then, if you shall be expressly ordered to take the station allotted to you?'

'Why, sir,' Admiral Elphinston replied with the utmost scorn, 'I will do my duty.'

By eleven o'clock each commander had returned on board his own ship, at which hour the signal was made for prayers throughout the fleet to supplicate the Almighty to crown them with victory. There followed then an awful and profound silence in both fleets. It seemed to Samuel as he paced the quarterdeck in the midday heat that both sides must be penetrated with proper ideas of the great importance of the day and that every man jack, from the Commander-in-Chief to the youngest powder-monkey, had become aware of what he was to fight for and of how much the success of it depended upon his conduct and courage.

With forethought of any emergency which might require a special remedy, Samuel had attached to himself one of the younger Scottish officers, a Lieutenant Dugdale, whose expertise both in seamanship and gunnery was a welcome complement to his own, and whose red hair and freckles reminded him slightly of the child which Sarah had once been.

'Have you confidence in our Russian sailors?' Samuel enquired as they took a turn up and down the deck.

'I have the utmost confidence that they will fight as well as if they were Scotsmen,' Dugdale replied. 'They are sensible that they serve a sovereign of liberal sentiment so far as her fighting men are concerned, who takes a pleasure in rewarding merit even when unfortunate.'

'And do you consider them also aware – since it has been

explained to them often enough – that should we lose this battle, we have no friendly port in which to secure ourselves from the destruction that must inevitably follow a defeat?'

'Likewise the Turks, sir,' Dugdale commented, glancing across at their prey, 'they cannot escape the conclusion staring them in the face that should *they* lose the dominion of their own seas, which we intend to deny them, then their reward will be the severe frown of their haughty master, the Sultan, which I am told is the equivalent of a sudden and violent death.'

At noon Count Orlov threw out the red flag as the signal to attack and the Russian fleet, fully ranged in order of battle, descended upon the enemy like a gathering storm, every brave man now wishing either to survive with glory or die with honour.

Leading the van, Admiral Spiritdoff bore down upon the head-most of the enemy, the *Capitana Ali Bey* of a hundred guns. In the course of this approach, he received the fire of the other four Turkish ships in a position to respond to the Russian attack. At least a hundred of his men were killed outright, but Admiral Spiritdoff wisely reserved his own fire till he found himself within musket shot. Then, as if this delay had doubled the power of shock, he poured into the Turk a terrible holocaust of shot.

The compliment was as boldly returned, the which shot away the greater part of his rigging. Being thus disabled he endeavoured to stand out of the line to repair the damages with all dispatch but was prevented from so doing by a ball which carried away his starboard main-brace. The next shot unfortunately cut in two the larboard main topsail sheet so that his ship no longer answered her helm, and being to windward and as they neglected to let go an anchor, she fell with her broadside on board the Turk.

The crews of both ships now fought each other with redoubled fury, the Russians succeeding in driving the enemy from their deck, boarding them and then at once compelling them to strike their colours.

'By God, the Turk has been fairly taken,' Samuel

called out to Orlov through the noise of the bombardment they were themselves carrying out on another Turkish ship.

'And so has poor Fort,' Dugdale said at his side. Monsieur Fort, known on board as 'the French gentleman' was another of Samuel's foreign Lieutenants, and looking amidships Samuel saw that a Turkish shot had carried away his right arm, upon which he had fallen to the deck.

'Take him below to the surgeon, Mr Dugdale, and replace him yourself,' Samuel ordered, but as Dugdale leapt forward to obey it was already too late. The gallant Frenchman had begun to struggle to his feet when another Turkish ball cut him in two, mercifully putting an instant end to his life. Then as they looked away in horror—

'The Pasha's ship is afire!' one of the lookouts called down. Now that Spiritdoff's ship and the Turk had grappled together and a fierce hand-to-hand fight was in progress, the situation for both ships became critical in a matter of minutes.

'We shall lose them both,' Samuel called out to Orlov as, appalled, they watched a column of flame and smoke burst out from the Turkish Admiral's starboard quarter gallery. The sight compounded by the thunderous cannonade going on all around them, was dire enough to make the stoutest heart tremble. Confusion now reigned through both ships, as the fire increasing with lightning speed on board the Pasha's ship, proceeded to engulf the rigging, masts and sails of the Russian ship.

The crews of both, equally exposed to the same calamity, promptly forgot their animosities. They suspended firing upon each other and set their intention solely on the means of escape from those dreadful elements of fire and water. The Turk was now in a general blaze and, being to windward, exposed other of his ships to the same catastrophe. Struck with a panic, the whole fleet now took the fatal resolution, cut their cables and ran into the Bay of Chesme, which, being a mere mile in width and two in depth, afforded them but little prospect of security.

'Are we to improve the advantage, sir, by following them

in?' Samuel asked Orlov as they set about picking up survivors from the Russian and Turkish ships, amongst whom was a singed but otherwise undamaged Admiral Spiritdoff himself.

'The Grand Pasha has already suffered a shattering defeat,' Orlov replied, looking at the helter-skelter disorder inside the Turkish harbour. 'Let us benefit from this by recuperating ourselves and remaining here as a threat.'

'And allow them time to repair the damages they have suffered?'

The Commander-in-Chief looked haughtily from Samuel to Spiritdoff, who was leaning against a capstan physically bedraggled but with a justifiably triumphant look on his face.

'I trust that Admiral Spiritdoff has now disproved to your satisfaction the notions which you and the other British officers appear to hold that we Russians are dilatory in facing the enemy.'

'It is not a question of courage,' Samuel retorted. 'I never saw any lack of that – and I congratulate you, sir,' he went on to Spiritdoff, 'on the warm time you have just given the Turk. But we must press the advantage, we may not benefit from such a favourable circumstance again. We have them in disarray, bottled up in a most inconvenient port. Detach me a couple of fireships and I will finish them off.'

'Fireships are the province of General Hannibal, the Black,' Orlov said and ordered the Master of the Train to be summoned to his presence.

This officer, whose father had been presented by Louis XIV of France to Peter the Great, and who had been greatly raised in consequence, did not succeed in his preparation of the fireships till the following night, and this delay might well have proved fatal to the enterprise. In consequence, Samuel considered, the Turks in their critical situation might be supposed to come out and engage the Russians the following morning, or at the very least to mount sufficient batteries at the mouth of the harbour to prevent a Russian ingress. In fact they did contrive such a hazard but, perhaps on account of the haste with which it was prepared, it proved to be ineffectual.

At this point Samuel came into his own. With the consent and support of Count Orlov, he pressed on at full speed with the preparation of three old Greek vessels as fireships which were to follow him into the harbour in the *Rasa Slav*, in company with the *Netromena* and the *Europa*.

All was got ready by the following night. 'Commodore Greig is to hoist his Broad Pendant on board the *Rasa Slav*,' the Commander-in-Chief ordered and privately said to him:

'I approve your proposal to appoint Lieutenants Dugdale and Mackenzie to the two largest fireships and Lieutenant Borisovich to the third. May God speed and favour your endeavours, Samuel Karlovich, and rest assured that I have the utmost confidence in the success with which I am sure the operation will be crowned.'

Whilst in no way doubting the sincerity of His Excellency the Count Orlov, Samuel could not but reflect that it was one thing to stride up and down a flagship's poop deck, giving orders and receiving reports, quite another to lead three warships into a defended port which you are intending to destroy.

So Samuel once again commended his soul to his Maker and, when the hour struck, hoisted the signal to attack. Leading the way in the *Rasa Slav*, Samuel realized with something akin to an illumination of the spirit that danger had become the real climate of his life. He had never felt more alive than now, when there was every chance of his losing both life and limb, which engendered an exhilaration rare, dynamic and curiously whole in itself. 'It is only when all is at stake,' he afterwards told Sarah, that a man is all of a piece. We are none of us more than chessmen on God's chequerboard. Acceptance of that fact provokes an enveloping, protective calm of the spirit in the midst of the turmoil of battle. You forget about the danger and simply do what has to be done.'

The batteries which the Turks had contrived at the harbour mouth failed to stop the progress into the harbour of the Russian squadron, and as soon as they were inside, Samuel brought the broadsides of the *Rasa Slav*, the *Netromena* and the *Europa* to bear on the largest of the enemy's ships. It was a situation after his own heart. As the rain of fire began, he was pleased to observe that the Turkish fleet had been so crammed and crowded together that many of the smaller vessels had been hauled up on shore behind the greater ships, there not being sufficient sea room.

The Russian assault started with the conventional thunder of cannonballs and then after a short time Samuel introduced his new shells which seemed greatly to surprise the Turks. Stopping their own fire they watched these burning meteors flying at them and threatening destruction wherever they fell. However the surprise proved to be only momentary, and then the battle was resumed with increased vigour as all Turkish attention became directed on Samuel's three great ships. In the meantime, obedient to a previous signal, Lieutenant Dugdale led in the three fireships.

A further distraction of attention from the approach of the fireships occurred when a lucky shell from Samuel's ship fell into the bunt of the fore top-gallant sail of the weathermost Turk. The sail, being made of cotton, was set instantly in a blaze and 'almost sooner than it is possible to conceive, the ship lay all in flames'.

The leading fireship under Lieutenant Dugdale's command was now in a position to be fired, and thus to encompass the complete destruction of the enemy. However the men with him, who were to bring him off, either mistaking his orders or dreading to stay in the face of so much danger, jumped into the boat and rowed away as fast as they could whilst she was going with all her sails set down upon the enemy.

The gallant officer, although fully aware of the situation he was in, yet preferred his duty to his safety. Alone he remained, and when near enough, as he imagined, to take effect fired his pistol into the train, stayed to see it take fire and then boldly leaped into the sea. By great good fortune a Greek boat that was passing took him up just as he was sinking with fatigue.

The Turkish fleet appeared now to blend into one general blaze. Even to Samuel's long experienced eyes it nevertheless struck him as the very picture of distress and horror. Of the two hundred sail caught in the trap, but one sixty-four-gun ship and a few galleys escaped from the harbour.

'The rest, sir, went up in smoke,' Samuel reported to the Commander-in-Chief, after the action had been brought to an end and he had returned to the main fleet.

'The appearance from here,' Orlov said in his elegant drawl, 'was one of a dreadful sublimity – so complete has been the Turkish ruin! So complete our victory! I shall ask the Little Mother to reward you all suitably for what has been achieved. Now take you some rest.'

After their fleet had thus been destroyed, the Turks abandoned the town of Chesme and 'flew in a great wrath to the city of Smyrna some thirty miles away where they fell upon the Greeks (whom they regarded as friends to the Russians) and without distinction put hundreds of men, women and children to the sword before the Governors and Magistrates could stop their savage fury.'

Count Orlov made the signal for a general thanksgiving to the God of battles and the giver of victory, for the success of the Russian arms, the solemnity of which was greatly heightened by the attendance of the Greek clergy, who came from shore in their boats in regular procession, rowed round the fleet and then gave their benediction upon the whole.

Festivity and good humour now took possession of the Russian fleet. All the commanders were summoned to dine on board with His Excellency Count Orlov, the Lord High Admiral, where they were thanked in the name of Her Imperial Majesty. Lieutenant Dugdale was made a Captain of the first rank and rewarded with a ship. Samuel was raised to the rank of Rear Admiral and honoured with the second order of merit. He was later presented with an elegant inlaid dressing table, the late property of the Turkish Commander-in-Chief.

'So all is concluded for the best,' he wrote to his Sarah, 'except that I am gone hard of hearing in one ear, the which perhaps will remedy itself with the passing of time. Now for the Dardanelles!'

Reports of the great exploit were excellently well received in St Petersburg. The naval victory, in addition to progress by the army towards the Crimea, suited the Empress very well indeed. During her reign Russia had already been accepted as a major power in the world to a degree which Catherine's predecessors would have thought astonishing. The *réclame* brought her by the destruction of Turkish naval power at Chesme strengthened her hand both abroad and at home, and she was quick to express her gratitude in honours and also in more material ways to those who had served her so well.

Yet the crown still sat uneasily on her head. It was rumoured that the favourite was tiring and this later proved to be true. 'Her' Orlov was becoming increasingly careless in the extra-curricular pleasures he saw fit to take, and when knowledge of this behaviour could no longer be hidden from Catherine, it nearly broke her heart.

'During this time', she later wrote, 'I grieved more than I can say and never more than when other people were satisfied. Every act of tenderness caused my tears to flow and I believe I have never wept so much since I was born as in this year and a half.' She was a lonely, full-blooded woman in great need of love. 'If Fate had given me in youth a husband whom I could have loved, I should have remained always true to him.'

Fate, however, had not obliged her in this way and the offspring of her unhappy marriage to Peter III, the heir to the throne, was also causing her anxiety in ways she had hoped to avoid. The Grand Duke Paul was now in his teens. If he did not in absolute truth hate his mother, he gave a remarkably good impression of so doing and he held rigidly to the notion that she had had his father murdered. Such a 'Hamlet situation', foreign observers noted, did not make for easy relationships at court, the more so because ever since her elevation to the throne, the Empress had reposed no real confidence in anyone other than the Orlov brothers and their close associates.

The British Ambassador had written in one of his dispatches that 'since the Empress feels her title to the crown to be so precarious, she was forced after her accession to attempt to gain the love of her subjects. In an Empire such as Russia where the sovereign enjoys so much power, the best thing that can happen is that the monarch sees fit to govern with equity and moderation. This country has already felt the good effects of such a policy more evidently, perhaps, at the beginning of the reign than at present, since the Empress feels and acts more boldly the more secure in her power she feels.

'No one could be more active, could inform herself more thoroughly as to the genius of her subjects not study with more attentiveness the ways and means of ameliorating their condition. She is highly suspicious and dissimulates with those who do not blindly share her views. She treats the interests of the Orlov faction as her own and funnels through them all civil and military preferment. Aided by Monsieur Diderot, she is establishing a code of law. She is also founding, with much pomp and ceremony, academies, universities and schools for the education of her people. But when her real object is seen to have been obtained – namely that civilized Europe should be made fully aware of her generous views – culminating in the fact that even the Philosophes of Paris have promoted as opposition to the intolerant government of France the liberal ideas of the Russian Empress – "it is from the North that the Light has come" – then she leaves unfinished those establishments, begun at such cost, to house her schools and academies, and occupies herself with other things.'

Now with the waning of the Orlov influence, that of the Vorontsovs, the Panins and the Teplovs increased and soon there would be a new and permanent power behind the throne – that of Prince Potemkin, who had been no more than a Sergeant of the Guard at the time of the Empress's accession. Into this kaleidoscopic society Sarah and her mother had contrived to fit themselves, first as no more than the appendages of a foreign officer in the Imperial service but later, as Sarah's intelligence and charm began to make its mark, in their own right.

The foreign community of St Petersburg at that time formed what was perhaps the only effective link between Russia and civilization. The city had become an open window looking to the west. Since the principal communication to and from the Russian capital had perforce to be by the sea. it might be said that Petersburg stood at the very far point of a long maritime sock or peninsula, if the roles of land and sea were interchanged for purposes of the metaphor. Petersburg marked the end of the line – the terminus where ships turned round to begin the long voyage back.

Landward Petersburg looked east over a barren area of decreasing civilization which, with the exception of Moscow and one or two similar cities, stretched in unrelieved, savage, animal ferocity of climate, terrain and human values all the way to the Urals and then on through Siberia to China. Here serfdom and brute strength set the tone for all life, except that of the nobles living in medieval sloth on their vast lonely estates. Existence east and south-east of St Petersburg remained virtually untroubled by thought, whereas in the city itself the art of living together in a constantly growing and generally thriving community was increasingly being acquired. The Court attempted to set the tone, but in reality the quality of life depended upon, or at least was fed by, the foreign professional and trading community, a colourful conglomeration of every class and nationality.

Further along the coast an Irishman, Count George Browne, had been appointed Governor General of Riga. A Scotsman, Count James Bruce, was Governor-General of St Petersburg. There were German soldiers and Scottish sailors: there were Swiss, Dutch and English doctors,

French and Italian architects, a mixed collection of opera and theatre people and of poets, philosophers and artists of every nationality. The communities were under the overall tutelage of their countries' ambassadors, and of course their original language and common interest resulted more often than not in the same nationalities congregating together for social purposes.

The British community, perhaps because of the ancient City of London attitude to trade, was one of the more liberal collections of foreigners in St Petersburg. It included an English gardener who was advising the Empress on the gardens at Peterhof and the Winter Palace, a Scottish banker called Forbes who was also an author, and even a lady sculptress called Anne Seymour Damer. Merchants and the professional classes tended to live near the Moika Canal, and whilst high society in Petersburg became all the time more glittering and spendthrift, the English community with its gentlemanly, self-controlled virtues of tolerance, decency and an innate sense of fair play became a corrective to the oppression, unrest and violence which the great Russian families and their bailiffs were engendering in the environs of St Petersburg, together with the bitter crop of class hatred which was to follow.

Whilst the Court had always tried to model itself on Versailles, and such old Russian social values as there had been – and there were not many – were all the time being replaced by the new corrupt values of the Louvre and of Versailles, the small British community lived in unostentatious elegance, conscious of their 'apartness', distinguished by a sense of humour and valuing the civilized virtues of restraint.

Naturally the British, however prudish their detractors might make them out to be, were, like all human beings of all times, exposed to the temptations of love affairs and of personal intrigue. They were no strangers to the playing of cards for high stakes, the backbiting and the amorous disasters which social life in any civilized country at that time entailed, and they proved as adept as any native Russian in navigating the dark passages and secret stairways, in dealing with the bribery and the spying and in relishing the wining, the dining and the dancing which were inseparable from the masquerades, the follies and the pleasures of St Petersburg life.

From time to time the British Ambassador, who kept more closely in touch with his compatriots than did his French, Austrian or Prussian counterparts, would give a reception at his Embassy for the British community alone. This was thought privately by other foreign envoys to be a somewhat questionable habit, bordering on bad taste, since all classes from visiting Lords to resident shopkeepers would be invited and would freely, and for the most part unsnobbishly, mingle together. However from the British Ambassador's point of view, these gatherings yielded one paramount value – there took place an exchange of information and of ideas to which his brother Ambassadors had but little similar access.

'And what is the opinion of the Vorontsov family?' the British Ambassador enquired of Sarah at a reception he gave for the British community of St Petersburg some little time after the news of Chesme had been received and digested.

'As to what, my Lord?'

'Why as to this latest exploit of the Orlov clan – so ably assisted by your distinguished husband and by Admiral Elphinston. Will it restore the favourite?'

Sarah studied her questioner with a careful attention before answering. She had already learnt to exercise restraint in giving forth opinions in Russia.

'The Vorontsovs are persuaded that once the Empress makes up her mind, then woe betide anyone who attempts to reverse such a decision.'

'All then is lost *chez* Orlov?'

'Your Lordship would be better informed as to that than a mere grass widow,' Sarah said with a twinkle. She liked Lord Cathcart but thought him even more devious than Monsieur Sabatier, his French equivalent, who also made consistent attempts to pick her brains. 'Doubtless Your Lordship has heard it said that the habit of the favourite of "distancing himself" from the Empress in order to go – shall we say – hunting, is now likely to result in his being "distanced" for ever.'

'*La jalousie?*'

'I do not believe the Orlovs use the French language,' Sarah countered, 'but then equally I do not imagine that the Empress has much use for gross Finnish girls . . .'

'You are well informed,' the Ambassador remarked.

'I have a friend whose house is adjacent to that of Monsieur Saurin,' Sarah said, 'the *valet de chambre* who has been elevated to the rank of Chamberlain, but without the right of appearing at court.'

'You are *very* well informed,' the Ambassador said drily. 'And how is the child?'

'There are three children,' Sarah said, 'and Saurin has the care of them. The Empress sees them from time to time, but only on rare and very discreet occasions.'

She paused and studied the Ambassador, whose expression told her that he was aware of the situation to which she referred. She therefore decided to continue and said with a smile:

'There are many people who believe that a secret marriage took place before the Coronation but that Monsieur Panin would never agree to a public announcement.'

The Ambassador nodded his agreement.

'Count Panin may yet be appointed Chancellor, since he appears to have more state secrets in his keeping than any other official of the court.'

'Or perhaps be appointed to Siberia, my Lord.'

'Not whilst he retains his present responsibilities and the confidence of the Grand Duke Paul – though what will transpire if the young man allows himself to be pushed into this Prussian marriage lies in the lap of the Gods.'

Sarah decided to bring the conversation round to a more personal plane.

'What would your Excellency say, were my mother and I to journey south to Tuscany later in the year?' she enquired. 'I believe that my husband's squadron will need to put into Leghorn for refurbishment.'

The Ambassador considered this question for a moment or so before answering.

'I will enquire of Her Majesty,' he said in the end. 'Admiral Greig is highly considered by his Commander-in-Chief, but in view of what we have a moment ago been discussing, perhaps there will be a change in the high command. I comprehend that Admiral Elphinston is on such uneasy terms with Orlov and the other Russian officers that he is being desired to go to Leghorn under an assumed name – so as not to detract from the glory attaching to the Commander-in-Chief. Perhaps matters are not all as they should be in the Russian fleet. Once again it appears to be jealousy which rules the roost. I am informed that had it not been for the gallant actions of Admiral Elphinston and of your husband, there might well have been no victory to celebrate, and that their plan to penetrate the Dardanelles has been thwarted in the interests of security – or as some would prefer to call it "apathy".'

He looked away into the distance and then concluded by saying:

'I think it an excellent idea for you to visit Leghorn – provided, of course, that Her Majesty agrees.'

This suggestion met with a good reception. A little later Sarah was summoned to a private audience of the Empress. Although Her Imperial Majesty was pleased to indicate that she favoured Madame Greig with her trust and that accordingly she was in a privileged position, Sarah nevertheless felt herself overawed every time those piercing blue eyes rested their attention on her. The Empress, in turn, was fully aware of the effect she had on those brought into her presence, and from time to time she plainly enjoyed the exercise of her power. She bade Sarah feel at ease, a command easier to give than obey, and then quickly came to the point.

'We understand that you seek a *congé* to be with your husband at Leghorn,' the Empress began, 'and to this we assent. There is one condition, however.' The Empress paused reflectively, staring at Sarah, and then continued:

'You are to correspond with us in private – under seal

– as to the state of affairs you find on your arrival and during your stay in Tuscany. You are to be completely free in the expression of your opinions. You are to write what you see and hear. Above all you are not to report to us what you imagine it would please us to hear but only what you discover, and yourself consider to be the truth.'

'I am a poor hand at gossip, Your Majesty,' Sarah said, deferentially looking away. She had no relish for being appointed a spy and it was on the tip of her tongue to say so. The Empress read her thoughts like an open book.

'We appreciate that you have but little of our Russian taste for servile flattery and that is why we are assigning you this simple task. We are not interested in gossip. We do, however, need a fresh and honest eye on matters on which we may later require to pass judgment.'

The Empress picked up a paper from her writing table and read from it with a sardonic smile.

' "The greater part of those composing the court are animated by no other passions than a low and implacable jealousy, a love of gold and every element of a gross and ostentatious vanity. Friendship, virtue, manners, consideration of others and integrity are here devoid of sense. Their only interest is self-interest and the preferment of those who will be either their patrons or their creatures." Thus wrote a French Ambassador to his King. A similar opinion was furnished to the English King by Lord Cathcart's predecessor. "Our error over Russia is to consider it a civilized nation and to behave accordingly. Russia in no way merits such a title – in spite of the opinion of those who know it not – pride is the son of ignorance and no one need be surprised to see the proceedings of this court stamped with arrogance and vanity ... there is not one Minister here who understands Latin and nothing is rarer than the first elements of literature. I might as well cite Clarke and Tillotson to the Divan of Constantinople as invoke the authority of Grotius or Puffendorf when treating with the Russian Ministers." '

The Empress paused, judging the effect of the documents she had just read on the Admiral's lady. As Sarah maintained an interested silence, the Empress eventually continued:

'Thus you will comprehend, madame, that we are not unaware of the real opinion in which we are held, despite our success in arms. We cannot come to a right conclusion on subjects requiring decision if flattery, vanity and self-interest besmear the reports we receive.'

'I am honoured to be so trusted by Your Majesty,' Sarah said, privately hating the task she had been given and wondering by what means the Empress had come into possession of the dispatches she had just read out.

'In that event,' the Empress said briskly, indicating the audience to be at an end, 'see that in turn you honour our trust and tell your husband, the Admiral, that we will send him whatever he considers necessary for a continuing successful prosecution of the war, since we also comprehend that in making any such demands, self-interest will be kept to a minimum. We are aware that certain other of our Admirals are minded differently.'

11

Conflict at Leghorn

By the time Samuel and Sarah were reunited in Leghorn, thanks to the will of the Empress and the good offices of the Grand Duke of Tuscany, an almost unbridgeable chasm had opened between the Commander-in-Chief, Count Orlov, and Admiral Elphinston, the senior British officer under his command.

This had come about primarily because Admiral Elphinston, in his gruff outspoken manner, made little effort to conceal the low opinion he held of Admiral Spiritdoff and of what he had dubbed 'the useless brigade'. Elphinston took every opportunity – and there were many – of laying complaint as to the Russian's slackness in general and his particular wish, as it seemed to Elphinston, of avoiding aggressive action at all times when advantage might have been gained over the Turkish enemy.

When Count Orlov refused to pay attention to such strictures, Admiral Elphinston extended his comments indirectly to include the Commander-in-Chief himself. The relationship between them thus became cool. In this unfortunate clash of personality Samuel endeavoured to put the deafness he had acquired in battle to a practical use and to avoid being drawn into the polemics of a divided command. He remained the closest to Count Orlov of all the British contingent and therefore 'the first to do duty as a whipping boy' Fortescue Fynne observed to Sarah, when they were all three dining together in the house which had been put at their disposal in Leghorn.

'However,' he went on with a wink and a smile, 'if our Honest Sam can survive a little longer, he may yet outlast the Lord High Admiral himself, whose knowledge of the sea remains as perfunctory as his social graces are charming.'

'I should have thought a good social manner to be

scarcely an ideal attribute for command at sea,' Sarah remarked. This 'interference' from the distaff side did not commend itself to the recently promoted Admiral, who quickly put in:

'And I would have thought it scarcely the province of a lady to pass judgment on such matters.'

Sarah glanced at Fortie who was studying them both with a close attention. She knew if need arose that she could rely on the support of Samuel's oldest friend. Although a young man in spirit, Fortie's hair had by now turned almost white. This seemed to give him a dignity and certainly a 'presence', belied only by the perennial levity of his outlook which had stamped on to his features an ironic twist. He was still — perhaps more than he had been in earlier years – an attractive man to Sarah, who was fully aware that he found her 'an engaging creature' himself.

During that first winter in Crondstadt, indeed shortly after she and Samuel had been married – which now seemed so long ago – Fortie had once seized the advantage of an ill-lit passage to slip his hand quickly up her skirt and although she had soundly rebuffed him, pointing out that if his advances were abominable, his timing was even more lamentable, she had not only been flattered but, being an honest and direct woman, had admitted to herself that she, too, found Fortie a charming and compelling man with whom it would have been only too agreeable to go to bed. But Sarah was never minded to be unfaithful to the man whom she really adored with all her heart. So Fortie remained what he had always been – a good friend to both of them, and from time to time both were able to employ his services in resolving matters between them on which there was disagreement.

'You will observe, my dear Sarah,' Fortie now said, 'that your husband the Admiral's deafness miraculously disappears when occasion demands his close attention.'

'Keep your opinions to yourself, you aged goat,' Samuel said sharply. 'Sarah is not in my good books tonight, as well she knows.'

Sarah drew herself up and her eyes seemed to flash with a green fire.

'Because I am merely doing my duty,' she said, 'and since when has duty been the prerogative of the male sex?'

'Come, come, madam, enlighten this aged goat. What duty is it which has so discountenanced the Admiral?'

'Why sir, my duty to the Empress,' Sarah replied, and proceeded to reveal to Fortie, under an oath of secrecy, the reporting assignment she had been given by the Empress.

'When I acquainted my husband of this,' Sarah went on with a hard look at Samuel, 'the which task I undertook immediately before your arrival tonight, you would have imagined me to have absconded with the Crown jewels.'

'A domestic Court of Enquiry?' Fortie said. 'Your Admiral is something of a specialist in naval courts-martial. Ask him about the loss of the *Svetislov*.'

'You will do no such thing,' Samuel said, beetling his brows at Sarah.

'My husband has taken great offence because the Empress, to whom he is also sworn, has appointed me – very much to my distaste – her spy here in Leghorn. The Empress is a law unto herself. That fact is well known to all who serve her, whether at a distance or close at hand. What option in such an assignment do any of us have?'

'It is a shock to discover one's own wife a common informer.'

'It is a shock to discover an old friend to be no more than a pompous ass,' Fortie remarked drily. 'And should your wife find her life to be intolerable married to such an old Scottish hypocrite, then she knows to whom she can turn.'

'Aye,' said Samuel, a twinkle returning to his eye, 'you'd like to get your hands on her, would you not, you profligate Sassenach? Well, you'll not be doing anything of the sort, Master Fynne.'

'Captain Fynne, if you please,' Fortie said, realizing that the danger had passed. 'Now Sam, when you have replenished our glasses, regale our delicious and delectable Sarah with your standard account of the stranding of one of Her Majesty's finest ships. She may find it of value in her next secret despatch. Of course,' he went on to Sarah, 'this was a purely naval disaster which took place in a driving storm, but it will in some measure convey to you what service in the Russian fleet can entail. Now, Sam, the floor is yours.'

For a moment or so Sam scratched his head, wondering if Fortie and Sarah were in collusion to make a fool of him and then launched out into a story which Fortie had described as 'standard', but which he had had to tell many times to Orlov and other of the senior officers.

'In the court of enquiry which I held concerning the loss of this ship,' Samuel said, 'it appeared that the wind had changed four points after the Captain had delivered his orders and retired to his cabin. The Master or Pilot said that he had been on deck at one o'clock on the Monday morning, and on observing that the wind had veered four points, he desired that the Lieutenant – a Russian – should put the ship about directly, for fear of the shoals of Lemnos. But he refused, saying he should abide by the Captain's order which was not to put her about till two o'clock. He was then desired to go down and acquaint the Captain with the change that had happened, which he also refused, whereupon the master told the lieutenant that unless he tacked about immediately, he would throw up the charge of the ship and retire to his cabin, which he did; and heard no more of her till she struck on the shoals. Thus by carelessness and obstinacy perished the best ship in the whole fleet. A tragedy of this nature would be unthinkable in a British man-of-war. Alas, in the fleet in which we serve, a different attitude prevails.'

'And will the Empress be so informed?' Sarah enquired.

'The Empress will receive the report of the court of enquiry,' Samuel said, looking into the distance. 'I doubt, though, that she will have other than a biased account of our failure at Lemnos since that would reflect upon the competence of the Russian officers concerned.'

He looked angrily at his young wife as if it were in some way her fault that the Empress had required her to report in the way she had described.

'This imperial command to spy on the behaviour of brother officers I find to be highly distasteful,' he said, and then, observing that Fortescue Fynne was suppressing a smile, went on: 'You still appear able to find an element of humour in this . . .'

'How else can it be regarded?' his old friend retorted. 'Are we not both under a similar obligation to the Lords Commissioners of our Sacred British Admiralty? The raiment of a vestal virgin ill becomes you, Samuel. It might trip you up, causing you to fall down the hatch arse over tip – if Madame will excuse a vulgar naval expression.'

'And what was the failure at Lemnos?' Sarah enquired. There was once more a hard, business-like look in her eye which, on a previous occasion, had caused Fortescue Fynne to bow towards her and murmur, 'I name this warship *HMS Implacable*', after which he had not been invited to share their company for several days. Captain Fynne did not appear invariably seized of the gravity of naval service and indeed was accused of occasionally laughing out of turn, an action indecorous to an officer and a gentleman. It had long been Fortie's opinion, backed by the red-headed Sarah, that Samuel would go to the top and that this was indeed his rightful position. So far as Fortie himself was concerned, he accepted that his more easy-going nature would always delay a preferment, but this did not cause him undue anxiety.

'Well, Sam,' he said, 'pray poke another disaster through the hawsehole for the benefit of Madame and the Imperial ear.'

'The island of Lemnos', Samuel began, 'is of quadrangular form and somewhat greater in size than Malta, being, I believe, some twenty-five miles in length by fifteen in breadth.'

Fortie suppressed a yawn and then gave Sarah a wink.

'I don't suppose the Empress wants a lesson in geography,' he said.

'Well she's going to have one,' Sam said. 'If you do not set the scene, how can the play be understood? So just you trice your ears out on a bowline and hold your tongue for a while.'

'You see what Orlov has had to endure?' Fortie said with another little smirk at Sarah, but Samuel did not catch the remark or the look and had again launched out on his tale.

'Lemnos has a good harbour in Mudros which could serve as a convenient base for the fleet, since from it the Dardanelles and thus Constantinople might well be placed under Russian control. When the island was possessed by the Venetians, the villages were populous producing corn and wine, whereas now they are but thinly inhabited.'

Fortie now made a circular gesture with his hand as if winding something up.

'And what, pray, does that signify?' Samuel asked.

'I was keeping the hurdy-gurdy in motion.'

'If you bait a bull too far, he will certainly charge,' Sarah said warningly to Fortie.

'It is high time you got yourself a wife of your own,' Sam said, 'instead of trying to drive a wedge between Sarah and me.'

'Och away, mon. Where would be the fun in that?'

Sarah went across and put her arm round her husband's shoulder and then kissed the top of his head.

'It takes a man to get a wife,' she said, and put her tongue out in a very vulgar manner at Fortie. 'Now go on about Lemnos.'

'Well,' said Sam, instantly mollified by the touch of her lips and the show of affection, 'the town of Lemnos itself is small and defenceless, not containing above twenty houses which are of stone. However the Turkish garrison at that time consisted of some fifteen hundred men. Now then, as soon as the Russians had landed their troops and began to throw shells into it, the Turks retired into the castle and prepared for a vigorous defence.

'The Russians, assisted by Greeks and Albanians, turned all their attention to the reduction of Lemnos and expected that a surrender would soon follow; but finding that this plan did not succeed, they resolved to batter the walls and endeavour to take it by storm. Two breaches were soon effected and an attempt made on one of them, but either for want of resolution in the assailants who made the real attack, or because of the neglect of those who were to have made the false one, it proved unsuccessful. The Greeks and Albanians then had considerable offers made them to induce a trial of their fortune a second time alone. They absolutely refused, unless joined by the Russians of whose lives the Commander-in-Chief was very tender, and therefore it was resolved to turn the siege into a blockade.

'Thus they went on from day to lay without anything material happening, except frequent proposals from the enemy who began to fear that without some seasonable showers to fill their reservoirs, they should inevitably be obliged to surrender at discretion.

'About a month later, some forty or fifty English and Swedish seamen who were just arrived in a vessel purchased here at Leghorn, sent a letter to the English in the fleet who had before voluntarily offered to mount the breach under the command of Lord Effingham, that they were desirous of sharing this honour with them. The next day thirty more Englishmen from different vessels desired that they might be permitted to join their countrymen in the same hazardous undertaking. I then settled matters and agreed on a plan of attack by which the English were first to mount the breach with cutlasses and pistols, supported by a hundred of the bravest Greeks, two hundred of the Russian troops being employed to close the assault, whilst other Greeks were to be employed in bringing up sandbags and fascines to form a lodgement. Everyone now wished for the hour of attack. Success seemed to us to be pretty certain, crowning us with honour. It appeared that the number of assailants would have been considerably greater than the Turks could have brought to the defence of the breach, as their force would have been divided by our making three false attacks at the same time.'

'And how said the Russian commander?' Sarah asked, by now completely absorbed by the story.

Samuel raised his eyebrows and then said with an ironic tone in his voice:

'Why – that the enemy being greatly distressed for water would probably soon surrender; but if at any time the attack of the breach should be thought necessary, then the English might be assured of having the honour to lead it.'

The two British naval officers looked at each other, pursing their lips. Comment upon this matter seemed to be superfluous, even to Sarah.

'Then three weeks later', Fortescue Fynne put in, 'the fatal news arrived of the *Svetislov* being lost. This greatly damped the spirits of the besiegers and gave new vigour to the besieged.'

'Nevertheless,' Samuel continued, 'two months after the blockade began, no relief being sent and their water quite exhausted, the capitulation was finally settled on both sides, the Turks giving hostages to deliver up the place as soon as the vessels arrived to transport them to the port agreed upon. What then took place? The next afternoon, almost before I knew what was happening and certainly before I had the courtesy of a forewarning, the tents in the camp were suddenly struck and the troops ordered to a post not distant from the side of a hill.'

'And why was that?' asked Sarah.

'There was an alarm that a body of Turks had been landed on the north-west side of the island to attempt a raising of the siege. This resulted in orders being sent in the night for all the people to embark on board the ships.'

'No bono panico,' Fortescue Fynne remarked and Samuel nodded.

'It was, I vouchsafe, as certain as I am standing here now that those landed by the Turks could not have exceeded a thousand men. A mere thousand men on a basically hostile shore – whereas the Russians and the Greeks must have doubled that number, to which must be added the seamen who could have been spared from the fleet. These amounted to no less than a thousand, three hundred of whom would, in my consideration, have been sufficient to keep the garrison blocked up whilst the remainder, if suitably disposed of in the suburbs, would most undoubtedly have been able to oppose and to defeat a greater number of troops coming, as did these Turks, with scant ammunition and no cannon whatever.'

'But His Excellency the Count thought otherwise?' Sarah enquired.

'Alas, yes,' Samuel said, 'the Commander-in-Chief maturely weighed the advantages and disadvantages – and then decided to raise the siege. Thus no Russian life would be lost, only some three months of time spent in the purchase of an object which was later to be senselessly abandoned until reinforcements could be obtained. The favourable moment was lost.'

A brief silence fell on the two officers as they thought back on the event just described.

'What happened then?' Sarah asked.

'I regret to tell you that our Greek allies expressed a scathing contempt for such faint-heartedness. And who can deny they were right? Yet worse was to follow. Later, when the fleet was wintering in Mudros harbour, the Russians erected their ovens on shore. One day in view of the whole fleet, the Turks sallied from their castle, burnt the bakehouses and kitchens and then retired in good order without the least interruption from the Russians who, by landing a few hundred men on the neck of land between the harbour and the castle, might have cut them off.

'Then, when intelligence was received that the Sublime Porte would shortly be reinforcing the island, Count Orlov and his brother removed themselves to Leghorn, followed by Admiral Spiritdoff. In all, what does this singular conduct imply – especially bearing in mind that when Admiral Elphinston was later desired to come to Leghorn, he was required to do so incognito under the name of Howard?'

Samuel looked from his wife to Fortescue Fynne. The truth was only too apparent to all of them, and it did not redound to the credit of Orlov or of the Russian High Command. Another silence followed. Then Samuel continued with a glance at Sarah:

'Since Admiral Elphinston has now been summoned to Petersburg, it is important that Her Imperial Majesty be enabled to see through the malicious motives of his enemies in the Fleet.'

'Indeed!' said Sarah, embracing her husband affectionately but unable to resist taking advantage of the opening he had given her. 'Did you not remark earlier that it is scarcely the province of a lady to pass judgment on such matters? Even a lady with a special assignation from the Empress herself?'

'I fear the Admiral's deafness will suddenly return,' Fortescue Fynne remarked with a smile at Sarah, 'but in the meantime you have certainly scored a broadside on his flagship. You had better board him with another flagon of wine to repair the damage.'

Over the next few years Samuel contrived not only to survive – a feat in itself – but also successfully to adapt to the new naval, social and political conditions of a decade charged with extraordinary events not only in Russia but in the rest of the civilized world. These were to alter life in a number of different but significant ways. 1770 – for Samuel the year of his first major victory against the Turkish fleet – saw elsewhere the discovery of Botany Bay in the Antipodes by James Cook, claimed by Sarah's mother to be a distant cousin. Exploration, Discovery and Progress were in the air. A couple of years later the first carriage traffic over the Brenner Pass began. Communications generally were opening up. Science leapt forward with the discovery of oxygen and James Watt invented the steam engine. But progress often also brought revolution in its train. Before Samuel returned to St Petersburg after the ending of the war, a Pretender to the Russian throne called Pougatchev was to lead a Cossack revolt in the south-east which delayed the Crimean victory and ended by his being sent to his Empress in a cage. Across the Atlantic ocean the British were already in deep trouble with their American colonies, and in France Louis XVI had been compelled by general unrest to recall the Parlements and to appoint Turgot as Controller-General.

As had been forecast in Leghorn, Admiral Elphinston decided to relinquish his command, returning to St Petersburg where he was duly honoured and rewarded by the Empress, somewhat to the surprise of the Counts Orlov and to the chagrin of the subordinate Russian Admirals. Elphinston then reverted to service in the British Royal Navy, being appointed in a dim glow of anticlimax to the Captaincy of a guardship at Portsmouth. His departure left Samuel unquestionably and firmly established as the senior British officer in the Russian service. This strengthened his authority, yet Orlov remained his jealous and watchful Commander-in-Chief and Samuel still found himself in uneasy harness with Admiral Spiritdoff and other Russian commanders who, in Samuel's opinion, had 'dodged out from under' when the going was hot, or in blunter phraseology had simply run away when victory lay in their grasp.

'We shall never come to a final conclusion with the Turk,' he had told Orlov, 'until the discipline in the fleet you command is such that an order from the flagship is obeyed instantly and without demur upon pain of death.'

Orlov had given a ready agreement to this and had promised corrective measures. However he had also agreed with Admiral Spiritdoff that the Russian Navy would never come into its own whilst it was dominated by officers from abroad. 'We will do things in our own manner,' Admiral Spiritdoff had suggested and Count Orlov had also assented to this.

The time, therefore, between the Battle of Chesme in 1770 and the equally definitive battle of Shumla in 1774 was spent by the fleet, based on Leghorn, in forays and expeditions to destroy Ottoman fortifications and stores in the Archipelago, but in no way to replace the Turks as the occupying power. When the Sublime Porte was at last driven to sue for peace and Russia acquired her outlet to the Black Sea which had been the prime object of the war, Samuel sailed with 'his' fleet back to St Petersburg. By then, however, the power of the Orlov clan was in process of being broken.

'We have here a change in the decoration,' the British envoy reported to his Foreign Secretary in March 1774. This change he proceeded to analyse as the most important matter meriting attention since Catherine had first taken over the reins of state. The interregnum in the Imperial bed, which had followed Gregory Orlov's dismissal, had been filled by a young cornet in the House Guards called Vassilitchikov. This new favourite was fifteen years younger than his Imperial mistress. But apart from the prowess for which he had been selected, his only notable achievement lay in nearly boring the Empress to death. His singular lack of intelligence, wit or conversation, however, commended him to those courtiers closest to the throne, since a few minutes in the young man's company sufficed to make it unquestionably clear that any influence he might wish to exercise on affairs of state would be nullified by his crashing stupidity.

Then, in the spring of 1774, General Potemkin arrived back from service on the eastern front where, it was rumoured, he had been *universellement détesté*. Initially a friend of the Orlov brothers, his role as Sergeant of the Guard at the seizure of power twelve years previously had brought him into frequent contact with the Empress. This inevitably aroused jealousy among the reigning favourites. 'In consequence and on what pretext I do not know,' the Ambassador continued, 'he was hurried off to Sweden and, after his return, prudently lived in retirement until the commencement of the war when he again took up military duty in the somewhat advanced rank of Major-General. He possesses a gigantic and ill-proportioned body and his physiognomy is far from pleasant. But from all I have been told he has a considerable knowledge of men and a discernment unusual in a Russian. Despite his debauched way of life, he maintains a close liaison with the clergy. Armed with such qualities and thanks to the indolence of his adversaries, he can flatter himself with a reasonable prospect of achieving what is undoubtedly a soaring ambition.'

Such then was the general setting of the scene at court when Samuel found himself back in St Petersburg in the late summer of 1774. Sarah had proceeded overland the previous year with her mother, who had for some time been in a decline, an anxiety which ended with her demise during the hard northern winter which followed.

The joy with which Samuel became reunited with his sprightly, red-haired, straightbodied Sarah was marred only by the memory of an irksome, indeed loathsome duty he had been compelled by the Commander-in-Chief to undertake. This was the conveyance to Petersburg in his ship of the 'Princess' Tarakhanova, who had been inveigled on board at Leghorn through one of the meanest tricks in the Orlov repertoire – and the last which, in the event, it was to lie within Count Alexei's power to play.

The Princess Elizabeth Tarakhanova was an attractive young woman who had been 'discovered' by the French court – some might have used the word 'contrived' – and whose brief career was deliberately exploited with the design of embarrassing the Empress Catherine. This Princess Elizabeth claimed herself to be the rightful monarch of all the Russias since she was, she announced, the daughter of the late Empress Elizabeth I, Catherine's predecessor, by a secret marriage.

Whether or not this was true, such a pretence to the throne could naturally not be overlooked and its continuance became a source of great annoyance to St Petersburg. Once this irritant had been established, Versailles compounded the damage by providing the gay and somewhat empty-headed girl with a Polish prince of great wealth who took her under his protection, lavished jewels on her and then departed with her to Italy in an endeavour to secure recognition of her claim to the Russian throne by the various Italian states. To begin with this had prospered, but whilst in Tuscany, the Grand Duke, who remained a true ally of Catherine, had had her movements spied on, and subsequently reported to the Empress via Count Alexei Orlov, who feigned a ready sympathy for the Russian pretender.

Samuel never discovered whether the idea emanated from the Empress herself or in the fertile brain of her Commander-in-Chief, whose diplomatic procedures were by now well known to Samuel in their full range. Whatever the provenance, the ending of the Turkish war coincided with the sudden departure from Leghorn of the Polish prince. The reason for this was not apparent, but he took with him the jewels he had once bestowed on his luckless *protégée*, at the same time leaving her behind in a state of penury.

Samuel first learnt of the plot two days before sailing for St Petersburg. Fortescue Fynne, captain of another of the line of battle ships which were to sail in company, came storming on board the flagship.

'Are you aware, Sam, of what is being hatched out behind your back? I refer to the Princess Tarakhanova with whom, as you are doubtless aware, I have maintained a tender relationship since the departure of that pestilential Pole.'

'There are so many plots for, against and concerning the lady—' Samuel began.

'Is Orlov sailing with us?'

Samuel shook his head.

'It is the Commander-in-Chief's intention to proceed overland. The long sea voyage would remove him from the seat of power for too long a time.'

'I do not take issue with that, Samuel, but are you aware that he has persuaded my poor misguided Elizabeth of his good faith in supporting her claim to the throne? He had gone further. He assures her that the great fleet under his command will also rally to her side. He has told her that she must take passage as an honoured guest, that on arrival at St Petersburg, protected by the guns of our warships, she will lay claim to be rightfully enthroned, that Catherine will be forced to abdicate, and that then the Empress Elizabeth II, acclaimed by the entire long-suffering Russian nation, will forthwith be elevated to power. Have you ever heard of such a rigmarole of nonsense in all your life?'

'And your Princess believes him?'

'She even asked if she might take passage in my ship. I told the Commander-in-Chief that if I were given orders to that effect, I would resign my commission on the spot.'

The two officers looked at each other, calculating the effects of the action proposed.

'Has she not heard of Pougatchev?' Samuel asked.

'She dismisses him as a mere pretender.'

'Then what is the lady herself?'

'What she is in very truth we none of us know, nor in all likelihood ever will. In her own eyes she is the legitimate heir to the throne. And there is no manner – at least no manner of which I know – to convince her of the folly of this dangerous behaviour.'

'If she sets foot in Russia, she will lose her head.'

'As to that, who can possibly tell? But she will not heed advice. She is a hot-headed, adorable creature who must be protected from herself.'

'A duty you would prefer to that of conveying her to her possible doom?'

'I have told you where I stand in the matter, Sam. You may be minded otherwise – and you may be right in being so minded. I do not know. But the consequences are of no great importance to me so far as my career is concerned. As I fancy you suspect, I would as lief follow old Elphinston back to England—'

'And half pay?'

'What is to be our future here now that the war is won?'

Samuel shrugged his shoulders and turned away.

'I would have thought it better to chance your luck by continuing in the Russian service than to moulder away in some guardship at home. We must find you a suitable wife. Unfortunately the Princess Tarakhanova, even if she would have you, scarce fits that particular bill.'

After calming his old friend, Samuel sought out Orlov to discover the official intent. He found him in the company of Admiral Spiritdoff, both of them looking as devious as ever. When taxed with the morality of such trickery, if trickery it were, Orlov at once 'became the Commander-in-Chief', as Samuel later explained it to Sarah, 'which he no longer affected to do with me except he be very unsure of his ground.'

Brusquely he intimated that the matter had already been decided. The lady would be conducted on board the flagship the following day, a few hours before the fleet had been ordered to sail, full honours would be paid her as she stepped on board and she was to be regally entertained until the ship was out of sight of land.

'From that moment on', Orlov decreed, a hard glitter in his eye, 'the so-called Princess Tarakhanova becomes the prisoner of Her Imperial Majesty, to be conveyed to the Peter and Paul Fortress at St Petersburg to await Her Majesty's pleasure.'

'I desire to be excused this offensive and dishonourable task.'

But this possibility had been foreseen.

'No, sir,' said Orlov, 'your written orders lie on that table there. You will take them with you when you leave, and I observe from your restless mien that you do not wish to delay your departure.'

He offered his hand but this Samuel refused to accept.

'I will obey Your Excellency's order,' he said stiffly, 'since your authority derives directly from the Empress to whom I am sworn. But shake hands on this shabby piece of tavern trickery – no, sir!'

Turning on his heel, he picked up the orders and left Orlov's presence. As he went he heard Spiritdoff murmur to the Commander-in-Chief in Russian: 'It is time these foreigners were declared superfluous to the imperial service, Alexei Gregorievich.'

12

The salons of St Petersburg

In the event it was the Orlov clan itself which proved to be superfluous. By the time Samuel reached Crondstadt, the new favourite Potemkin had extended his tentacles of power in a dozen subtle ways unknown to, or at least unexplored by, his predecessors. Potemkin had turned himself into a skilful general in the Crimea and he had made a careful survey of the St Petersburg battlefield before entering upon it. He had marshalled his own resources, deciding who would and who would not become his creatures. He had assessed his enemies, of which he was to discover there would never be a shortage, and he then proceeded to woo his Empress as she had not been wooed before.

He had elected to play a dangerous game at a highly perilous time. The Empress had been nearly fifteen years on the throne and her personal popularity now stood at its lowest ebb. The Russian peoples, in so far as they possessed a political voice, had been strongly against the Turkish war. Success had mollified this feeling but it still left them in continuing distress over the progressive worsening of their finances.

'You should know', the British Ambassador told Samuel when they were surveying affairs at the Petersburg court after his return, 'that when I went to Moscow in the company of the diplomatic corps to be present at the State Entry of the Empress, the Grand Duke and the Grand Duchess into that capital, the crowd witnessing their arrival raised scarcely a murmur of acclamation. It was regrettably obvious that such a visit was far from welcome to the inhabitants of Moscow, whether nobility or commoners – and of this Her Majesty became fully aware. Indeed it is fortunate for her that the wretched Pougatchev proved so lacking in judgment and commonsense as to be incapable of devising any sort of plan of campaign. Had he marched on Moscow, there is not the slightest doubt that the entire population would have joined him, and the natural timidity of most of the nobles would have prevented their taking any measures to resist him. In that circumstance the blaze would have spread right through the Empire.'

Samuel, however, was not concerned with such an aspect of Russian life. His own welcome back to St Petersburg both by the Empress and, as he was soon to discover, the new favourite had been of a marked warmth and friendliness. When peace with the Ottoman Empire had been solemnly declared, the Empress promoted Samuel Karlovich Greig to be Vice Admiral in the Imperial Russian Navy. A little later she appointed him to the post of Commander-in-Chief of the Port of Crondstadt. This was a cardinal move in his life. He had now reached the top echelon of command. Congratulations, sincere and not so sincere, poured in from all his friends and acquaintances.

'And I am directed to convey to you', the British Ambassador said a little later, 'the private congratulation of His Majesty King George III. Doubtless when you are established at Crondstadt – and should the peace prevail – you will consider a visit to England to be both timely and appropriate. I have already sounded out Monsieur Potemkin on this matter and he will invite the Empress's approval for such a voyage.'

The Orlov brothers were now to be kept at arm's length. The old favourite himself was banished to the Castle of Gatchina some forty-five *versts* south west of St Petersburg and his brothers retired from active service to their own considerable estates. To the great satisfaction of Samuel and of Fortescue Fynne, now himself a Rear Admiral and secured by Samuel as his Chief of Staff at Crondstadt, the Empress gave her assent to the employment of yet more British officers in the fleet. Admiral Spiritdoff and Russian officers of a similar seniority were honourably retired and Samuel was desired in a personal audience of the Empress, 'to remodel the discipline, institute new methods of training and in general raise the standard of efficiency in our

Fleet.' Again with a smile of understanding, the Empress said:

'You are to report directly to us upon any matter which in your opinion merits our attention and you will be given any material you require. You need do no more than ask. As no doubt you comprehend, this is not an authority we have given, nor are we likely to give, to anyone else.'

Thus a remarkable power was conferred on him, concurrently with a sum of money and the Orders of St George and St Vladimir. It seemed a long, long way from Burnt Island and the threadbare life of his boyhood. Sarah, too, kept through this time a sense of wonderment at the good things which were being showered upon them. Her own response to this sudden access of honour and acclaim was to present Samuel with a son, 'the crowning joy of all', and a year later she repeated the compliment. The few years after the ending of the Turkish war were unquestionably the happiest period of their lives for both Samuel and Sarah. Their good fortune seemed almost too overpowering to be true.

The Empress, too, now began to enjoy a personal tranquillity for which she had all but given up hope. She was loved and flattered as if she were still a young girl instead of the slightly obese woman who would soon be fifty years old. She was privately and intensely grateful to her new Prince, and both of them exercised a growing intelligence not only with each other but also upon the social and political world in which they had their being. Potemkin was no fool. Success had come to him comparatively late in life and he soon proved to be more responsible than any previous personage close to the throne.

Pougatchev had represented by far the most serious threat to Catherine which had yet arisen, but Potemkin had put his own brother in charge of the army sent to capture the rebel and this gamble had paid a handsome reward. However neither Potemkin nor Catherine deceived themselves as to the realities of the situation. The officer bringing the news that Pougatchev had been beaten near Astrakhan was encouraged to speak with a frankness which previous autocrats would never have tolerated. He was asked why he thought that Pougatchev had succeeded to the extent he had.

'The discontentment of the people is almost universal,' the officer replied, 'and even at the gates of the capital the peasants called him by no other name than Tsar. The nobility and the clergy are both complaining that they have suffered just as much from the Imperial troops as from those of Pougatchev. I would thus urge Your Majesty to apply any and every remedy which may be to hand,' the officer dared to conclude, 'in order to stifle the bad feelings which are now spreading over the land.'

It was a timely warning, and when Pougatchev had been delivered first to the Empress and then by her to the Senate for justice to be executed in the best way seen fit (he was hung, drawn and quartered), the lancing of this boil, together with the ending of the Turkish war, ushered in a new era of prosperity. The salt and other taxes were reduced, and the British Ambassador was soon able to write a dispatch in which he remarked that 'I have never seen the interior of the Court so peaceful since my arrival and with so comparatively few intrigues for over a month. Even the disquieting and turbulent spirit of the Princess Dashkov has proved incapable of disrupting the calm which reigns. This may undoubtedly be attributed to the absence of Count Zacharias Tchernikov who is the lynch pin of most intrigues at this court.'

The British Ambassador's sharp intelligence now began to think of ways of increasing British influence during this quiet time.

'And one of these ideas, indeed my favourite one, concerns your wife,' he remarked one evening to Samuel, when the ladies had left the two men to their port. The Greigs had been bidden to dinner at the Embassy in St Petersburg, both slightly surprised to be the only guests. Now the reason was to be revealed.

'You have been blessed with a wife who is not only of rare beauty,' the Ambassador continued, pouring out a further glass of port for Samuel, 'but who also enjoys the confidence of the Empress and of many of the close advisers to the Throne, principal among them being Prince Potemkin.'

'I am obliged to you for the compliment,' Samuel said formally. He wondered what was coming next. He distrusted the Ambassador and frankly had a diminishing taste for these rare social expeditions to St Petersburg. He enjoyed the Imperial Conferences at which he could put ideas and demands to the Empress and receive her assent, but in general he much preferred the nautical world of Crondstadt where he could make it clear that he was Commander-in-Chief not only in name but also in everyday visible fact. The older he got, the more of the bluff sailor he tended to become and Sarah had once told him in one of their few disagreements that he so obviously enjoyed strutting about in his splendid uniform 'showing off', that he would have done better to go on the stage as an actor. There had not been much conversation in the Greig household for some days after that. Now, as if reading his thoughts, the Ambassador who had been watching him closely said with a little smile:

'Pray do not think that I am trying to steal your Sarah. I would, however, like to purloin you both from time to time for what might be described as courtly manoeuvres. In other words, Sam, I would like Sarah to begin entertaining here in St Petersburg in the quiet style she has made her own at Crondstadt.'

'You have just ruined the excellent dinner you have given us.'

'Come come, Sam, I am not making a *plaisanterie*. I realize that such activities are not to your taste but you *have* become the principal naval adviser to Her Majesty. She holds you in great and increasing esteem, and in this your lady shares as an equal partner. It would please the "Semiramis of the North" – as I believe the Empress has been dubbed by Monsieur Voltaire – were you both to take a greater part in the social life of St Petersburg.'

Samuel sighed but managed to contrive a somewhat wan smile.

'I would venture to guess that you have already made some tactful enquiries of the Empress or Prince Potemkin,' he said, looking up from under his bushy eyebrows.

'You have guessed correctly,' the Ambassador said, 'and the response was extremely favourable. I was told that, were your wife to agree to establish her salon in the house which Count Razumovsky had been kind enough to let me acquire, she would become a civilized corrective to some of the flamboyant elements with which the Russian court bedizens itself. Do you fancy we could secure an agreement from Sarah?'

'If I give my permission she will, of course, agree,' Samuel countered, a little testily.

'Naturally,' the Ambassador said, carefully suppressing a smile by suddenly having to blow his nose.

'But if we are to employ Count Razumovsky's house for the purpose—'

'In effect, it is his second or third establishment.'

'I care not if it be his hundredth whore-house,' Samuel said, 'provided the Count and his sons keep well away. I have no intention of exposing Sarah to any of the dubious manoeuvres of *that* scandalous entourage.'

'You refer to the unfortunate gossip which has begun to circulate concerning the Grand Duke Paul?'

'I do,' Samuel said, every inch of him bristling, as Fortescue Fynne would have put it, with Scottish pawkiness. 'Or rather, to the Grand Duchess and that young Razumovsky rat.'

'No breath of scandal shall ever attach to Sarah,' the Ambassador said, wondering how he dared to talk in such a way since how could anyone prevent any scandal at any court? 'But the Tchernikovs, the Razumovskys, the Vorontsovs and the Panins are now the families of position and power, whom Potemkin plays off one against another for the amusement of his royal mistress. I have no doubt that Sarah will conquer the denizens of the Winter Palace with the same *élan* as her husband conducted his fleet in Turkish waters.'

'There is no requirement for flattery,' Samuel said. 'Let

us discover what Sarah herself feels about this tedious proposal.'

So a new era in their lives began. Initially Sarah felt some uncertainty in her ability to control this extension of their activities. But, as the British Ambassador had suggested, she soon became fascinated by the various intrigues and intriguers – 'as would any woman of character and spirit', Fortie remarked to Samuel later on, 'let alone one with as firm and charming a character as Sarah.'

Yet even when her salon had become an acknowledged success, Sarah still suspected that it did not please her husband. She accepted the fact that Samuel trusted her implicitly – a trust she had never betrayed – but like so many sailors' wives throughout the ages she had also to accept that her husband's first love remained the Navy, which had for so long been nine-tenths of his life.

From time to time she brought these feelings out into the open, taking soundings as to Samuel's real attitude. She had noticed that whenever possible the Admiral would 'get out from under', for service reasons which seemed to be increasingly far-fetched.

'So that if you consider that it is not the function of a Commander-in-Chief's wife to indulge in socialities of this nature,' she said one day, when Samuel had excused himself from yet another of her soirées on the plea of 'forthcoming manoeuvres', 'I shall, of course, desist. You have only to say the word.'

Samuel looked up into the distance as if some enemy fleet had been descried on the horizon and then, as was his wont, took a turn up and down the room to consider the matter before giving his decision.

'My service with Orlov', he said after a pause, 'provided me with sufficient experience of diplomatic procedures to last me a lifetime. As you rightly suspect, Sarah, such frivolities are not to my taste. However I cannot but agree that, like it or not, they form an essential part of our life here in St Petersburg. I am, therefore, only too pleased to have a wife who will so engagingly remove the weight from my shoulders. I am also cognizant of the confidence reposed in you by Her Imperial Majesty.'

'And in you, Samuel.'

'I dare say that is true. But Her Majesty looks to me for her fleet and not for the poodle-faking activities you seem to enjoy.'

'I can only continue to enjoy them provided I have your assurance that you do not secretly find them offensive.'

He strode across and took her impulsively in his arms.

'Offend me? The very opposite is true. Were you not here at my side, I should be compelled to engage in them myself. As it is, I am delighted to have all such responsibilities removed from my brow and to be your servant in these matters to any extent that you may see fit. Do as you wish, but spare me as much as you can.'

So, assisted by the British Ambassador who saw in her a discreet provider of confidential intelligence, Sarah continued to build her reputation in the social world of St Petersburg, 'learning to navigate the shoals of precedent and protocol', as Samuel commented. She quickly became skilled in sensing whom to invite with whom, or perhaps more importantly whom not to invite with whom.

In this she was urged by the British Ambassador to seek the private counsel of Prince Potemkin, 'since we shall see the credit of this wily courtier constantly augment', the Ambassador remarked, 'and soon he will have each and every string in his hand. Unlike Orlov he has no wish, so far as I can tell, to be consort in name. He is content to stay in the shadows, from where he can exercise more power than any similar personage in any other European court. He has disposed of the Orlovs. Next it will be the turn of Monsieur Panin under whose great shade he rests whilst secretly doing his best with the Empress, if not to ruin him (which would be difficult), then at least to lessen his influence. With this in mind he is promoting the interest in foreign affairs of the son of old Chancellor Ostermann. To my knowledge two or three important matters have lately been expedited by Monsieur Ostermann without Count Panin being aware of what had been arranged behind his back.'

'And where does Prince Potemkin stand in the matter of Prince André Razumovsky and the Grand Duchess?'

The Ambassador studied the Admiral's wife, trying to decide in his mind how much of this disreputable scandal she knew and then said, after a pause:

'Monsieur Potemkin identifies himself utterly and completely with the exclusive interest of the Empress, though how that interest can best be advanced it is not always possible to ascertain – especially in so far as the Grand Duke, her son, is concerned. The Empress is jealous of any popularity which her son may acquire. In the early days of the young man's marriage, the Empress looked to her daughter-in-law, the Grand Duchess – after all a German like herself – to keep her husband contented and in the background happily playing at soldiers as did his father. To this end, and as a reward for acting as her son's "keeper", she encouraged the young woman to indulge herself with the young Prince André Razumovsky in the way known to everyone at Court, with the exception of the Grand Duke himself.'

'The Grand Duke is nevertheless more popular, would you not agree, than a cuckold might be expected to be?'

'Indeed that is so. The Count considers that the Grand Duke is of the blood royal, such as it is in Russia, whereas the mother will always be a foreigner and a usurper. The Grand Duke is aware of this feeling and since he detests Monsieur Potemkin, the latter no doubt suggested to his Imperial mistress the vile notion of advising the Grand Duke of the extent of the familiarity in which young Razumovsky is held by the Grand Duchess. This odious confidence caused the Grand Duke a chagrin he has attempted to hide, with an entire lack of success. In the end the Grand Duchess was compelled to make a clean breast of the affair to her husband, and this reduced both of them to tears for a period of days. It also demonstrated the malignity of some of those who surround the heir to the throne, and has increased the loathing the Grand Duke already bears his mother. Unfortunately for the Empress, the Grand Duke continues to entertain a profound and lively affection for his wife. He believed in her protestations and in her tears. All was forgiven and forgotten.'

'And the result?'

'He takes every opportunity available to him to parade his own popularity and to humiliate, whenever possible, his mother's favourite. In this, alas for himself, he achieves but little success. The Empress – and Potemkin – possess the ultimate sanction, namely that of the purse. On his last birthday the Empress presented her son with a watch of but little value. Monsieur Potemkin received 50,000 roubles, a sum of money of which the Grand Duke had a pressing need. This has embittered him against his mother even more than before, since he sees the favourite disposing of everything whereas he, who should himself be on the throne, remains in indigence.'

Although Samuel made in the main some genuine attempts to attend in St Petersburg when Sarah held her salons or they were invited to other official or semi-official functions, many occasions cropped up when Sarah had to 'represent the Commander-in-Chief' alone. There were manoeuvres. There were inspections of distant naval establishments, and there were days when there were neither but Samuel let it be thought that there were.

However if it were possible, and also to salve his conscience, he would command his Chief of Staff, Rear Admiral Fortescue Fynne, to take his place and to squire Sarah, since Fortie had still not achieved a wife of his own despite several gruelling campaigns, mounted by the matriarchy of the capital, to 'get him hooked'. By now Fortie and Sarah's friendship was of such long standing that both recognized they were, or had been, a little in love with each other, although neither put this into words, and each had a protective affection for the other.

With Fortie this took the form of an attentiveness unmatchable even by Samuel, and Sarah, in turn, kept a careful watch on the various sly assaults upon Fortie's eligibility which Russian mothers were apt to make with their younger and less well-endowed progeny in mind. In many ways it was a game which both enjoyed. They played it to firm, though unwritten, rules. There was usually an element of risk and both relished the keen cut and thrust of court socialities which, though not on a par with Versailles, were certainly sharpening and being refined with each passing year.

On one such occasion Sarah was accompanied by Fortie to a Ball at the Winter Palace when young Prince André Razumovsky decided to seek her acquaintance. The Winter Palace that evening was at its glittering best, the brilliance of the chandeliers illuminating the damask walls (white paint had gone out in the early days of the late Empress Elizabeth's reign) and showing off to effect the rich brocades worn by the men and the dresses, lavishly decorated with gold and silver, which would be the talk of the town for weeks. By comparison with the dazzling bejewelled uniform of a courtier such as Serge Naryshkin, Prince André appeared to be almost modestly dressed, and Sarah was curious to discover what it was about the young man which had so commended him to the Grand Duchess. She was soon to find out.

'A single dance on an evening such as this', the Prince murmured in her ear as he conducted her back to her seat, 'is scarcely adequate to make the acquaintance of the most ravishing, the most beautiful and the most intelligent woman in this great vulgar hall.'

His animal magnetism seemed to Sarah to be only slightly disguised by his elegant manners, and there could be no doubt about the powerful attraction he was deliberately exercising upon her person.

'You are very flattering, sir,' Sarah answered, 'but you will not, I hope, think me impolite if I remark that the words you employ appear to have been well worn in a previous usage. Are they not, perhaps, your opening remarks upon making any new acquaintance?'

'Naturally they do that duty,' Prince André quickly agreed with a sparkle in the eye. 'They break the ice, and what lies beneath the surface can then be explored.'

'And is it your proposition to explore me in a similar

fashion to that which you carried out with – another personage of the court?'

'Wicked remarks of that nature will in no way advance our knowledge of each other. I see that your beauty is matched by a mordant tongue.'

'And a Scottish commonsense,' Sarah said, but not unkindly.

'I should like to dispose of that commonsense, as you call it, in another place and in a way of my own.'

'Thus providing the gossips with a fresh portion of pleasure?'

'It is not the gossips I would pleasure.'

'I dare say not,' Sarah said, observing Fortie approaching them from behind the young Prince's back. 'You are a very desirable young man, but unlike the Grand Duchess I am married to a man I consider even more desirable myself.'

'A pox on that impeccable reputation of yours. What virtue is this which requires such preservation by "commonsense"?'

'Sir, I have already been blessed by two sons and I am not required to produce an heir to the throne.'

'What is this impropriety I hear?' Fortie demanded in an angry tone of voice.

'You were not required to hear anything, Admiral,' the Prince retorted with an insolent sneer.

'Indeed, sir?' Fortie said coldly. 'When I seek advice from—'

'Now, Fortie,' Sarah put in quickly, 'do not excite yourself in this way. Prince André and I were simply indulging in an exchange of badinage which would in any event have been brought to an end by the next gavotte.'

She bowed slightly at Razumovsky who had the intelligence to return her bow, kiss her hand and leave her presence.

'It was gallant of you, dear Fortie,' she said quietly, touching his hand, 'but do you not see where it would have led? To the inevitable dawn meeting with seconds in attendance, which would have settled nothing and in which you might perhaps have lost your life. No stupid proposition from a hot-blooded young man is worth anything of that nature.'

'They hate us,' Fortie said, for once unsmiling and of serious mien; 'they want any excuse to send us all away.'

'Not while the Empress is here to protect us,' Sarah said. 'She and Potemkin are more than a match for the Razumovskys of this court.'

'If Sam had been here—'

'Dear Fortie, you have stood well in his place. I cannot see you harmed, and that is why I did not want you to rush to my aid. He is certainly an arrogant young man but there are other ways of setting him back in his place which you can safely leave to me when I next see Prince Potemkin. And above all Sam is not to hear a word of this. Do I have your promise?'

'Reluctantly, Sarah, reluctantly,' Fortie said, nodding, 'but then you can have anything of me you care to ask.'

Later when considering the implications of that evening, Sarah realized yet again how close to the wind she and Sam were always being forced to sail in this cabbalistic Asiatic court. Nothing was ever direct. There was no smile which did not disguise some crafty endeavour, no forest of innocent-looking trees which did not shelter a pack of wolves. And now she had not only Sam to care for but two growing sons. In Russia tread softly, tread carefully, she had been warned, because there *vous marchez les oeufs*. It was an undeniable fact of life. Another undeniable fact continued to be the paramount value to the Russian Empress of her British-born Naval Commander-in-Chief. This single factor in the end was what mattered the most.

'I have discussed your sons' education with the Empress,' the British Ambassador informed Sarah a little later on. 'I acquainted Her Majesty with your desire to have them educated in Scotland. This was a delicate subject to broach, and at first the Empress took it as a reflection on the great efforts she has been making to improve education in this barbarous land. However once she ascertained that it is the Admiral's intention for his sons to follow him in the naval service, she expressed her consent to your proposal. Indeed she there and then gave the necessary instruction, and here is a letter from Count Bezborodzko to the Admiral giving this effect.'

The Ambassador handed Sarah the following letter, which he had had copied for the benefit of the British Admiralty.

> 'My dear Sir, Samuel Karlovich, [it began] Her Imperial Majesty has not only affectionately consented, but has also graciously commended the desire of Your Excellency to send your two sons for education to Scotland. Assuming, my dear Sir, that for your younger son you will also choose service in the Navy in preference to any other, Her Imperial Majesty has graciously appointed him to be Midshipman of the Fleet. Of the above I hasten to apprise His Illustrious Count Ivan Gregorievitch Tchernikov and beg to congratulate Your Excellency upon this Imperial favour.'

Other marks of approval were shown the Admiral during this period following the successful conclusion of the Turkish war, and although there were naturally Russian Admirals of a greater seniority than himself, it was Samuel Karlovich Greig, descendant of a clan once proscribed in Scotland for two hundred years, who effectively controlled the affairs of the fleet and who thus acquired for himself a status in the Imperial Russian Navy equivalent to that of the First Sea Lord in the British Admiralty.

13

The Crondstadt Plot

'Heigh! heigh! heigh!' Samuel said, striding into his drawing-room at Crondstadt and clasping Sarah to him in an unexpected and warm embrace. He had just returned from a conference with the Empress. 'The Greig family is to be sent home *en prince* to the United Kingdom,' he went on, the excitement in his voice reminding Sarah of the gauche yet eager young man she had first fallen for when a girl so many years ago. 'A frigate is to be put at my disposal next summer. We shall convey Alexis and young Samuel to school in Edinburgh, and the Empress is writing privately to King George III who, she says, will condescend to receive us and intends conferring a Knighthood on me. What does your wee future Ladyship say to that?'

'That she will be very pleasantly surprised should it really take place,' Sarah said, hugging him fondly, 'and even more delighted should we return to Russia without discovering that Admiral Sir Samuel Greig's next appointment is to some rowing boat on a lake in Siberia.'

'Aye!' Samuel said, the pleasure already draining out of him, 'only a fool would not be aware of the dangers in leaving the seat of power. I know certain people will be only too pleased to see the back of me.'

'Stryalokov?'

'And other contractors. I believe Fortie has decided to jump overboard at last – into matrimony with a niece of Count Steckelberg.'

'That will complicate matters.'

Sarah had been aware of this possibility for some time but had kept this news to herself. Steckelberg, as both she and Samuel knew, was a man of power, unscrupulous and ever ready to exploit any monopoly or advantage on which he could lay his hands.

'It may do so for poor Fortie. It will do no such thing

for me,' Samuel said. 'I'll have that reprobate out of Crondstadt before ever we leave for England.'

'Was it not old Steckelberg, the father, who so flattered the Empress Elizabeth that she gave him a hundred thousand serfs to enable him to maintain a proper appearance at court?'

Samuel nodded.

'And that was but a part of it. The father collected monopolies much as the old Empress acquired gowns. The son is no better. He is devoted to the use of bribery and corruption as being the shortest distance between two desirable objects. He is as honest as a bow oar; in other words he is a thorough-paced rogue. There is not a purser in the fleet without experience of the rotten meat and the watered brandy issuing from the Steckelberg warehouses – nor also of the mean sum of roubles thought necessary for Mr Nipcheese which accompany these contaminated supplies. I can stop his practices here in Crondstadt, I cannot bring the Steckelberg family more generally to book. And now if Fortie is to marry the niece....'

'Why, we shall have a spy in the enemy camp,' Sarah said brightly, 'and one on whom we know we can rely. She is also a pretty girl, so Fortie will have his hands full in other departments. Now, Sam, will you go over our list of guests for the Royal Inspection before you go in to dinner?'

During this long final period of his life which began with his appointment as Commander-in-Chief of Crondstadt, Samuel developed into full maturity. Always a firm disciplinarian success had strangely enough increased his tolerance, but this was based not on weakness but on understanding. This was the Admiral who was to stamp his beliefs, his standards and his breadth of vision on the Russian naval service for the better part of a century, since the ideas which he put into practice were later continued and developed by his son, who himself became a Commander-in-Chief, and by the Russian naval officers who rose to high positions of command under the Greig aegis. Strangely enough, although initially imposed, these ideas and policies were generally welcomed and accepted because any storms which they encountered – and to begin with there was plenty of opposition – were usually overcome by the application of Samuel's Greig's understanding, his warm humanity and his essential good humour.

Yet this proved to be no simple nor accidental process. Nor was it painless. 'I hear a deep cry for order,' he remarked to the Empress at one of the unofficial auditions to which she summoned him from time to time, 'but the cry quickly becomes lost in the confusion from below which is forever attempting to reimpose itself. This drift into procrastination and chaos is so pronounced that I venture to say that were it not for the trust with which Your Majesty has seen fit to honour me, I would long ago have requested my release from the Russian service.'

The Empress studied him with those cold but amused blue eyes which could so instantly strike terror into her subjects.

'I am fully informed of the difficulties which beset you at Crondstadt,' she said, and then added with a smile, 'but I never yet had a good servant who himself acquired no enemies. I understand you have refused to submit the estimates for the rebuilding in stone of the Citadel, proposed to you by Monsieur Steckelberg.'

'I have today brought Your Majesty a revised estimate for the work, calculated by myself, which exhibits a saving of over a million roubles. It will also result in a sounder fortification.'

The Empress nodded.

'You have precisely confirmed what I have said. You need not search for trouble if you have a contractor for a friend.'

'Count Steckelberg is no friend of mine,' Samuel observed, 'though I have but little doubt as to which of us will die the richer.'

'You may live longer, Samuel Karlovich,' the Empress said in a tone of voice which would certainly have struck a chill into the contractor had he been present, 'and as to your wealth you may safely leave that matter in our hands.'

Samuel and Sarah did, in fact, now enjoy an established and privileged place in the Empress's thoughts. Catherine had realized at a very early stage that her favourite Admiral lived and would continue to live by principle. Not a day passed that did not begin with a reading from the Bible and a visit, where this was expedient, to the Scottish Chapel at Crondstadt or to the English or French Reformed Churches at St Petersburg. Aided by his Masonic connection, Samuel had been elected to the College of Commerce where he read a series of important papers.

But whereas the Greigs entertained not only at Crondstadt and later at the Livonian country house which the Empress had given him, they were sparing in the return invitations they accepted and invariably refused any engagement in which an interest might be seen to accrue to the host. Samuel's memories of dockyard 'hampering' in England were vivid enough to induce him never to accept a gift of any kind or size which might lay him open to a charge of bribery. He would have merchants, purveyors and contractors to his table from time to time: he would never be seen at theirs.

This incorruptibility made him many a foe, as the Empress had foreseen, and powerful forces waited in the shadows for the day when this 'too good to be true' British Admiral might stumble and fall, and revenge be had. His adversaries, principal among them being, strangely enough, the Grand Duke Paul who disliked all foreigners and especially those in positions of power, might dub Greig a pawky and complacent Scot; the truth was otherwise and, so far as discipline was concerned, whilst he did little to diminish the application of the many harsh punishments in force, he tempered his judgment wherever possible with a compassion sometimes incredible to Russian eyes.

'When considering a mistake or a crime,' he gave it out in his orders, 'Commanding Officers will endeavour to distinguish between the faults of the head and those of the heart. The former will be dealt with more leniently than the latter. A navigational error, even though it result in disaster, is not of the same order as mutiny or a refusal to engage the enemy.'

Thus cowardice, however disguised by inefficiency or sloth, continued to be punished with the full medieval severity of which there was certainly no lack in the serfdom of Russia. In all this Samuel was constantly observed and assessed not only by his Empress but also at one remove by the English king whose service he had left, and who was now facing a revolt of his American colonies.

The conduct of a foreign navy, especially in a country as powerful as emerging Russia, had always been and would continue to be, of very considerable interest to the British; and it was not without misgiving – and indeed only after a lengthy debate between herself, Prince Potemkin and Count Panin – that the Empress decided to put a frigate at the disposal of the Commander-in-Chief for the purpose of the visit to England which she had promised him. Once her favourite Admiral found himself back in England, would the wily British not contrive by some means or other to retain his services there? The Royal Navy now had a colonial war on its hands ... instead of a glut, there was once again a shortage of trained naval personnel.

However written orders for the visit to take place the following year were duly made out and conveyed to Samuel during the summer of 1776, when the Empress paid a State Visit to her fleet at Crondstadt. No such magnificent nor auspicious event had previously occurred on the island fortress. The great Peter had constructed Crondstadt as a protection to the mouth of the river Neva, on which his 'infant capital', later to bear his name, was rising from the marshy swamps. Crondstadt had become an impressive enough fortification in itself. The drawings for this fortress had been done by Peter's own hand and were proudly produced by Samuel for inspection by the Empress during her visit.

'They are of such excellence,' Samuel observed, 'and the works they provoked so strong, that no additions of importance are necessary except for the replacement of wood by Finnish stone, which as Your Majesty can see is now in an advanced state of completion.'

Crondstadt is only five miles long by approximately one in width, and the Empress was ceremoniously rowed past her ships which were dressed overall for the occasion in a style copied from the Royal Navy. A royal salute of 101 guns was fired whilst the imperial barge moved slowly along the line, the Empress being seated under an embroidered canopy, accompanied by her Commander-in-Chief. It was with obvious pride that Samuel pointed out the basins, docks, canals and spacious moles which the calculations of Peter, and the wise expenditure of the present Empress, had brought into being.

'Every convenience that is necessary in a maritime depot is now to be found at Crondstadt,' Samuel informed her, 'and it may surprise Your Majesty to count the number of trading vessels lying in the adjacent commercial harbour. Several hundred ships of every nation now visit us here each year, riding at ease and in safety under the protection of Your Majesty's guns.'

The Empress then accompanied her Governor to the commanding heights of the fortress, from which a panoramic view of the whole gulf was to be had.

'Your great predecessor's judgment and foresight have been proved to be extraordinary in many different directions,' Samuel said as the Empress surveyed the scene. 'Before fortifying the place on which we now stand, he made a careful chart of the shoals lying at the mouth of the Neva. The result is that this fortress has been made all but impregnable in itself. Coupled with the underwater impediments between here and St Petersburg, the whole renders Your Majesty's capital secure against any major attack from the sea. Indeed we experience considerable difficulty ourselves in passing ships built in St Petersburg over the shoals when they are en route to Crondstadt for the installation of their guns. Once the guns are in place and the dead weight of the ships increased, it would be impossible for them to return to Petersburg without running aground. Were an enemy to attempt such an expedition, his ships would thus become sitting targets and could be much annoyed by our cannon, installed with exactly this purpose in mind.'

Later Her Majesty did the Commander-in-Chief the honour of dining on board his flagship, where she dubbed him a knight of the orders of St Andrew, St George and St Anne, pinning upon his breast the star of St Alexander Nevski. He was forty-one years of age.

So it happened that the following summer, accompanied by Sarah and the two boys who were to be sent to Edinburgh for their schooling, the frigate *Nadishda* set off for England, calling in at Copenhagen where Sir Samuel and Lady Greig were received by the King of Denmark and his consort the 'amiable but unfortunate' Matilda.

'She conversed long with the Admiral,' Sarah subsequently reported in a private letter to the Empress, 'and treated him with the most flattering condescension. On our arrival at London we were soon presented by the First Lord of the Admiralty to His Majesty King George III. The King received us most graciously and declared that he was very pleased to see one of his subjects who had distinguished himself in so brilliant a manner. The Admiral, in turn, told me how astonished he was at the knowledge which His Majesty displayed in naval affairs, and the number of pertinent questions he put relative to the Russian fleet, demonstrating how well he was acquainted with the minutest details of his own.'

'It will do the English king no harm', the Empress remarked to Potemkin, when she showed him this letter, 'to be apprised in so expert a fashion as to our naval strength.'

Whilst agreeing with this sentiment, Potemkin observed that he had again received from the Grand Duke, her son, yet another remonstrance about the number of foreign officers employed in the Imperial Navy.

'He is reported to have said that our foreign policy is now clearly dependent on the good-will of the aliens in our service and further that, when he ascends the throne himself, his first action will be to order every English resident at Crondstadt to be sent, during the severities of a very inclement winter, many thousand *versts* up the country. This is scarcely likely to increase the loyalty of those to whom he refers.'

'I would prefer to rely on the present loyalty of my Scottish sailors,' the Empress replied, 'rather than on any whim of my miserable and luckless son.'

'With that there can be no argument,' Potemkin said. 'However the Grand Duke is correct in one direction. I do not see our Navy opening fire on a British fleet should we find ourselves at war with the United Kingdom.'

'I can conceive of no circumstance in which any such state of affairs could come about. Our interests and those of England are too close.'

'And should the Royal Navy stop, search and perhaps seize our merchant vessels in pursuance of suppressing this American revolt? Their definition of contraband may not tally with ours.'

'Then in Admiral Greig we possess a first-class requirement to desist. He and his brother officers carry more influence by their presence and behaviour here than by any physical action necessarily undertaken by ships of the Imperial Navy.'

'I agree with Your Majesty's assessment,' Potemkin said, raising his eyebrows, 'yet there remains a faction here at the court which holds to a very different point of view.'

Potemkin was right. Not only did there exist an amorphous group of sailors, soldiers and courtiers with jealousy and xenophobia as their underlying and unifying emotion, there were those among them who were even prepared to do something about it. Greig was out of Russia, they said, let him remain abroad. It was a measure of how dangerously they misjudged the temper of their 'little Mother' that during his visit to England, Greig was thought by them to be removable from office and to be replaceable by one of the elder figurehead Admirals who remained, senior to Samuel, on the Active List. To this end they concocted a plot.

The leader of this faction was a Russian Rear Admiral called Vladimir Nemikovsky who detested the British

Commander-in-Chief for the best of all reasons – Samuel had once done him a favour. For this he was not to be forgiven. The favour in question was the not inconsiderable one of saving Nemikovsky from a court-martial for cowardice. The incident had occurred when Captain Vladimir had been in command of a sixty-six-gun at the last battle of the Turkish campaign, that of Shumla in 1774. Nemikovsky's ship had been ordered into the van but instead of taking station as signalled he had – accidentally as he later claimed – stranded his ship on a shoal about which every Captain had been specially warned.

Both Orlov and Samuel had been furious at this display of crass bad-seamanship, the more so since at the Court of Enquiry it transpired that Captain Vladimir had specifically countermanded the advice of his Master who was navigating the ship and who also happened to be Scottish. The circumstances, though highly suspect to Samuel, were of such complexity that there had had inevitably to be an element of doubt as to whether an error in language and communication on board Nemikovsky's ship might not justifiably be held to be the cause of the accident. Moreover, throughout the commission Captain Vladimir and his Scottish navigator had been scarcely on speaking terms. Nemikovsky had then appealed directly to the Commander-in-Chief, and Orlov, who by that time had had enough of the Elphinston Eccentrics and his foreign contingent in general, had decided to court-martial the Master of the ship in place of the Captain. Since this went counter to all good naval discipline, Samuel had recommended that the case be dropped, and with it any implication of cowardice or a desire to hold back in the heat of battle, although in Samuel's own mind the facts of the case were clear.

With the passing of time and the return of the fleet to Crondstadt, the contract of service of Nemikovsky's Scottish Lieutenant had been brought to an end on some trumped-up charge, and the officer had returned to the United Kingdom and further service in the Royal Navy. Nemikovsky had been promoted Rear Admiral and given a shore appointment in charge of one of the dockyard departments at Crondstadt. There whilst sedulously obeying the letter of the regulations and 'dancing attendance', as Samuel put it privately to Sarah, he lost no opportunity of denigrating 'Honest Sam' behind his back and of suggesting whenever possible to willing ears that the Commander-in-Chief was 'in on the gravy'.

He also did his best, aided by contractors such as Steckelberg, to drive a wedge between the Russian lower deck and the foreign officers. In this he had only a partial success, since Samuel's disciplinary methods, allied to his British sense of fair play, had rendered him far more popular to the nautical *moujiks* than the Russian officers, to whom oppression and a cruel despotism were second nature.

Indeed stern disciplinarian though Samuel continued always to be, his attitude had taken on the aspect not of a tyrant but more of a father chastening a favourite son. In consequence he became known to all his sailors as 'Father Greig', and such was the veneration and respect in which they held him that there was no place unsafe for him to go; although there were occasions when this 'passport' might be thought to entail an undue risk by the Empress and her close advisers.

Yet throughout this time the Admiral's enemies, some of whom had become very powerful, took every opportunity of blackening his character in subtle ways to the Empress. 'You cannot touch money without getting your fingers dirty,' they whispered. 'Was it not true', they went on to suggest, 'that the Admiral rendered the naval accounts in so many instances directly to the Empress, without the Russian Admiralty being given a chance to consider them?' This may well have been at Her Imperial Majesty's behest, but in the process 'how many roubles found their way into Father Greig's pocket?'

In such a way, then, had the stage been set at the time the Greigs departed for England. Now the plotters would have to strike whilst the iron was hot. Evidence of corruption and a covering up of 'gross peculation' had been carefully manufactured but to make such charges plausible it would be necessary to remove from the scene Fortescue

Fynne, who was not only Samuel's Chief of Staff with the control of every naval department in his hand, but was also about to marry into the Steckelberg family.

This latter reason could well become an embarrassment, and it was an awareness of this possibility which alerted Potemkin to what was really going on. Before leaving Russia, Samuel had insisted to Potemkin, and also to the Empress herself, that whilst he was away, Fortescue Fynne must remain in charge at Crondstadt.

'If for any reason whatever the Russian Admiralty decide to send him elsewhere in my absence,' Samuel had said, 'you may take it as a signal that some overthrow of authority is in the air ...' He had not needed to specify it further. Her Imperial Majesty and Potemkin knew only too well the anatomy of a plot.

When, therefore, Rear Admiral Fortescue Fynne was unexpectedly requested at short notice to make an urgent inspection of the naval fortifications at Reval, which would have entailed an absence of several days from Crondstadt, he quietly forwarded the orders to Potemkin, pleading to the Russian Admiralty a sudden indisposition which kept him in bed in the fortress of Crondstadt.

Potemkin acted at once. Who, he secretly enquired, was intended to take the place of Rear Admiral Fortescue Fynne on this voyage the Admiralty had abruptly proposed? The plotters had not meant any of this to come to Potemkin's ears until he could be faced with a *fait accompli*, and when they were then forced to reveal that the intended replacement would be none other than Rear Admiral Vladimir Nemikovsky himself, everything fell into place.

'Pray attend me at the Winter Palace,' Potemkin sent by hand to Fortescue Fynne, 'as soon as you have recovered from your unfortunate indisposition,' and Fortie sent back a message that he would be in Petersburg the following day.

No sooner had he arrived at the Palace than he was at once ushered into Potemkin's private room which gave directly on to that of the Empress. The Prince wasted no time, and it struck Fortie that there was a certain cruel streak of pleasure in the way this great ugly man of power went about his work. Tapping a dossier in front of him on the wide plain table he had had constructed for his papers, Potemkin said:

'We have here all the necessary documentation and we need waste no time in a study of the detail. But what is to be done?'

Then as Fortie did not immediately answer, the Prince walked across to the window and looked reflectively at the park, where the grass was already beginning to yellow in the summer sun. So with the grass, so with men's lives, Fortie thought, they yellow too.

'I have but to step through that door,' Potemkin eventually said, nodding towards the Empress's inner closet, 'and Admiral Nemikovsky and his associates will be removed forthwith to the dungeons of the Peter and Paul fortress, from which they will never emerge. I can have their lands forfeit and their families banished to Siberia. One word is enough. In the absence of Admiral Greig, what is your recommendation?'

Again Fortie hesitated, privately finding this arbitrary despotism extremely distasteful, even though another side of him fully comprehended the need for such an iron attitude.

'I have had an independent and private report on Admiral Nemikovsky,' Potemkin went on, a sly smile twisting the corners of his fleshy lips. 'He has been described as timid in war, courageous in peace, unskilled in business affairs, devious in his dealings with our Court, generous with other people's money, parsimonious with his own.'

'I cannot arge with that assessment,' Fortie said gravely, running his fingers nervously through his unwigged white hair, 'except that both Admiral Greig and I would award him a higher mark for his services at sea.'

'Even allowing for the stranding of his ship at the battle of Shumla?'

'There must always be a second chance for a man of quality.'

'Not always in Russia,' the Prince snapped impatiently.

'Nemikovsky is by no means all bad and as to his skill in business affairs – his department in the Dockyard is not noticeably corrupt or at fault.'

'And you are to marry Count Steckelberg's niece, I understand,' Potemkin said, giving him a hard look. Fortie countered this with a smile.

'I would not be so foolish as to recommend a man for the galleys and then try and step into his shoes. It has been said that Admiral Greig has no guile and I no malice. I think both you and the Empress read your Scottish officers like an open book. We have nothing to fear on that account.'

'Not whilst the Empress and I are here to protect you,' Potemkin said, and Fortie wondered how many similar secrets this close personal adviser was privy to. Not for all the roubles in Russia would he be in Prince Potemkin's ornately buckled shoes.

'So—' Potemkin went on, 'your inclination is to mercy?'

'It is. And I am also persuaded that such would be the thinking of the Commander-in-Chief.'

A pause ensued, which Potemkin employed in taking snuff.

'It would certainly please the Grand Duke Paul. It would also give us another handle to use.

'And perhaps induce His Imperial Highness to accept his British naval contingent with a slightly better grace?'

'As to that,' Potemkin remarked, 'we shall see. The inability to leave things alone is the Grand Duke's particular curse. The Empress totally relies on her British naval contingent. I have warned her of the dangers of this, not,' he added quickly, seeing a frown on Fortie's face, 'for any personal reasons connected with yourselves, but because the worldwide success and effectiveness of the Royal Navy at this time has engendered a growth of British influence not only at St Petersburg but also in other ports of strategic importance such as Naples, where you have already displaced the French.'

'That is true,' Fortie agreed, 'and no matter how brutal the Grand Duke may be in the expression of his feelings, there is no doubt that Imperial Russia finds herself undeniably dependent on her foreign specialists of every kind.'

'They swarm in Petersburg. Look at our Italian architects, our French opera, our doctors, our Austrian and English painters, musicians and men of letters. This apart from you British in the Navy and the German military command. Add to this that the whole international community here is supported by, and relies upon, a polyglot collection of merchants from almost every country in the world and you see a certain validity in the Grand Duke's point of view.'

'Perhaps if the Russian nobility were to hold us in less disdain, the situation might generally improve. But from all such influence they keep themselves untarnished whenever this is possible.'

Potemkin nodded and picked up a letter from his writing table.

'The Secret Chancery intercepted a letter from one of your English painters here at court who shall remain anonymous,' the Prince observed and proceeded to read it out.

' "To us who regard our merchants as the pillars of our country," he begins, "it is surprising to see the prejudices of the Russian nobility against the mercantile profession. Indeed all professions, excepting arms, are held in sovereign contempt by this lofty order of men. None but slaves, or persons derived from that race, ever in Russia become merchants, physicians etc. etc. Hence it is very difficult for nobles who have never been beyond the Empire, to be made to understand that all those vocations are often filled in England by persons related to the best families. So far is the distinction carried, that a merchant of whatever wealth is not allowed to travel with more than three horses on the road, and two in the city. A noble never drives less than four, and frequently six. However, nothwithstanding this general prejudice, I have sometimes met with a few (but very rarely) of both sexes of the Russian noblesse at the houses of our merchants, but they have always been persons of an extraordinarily enlarged mind, rendered still more liberal by travelling, and possibly a residence in England." ... How say you to that?'

'Why sir, it is true in fact,' Fortie said, 'and very fair in its judgment.'

Potemkin laid down the letter and again walked over to the window, studying the park outside with a generally unseeing gaze. In this previous diversion of interest he had evidently been making up his mind.

'Very well,' he said in the end, 'I shall deal with Admiral Nemikovsky myself. You will have no further trouble from that direction. You will find him requesting a rustication of the Commander-in-Chief for personal reasons. To this the Empress will agree and this will continue until Admiral Sir Samuel Greig returns to his post.'

Thus matters were arranged until Samuel and Sarah were once more at Crondstadt, and the attempt to remove the British Commander-in-Chief from his seat of power had been fully threshed out and the secret dossier put away.

Once the Greigs had again settled into the life of Crondstadt and St Petersburg – and Fortie had duly married his Russian Countess – the Empress and Potemkin fell into the habit of seeking their comments upon other than strictly naval topics. This enabled Samuel to draw attention to the other side of the 'anti-foreigner' coin. This was the autocratic and often extremely stupid way in which the daily life of the city and its environs was administered. One order in particular from the Chief of Police gave Samuel a few moments of sardonic pleasure before it was hastily withdrawn.

'In the case of fire', the order read, 'all landowners will notify the Chief of Police three days in advance.'

The civilizing effect of the foreign element in Crondstadt and St Petersburg – of which Samuel had by now become a leader – depended in essence on the daily application of ideas and principles which the turgid and backward nobility continued to find it disagreeable to accept.

'I cannot change them,' the Empress remarked at one

of her discussions with Samuel. 'They prefer their ancient arrogance, ignorance and laziness. They do not deserve the many ameliorations of life which are being strewn in their path. Did you hear that that fool Ryelev went to the theatre a few nights ago and was later asked what the play was about. He replied that as it was pouring with rain he never managed to read the poster outside and he thus spent the entire evening in stupefied ignorance. What can we do with such a man?'

'Why not appoint him a Governor in some distant place?' Samuel suggested. 'There are not many theatres to the east of Moscow.'

In one respect the Empress and Potemkin were more 'foreign' than the foreigners themselves. They were industrious in a way which put the greater part of the nobility to shame. Frequently they worked fourteen hours out of the twenty-four. This energy and skill in government was matched by Catherine's acute judgment of those whom she chose for close consultation.

Thus it came about at this time that although there were two Russian Admirals senior to Samuel, it was the Scotsman's opinion which was most often sought by the Empress, and this process extended itself little by little into political matters, especially in the area of foreign affairs. This was naturally observed by the British and reported confidentially to London:

> 'Greig's penetrating mind and sound judgment enables him on the most intricate points to give salutary advice. His elaborate dissertation on the Nature of Exchange relative to the College of Commerce has procured him the Empress's thanks, accompanied by a magnificent snuff box with her picture surrounded with brilliants. The Empress frequently sends couriers to him writing in her own hand in Russian. I am informed that Admiral Greig whilst he understands the Russ tongue prefers, when he does not have the services of a secretary available, to answers these letters in French. The Empress is a woman

of acute discernment and Sir Samuel continues in the full bloom of favour and reputation.'

Inevitably, and to the private disgust of the Grand Duke, this redounded to the credit of the Admiral's native land.

14

'Turn out the Guard!'

During the year after Samuel's return from his visit to England, and with the British war against their American colonies still waxing and waning, France sought to gain an advantage over the hereditary enemy by signing an offensive and defensive alliance with the American colonists. These military arrangements were then backed up by a commercial treaty. Inevitably Great Britain declared war on France. The following year, fired by a French promise of assistance in the recapture of Gibraltar and Florida, Spain declared war on Great Britain and the four-year siege of Gibraltar began.

Whilst these events were in progress elsewhere in the world, Samuel maintained his close acquaintanceship with the various Ambassadors to the Russian court who frequently graced his table with their presence and whose opinions on pressing matters of moment were in due course reported to London, as indeed were Samuel's to the other capitals concerned. Crondstadt acquired honour and distinction through visits from the Emperor Joseph of Austria and Prince Henry of Prussia, these monarchs having compounded, compromised and composed their differences on the Bavarian succession by the Peace of Teschen in 1779. They and 'other illustrious personages', reported the British Ambassador, 'not only expressed their utmost satisfaction but also left tokens of value by which our Admiral should remember them.'

Indeed at this time when an 'Armed Neutrality' had been declared by Russia in an attempt to prevent British ships from searching neutral vessels for contraband of war, Samuel's hospitable table frequently welcomed the envoys of Spain, France, Austria, Prussia, Denmark and Sweden – precisely those countries which had joined themselves with Russia in that declaration, known locally as the

'Armed Nullity'. This civilized exchange of opinion which took place under diplomatic privilege in a country but little concerned with, or rather not actively concerned in, the wars then in progress, developed into a forum of considerable value not only to those who took part but also to the Empress, who received a distillation of their various debates either from Samuel himself or, more frequently and informally, from Sarah.

Sir James Harris, the British Minister at Petersburg during this period, became a particular friend of the Greigs and his shrewd, observing mind enlightened these informal discussions more, perhaps, than any other of those invited to the Commander-in-Chief's table. Naturally not every matter under discussion came to the ears of the Empress. In particular the rise and decline of Her Majesty's favourites, now that Prince Potemkin had retired, so to speak, to the anteroom, became the principal and most delicate of such topics to be declared *verboten.*

'I sometimes wonder,' Harris remarked one day to Samuel when the various problems provoked by the 'armed nullity' were at their height, 'whether our friends at home consider how difficult a task they have imposed upon me in my attempts to subvert the various influences at this Asiatic court which are better paid than our own.'

'Yet I have heard you say that the amiable Count Panin – with his wonderful desire to be thought open and frank – is beyond the reach of corruption.'

'Only because from the very beginning he has been better paid by Frederick the Great than by anyone else.'

'I would hazard a guess', Samuel said, 'that this country, whilst it thinks itself the epitome of glory and political perfection, stands perhaps in the most dangerous crisis it has ever endured. Yet the great good fortune of the Empress, joined to her resolution and parts, may still supply the many deficiencies of her Generals and Statesmen.'

'If her worst enemies do not get the better of her.'

'And who are they – or how would you define such enemies?'

'Why – flattery and her own passions,' the Ambassador said. 'She never turns a deaf ear to the first, let it be ever so gross, and her inclination for gratifying the latter appears to grow upon her with age.'

'I hear she is disposed to amuse the public with hopes of a new accommodation with the Porte. Yet what are the grounds for such an idea? The Turks are preparing a really formidable fleet in the Black Sea and are taking many more efficacious steps towards forming a regular army, I am informed, than any they have yet attempted.'

'And in the meantime the system of the court goes on here in its old train – immense prodigality harnessed to an ineradicable habit of indolence and procrastination which reigns from the first to the last.'

The Ambassador paused, favouring the Admiral with one of his penetrating looks.

'How then do you interpret the recent treaty with Austria,' he enquired, 'by which it is hoped to drive the Turks out of Europe? Her Imperial Majesty's grandson, Constantine, is to be placed at the head of a restored Greek Empire to be called the Kingdom of Dacia, as I comprehend – the western Balkans and Serbia being allocated to Austria and the Morea, Candia and Cyprus to Venice. Are we now to have another Turkish war?'

The Admiral did not immediately reply but after consideration smiled and then said:

'Her Imperial Majesty recently visited Crondstadt, as I believe you know, for the purpose of laying the keel of her latest hundred-gun ship of the line and after this ceremony had been performed, she did me the honour of calling at my house. She had expressed a wish to drink a dish of tea but after resting herself in our salon, she intimated to me that she understood I had some fine old Greek wines in my cellar and that she would be glad to see a sample of them. I instantly presented her with a small glass of Cyprus. She pronounced the quality of this to be excellent.'

'As indeed it is,' the Ambassador interjected.

' "I hope you have a good stock," she went on, to which

I replied "Alas! my cellar is almost empty and I have absolute need of another Greek war to replenish it." She smiled graciously and in such a manner as to indicate that a project of this kind was certainly not foreign to her thoughts.'

One early October evening in that same year of 1782 the recently appointed Spanish Ambassador, the Marquis de las Torres, joined his French and British colleagues at Greig's hospitable table, during which time a discussion of the beleaguerment of Gibraltar took place. This redoubtable siege had then been in progress for over three years and the Marquis himself had been present during its early stages.

'I assisted at the commencement of that siege,' the Marquis remarked, 'in the role of second-in-command. Luckily for my reputation I did not foretell its speedy reduction, as my Commander-in-Chief was unwise enough to claim.'

'However, my lord,' Samuel interrupted with a smile, 'you have now been sent copies of the new plans for the floating batteries destined to reduce that stubborn rock.'

Barely concealing his surprise, the Marquis enquired how such intelligence had come into the Admiral's possession.

'Why, sir,' the British Ambassador put in, 'the Empress sent them by courier to our host for what she is pleased to call a professional opinion.'

'And since we are met here in our private capacities,' the Spaniard said, 'what in substance was the reply you gave?'

'I said I could not but admire the ingenious construction of the batteries,' Samuel answered. 'Nothing in my opinion could exceed their solidity. They might even prove to be bombproof.'

'But . . .?'

'They would not be effective in resisting red-hot shot. At least I thought it unlikely.'

The astonishment evinced by the Marquis now exceeded all bounds.

'Does every Scotsman possess the second sight?' he asked.

'No, my lord,' Samuel said, 'I lay no claims myself to such a propensity. But I am a practical sailor well versed in this kind of problem. Why do you ask?'

'Because I have only yesterday received a dispatch from Madrid which exactly confirms your suspicions. The mode of destruction of these batteries by the gallant Elliot was precisely that of attacking them with red-hot shot.'

This opinion, or, as his enemies maintained, this well-founded guess added in no small measure to the high esteem in which Her Imperial Majesty continued to hold her Commander-in-Chief. This consideration in the multiplicity of affairs which at times threatened to swamp his life proved to be the sustaining force which enabled the Admiral to bring order into every matter engaging his attention. Any problem not susceptible to a ready solution would be subjected to scrutiny in the minutest detail, and one such matter resulted in his being elected to the Royal Society of London.

This came about because at that time a fire broke out in Crondstadt for no reason which was immediately apparent. After the most searching enquiry, Samuel established that the fire had not been started by a human hand. It had generated itself in the carpenter's shop where a quantity of lampblack and oil had been mixed together for the purpose of painting the yards. After much trial and error, Samuel discovered that these substances mixed in different proportions and covered up close will take fire at a given time.

Once remedial precautions had been instituted in the Russian Navy, Samuel hastened to report his discovery to Lord Sandwich at the British Admiralty. For this he received His Lordship's thanks and his subsequent election as a Fellow of the illustrious Royal Society of London. At much the same time Samuel became one of the first recipients of the Grand Cross of St Vladimir, a new order of knighthood instituted by the Empress. There were to be but twelve members of the first grade of this new honour, and of these twelve, Her Imperial Majesty declared, Sir

Samuel Karlovich was to be the premier. At the same time she caused his portrait in oils to be executed by her court painter Levitsky, the which was to hang in the hall of that order. By now Samuel's fame had spread to all quarters of the Russian Empire.

But 'Father Greig' still had his enemies, not only in the higher ranks but also among the 'woodlice of the dockyard'. Steckelberg and his associates had been driven back into the shadows, they had not been destroyed. No sooner had one monopoly been liquidated than attempts were quietly made to set up two others in its place. A fleet must have its suppliers, chandlers and repairers. This naturally entailed a running account of millions of roubles, on which inevitably there were monopolies and through which various contractors inevitably grew prosperous and fat. Unfortunately for the generality of these contractors, however, Samuel had imported yet another Scottish principle into the management of his Crondstadt command. He paid his bills in cash on demand, at the same time securing a discount for prompt payment – a practice all but unknown in Russia.

This had a revolutionary effect on the contractors supplying the Navy since – like the Kings of France – they had hitherto lived in a world where almost any amount might be signed for, borrowed, deferred or otherwise made a consideration, provided the transaction was merely recorded on paper, whereas the finding of a few roubles in hard cash would take days and sometimes months of negotiation, the whole frequently ending in a vacuum of inaction. However these cash payments, as contractors very smartly discovered, were designed to be passed on with equal celerity to the carpenters, shipwrights and artisans who made or worked the articles needed by the fleet and to the victuallers who kept it supplied. If Father Greig were to hear of any delay in these 'on payments' – and he made sure he did – then he sent immediately for the contractor in question, addressed him a verbal broadside and deducted a painful fine from the next payment due.

In one of these grey transactions, as Samuel phrased them, his old colleague, Fortescue Fynne, became unwittingly involved. By this time the light-hearted excesses and penury of Fortie's early life had been brought to an end by his marriage to the young Baltic beauty, the Countess Anna Feodorovna. On an intimate and domestic level this marriage was a great success. She was very much younger than he was. She doted on him, and Fortie, in turn, took a boyish delight in the attentions of one so elegant and sweet. In due course a family of their own was begun and this – to Fortie – unexpected marital bliss continued undisturbed except for the fact that he was never allowed to forget that she was the niece of Count Steckelberg, the contractor whose estimate for the rebuilding of Crondstadt had been rejected but who had then made up for this disappointment by securing the brandy monopoly. Any state monopoly is an important affair, and the Steckelberg family fortunes gained very considerably in consequence. Alas! greed came to dominate the Count's calculations in the supply of brandy as it had done in the furnishing of stone for the fortification of Crondstadt, and one day towards Easter, the Count's presence was requested in the office of the Commander-in-Chief. With some reluctance and a show of hauteur, the Count presented himself as requested. After civilities had been exchanged, Samuel came straight to the point.

'I have received continuous and growing complaint from my sailors that the brandy supplied to Crondstadt is being watered and is not up to strength.'

'That may well be,' the Count replied with a bland condescension. 'The spirit I supply is certainly up to its proof as the Imperial Inspector will tell you. However there is no way of preventing an individual seller of brandy from increasing his profit by adding a little water to the cask. Such minor peculations are nothing to do with me and are beyond my control.'

'It is said that you pay the Imperial Inspector very well for his services, that as a consequence many a cask passes through his hands without a proper check and that the cases already investigated show beyond any doubt that water has been added before the arrival in the shop of the casks concerned. So I give you warning, Count, that the practice is to cease forthwith. How you cause it to cease is your affair, but cease it will.'

'You do not threaten Count Steckelberg,' the Count said haughtily.

'And you, sir, do not from now on supply the Imperial Russian Navy with adulterated spirit.'

'Good day to you, sir,' the Count said and abruptly took his leave. Unfortunately as he left the Admiral's office he met Fortescue Fynne on his way in. The latter naturally enquired of his wife's uncle the reason for his visit, and on briefly acquainting him of this, Count Steckelberg added with a smile:

'Though I would have thought a weakening of the brandy supplied to these sailor serfs of yours might better be a cause for a congratulation, since there will assuredly be less drunkenness in Crondstadt during the Easter holidays.'

This casual remark, being overheard, was immediately and quietly put to good use by the Admiral's enemies who bruited it around that the contractor and the Commander-in-Chief were 'in consent' and were dividing 'the profits of water' between them. Rumours are rumours: watered brandy had another and more violent result. Insinuations were made with much industry to the sailors that it was in vain to complain, but that they should in a body do themselves justice. This, on Easter Sunday, they put into practice.

The Greek and Russian Orthodox Churches require of their adherents a strict observance of Lent. No flesh is to be eaten, no fermented liquor to be drunk in the period culminating in Good Friday. By Easter Sunday, however, those rigours are drowned when the floodgates of indulgence are opened. Then each little community will roast a whole sheep over a spit in the village square and this will be washed down by casks of wine and spirit so that full drunken advantage may be taken of the holiday which follows.

On this Easter Sunday the sailors of Crondstadt assembled in thousands and began their celebrations by going from one brandy shop to another and by almost beating to death the unfortunate brandy sellers. 'And consider yourselves lucky,' they shouted to those they considered the worst profiteers by water, 'that we do not roast you alive in the square in place of the sheep.'

They then drank as much as they could manage in the wrecked shops, endeavouring to carry off the remainder in buckets and hats. A very considerable havoc was wrought and when the Duty Officer of Marines attempted to put an end to the tumult, his own end was nearly achieved with a sharp shower of stones. Wasting no further time, this officer whose cheek had been half torn off, ran to his Commander-in-Chief and burst into Admiralty House where Samuel was at dinner with a few friends amongst whom was Fortescue Fynne.

'Sir!' he cried out, 'the mob is looting the brandy shops and may soon have the whole dockyard on fire.'

'Turn out the Guard,' Samuel ordered and summoning his Aide-de-Camp strode off towards the heart of the trouble with Fortie at his heels. 'By God!' he exclaimed, 'I'll have Steckelberg for this.'

By the time Samuel and his small party reached the principal brandy shop which had already gone up in flames, a full-scale riot was under way. In recent times reports had come in of country estates where the serfs, driven beyond human endurance, had risen and slaughtered their owners. Now, it seemed to Samuel as he surveyed the scene, he had the same trouble in his own back yard.

'Where's the damned Guard?' he called out in a fury, but although the alarm had been raised on Samuel's departure from Admiralty House, no sign of the duty officers and the regulating squad was to be seen for nearly an hour. Indeed long before they arrived on the scene, Samuel had decided to make his presence felt.

When the mob had first caught sight of their much loved

Commander-in-Chief, they had run off pell-mell to a distance, but still within earshot. There in a great mass of angry men, they took counsel of one another but very soon anarchy took over and they began to plunder and pillage once more.

'Stop this violence at once!' Samuel called out. 'Step forward the leaders! D'ye hear there? In the name of the Empress.'

'In the name of brandy the strength of piss,' the answer came back accompanied by shouts and jeers.

'Follow me,' Samuel said to those who were with him. 'I shall settle this crackerhash once and for all. Fortie, put away your sword. We can do this without striking a blow.'

'Perhaps,' Fortie said under his breath, 'perhaps not.'

So, completely unarmed, Samuel strode into the very midst of the mob, which reacted to this gesture of authority with a frightened but temporary paralysis.

'I know you, Ivan Kyrilovich,' Samuel rasped out, recognizing a well-known trouble-maker from earlier days, and seizing him by the arms, forced him to kneel on the ground. 'Now who else of you call yourselves leaders?' he shouted and as no one answered, Fortie and the ADC, helped by two other officers who had arrived on the scene, grabbed the rioters nearest to them and frog-marched them out of the mêlée. In the course of this Fortie received a black eye and the ADC a severe cut on the shoulder. But for the moment the power of the mob had been broken by the removal of five of their most vociferous ringleaders.

At last the Guard arrived and were ordered by Samuel to remove these five to prison. This again proved to be too much for the mob. Although the Guard was of course armed, the crowd fell on them with shouts of anger and vengeance in order to secure the release of their companions. In this scuffle a sailor was killed by the thrust of a bayonet. At length, awed by Samuel's commanding presence and the dire penalties he promised them all if they did not immediately desist, and which, to a man, they knew he would enforce, a semblance of order was restored and the mob returned to its barracks. Samuel then turned his attention to the dilatory appearance on the scene of the Duty Officers and the Guard. Their lame excuse rested upon a faulty communication.

'That I do not accept,' Samuel remarked tersely. 'However you shall have a choice. Either suffer a court martial which I shall summon tomorrow, or you shall accompany me this very evening on a tour of the brandy shops which are to be reopened with such stock as is left. I shall sample the brandy myself and pronounce on its strength.'

The Guard, realizing well enough the likely outcome of a court-martal conducted under the direct eye of their Commander-in-Chief, chose to tour Crondstadt that evening and heroic efforts were made (with doubtless some unadulterated stock being brought up specially from the cellars) to get the place 'ship-shape and Bristol fashion'. The tour itself thus became something of a triumphal progress, since the affection of the great mass of the sailors for Samuel was amply demonstrated and Samuel, in turn, tasted the brandy in each of the shops and pronounced it 'suitable in all respects for the purpose of intoxication'.

'And now for Count Steckelberg,' Samuel said to Fortie, as they returned to Admiralty House. 'Your wife's uncle shall be put to the trouble of a full explanation and, if I have my way, of a reimbursement of the Crown's expense in restoring today's damage in full.'

In the meantime news of the riot had been reported express to the Grand Duke Paul in Petersburg by one of the subordinate officers who had taken good care not to appear on the scene until all of it was over. 'I saw the Admiral kill four or five sailors with his own hands,' this informer told the Grand Duke, who then conveyed this intelligence which, he said, reflected on the Admiral's honour, to the Empress herself.

Once again Her Imperial Majesty, having had the matter independently investigated, expressed herself entirely satisfied with the Admiral's conduct. The officer who had propagated the evil news was stripped of his rank and sent to the hulks. Others who had been dilatory were likewise punished, and an Imperial reprimand was addressed to all flag officers and subordinates at Crondstadt.

On the next occasion that Samuel appeared at court, he complained to the Empress in a private audience how ill he had been treated by injurious reports.

'Do not be surprised that your enemies are vocal,' the Empress declared and then added with a frown, 'Moreover I am seriously displeased with your conduct on this occasion.'

'May I presume to ask Your Imperial Majesty in what respect?' Samuel replied, unable to keep an indignant note from his voice.

'Why, by risking your life, Samuel Karlovich. You ventured into the midst of an enraged mob.'

'But I was not alone.'

The Empress stared at her Admiral and then, with the glint of a smile, indicated her displeasure to be more simulated than real.

'Do not think I am ignorant of anything that passed,' the Empress eventually commented, 'but you only had two or three of your own countrymen with you. Such a bodyguard is scarcely adequate to its purpose. In future you will please to take greater care of a life that is so precious to me – and to the Empire.'

15

'On the side of the Spartans'

Some twelve years after Russia had first annexed the Crimea, and with hostilities against the Sublime Porte still intermittently in progress, the fortification of Sevastopol and the creation of a Russian Black Sea fleet did not seem to the Empress to be making the progress she required. Late in 1782, therefore, when elsewhere in the world the American War of Independence was about to end, when Gibraltar had been relieved and when Austro-Russian pressure against the Turks was all the time increasing, Samuel found himself requested to attend one day on Prince Potemkin, who drew him into his private closet and said:

'Her Imperial Majesty has it in mind to send you on a visit of inspection to the Crimea, if the temporary delegation of your duties at Crondstadt can be arranged. However the Empress does not wish to issue her orders without first ascertaining your feelings in the matter.'

'As Your Excellency is surely aware,' Samuel replied, 'I will obey whatever commands Her Majesty desires to give me.'

Potemkin nodded his approval and reminded Samuel that one of his compatriots, General Sir Samuel Bentham, had been given charge of the arsenal at Kherson.

'However there is another General, a Russian General, presently on one of his very rare visits to court whom the Empress desires you to meet in private before you undertake the long journey south. I do not think you have previously made General Suvorov's acquaintance and I consider a word of caution appropriate before you do so. Of his military reputation you will no doubt be fully cognizant: of his other attributes and personal characteristics, you may be less well informed.'

'I know he is nicknamed Alexander Diogenes.'

Prince Potemkin allowed himself a sly smile.

'Our Potsdam friends would call him a "Feldherr", I imagine. A man for the battleground, not for the court. It was Comte Ségur, I believe, who once enquired of him whether he always slept in his clothes, to which he replied that he did but that if he really wanted a comfortable night he sometimes took off a spur.'

'Yet I am told he can command a loyalty from his troops exceeding that of any other general in the service of the Empress.'

'That is true,' said the Prince, 'and the Empress has also observed that this is a quality he shares with "Father" Greig. However he somewhat lacks your English manners and behaviour – when such behaviour would be politic and appropriate. At one of the full courts he attended, he looked scornfully round the assembled company, clapped me on the shoulder and remarked: "What a host of troubadours Your Excellency has!"'

Prince Potemkin smiled thinly. It was apparent to Samuel that he did not find this comment especially amusing.

When the meeting duly took place, the British sailor and the Russian general found themselves in instant accord. Samuel invited Suvorov to visit Crondstadt before returning to the Crimea and, although at first reluctant to delay his departure from Petersburg a day longer than necessary, the doughty general accepted the invitation, being pleased to congratulate Samuel on what he observed.

'I comprehend that you and I are endeavouring to apply in our respective services the same idea of discipline,' he remarked, 'namely that it should be founded upon understanding, the use of force only being applied as a last resort. If a man understands, he need not tremble before anyone, including his Commander-in-Chief. But then—' he added with an angry spark in his eye, 'you do not suffer in the naval service from the regiment of Guards. My problems lie more with my officers than with the men they command.'

'Ah! but I do have similar difficulties,' Samuel said and endeavoured to draw him further on this point.

'The court', Suvorov said in a tone of acid contempt,

'is the breeding ground of that most detestable of characters who, unchecked, will destroy all military order. I refer to that source of everything that is dangerous in an army – the mannered fop, the damned fellow who "doesn't know", the hint-dropper, the poser of riddles, the word-spinner, the two-faced incoherent womanizer and drunkard.'

'You are known to be on the side of the Spartans,' Samuel remarked. It struck him that talking to General Suvorov was like lifting the lid from a boiling kettle.

'I will not have near me one of those courtly fellows who insinuates himself into the favour of his superiors by sweet and ambiguous talk. I know them too well. It is thus that they attempt to hide their own insufficiencies. In such a man hypocrisy replaces humility and manners, experience. When he becomes a general he remains essentially the same. He then has power but yet no understanding of responsibility. Ugh! For war we need other qualities, more practical, more down-to-earth. I can find here at the Petersburg court no trace of the breed of leader the Imperial forces require.'

'The Empress herself knows what she is about.'

'Our little mother will never admit to the possibility of defeat,' Suvorov said, 'and in that point of view I proudly share. It makes for no popularity with the hereditary nobles who infest the court, that self-indulgent rabble which merely mimics the French in their dress, their morals and their manners.'

'Not everyone is so tainted,' Samuel observed, 'and the man closest to the throne, the Prince Potemkin, has been a "practical soldier" himself, much I fancy in the mould you so admire. You may not find him agreeable. You may not even trust him to any depth, but his military experience in the field is undeniable. The same can also be said, though in a lesser degree, of another past favourite of Her Imperial Majesty, the Count Alexei Orlov. Whatever his private faults, there can be no doubt about his martial attributes.'

'We will not speak of the Orlovs,' Suvorov said. 'Come to the Crimea and see for yourself how we order things in that part of the Empire in which it is my lot to serve.'

The significance of this meeting between Greig and Suvorov thus late in their careers was that each had clearly shown himself to be unique in his own sphere. Both had arrived at their essentially commanding, essentially indispensable positions by a strict adherence to principle, a deep courage and an undauntable will to achieve what they set out to do.

'And what was your opinion of our distinguished visitor?' Samuel asked Sarah after Suvorov had taken his leave.

'I should not care to be his wife. He may be a great soldier ...'

'He is certainly that.'

'But he is only a partial man. That story about the spurs is revealing. No doubt he is the man for a hard campaign. But do you suppose he removes his spurs when he tries to be agreeable to a woman?'

'I fancy there has been little enough of that in his life,' Samuel said. 'His marriage could scarcely be described as successful.'

'That does not surprise me at all,' Sarah said, seeking the comfort of Samuel's arms as she always did when she wished to feel secure. 'One might as well be married to a monk. There is a limit to austerity so far as a woman is concerned.'

The next visitor to the Greig mansion, after Suvorov had departed, happened to be Sir James Harris, the British Ambassador. To him Samuel described the General's visit and his opinion of the effect of such a character on the conduct of Russian affairs.

It was high summer and Samuel had taken the Ambassador for a sail round the great harbour of Crondstadt in the green-painted caravel he had had built to his own design. This form of entertainment, which Samuel reserved for those he most respected, was usually followed by a climb to the 'crow's nest' – a nautical gazebo Samuel had had constructed on the commanding heights of the fortress.

Here he had installed a powerful telescope with which he and his visitors could survey the whole port. His steward would follow with suitable refreshment, and since it required an effort to reach, was entirely private and could be kept comparatively cool by an ingenious system of canvas shading, the Admiral's eyrie was conducive to reflection and, if matched by the intellect of the visitor, formed an ideal background to discussions in depth.

Samuel would always mount to this point when there were matters he wished to think out by himself, and now as the Ambassador looked down on the rugged battlements below, over the masts and sails of the huge ships of the line alongside the moles or anchored imposingly in the harbour, and then on to the coastline leading to St Petersburg, the place had evidently the same effect of persuading his mind to range back in time as it had on Samuel.

'The longer I remain *en poste* at Petersburg,' the Ambassador said, 'the more incredible appears to be the lead which this court seems able to take in the great transactions of Europe. Why is this? The public success of Russia and the supine inefficiency of its administration are incompatible – and yet they co-exist.'

'I am told by those who visit me here and have never lived in Russia, that the Empire appears to be conducted with a superior judgment, being defective in no one essential point of its government. I find this to be incredible and so, I think, would every foreign officer under my command. We simply cannot get them to accept ideas. They nod their heads in a wise way and then go on exactly as they did before.'

'To what then do you ascribe their success in the other great courts of Europe?' the Ambassador asked, looking over the rim of his glass down on 'the Admiral's parish'. The Navy he knew to be almost the only exception to the lawless disorder which prevailed in other Russian government services. He snorted with indignation at the memory of some of the local transactions he had been forced to undertake.

'To those of us here', he continued, 'who perceive the unaccountable and imperfect manner in which all plans are traced, together with the improper instruments selected for their execution, it is a matter of constant astonishment that they do not fail in every single thing they undertake.'

Samuel nodded his agreement and then took up the Ambassador's train of thought.

'Since we live our daily lives in confusion and anarchy, except where we bring our own intelligence and powers to bear, I would venture to say that a kind of pre-ordination of good luck attends the operation of this court – at least as I see matters here at Crondstadt. This has not only saved Russia from the most imminent dangers, it raises the country to a degree of power I doubt even Her Imperial Majesty had expected to attain.'

'However, the endurance, or let us say the permanency, of this superior influence', the Ambassador remarked, 'gives rise to much greater doubt. Her Imperial Majesty, before she took the reins of Empire in her hands, had long and diligently prepared her mind to govern. With very fine parts, she employed her many leisure hours as Grand Duchess in laying in those materials which have made the first seven or eight years of her reign the most brilliant period, I would say, in the Russian history. She then governed systematically, judiciously and with dignity. But now Monsieur de Voltaire is dead and the Orlovs dismissed from favour. Certainly from this latter event we can date her political errors. And now her court, from being conducted with the greatest dignity and exterior decorum, is gradually become a scene of depravation and immorality. A Korsakov follows a Zoritz into her bed, and now we have a Lanskoi in competition with a Mordnivov – the whole circus controlled by a ringmaster called Potemkin who rules over her with an absolute sway operating as and when he may choose upon her weaknesses, her desires and her passions.'

'And the Grand Duke – with his declared aversion to all foreigners and especially to ourselves?'

The Ambassador thought for a while before answering and then said:

'Mercifully I doubt him to be capable of justifying the fears with which Potemkin inspires the Empress. The Grand

Duke is innately timid. He also possesses a levity of temper – perhaps vacuity of temper would be a better description – which appears not to diminish with age. I apprehend him as perfectly unfit to govern this immense and turbulent empire. His wife, it is true, has every mark of a virtuous, well-informed mind and her conduct – now – is judicious. But these are qualifies which do not appear to survive an elevation to the throne. Certainly no Empress has ever carried them with her to the grave. The criterion for the Grand Duchess will be when her husband comes to the throne or when he violates those conjugal ties he now observes with such un-Russian severity.'

'I find the Empress herself still to be as much "English" as – shall we say – "French" or "Prussian", but I may gain this impression from the special favour in which she appears to hold her British naval contingent.'

The Ambassador considered this and then slightly changed the course of the discussion.

'Are you acquainted with the fact that Count Alexei Orlov, though out of favour in one respect, still carries great weight whenever he speaks to the Empress?'

The Admiral nodded his agreement.

'My old Commander-in-Chief was always clear in his language and generally happy in his expressions,' Samuel said, thinking back to his service with him in the Turkish war, and then went on: 'And now that you have mentioned the Count, I must say that he has always been a staunch friend to the British. I had a conversation with him on his return from abroad in which he informed me that the Empress had taken him to task for not including England in his travels. "Why, madame," he retorted, "with our adhesion to this Armed Neutrality so recently in mind, I would have been ashamed to show myself in a kingdom to whom Russia was under so great obligations. If I had appeared in London, I must have expected my old Mediterranean acquaintance to turn their backs on me." I asked him how this had been received by Her Imperial Majesty and he said "not very well at the time" but that she had later sent for him in private and had confessed herself not quite pleased with her own behaviour towards the English. She then asked his opinion on the present situation of affairs. Orlov replied that his political sentiments had ever been the same; that he considered the French as a faithless, false nation, enemies to her and to her Empire and that if their conduct was changed, yet their designs were not. He added with a smile that he granted the English were *less polite* than the French: however they were much *more sincere* and they were also the only true and useful friends Russia could have. If, he said, the Empress remained indifferent to the esteem and regard of a nation like ours, then she ought not lightly to lose our goodwill and friendship.'

'I, too, have had conversations with Count Alexis,' Sir James Harris said. 'These could well have been embarrassing as naturally I did not hide from him my many obligations to his successor, Prince Potemkin, nor the strong and daily proofs I receive of Potemkin's friendship, to which alone I attribute the maintenance here of my ground. I added, however, that my opponents having fixed in the Empress's mind an idea that Prince Potemkin receives all his political impressions from me, she would not, when he talked to her on foreign affairs, pay that deference to his opinion the which she afforded him in most others. I therefore considered it to be in the power of Count Alexis on the other hand to do me a very essential service, particularly on two points of the greatest importance to England, on one of which he was the properest person in the Empire to speak. The first, I said, was to convince Her Imperial Majesty of the necessity that America should remain entirely dependent on her mother country – England – not less for her sake than ours. The second was to prevent the Empress from attempting to foist into a treaty of peace the principles of the Armed Neutrality. On these matters, I observed, no one could talk so pertinently to her as himself, who had commanded her fleet in the Mediterranean, assisted by the man she had now promoted to be her Commander-in-Chief at Crondstadt, namely yourself. The Count entered with a cordial conviction into everything I advanced and added, "The Empress cannot but admit the truth of what you say when she hears it from two such different persons as Prince Potemkin and myself, who never till now thought alike."'

The friendship of Sir James and Lady Harris, and a frequent contact with the Ambassador's informed and lively mind, became to the Greigs not only a sustenance but a solace. Like speaks to like, and each man brought a ready understanding and an intelligence to the problems facing the other. Both were men of integrity, conducting their affairs in a milieu in which every word could become almost a term of abuse. Over them and the few others of a similar nature, and over the bustling antheap of the Petersburg court, loomed the increasingly sombre, corpulent figure of the great Empress, the autocrat whose whim could spell life or death to any of her subjects brought either by fate or by their own contrivance into the magic circle of power surrounding the throne.

Those revolutionary forces which would so soon erupt in France were still contained underground, in seed form, perhaps, but nowhere near the possibility of germination in Russia. The Austrian Emperor, Joseph II, who had visited St Petersburg and to whom the Russian Empress felt more cordial than to any other of the European monarchs, had recently abolished serfdom, had freed his country's monastic orders from the dictatorship of Rome (despite a visit of protest to Vienna by the Pope) and had allowed a new tolerance to the press. The Empress Catherine, whilst striving to establish Monsieur Diderot's code of law and other structures of civilization in the barbaric vastness of her realm, remained shackled by the indolence, greed and corruption of those upon whom she was compelled to rely for the execution of her orders.

Such, then, was the world in which Samuel lived out the last decade of his life. As a trusted servant – and for all practical purposes the head of one of the two armed forces on whom ultimately the throne relied for its authority – Samuel found himself consulted more often than he would have wished on matters not strictly in his domain.

He duly toured the Crimean theatre of war and advised the Empress on what he saw in those recently acquired parts of Empire. More and more British naval officers were secured for the Russian service, and a substantial fleet grew into being year by year at Crondstadt.

There were other British influences, or perhaps it would be more accurate to say mainly North British influences, which had taken root in that harsh, inhospitable climate. There were Scottish philosophers, historians and doctors – one of whom had successfully inoculated the Empress against smallpox (at the same time taking the precaution of having a carriage and horses kept at the ready for a speedy escape in the event of the inoculation failing). There was also an English gardener – the 'Repton of Russia' – who planned and superintended the pleasure grounds of the Winter Palace, which he laid out in the English style of extensive shrubberies, romantic walks, rustic retreats, hot-houses and conservatories – the whole being supervised by the remarkable Mr Gould. Indeed this Englishman's honesty, excellent heart and generous hospitality helped materially to build up that respect for the British character in Petersburg which Samuel and Sarah had in their turn done so much to establish. Ironically enough these were the people whom the Grand Duke, the heir to the throne, in his jealousy wished to extirpate from the Russian life.

16

Final endeavour

In the autumn of 1787, as the first snows began to fall during that magic season when the burnt-out land begins to refresh itself, soon to lie silent and still under its winter covering of snow stretching away, dazzling white into the distance, as far as the eye could see, the Empress returned to St Petersburg after a long visit to the Crimea.

'And the troubles in that region threaten very serious consequences,' the British Ambassador confided to Samuel, as they watched the snow catching on and weighing down the dark-green fir trees which lined the courtyard of the Petersburg house. Sir James Harris and his lady had been invited to an informal dinner with the Greigs – an event enjoyed by all four of them – and all took 'the alien's pleasure' in watching the slow transformation of the buildings and the landscape as the lead-coloured sky shed an endless, drifting load of snow.

It was the first big fall of the late autumn, and somehow to Sarah it symbolized what seemed to have become the almost changeless pattern of their lives. To Sarah, the year began with the hard lengthy winter when most activity in the house would centre around the tall wood-burning stoves and on the importance of keeping warm. Outside it would be fur coats and sleighs, and more often than not a razor-sharp icy wind.

Then these long long nights and short days were followed by that brief period of slushy thaw out of which burst the brilliant spring, when all life seemed to start again. Spring to the watchful Greigs meant great resolutions being made to improve the quality of existence on their country estate by bringing in more of the new agricultural methods already proved in England, such as the rotation of crops – which of course, were begun in the usual Russian way and then abandoned as soon as the prospect of hard work became reality. Every year Samuel would say:

'Had I not been compelled to attend to my duties at Crondstadt and at sea, I would have battened down those lazy, good-for-nothing idlers who cannot hoist in the idea—'

'—that without effort no improvement can result,' Sarah always finished the sentence for him. This occasioned first a frown and then a smile from the husband she adored but who was now, she was forced to admit, becoming an old man.

Tonight was the first opportunity they had had for some time to see Sir James and his wife, and perhaps because of the changing weather, perhaps because all had reached that stage in their lives when the day-to-day minutiae no longer swamped every passing moment but allowed them time to consider and reflect, all were in a somewhat nostalgic mood. This was enhanced by the fact that a long run of bad health had caused Sir James to ask for his recall to London, which had been granted, so that this dinner party might well be the last time the four friends would meet together in such relaxed circumstances.

'You are soon to return to England,' Sarah said, as they left the window and proceeded through into the dining room. 'I wonder if we shall ever see our homeland again...'

'Our homeland is now Russia,' Samuel put in, 'a fact I have long accepted but which Sarah, alas, has not.'

Lady Harris exchanged an understanding smile with her hostess.

'However, Sam, I note that you console yourself with your Fieldings and your Smolletts, and by ensuring the regular arrival of the *Gentleman's Magazine*.'

'He needs an English chuckle from time to time,' Sarah said, a trifle wistfully, 'and there are no Russian authors to supply that requirement.'

'Aye, that is so,' Samuel conceded. 'The life here is harder on Sarah than it is on me.'

'I would certainly be in agreement with that,' Lady Harris said, 'but your sons will soon be away to sea themselves. Perhaps then you could allow your wife a little home leave?'

'I could never abandon him here alone,' Sarah quickly retorted. 'Such is not my desire, even for a short period of refreshment and recuperation.'

'I would assuredly be lost without her,' Samuel said, 'and so great a part of our lives has perforce been spent apart that we relish whatever time together Fate will allow us.'

'I think you will soon have another Turkish adventure on your hands,' the British Ambassador opined. 'The Empress has set her mind on it, I am convinced.'

'And so am I,' Samuel agreed. 'Indeed we are pressing ahead with our plans for next summer. Perhaps when I am occupied in the eastern Mediterranean and the Black Sea, Sarah can be allowed her visit to England.'

The Ambassador nodded, but his mind was on greater affairs of state.

'There is no stopping the Empress these days once she gets a firm notion in her head.'

'There never has been,' Samuel agreed.

'She thinks herself quite sure of the Austrian Emperor,' the Ambassador said, looking into the distance. 'When he joined her at Sevastopol this summer, she was convinced that he had agreed to a new defensive alliance. An active war against Turkey is now probable and, bearing in mind General Suvorov's aggressive power, perhaps inevitable. I fear that she has in herself determined that the moment for carrying such a romantic plan into execution is at hand. My view is that the Austrian Emperor, "her dearly beloved Joseph", will keep it up until he has got Bosnia and Servia. He will then plant Her Imperial Majesty and leave her to the formation of an eastern empire on her own bottom. This will be the breaking up of their union but before that, many events may arise, and Europe be in combustion. I have advised keeping aloof at home and not committing ourselves on any side too far. We stand on good grounds, as I have emphasized to the Foreign Secretary. I trust our enemies will be too intoxicated with their numbers and prospect of success to hold out anything like reasonable terms of pacification, and that we shall be able to breathe moderation and forbearance in our political conduct, and use neither one nor the other in our military activity.'

'Although I am not concerned directly with politics,' Samuel said, 'I consider that Her Imperial Majesty now has innate force enough not only to refuse concessions but further to compel those who urge them on her to seek pardon for their presumption.'

'Pride has begun its dangerous sway over the martial powers of Europe,' the Ambassador remarked. Neither he nor Samuel could know that the revolution in France which would change the civilized world for ever lay only two years ahead.

'Aye,' said Samuel, 'fighting, not negotiating, is the Russian *forte*. And who is really to say the Empress is in error? It has paid her a handsome dividend to date.'

With these forthcoming Turkish adventures in mind, the Empress gave orders for the fitting out at Crondstadt of a very considerable naval force for the spring of 1788. 'The fleet of ships of war and of transports', her orders read, 'is to be prepared to take on board a body of excellent troops together with many thousand stands of arms for the Greeks and Albanians who, it is expected, will flock to the Imperial Standard.'

Count Alexis Orlov was again sent for from Moscow, and the command of this formidable armament offered. However he excused himself on the score of his age and infirmities, and by his advice the sole command was conferred upon the Admiral, who was appointed not only naval and military Commander-in-Chief but also Minister Plenipotentiary to the various states in whose neighbourhood the scene of his future operations lay. Indeed discretionary powers were given him by the Empress unlimited beyond any former example. They were, alas, never to be used.

The Admiral approached the fulfilment of this new and daunting task with his usual and indefatigable zeal. By the month of May 1788, the whole force – or to be accurate, the ships at least – were ready to put to sea. They were sufficiently armed, stored and victualled to leave the Baltic and proceed in their formidable strength to the Mediterranean theatre of operations.

At that moment an unexpected event altered the course of history. In his subsequent report to London, Lord Carmarthen, the new British Ambassador, remarked that the Russian court 'seemed to be perfectly unaware of the aggressive attitude of the King of Sweden who has been incited by ambition, the which had been fired by a sizeable sum of good Turkish sequins.' The Swedish fleet had put to sea, but its real intention was improperly suspected, 'notwithstanding the testimony of several British ship masters – still less that the fleet in question had hostile views.'

It had been decided to sail the Russian fleet to the Mediterranean in several divisions. This move had been ordered contrary to the Admiral's better judgment, because the process of taking on board the motley collection of Tartars, Tchevesses, Asliks and so on, who were to fight the Turks, had not been completed. These men, moreover, were ignorant of the Russian language and had never before seen a ship. 'It is no small praise to the Admiral,' the report continued, 'that in the course of a very few days such weird men were taught the most necessary parts of their duty and were able to distinguish themselves to the extent they did in the subsequent action.'

The first division of the Russian fleet which had been ordered to sea, all unknowing of what lay ahead, consisted of three first-rates under the command of Vice Admiral von Desin, a German officer for whom the Admiral had but little regard. This squadron had not even left the Gulf of Finland when, between Sveaborg and Reval, it was set upon by the Swedish fleet and captured without a fight. Intelligence of this strange conduct by his subordinate Admiral was received by the Commander-in-Chief at Crondstadt after two frigates had sailed for the annual exercising of marine cadets. These two ships were likewise captured by the Swedes, whose real purpose had now become disagreeably clear. However the Swedish fleet showed itself reluctant to follow up the advantage of surprise on which it had depended until now.

'Had they pressed on to Crondstadt,' the Admiral informed the Empress in a dispatch giving details of what had happened, and of his own intentions to sail forthwith, 'it is impossible to say what the consequences might have been. My ships are replete with untrained landsmen as yet unable to comprehend even the orders they are given. Be that as it may, we sail at dawn tomorrow in order to teach the King of Sweden a lesson and to restore Your Majesty's honour.'

On receipt of the Admiral's dispatch, the Empress at once swept out of the reception she was attending, ordered her fastest carriage and at once drove to Crondstadt with a company of the Guard, an Imperial outrider galloping on ahead to warn the Admiral not to sail before Her Majesty had arrived to wish them God speed. It was a dramatic sight.

The main squadron was anchored out in the harbour and Samuel had been about to join them when the messenger arrived post-haste. Samuel then ordered the flagship, the *Rotislav*, to remain alongside, and by the time the Imperial cortège arrived, with the dawn light gleaming on the golden breastplates of the cavalry officers and the magnificent Tartar horses drawing the Empress's coach flecked with the sweat of their effort, the officers and ship's company of the great ship had been drawn up in one long straight line for Her Majesty's inspection.

As the coach was brought to a halt, a signal was made to the fortress of Crondstadt and the monarch was saluted with 101 guns. Slowly and with solemn dignity the Empress inspected her sailors, and then said for all to hear:

'I pray to God that He will bless you. I have entire confidence in you, Admiral, and in this mighty fleet you command. I am convinced that you will omit no favourable occasion which shall present itself of destroying our enemies. May Heaven bless all your enterprises! That is my ardent prayer which I offer for you and all the fleet.'

Samuel then called for three rousing cheers for Her Majesty, which all but blew down the fortress itself, and, after obtaining the Royal assent, dismissed the ship's company back on board to take up their stations for leaving harbour. The autocrat watched this manoeuvre with a smile on her lips. She stood there a lone, rather bulky, plainly-dressed figure offset against her magnificently uniformed guards. When all had returned on board except Samuel himself, the Empress stepped forward and taking the arm of her Commander-in-Chief walked away from the guard until they were out of earshot.

'My dear Admiral,' she said, 'I do not at all doubt that the motives of the King of Sweden are such as you suppose them to be. From all parts I hear that the steps taken by this King are regarded as a real extravagance. These are the very words used, among others, by my Lord Carmarthen. So, Admiral, it is the duty of my forces on land and at sea to make His Swedish Majesty repent of these unconsidered steps.'

'Have no fear on that account, Your Majesty. That shall be our constant intent and endeavour.'

Catherine rewarded him with a sideways smile and a gentle squeeze of the arm. Then, as they were nearing the end of the mole, they turned and began walking slowly back to where the coach was drawn up.

'As long as you are on the sea,' she continued, 'the Swedish descents in the neighbourhood of Reval are not to be feared, and in the winter the troops will be re-inforced in that part. Never has the ardour of our troops been stronger than against this perfidious enemy. The number of fighting men augments each day: they are coming from all the provinces. If I should let them have their way, all Russia would put itself on horseback.'

By now they were close to the coach, with the gangway to the ship a few paces in the other direction.

'I see that the disposition of the spirit of the fleet under your command keeps in perfect conformity with that which is good for the public ... adieu, my dear Admiral Greig, keep in good health personally and be assured of my esteem, of my confidence and of my very sincere friendship.'

Then with the eyes of all on board upon them and also now watched by a large and impromptu crowd which had gathered from the town of Crondstadt, the Empress withdrew her arm, bowed her head as Samuel saluted and watched his tall erect figure stride up the gangway of the *Rotislav*.

Whilst the gangway was being cast off, the Empress dispatched the Captain of the Guard to find Lady Greig and invite her to sit with the Empress in the Royal coach whilst the great ship was warped away from the jetty, the sails were set and the flagship proceeded to lead the fleet out of harbour. It was to be the last time the Empress was to see 'her' Admiral alive.

Although Fortescue Fynne had put in a special request for command of one of the squadrons, Samuel had felt his services at Crondstadt to be too valuable, so that he was left there in charge during Samuel's absence. Perhaps it would have been better to bring him along, Samuel reflected, whilst watching some of the bungling and delays being occasioned as the fleet put to sea. God knows they had practised the drill often enough. But then, Samuel thought ruefully, after a practice manoeuvre he, the Admiral, would visit the offending ships himself and give them a taste of his tongue: now that they were setting off for a real operation, it seemed that nothing went right, possibly because underneath it all there still lay a reluctance on the part of some to sail at all.

The Empress had done them all a great honour by herself coming to see them depart, and so far as the *Rotislav* was concerned the sailing had taken place without delay or mishap. With some of the other ships, it was the old, old story. Out in the bay Samuel fumed to his Flag Captain as a succession of signals went out to the offending ships, telling them in language they would certainly understand that they must smarten their drill if they were ever to be of the slightest use.

As always, the ships with the foreign officers went ahead,

the Russian-captained ships invariably lagging astern. He wondered how much of this the Empress would have observed and understood. He had warned her of the problem often enough. It was that eastern temperament, he told himself, that Asiatic element he had never been able to control. Suvorov was right – if a man cannot grasp an idea of his own accord, no progress is ever to be made; and it seemed to Samuel, as he watched the fumbling seamanship of some of his ships, that even after all this time he would never get them up to scratch, never induce in them an aggressive, as opposed to a defensive, fighting spirit. Even their trained seamen were landsmen at heart, reluctant to venture far from the shore, reluctant to bestir themselves unless driven by threat. There was nothing of the island spirit in Russia.

However, in the end, the entire fleet did get away to sea, the leading of the line being commanded by Admiral Elphinston's eldest son who, like Samuel's own progeny, had been entered for the Russian service when a mere boy of seven. Now the ten battleships and their attendant frigates were beating up the Gulf of Finland. It was a stirring sight. The sea conditions were moderate and a fresh wind blew in from the west, causing them to make lengthy tacks, observable from either shore, so that any hope of surprising the Swedes must have been lost at an early hour.

Samuel brought the enemy to battle off Hochland, and almost at once disaster struck. The Swedes, too, were foreign led, their Admiral being a German called von Wachmeister, and, perhaps encouraged by their previous easy successes they were resolute in attack. They did not wait, as the Turks had done all those years ago, safe under cover of their harbour guns. They sailed out in full combat order and at once engaged the most forward Russian ship, which was commanded by Captain Sam Elphinston.

'That youngster is as determined and aggressive as his father,' Samuel remarked to his Flag Captain, 'but where is the support? Why is Bletsikov so backward? God's teeth, he's even holding away. On the starboard tack, man, the starboard tack!'

Samuel might as well have saved his breath. He was shouting to himself. In any case the Russian centre squadron took good care to keep some way out of hailing distance. However they were undoubtedly well able to read the Commander-in-Chief's signal hoists. These not only ordered them to close the enemy but demanded to know why the signals had not so far been obeyed. The Bletsikov squadron paid no attention. Now they not only held back but at one time actually turned away.

'I know what they will claim,' Samuel said, ordering a frigate to come alongside; 'they will say the smoke of the battle obscured our yardarms. I have had enough of such nonsense. Go to Admiral Bletsikov,' he called down to the Captain of the frigate, 'and remind him in the strongest terms of his duty – unless he wishes to face an immediate court-martial.'

The frigate made off and succeeded in passing the message. The answer given was simple and bland. 'Tell the Commander-in-Chief that the range is too great for our guns. However we are endeavouring to close.'

Infuriated by this half-hearted answer and the continuing disobedience, Samuel decided himself to go to the assistance of young Captain Elphinston who was now in dire straits. Although starting from a greater distance from the heart of the battle than Rear Admiral Bletsikov and his timid ships, Samuel pressed on every inch of sail and soon came to close quarters with his Swedish opposite number. He found a situation approaching catastrophe for the Russian van.

Elphinston had been killed, his ships had been set on fire and looked to be in a very present danger of being sunk. The relief afforded by Samuel, however, and by the two closest ships of his division enabled this fate to be avoided. A short fierce engagement followed, after which the Swedish Admiral was compelled to strike his flag, suffering his ship to be taken as a trophy.

In the event the Swedish flagship became the only prize secured by the Russian fleet. Aided by an on-shore wind, the Swedes quickly fled into port, regaining the protection of their fortress guns and taking with them another Russian ship of the line which had been so disabled by the action that she could only run before the wind. The consequence of the battle was a resounding victory for the Russian fleet, but this had been marred by the timorous Rear Admiral Bletsikov, whose squadron had played no part whatever except to hold back from the scene until it was all too late.

Once the Swedish fleet had been bottled up in Sveaborg, Samuel ordered a Russian squadron to patrol off the mouth of the harbour, thus preventing their escape and, perhaps, provoking them into another sortie and a further engagement. Samuel himself put into Reval, disposed of the Swedish force which had previously landed there with aggressive intent, and then turned his attention to court-martialling the Rear Admiral and the defecting Captains under his command.

'Rarely have I seen the Commander-in-Chief in such a continuing rage,' the Flag Captain, who had charge of the courts-martial, reported, 'and when the offending Rear Admiral and his Captains had duly been tried and found guilty, the Admiral had them all lined up on his quarterdeck. He began by staring at them individually in silence, each one being given perhaps an uninterrupted minute. The weather was fine and sunny with a gentle breeze ruffling the surface of the harbour, reminding me of a summer's day in the Firth of Forth.' (The Flag Captain was, almost inevitably, another Scotsman.) 'The seagulls swooped and cawed overhead whilst these wretched and guilty men faced their Admiral, knowing that they could expect no mercy.'

'Scum!' Samuel eventually spat out. 'You're enough to make a dead man chew, that's all you are, a pack of curs with your tails between your legs, a disgrace to the Empress, a dishonour to your calling and a shame – a deep, deep shame to me. You held back through cowardice at a time when brave men were giving their lives in battle. You disgust me. Now hand over your swords. You shall be sent to the Peter and Paul to await the pleasure of Her Imperial Majesty.'

He turned and strode into his cabin. The offending officers were then formally relieved of their commands and sent overland to Petersburg in chains. News of these summary dismissals preceded the officers' arrival, and an immediate process of lobbying was then begun to invoke the Little Mother's mercy. But to no avail. 'You have ill-served the Empire,' the Empress decreed, 'at a time when the Empire had most need of your true and courageous service.' Stripping them of their rank, their lands and possessions, she dispatched them to the hulks, which was the equivalent of a lingering death.

Meanwhile Samuel led his fleet once more to sea. He did not intend to sail for the Mediterranean until he had disposed of the Swedish fleet, and this in the end was to prove his downfall. The immediate consequence of this decision, however, showed to the Russian advantage. The Swedish ships remained blocked up in Sveaborg for the remainder of the summer, making but one attempt to escape. This proved disastrous. No sooner had they left the protection of their fortress guns than they were set upon and trounced by the Russians. One of their ships was driven upon a rock, boarded and set on fire within sight of the rest of the fleet, which made no effort to prevent it. This particular action was undertaken by the Russian flagship, and during the course of it Samuel received a severe contusion on his thigh. This was caused by the wind of a shot which killed a Petty Officer standing at his side.

The main Russian fleet returned to the Bay of Reval, repairing the damage the ships had received and restoring the health of the ships' companies. As a token of her gratitude 'for the consequences of this Swedish repulse which are incalculable to our capital and empire', the Empress appointed her Commander-in-Chief to the first order of knighthood in Russia, that of St Andrew, 'to bandage your wound'. Whilst this honour delighted the Admiral, the earlier defection of so great a part of his fleet made a deep impression on his spirit and caused him to entertain grave doubts as to the reliability of the fleet he had so earnestly trained. This in turn developed in him a depression of mind which doubtless laid him open to the fatal disaster which was soon to carry him off.

Back at Crondstadt one day early in October, Fortescue Fynne called in on Sarah at Admiralty House on his way to Oranienbaum for a conference with Potemkin and the Empress.

'The news from Reval is very bad,' he said. 'A dangerous fever has been plaguing every ship of the fleet and I fear that Sam has caught the malady as well.'

'He has suffered many such fevers before,' Sarah said. 'Is the degree of this current one so very much worse?'

'The latest dispatch from Reval claims that sixty-five men and three officers have already died of the fever. Sam is usually proof against such contagion but this time he has succumbed. The fever is attended by an inflammation of the intestines which is both painful to bear and lowering of the spirits. Reading between the lines, Sarah, I think the situation is more serious than at first it appears. The dispatch was accompanied by a note from the Flag Captain which said that the Admiral has never recovered his equanimity since that Bletsikov defection. The fever brings with it an intermittent delirium and when Sam is under its grip, he raves about the cowardly rascals who so disgraced the good name of the fleet. As you know, the fleet is like another son to Sam, he is so proud of it, so determined that the standards of the Royal Navy shall prevail, and so utterly cast down when he is not supported as he should be.'

Sarah had listened to Fortie's words with a growing alarm. For a moment or so she stood still, looking into the distance. Then quickly she made up her mind.

'I shall go to Reval myself,' she said. 'If you are having an audience of Her Majesty, perhaps you would secure her formal approval to this journey on my behalf.'

The Empress and Potemkin were at once as fully seized of the gravity of the news as Sarah had been.

'Doctor Rogerson is to be fetched from Petersburg,' the

Empress decreed, and when her favourite physician, himself a Scotsman, had duly arrived and had tendered his advice, she ordered him to Reval without delay. 'The Admiral's health is the health of Russia,' she said. 'See to it that his life is not endangered. The Empire has more need of him today than ever before.'

But by the time Sarah and Dr Rogerson had separately arrived on board the *Rotislav*, matters had taken a turn for the worse. The ship lay out in the stream, since there was no jetty in the Livonian port with a depth of water alongside sufficient to accommodate the great flagship of the Russian fleet. All communication of persons and *matériel* between ship and shore had to be by boat, and therefore at times became as uncertain as the autumn weather which that year was early on the change.

Indeed the overcast skies and the intermittent high winds boded ill both for the fleet itself, and for the final decision against the Swedes for which Samuel had been so assiduously preparing in the last three months. At first sight of her husband, Sarah felt a dread clutching at her throat. She had never seen him as ill as this.

'He does not recognize you,' Dr Rogerson said. 'His mind has been entirely swamped by this dread delirium.'

Sarah tried unsuccessfully to suppress a gasp of horror.

'Is there no relief – no remedy you can give him?' she said, her eyes rounding with the terror she felt.

'The fever is burning him up. For three days now he has tossed and turned, cursing those "blackguards" he has had the misfortune to trust, swearing at them to take up their stations under penalty of the lash in a manner most terrible and shocking to hear.'

Sarah took hold of Sam's hand which was moving restlessly in the air as if trying to express in gesture the incoherent fury which was animating the prone figure. Samuel snatched it away.

'Touch me not! Stand away from me, you dastard!' he called out. 'By God, I'll have you strung up at the yardarm. I'll make you an example to the other curs and cowards. A pox on you all!'

'Sam, dear Sam!' Sarah cried out, falling to her knees beside the bunk. 'It is I – Sarah. Let him be, you devils . . .' she called out as if those invisible powers who had him in their thrall were dodging about the carved bulkhead above the bunk.

'I fear the end cannot be far away,' Dr Rogerson murmured. 'I have been sent for too late – though doubtless you have done your best,' he went on to the crestfallen ship's surgeon who was standing by, having tried everything in his knowledge from leeches to a succession of cold compresses. The stench in the cabin was very bad, and when night fell and the lamps were lit, it was as if some animal were dying in a cave. By now the storm which had begun to get up as Sarah had stepped on board, had greatly increased in violence. The ship moved to the wind, rolling in a slow, heavy, continuous motion which even though safely at anchor in harbour was sufficient to cause Sarah a bout of seasickness. This greatly increased her distress.

Outside on the quarterdeck the rain lashed down as if this storm heralded the beginning of a new flood. Lightning flickered and deep rumbles of thunder seemed ever nearer. The climax was evidently at hand – 'a sight most agonizing to a feeling heart', as Dr Rogerson later reported to the Empress – and just before dawn, on 27 October, 1788, with a terrible rattle in the throat, the Admiral died.

'He is gone,' Dr Rogerson murmured, after he had felt the pulse and with a primeval cry of horror, Sarah fainted clean away. Nor was there a dry eye elsewhere in the ship.

The effect on the Empress was equally dramatic. On hearing the news she clenched her fist, violently cursing on all who had helped to bring about the death of so great a man. 'The Empire is undone,' she called out, and forthwith cancelled every function, ceremony or activity of state for fourteen days. 'A light has been dowsed,' she cried to Potemkin, 'a light which will not be relit whilst you and I are alive,' and, beating her fist against the nearest wall, she gave herself over to an uncontrollable grief, lamenting the loss with a most unfeigned sorrow.

So the Grand Admiral departed this life. A general mourning was immediately ordered and a state funeral in the cathedral church at Reval took place. In due course a magnificent monument in Italian marble was erected over his grave, on which were carved the ships of the fleet with their flags at half-mast and with crossed yards. A large gold medal was also struck and was sent to Lady Greig by the Empress as a posthumous honour.

'Few men ever united all the great qualities of a chief with the mild ones of a private individual, in a greater degree than Admiral Greig,' wrote Adam Armstrong, one of the British captains who served under his command. 'He was, indeed, so superior in these capacities to the common herd of mankind that to delineate them faithfully has more the air of a panegyric than of fact.'

This was written the year before Nelson died at Trafalgar, and sixteen years after Samuel himself had been laid to rest. By then, too, the Empress Catherine the Second had herself died and her son, Paul, had been assassinated. Napoleon was ravaging Europe and in a few years would make his fatal lunge into Russia. But the spirit of this great expatriate Admiral lived on, his son Alexis rising in turn to become the Commander-in-Chief of the Black Seas Fleet.

'The groundwork of his character', Adam Armstrong continued, 'was the most heartfelt conviction of the truth of the Christian religion and the strictest adherence of its principles amidst the hurry of business and the allurements of courtly pleasure. It is this that gave lustre to his public character, supported him in the difficulties with which he had to struggle in many arduous scenes, and in private life rendered still more amiable the steady friend, the kind master, the affectionate husband and the indulgent parent. To the steadiness of his friendship and to his unwearied zeal for the service of those who applied to him for assistance, many living and most reputable characters can bear witness.'

Sarah and her family were left, but the heart had gone out of her life. Although honoured by the Empress and cared for by their many friends in the foreign community of St Petersburg, she no longer saw any point or purpose in her life. The sons were almost at the moment of leaving home and of going out into the world. Now that there would be no more weekend visits to the country for horse-back riding and shooting, now that she would no longer have to make last minute arrangements to entertain visiting Ambassadors who happened to call unexpectedly on the Commander-in-Chief, now that there would no longer be the slightly deaf, comfortable man laughing out loud over the pages of *Tom Jones* and *Peregrine Pickle* before taking her comfortably to bed, she composed herself with the Christian resignation which she knew Sam would have wanted her to display, and waited patiently for her own release from life.

She had no more than five years to wait, and by then both her sons had established themselves in the service their father had done so much to develop. Sarah passed away peaceably in her sleep at little more than forty years of age. Three years after that, the Empress Catherine died and her son Paul I succeeded to the Imperial throne, doing his luckless best in the five unhappy years of his reign to reverse all that his mother and her great Admiral had achieved.

Author's note

Almost all the characters and events in this book are based on fact and the story was derived from contemporary accounts, some in the London Library and some from the Greig family papers. These were made available to me by John Ramsay-Fairfax, a Greig descendant, to whom the story is dedicated with my gratitude for the interest he has devoted to the subject and the help he has given me personally in its pursuit.

Doubtless there are anachronisms and other mistakes which sharp-eyed students of the late eighteenth century will spot. My apologies for any of these which may give offence. However I wrote the story as fiction because it gave me the freedom to suggest motives and to develop relationships which I strongly fancy to be consonant with the characters concerned but for which, rather naturally, I could find no written evidence.

[illegible]

[illegible] Full [illegible]
reproduction of the cover illustration [illegible] print of this book is now available exclusively to purchasers of Warren Tute's Honours of War and Peace.

Printed on good quality art paper, this beautiful painting will enhance any art collection for years to come.

To obtain your free copy, just fill in the coupon below (in block capitals please) and send it, together with 20p (postal order or cheque made payable to Granada Publishing Ltd) to cover postage and packing costs to:

The Paperback Stationery Department
Granada Publishing Limited
PO Box 9, 29 Frogmore, St Albans, Herts AL2 2NF

This offer applies to the United Kingdom and Eire only and closes on 31st March 197[illegible]

Please allow 21 days for delivery.